EXPECTING
ROYAL TWINS!

BY
MELISSA McCLONE

AND

TO DANCE
WITH A PRINCE

BY
CARA COLTER

MILLS & BOON

Dear Reader,

Ever since my first 'royal' romance came out in 2000, I've wanted to write another one. But I struggled to find the right cast of characters and plot.

Enter His Royal Highness Crown Prince Nikola Kresimir of Vernonia. When Prince Niko popped into my imagination I knew I'd found my hero and a story would follow. It did!

Duty matters most to Prince Niko. He knows what his country needs to thrive in the future, but he doesn't have a clue what he needs to be happy. Forget about love. Niko plans to marry to provide Vernonia with a princess bride's dowry and an heir.

Isabel Poussard is an American car mechanic who dreams of working on a racing team's pit crew. Izzy hates the colour pink and doesn't own a dress. No way does she want to be a princess. No matter what Prince Hottie thinks!

As Niko and Izzy will learn, sometimes what we want isn't what we need to find our happily-ever-after. Enjoy!

Melissa

EXPECTING
ROYAL TWINS!

BY
MELISSA McCLONE

First published in Great Britain 2011
Harlequin Mills & Boon Limited,
Eton House, 18-24 Paradise Road, Richmond, Surrey TW9 1SR

© Melissa Martinez McClone 2011

ISBN: 978 0 263 88866 9

23-0311

Harlequin Mills & Boon policy is to use papers that are natural, renewable and recyclable products and made from wood grown in sustainable forests. The logging and manufacturing processes conform to the legal environmental regulations of the country of origin.

Printed and bound in Spain
by Litografia Rosés S.A., Barcelona

With a degree in mechanical engineering from Stanford University, the last thing **Melissa McClone** ever thought she would be doing was writing romance novels. But analyzing engines for a major US airline just couldn't compete with her 'happily-ever-afters'. When she isn't writing, caring for her three young children or doing laundry, Melissa loves to curl up on the couch with a cup of tea, her cats and a good book. She enjoys watching home decorating shows to get ideas for her house—a 1939 cottage that is *slowly* being renovated. Melissa lives in Lake Oswego, Oregon, with her own real-life hero husband, two daughters, a son, two loveable but oh-so-spoiled indoor cats and a no-longer-stray outdoor kitty that decided to call the garage home. Melissa loves to her from her readers. You can write to her at PO Box 63, Lake Oswego, OR 97034, USA, or contact her via her website: www.melissamcclone.com

For Tom, Mackenna, Finn, Rose, Smalls,
Rocket, Spirit, Chaos and Yoda.
The best family a writer could have!

Special thanks to: Elizabeth Boyle, Drew Brayshaw,
Roger Carstens, Amy Danicic, John Fenzel, Terri Reed,
Robert Williams and Camas Physical Therapy.

CHAPTER ONE

NIKOLA TOMISLAV KRESIMIR, Crown Prince of Vernonia, strode past his father's assistant and the two palace guards standing watch. As soon as he entered the king's office, Niko heard the door close behind him.

He grimaced.

Niko didn't have time for another impromptu assignment. His in-box was overflowing. The upcoming trade conference was turning into a logistical nightmare. Princess Julianna of Aliestle was patiently waiting to have lunch with him.

He was used to juggling competing demands, thrived on them actually, but the collar of his dress shirt seemed to have shrunk two inches since he'd left his own office three minutes ago. He tugged on his tie.

Not that it lessened his frustration level.

A summons from the king trumped everything else and often messed up Niko's schedule for the rest of the day, sometimes week. Not to mention the havoc royal protocol played with his priority of turning their provincial country into a modern nation. But he followed his father's orders out of respect and for the good of the country.

King Dmitar sat behind his large mahogany desk staring at a manila file folder in his hands. His once dark hair was now as white as the snowcapped peaks of the Balkans and Carpathians. His face, like Niko's own, was as rugged as those same mountain ranges. His wire-rimmed reading glasses rested low on his nose, making him look more like a professor than a soldier or a king who had spent the majority of his rule trying to unite his country against all odds.

Niko stood ten feet away, waiting.

A breeze blew through an open window, carrying the sweet fragrance of flowers from the royal gardens. A vast improvement over the acrid smell of gunpowder and sickening scent of blood that used to taint the air around here.

Five years had passed since the ratification of the peace treaty. Tensions between the two warring factions erupted occasionally, but peace prevailed. Niko intended to ensure it always would. A totally united Vernonia, however, seemed like a far off dream. A fairy tale, really.

Not wanting to waste more time, he cleared his throat.

His father looked up. Dark circles ringed his eyes.

"You sent for me, sir," Niko said.

The lines on his father's face seemed deeper, more pronounced, than they used to be. The conflict had aged him; so had grief. But still the corners of his mouth curved upward into a rare smile. "I have good news, my son."

The best news would be that Vernonia had been accepted into the European Union, but Niko knew they still had too many improvement projects to complete first. He stepped closer to the desk. "I've spent the morning wading through the demands of the trade delegations. Good news will be a welcome relief, Father."

"Your bride box has been located."

Not located. *Found.*

The unexpected news sunk in. Niko respected the past, but the fact something as important as his marriage was dependent on such on antiquated custom as presenting his wife a family heirloom on their wedding day irritated him. Traditions could only take his country so far. "You are certain it is mine?"

"As certain as we can be until we have the box in hand."

His bride box hadn't been seen in over twenty years. Not since the collapse of the Soviet Union brought turmoil to many Balkan countries. Vernonia had avoided the ethnic strife that ravaged many of its neighbors, but terrorist acts had led to a deadly civil war that tore the country apart and nearly destroyed its economy. "Where is the box?"

"The United States." His father adjusted his glasses and studied the folder. "Charlotte, North Carolina, to be exact."

"A long way from home."

"Yes."

The location wasn't really important. Niko would have the box back. Tradition—and his father—would be satisfied. Nothing would stand in the way of Niko's marriage to Julianna. He could finally fulfill his duty as his parents and people wished him to do. The marriage would give him the means and opportunity to do what he wanted—needed—to do with Vernonia.

Plans formed in his mind, but he couldn't get too far ahead of himself. Nothing could happen until he had possession of the box. "How was it discovered?"

"The internet." His father shuffled through papers in the file. "Someone posted on an antiques forum looking for the key. After a few exchanges verifying the seriousness of our interest, we were sent a picture that confirmed our suspicions. The box is yours."

"Incredible." Niko considered the number of private investigators and treasure hunters hired to find the heirloom. He laughed at the irony. "Technology to the rescue of an Old World custom."

"Technology may be useful at times, but our people desire tradition. You must remember that when you wear the crown."

"Everything I've ever done has been for Vernonia." Niko's family had ruled for eight centuries. The country was in their blood and hearts. Duty always came first. "But we must modernize if we are to succeed in the twenty-first century."

"Yet you have agreed to an arranged marriage."

He shrugged, but the last thing he felt was indifference. His marriage would act as a bridge between the past and the future. He might not be the United Kingdom's Prince William, but Niko had the attention of royal watchers. The publicity surrounding a royal wedding would be good for his country's nascent tourist industry. He would use whatever he could to Vernonia's advantage. "I may not be a stickler for tradition, Father, but I will always do what is best for the country."

"As will I." His father placed the folder on his desk. "You have the key."

"Of course, sir." Niko always had the key. He had been wearing the damn thing ever since the decree that he could never take it off twenty odd years ago. The only thing that had changed since then was the size of the chain. He pulled the thick silver one from beneath his shirt. A key that looked more like a cross and heart welded together dangled from his fingers. "Can I finally stop wearing the necklace now?"

"No." The word resonated through the spacious office until the tapestries on the wall swallowed the sound. "You will need the key when you go to North Carolina tomorrow."

"Send Jovan. I can't travel to the United States right now. I'm needed here," Niko countered. "My schedule is full. Princess Julianna is here."

"The box is yours," his father said. "You will be the one to bring it home. The travel arrangements have already been made. Your aide will be provided with an itinerary and the necessary information."

Niko bit his tongue. Further resistance would be futile. The king's word was final even if it made little sense under the current circumstances. "Fine, but you do realize I have never seen the box."

"You have seen it. You were a child, so you don't remember."

What Niko remembered from his childhood and early adulthood was war, the one thing he wanted and hoped to forget. Keeping peace and modernizing Vernonia were his main goals now. Though the parliament wanted him to provide an heir. Might as well get on with that, now that nothing stood in his way of marrying. Speaking of which...

"Do you wish for me to propose to Julianna before I leave for America or upon my return, Father?"

The king's face reddened. "There shall be no official proposal."

"What?" Niko remembered the open window and the people on the other side of the office door. He lowered his voice. "We've spent months negotiating with the Council of Elders in Aliestle. Even the Separatists are in favor of the marriage since King Alaric supported them during the conflict. The only obstacle to marriage has been the bride box. A delay will send the wrong—"

"No proposal."

Frustration mounted. Niko had searched for a suitable bride for almost a year. He didn't want to have to start over. "You agreed Julianna is an excellent choice for a wife and the future queen of Vernonia. That is why finding the bride box has been a priority."

"Julianna is more than suitable to be queen, but..." His father removed his glasses and rubbed his tired-looking eyes. "Are you in love with her?"

Love? Niko was surprised his traditional father had broached the subject. His parents' marriage hadn't been a love match. Niko had never expected one for himself after his older brother, Stefan, had been killed during the conflict.

"We get along well. She's beautiful and intelligent. I will be content with her as my wife," Niko stated honestly. He'd always known as crown prince he would marry for Vernonia's good, not his own. "The publicity surrounding a royal wedding will increase our visibility to the tourist industry. Most importantly, an alliance with Aliestle will give Vernonia the capital it requires to complete rebuilding. That will help our efforts to join the European Union."

"You've looked at all angles."

Niko bowed his head. "As you taught me, Father."

"And Julianna. Are her feelings engaged?"

"She...cares for me," Niko answered carefully. "As I do for her. She understands what is expected."

"But is she in love with you?"

Uncomfortable, Niko shifted his weight between his feet. "You've never spoken about love before. Only duty and what a state marriage would entail."

"You are old enough to know whether a woman has feelings for you or not. Answer my question."

Niko considered his outing with Julianna yesterday afternoon. They'd left their security detail on the shore and sailed on the lake. He'd kissed her for the first time. The kiss had been… pleasant, but Julianna seemed more interested in sailing than kissing him again. "I do not believe she is in love with me. In fact, I'm certain she isn't."

"Good."

"I do not understand what is going on, sir. If something has changed with Vernonia's relationship to Aliestle—"

"Nothing has changed there." His father's drawn out sigh would have made the parliament members' knees tremble beneath their heavy robes. "But a slight…complication in regards to you marrying Julianna has arisen."

Niko's muscles tensed. "What kind of complication?"

Inside Bay #2 at Rowdy's One Stop Garage in Charlotte, North Carolina, a Brad Paisley song blared from a nearby boom box. Oil, gasoline and grease scented the air. Isabel Poussard bent over a Chevy 350 small block engine. The bolt she needed to remove wouldn't budge, but she wasn't giving up or asking for help. She wanted the guys to see her as an equal, not a woman who couldn't make it on her own.

She adjusted the wrench. "Come on now. Turn for Izzy."

A swatch of light brown hair fell across her eyes so she couldn't see.

Darn ponytail. It never stayed put. If she had any extra money, she would get a short hairstyle so she wouldn't be bothered anymore. She didn't dare cut it herself. For years her uncle Frank had chopped her hair with whatever was handy, scissors or razor blades. She'd grown up looking more like a boy than a girl. Not that any dresses hung in her closet today.

Izzy tucked the stray strands behind her ear. She struggled to turn the wrench. Her palm sweated. The wrench slipped.

Frustrated, she blew out a puff of air. "No one is going to

let you work over the wall in the pits during a race if you can't loosen a little bolt."

She imagined the start of the Daytona 500. The roar of the crowd. The heat from the pavement. The smell of burning rubber. The rev of engines.

Excitement surged through her.

Being on a professional pit crew had been Uncle Frank's dream for as long as Izzy remembered. An aneurysm had cut his life short. Now it was up to her to turn his dream into a reality. He'd spent his life caring for her and sharing his skill and love of cars. More than once he'd had the opportunity to be on a pit crew, but he hadn't wanted to leave her. This was the least she could do for him.

As soon as she saved enough money, she would enroll in pit crew school. She wanted to put her days at dirt tracks and stock car circuits behind her and take a shot at the big leagues. For Uncle Frank and herself. She had bigger goals than just being on the pit crew. She wanted to be the crew chief. Izzy would show those kids who laughed at her grease-stained hands they were wrong. She would do something with her life. Something big.

She adjusted her grip on the wrench and tried again. The bolt turned. "Yes!"

"Hey, Izzy," the garage owner's son and her closest friend, Boyd, shouted to her over the Lady Antebellum song now playing on the radio. "Some folks here to see you."

Word of mouth about her skills kept spreading. She could not only fix old engines, but the new hybrids, too. Her understanding of the computer and electronics side of things coupled with a gift for diagnostics drew in new clients daily. Her boss, Rowdy, was so happy he'd given Izzy a raise. If this kept up, she could enroll in school in a few months.

With a smile, she placed her wrench and the bolt on the top of her toolbox.

Izzy stepped outside. Fresh air filled her lungs. Sunshine warmed her face. She loved spring days better than the humid ones summer brought with it.

In front of her, a black limousine gleamed beneath the midday sun. The engine idled perfectly. Darkened windows hid the identity of the car's passengers, but uniformed police officers stood nearby.

Not simply "some folks" wanting to see her. Must be a VIP inside the limo if police escorts were needed.

Izzy couldn't imagine what they wanted with her since the car sounded like it was running fine.

She wiped her dirty hands on the thighs of her cotton coveralls. Not exactly clean, especially with grease caked under her fingernails, but cleaner.

One of the police officers gave her the once-over, as if sizing up her danger potential. A good thing she'd left the wrench in the garage.

A chauffeur walked around the car and opened the back door. A blond man exited. He wore a designer suit and nicely polished black dress shoes. With a classically handsome face and short clipped hair, he was easy on the eyes. But his good looks seemed a little bland, like a bowl of vanilla ice cream without any hot fudge, whipped cream and candy sprinkles. She preferred men who weren't quite so pretty, men with a little more…character.

"Isabel Poussard?" the man asked.

She stiffened. The last time anyone used her real name had been during her high school graduation ceremony when she received her diploma. She'd always been Izzy, ever since she was a little girl. Uncle Frank had taught her to be careful and cautious around strangers. He'd worried about her and been very protective. She knew he'd be that way now if he were here.

Izzy raised her chin and stared down her nose. The gesture had sent more than one guy running in the opposite direction. "Who wants to know?"

Warm brown eyes met hers. The guy wasn't intimidated at all. He looked almost amused for some strange reason. "I am Jovan Novak, aide to His Royal Highness Crown Prince Nikola Tomislav Kresimir."

Jovan's accent sounded European. Interesting since this was

NASCAR country, not Formula 1 territory. "Never heard of him."

"He's from Vernonia."

"Vernonia." The name sounded vaguely familiar. Izzy rolled the word over in her mind. Suddenly she remembered. "That's one of those Balkan countries. Fairy-tale castles and snowcapped mountains. There was a civil war there."

"Yes."

"Hey, Izzy," Boyd shouted from behind her. "You need any help?"

She glanced back at the bear of a man who stood with a mallet in his hands and curiosity in his eyes. A grin tugged at her lips. She appreciated how Boyd treated her like a little sister, especially since she had no family. Of course that made things interesting the few times she had a date pick her up after work. "Not yet, Boyd, but I'll let you know if I do."

Jovan looked like he might be in shape, but she could probably take him without Boyd's help thanks to Uncle Frank. When she was younger, he used to barter his mechanic skills for her martial arts class tuition. Now she worked out every day to get in shape for the work necessary by a pit crew member during a race.

"Isabel. Izzy." Jovan's smile reached all the way to his eyes. He bowed. "It is such a pleasure to make your acquaintance, Your—"

"Is this about a car repair?" He acted so happy to meet her. That bothered Izzy. Most customers limited their interactions to questions about their cars. Some simply ignored her. The men who went out of their way to talk to her usually ended up propositioning her. "Or do you want something else? I'm in the middle of a job."

Not exactly the most friendly customer service, but something felt off. No customer would know her real name. And the guy smiled too much to be having car trouble.

"One moment please." Jovan ducked into the limousine.

Time ticked by. Seconds or minutes, Izzy couldn't tell since she wasn't wearing a watch. She used the clock hanging in the garage or her cell phone to keep track of time while she worked.

Izzy tapped her foot. She had to get the Chevy finished so she could work on the Dodge Grand Caravan. Somewhere a frazzled mom with four kids was waiting to get her minivan back. It was up to Izzy to get the job done.

Jovan stepped out of the limo finally.

About time, she thought.

Another man in a dark suit followed. Izzy took a closer look.

Smokin'.

The thought shot from her brain to the tips of her steel-toed boots and ricocheted back to the top of her head.

The guy was at least six feet tall with thick, shoulder-length brown hair and piercing blue-green eyes framed by dark lashes.

She straightened as if an extra inch could bring her closer to his height. Even then the top of her head would barely come to his chin.

But what a chin.

Izzy swallowed a sigh.

A strong nose, chiseled cheekbones, dark brows. Rugged features that made for an interesting—a handsome—combination in spite of a jagged scar on his right cheek.

Talk about character. He had it in spades.

Not that she was interested.

Spending her entire life surrounded by men, car mechanics, gave her an understanding of how the opposite sex thought and operated. The one standing in front of her wearing a nice suit and shiny shoes was trouble. Dangerous, too.

The limo, expensive clothing, personal aide and police escort meant he lived in a completely different world than her, a world where she was seen as nothing more than a servant or wallpaper or worse, a one-night stand. Having to deal with mysterious rich people intimidated her. She wanted nothing to do with him.

But she didn't mind looking. The man belonged on the cover of a glossy men's magazine. He moved with the grace and agility of an athlete. The fit of his suit made her wonder what was underneath the fancy fabric.

Everyone else around him seemed to fade into the background. She couldn't remember the last time she'd had this kind of reaction to a guy. No doubt the result of working too much overtime. Time to take a night off and have some fun. That would keep her from mooning over the next gorgeous guy who crossed her path.

"You are Isabel Poussard." His accent, a mix of British and something else, could melt a frozen stick of butter.

She nodded, not trusting her voice.

His assessing gaze traveled the length of her. Nothing in his eyes or on his face hinted if he liked what he saw.

Not that she cared. Not much anyway.

A hottie like him would never be interested in a grease monkey like her. Still he was a yummy piece of eye candy. One she could appreciate.

Izzy raised her chin again, but didn't stare down her nose the way she'd done with Jovan. She wasn't ready to send this one on his way just yet. "You know my name, but I don't know yours."

"I am Prince Nikola of Vernonia."

"A prince?"

"Yes."

She supposed a prince would have a police escort as well as an aide, but this was just the kind of prank Boyd would pull and kid Izzy about for the rest of her life. She glanced around looking for a camera. "Am I being punk'd?"

Jovan grinned.

Nikola pressed his lips together. "No."

Yeah, on second thought, she couldn't imagine the police participating in a joke. But she still had a hard time believing royalty would come to Rowdy's. This wasn't the worst part of town, but it wasn't the best, either. "Am I supposed to call you Your Highness or something?"

"Niko is fine," he said.

Better than fine, but he probably already knew that. Men as attractive as him usually did. "So Niko, why are you here?"

Jovan started to speak, but Niko held up his hand and silenced his aide.

Nice trick. Maybe he really was a prince. Or maybe he liked being the one to talk.

"You posted on the internet looking to find a key to a box," Niko said. "The box is mine."

She stared down her nose. "I don't think so, dude."

He winced.

"The box belonged to my mother," Izzy added. "I'm just looking for the key."

"I know you want the key, but the box in the picture never belonged to your mother."

Oh, boy. Rowdy and Boyd had told Izzy if she posted on the internet she would get some strange replies. But she'd received only one email from a person who described the box so perfectly she'd sent him a picture of it. "You're HRMKDK?"

"That's my father," Niko explained. "His Royal Majesty King Dmitar Kresimir."

Like a king would ever email a total stranger about a wooden box. Sure it was pretty, but it was old. Izzy had thought the only value was sentimental. Maybe she was wrong about its worth. "I did correspond with your, um, dad, but I already told you, the box belongs to me."

"The box is technically yours, but only because I gave it to you."

What a ridiculous statement. The box was Izzy's only connection to her mother who had died when Izzy was a baby. That was why she was desperate to find the missing key and open the bottom portion to see if anything was inside. With Uncle Frank gone, she had no family, no connection to her past. She wanted to know something…anything.

Fighting her disappointment over not finding the key, Izzy squared her shoulders. "I've heard of Vernonia, but I've never been there. I'm certain we've never met. I've had the box for as long as I remember."

"You have had the box for twenty-three years," Niko said. "I gave it to you when you were a baby."

"A baby," she repeated, as if hearing it a second time would make more sense than the first time. It didn't. The guy wasn't that much older than her—that would mean he'd been just a kid. Ludicrous.

"Yes," Niko admitted ruefully. "I must sound crazy."

If he wasn't, then she was. "You do."

"I can assure you I'm not crazy," Niko stated matter-of-factly. He glanced at his aide standing next to him. "Isn't that true, Jovan?"

"Not crazy," Jovan agreed, though he continued to look amused by what was going on.

"I'm guessing you're paid to agree with him, Jovan," Izzy said, irritated.

"Yes, but I'm also a lawyer if that adds to my credibility."

"It doesn't." Maybe this was how good-looking, eccentric royals wasted their time and money. She wished they would go bother someone else. "I think you both must be certifiable."

The two men looked at her with puzzled expressions.

"Insane." Izzy glanced at the police officers. She couldn't imagine them wasting their time and tax dollars protecting some mental case claiming to be a prince. Surely they would have checked him out and asked to see his diplomatic papers or passport or something. "Let's pretend what you say is true—"

"It is true," Niko said.

She took a deep breath to control her growing temper. "Why would you give a baby the box? Is there some significance to the gesture?"

"It's customary."

It was her turn to be confused. "Huh?"

"Tradition," Niko clarified. "When a Vernonian prince gets married, he presents his wife with a bride box on their wedding day."

"That still doesn't explain why you would give the box to me."

"Because I am your husband."

CHAPTER TWO

"MY HUSBAND?" Isabel's voice cracked. Her expression would have been comical if this were not such a serious matter.

"Yes." Niko understood her shock. He even sympathized. Discovering he had a wife had sent his world spinning off its axis. But her feelings—his feelings—would only delay the annulment needed to remedy this "complication" so he could marry Julianna and help his country. "It is a lot to take in."

"Take in?" Sharp, brown eyes bore into him. "Okay, Niko or whoever you are, cut the bull and tell me what's really going on here."

He stared at Isabel with the dirty, baggy coveralls, lopsided ponytail and grease on her hands and cheek. She might be half-way attractive with her oval face, high cheekbones and expressive eyes, if she weren't dressed like a man and covered in motor oil.

"Come on, Niko." She placed her hands on her hips. "Spill."

He expected her lack of protocol and manners, but the strength in her voice surprised him, as did her take-no-prisoner tone. Most people kowtowed to him. Few ever challenged him. He was...intrigued. "I am speaking the truth. I am your husband."

She pursued her full, unglossed lips and gave him a long, hard look. He was used to such a frank appraisal, but unlike most women, Isabel did not seem impressed by what she saw. He didn't know whether to be amused or annoyed by this woman who worked at a dilapidated garage fixing other people's broken-down vehicles.

"I told you. I've never seen you before," she said. "We can't be married."

"Indeed we can. You simply do not remember."

Isabel's gaze remained steady. "I think I'd remember getting married."

"Not if you were only a few months old at the time."

Her mouth formed a perfect O. "What?"

"I was only six years old when we married, and my memories are very vague."

Almost nonexistent, but he needed to convince Isabel of what had occurred twenty-three years ago, not add to the doubts shining in her pretty hazel eyes.

"Children marrying?" Isabel's nostrils flared. "There are laws against that kind of thing."

"Yes, and today it is illegal in Vernonia, but not twenty-three years ago."

"This is crazy." Her voice jumped an octave. "I'm an American."

"Your mother was American, but your father was Vernonian."

"My father…" Isabel's glanced toward Jovan as if seeking confirmation. At his nod, her hands balled into fists. "Now I know you're lying. My father's name isn't listed on my birth certificate. I have no idea who he is."

The hurt and anger in her voice suggested she was telling the truth. There was no reason for her to lie. She had too much to gain by accepting what Niko was telling her. His respect inched up. Opportunists or not, many women would have jumped at the chance to be his wife. "I have proof."

"You mean the box," she said.

"The bride box, yes, but also documentation and a photograph."

Curiosity flashed in Isabel's eyes. "What kind of documentation?"

Her interest loosened some of the tension in his shoulders. Maybe the paper would convince her of the truth. He motioned to Jovan, who removed a leather pouch from his inside suit pocket with a flourish and handed it over.

As Niko opened the flap, he noticed two tall men in coveralls watching them from the garage.

No doubt the limousine and police cars would attract attention. Niko wanted to avoid the media at all cost. The annulment needed to be handled quietly with no press coverage. Before departing for the United States, he had been upfront with Julianna about the situation, but others from Aliestle might not be as understanding about the sudden appearance of "his wife" on the front page of tabloids. He didn't want to risk losing her and what she would bring to Vernonia.

He glanced around. "I would prefer a more private place to discuss matters. Inside the limo perhaps?"

Isabel glared at him. "Do I look like the kind of woman who would get into a car with strangers?"

Niko assumed based on her reaction the answer wasn't yes. "I may be a stranger, but I am your husband."

"That remains to be seen."

She wasn't making this easy, but given her appearance he shouldn't be surprised. "Perhaps the garage or if there is an office—"

"Here."

He needed her cooperation. The last thing Niko wanted to do was upset her any more than he already had. He would allow her this much control.

"Fine. We shall remain here." He removed two folded pieces of paper from the pouch. "I took the liberty of having the marriage certificate translated."

She eyed him warily. "Marriage certificate, huh?"

He extended the papers toward her. "See for yourself."

Instead of reaching for the documents as Niko expected, Isabel wiped her hands on the thighs of her oversize coveralls. The same way she had when she'd walked out of the garage.

Not totally without manners, he realized, but a far cry from the grace and style of a woman like Julianna. "These are copies so it doesn't matter if they get dirty."

Isabel took the documents and unfolded them. As she read, she flipped back and forth between the two pages.

Niko appreciated her thoroughness. Now all he needed was her compliance. Given how things were proceeding so far, that might take time. Especially since he hadn't begun to explain the situation to her.

"The certificate actually looks legit," she said.

"It is."

"But it's wrong." She pointed her oil stained finger to the line with her mother's name. "My mother was never married."

He hesitated.

This "complication" went beyond Isabel Poussard being his child bride and standing in the way of him marrying Juliana and obtaining her significant dowry and trade support from Aliestle. Isabel might think she was a full-blooded American, but she wasn't. She was also Vernonian, the last of the royal Sachestian bloodline. Her family came from Sachestia, a region in the northern part of the country. She was one of his subjects, one who knew nothing of her parents, her homeland or her past. Isabel deserved to know the truth, but a part of him felt awkward about what he had to do, say. He wished it were already over.

"Your mother, Evangeline Poussard, was an American college student. She was backpacking through Europe when she met Prince Aleksander Zvonimir." Yesterday, Niko's parents had explained what happened so he could explain it to Isabel today. "The two fell in love and eloped."

She looked at Niko as if he'd grown horns. "My mother was married to a prince?"

"Yes."

Isabel's mouth quirked. She looked as if she was trying hard not to laugh. "So I suppose next you're going to tell me someone who looks like Julie Andrews is not only my grandmother, but also the queen?"

Niko had no idea what Isabel was talking about. He knew who the actress was, but couldn't connect to the reference. He looked at Jovan for an explanation.

"The Princess Diaries," Jovan explained quietly. "A series

of books and movies about an American who discovers she's a princess."

Niko had never heard of any such Princess Diaries, but at least he understood the context now.

"My mother is the queen," he said to Isabel. "Though she would be thrilled to be a grandmother, I can assure you she looks and sounds nothing like Mary Poppins."

Isabel didn't crack a smile.

So much for his attempt to lighten the mood.

She shook her head. "I just don't see how any of this can be true."

"The truth is not always clear, but that doesn't mean it isn't true."

As she studied the translated document, two lines formed above the bridge of Isabel's nose. He found the trait surprisingly endearing. It made her seem less in control and more open to possibility.

"Let's say my mother was married to this prince, and he's my father," Isabel said. "Why would she give birth to me in America?"

"She didn't," Niko said. "You were born in Vernonia."

"My birth certificate says I was born in the United States. I have a copy." Isabel pursed her lips. "One of the documents is fake. I'm guessing it's yours."

"Guess all you would like, but yours is the fake," he said. "Given the political unrest in Vernonia when you were born, I wouldn't be surprised if your parents had another birth certificate made omitting both Vernonia and Prince Aleksander's name."

"You sound as if you believe all this." Disbelief dripped from each of her words. "That Prince Aleksander was my father."

"Yes," Niko said firmly. "I believe you are Princess Isabel Poussard Zvonimir Kresimir."

She scrunched her nose. "Do I look like a princess?"

"You look like a car mechanic, but that doesn't change the facts. You are a princess of Vernonia and my wife."

Isabel stared at the marriage certificate. "Then how did I wind up here?"

"That's what we'd all like to know," Niko admitted. "My father's staff have been trying to figure that out."

She arched an eyebrow. "Where did they think I was?"

He didn't answer.

"Where?" she pressed.

"Buried in your family's cemetery."

She gasped. "You thought I was dead?"

"Not me. I was too young to remember you, but all of Vernonia believed you were killed with your parents in a car bombing a month after our wedding."

Isabel lowered the papers. "A car bombing?"

"By a splinter faction of Loyalists who were nothing more than terrorists." The way her eyes clouded bothered him. "It was a…troubled time, with two groups aligned to different royal bloodlines. That is in the past now."

The two little lines above the bridge of her nose returned.

Good, Niko thought. Isabel was thinking about all that he'd told her. She would see she had to believe—

"Look. I get that you're somebody. Otherwise you wouldn't have the limo, lawyer aide guy, documents or a police escort. You know my mother's name, but you have the wrong person. The Evangeline Poussard who was my mother never went to Europe. She never married. She never would have married off her baby. And she died due to complications with childbirth, not in a terrorist attack."

"What about the box?" Niko asked.

"I don't know. Maybe there are identical boxes. Yours and hers." Isabel shoved the papers at him. "I don't have time to deal with this. I have work to do."

With her head held high as if she were the Queen of England and not a lowly mechanic, Isabel turned away from him and marched toward the garage.

Niko's fingers crumpled the edges of the papers. He tried to remember the last person besides his father who had dismissed him so readily. "Isabel."

She didn't glance back.

What an infuriating woman. He wanted to slip into the limousine and forget he'd ever heard the name Isabel Poussard, except he couldn't. They were tied together. Legally. He needed to undo what had been done without their consent. "Wait."

She quickened her step. Most women ran toward him not away, but he had a feeling Isabel was different from the women he knew.

"Please," he added.

She stopped, but didn't turn around.

He forced himself not to clench his jaw. "Before you go, please look at the photograph."

Isabel glanced over her shoulder. "What photograph?"

She made him feel more like a peasant than a prince. Likening a wife to a ball and chain suddenly made sense to him if said wife happened to be a strong-willed woman like Isabel Zvonimir.

He removed the picture from the pouch. "The wedding photo."

She didn't come closer. "Look, I'm on the clock right now. My boss is watching. I can't afford to have my pay docked so you can pull a prank."

"This isn't a prank." The old garage needed a new roof and paint job. Niko wondered if Isabel's financial circumstances were similar to those of her place of employment. "I'll give you one hundred dollars for five minutes of your time."

She straightened. "Seriously?"

Now he had her attention. With the pouch and picture tucked between his arm and side, he removed his wallet, pulled out a hundred-dollar bill and held it up. "Quite serious."

She hurried toward him with her gaze fixed on the bill.

"You really are crazy, but for that kind of money you can have seven minutes." Isabel snatched the money from him and shoved it in her coverall pocket. "Hand over the picture."

Niko gave her the photograph. He didn't need to look at it again. After examining the picture so many times during the flight to Charlotte he had memorized everything about the twelve people in it. "You are the baby in the white gown with the tiara. Your mother is holding you. Your father is standing on the right of you. Your paternal grandparents are the two next to him."

Isabel held the photo with both hands. Niko watched her face for some sign of recognition of her mother, but saw nothing.

"This looks more like a picture from a baptism than a wedding," Isabel said.

"Only because of the baby." Niko repeated what his mother had said to him. "This is a traditional royal wedding pose with the bride and groom in the center and their families on either side."

Isabel narrowed her gaze. "You're the little boy in the suit with the light blue sash across your chest?"

"Yes."

She glanced up at him. "I don't see much of a resemblance."

"That was twenty-three years ago."

Isabel traced his boyhood image. "You don't look very happy."

Niko wasn't very happy right now. He wanted to be rid of this complication, of her. "I imagine a six-year-old boy would not be too happy about getting married."

"Who is the other boy?" Isabel asked.

"My older brother."

"Why didn't they marry the baby off to him?" she asked.

Niko noticed Isabel said "the baby" not "me." He took a calming breath to keep his patience under check. "Stefan was the crown prince and already betrothed."

She looked up. "Was?"

"Stefan was killed during the conflict seven years ago."

Her eyes grew serious. "I'm sorry for your loss."

Niko didn't want or need her pity, only her cooperation. "All Vernonians suffered losses during the conflict. I intend to make sure that doesn't happen again. I want to keep the peace and modernize the country."

"Worthy goals." Isabel refocused on the photo. "I'm sorry you came all this way for nothing. My uncle Frank had one picture of my mother that wasn't destroyed when their parents' house burned down. She looked nothing like this."

Niko recalled the dossier containing information about Isabel. She didn't have any living relatives. Her mother had been an only child and orphaned at nineteen following a train derailment that killed her parents. The Zvonimir side of Isabel's family tree had been killed during the conflict. Nowhere on either side of her family tree had anyone named Frank appeared.

"Who is Uncle Frank?" Niko asked.

"Frank Miroslav," Isabel said. "My mom's older half brother. He raised me after she died."

Miroslav. Niko recognized the surname, but had no idea how it related to Isabel and her American mother. He glanced at Jovan for clarification.

"The Miroslavs served the Zvonimirs for centuries," Jovan explained. "There was a deep tie and strong loyalty between the two families even though the relationship was master-servant. Franko Miroslav was Prince Aleksander's chauffeur, and I would go as far to say his best friend. It is rumored that Franko introduced the prince to Evangeline Poussard."

Isabel's mouth dropped open. She closed it.

"That would explain how you escaped out of Vernonia and ended up here," Niko said. "If they used another driver and a doll for the baby after you left the country—"

"No." Her lips tightened. "The woman in the photo is not my mother."

"Are you certain the woman in the picture your uncle Frank showed you is your mother?" Niko watched the range of emotions crossing her face. The vulnerability in her eyes surprisingly pulled at his heart. "I apologize, Isabel. I know this is difficult for you."

"What you're saying is impossible. Who would let a Vernonian chauffeur into the U.S. with a baby? Where would they get forged American documents? It's just not possible." She looked at the photograph as if trying to discover a secret hidden in it. "Uncle Frank wasn't a chauffeur. He wasn't a servant. He was a car mechanic from a little town outside Chicago. The town where he grew up with my mother. His little sister. He was like a father to me. Why would he lie to me about this?"

Niko respected the way she stood up for the man who raised her. Loyalty to one's family was important and would serve her well. "Perhaps Franko, your Uncle Frank, withheld certain truths for your own protection. You were his princess. A faction in Vernonia would have tried to kill you if they'd known you lived."

A faction that had been loyal to Niko's father even if the king hadn't approved of the group's methods and violence.

"It's so unbelievable."

Niko was not going to convince her with words, but perhaps he could show her. "There is a way to find out if what I say is true or not."

Her gaze jerked up from the photo to meet his. "How?"

He pulled the chain from beneath his shirt. "We can see if my key fits the lock."

Please don't fit. Please don't fit. Please don't fit.

The mantra had been running through Izzy's mind for the last half hour, ever since driving home with Boyd and Jovan to retrieve the box. Now she sat in Rowdy's office with the wooden box on her lap waiting for the others to join her.

That still doesn't explain why you would give the box to me.

Because I am your husband.

Her husband. Izzy's vision blurred. She felt light-headed.

She clutched the wooden box with its mother-of-pearl inlaid design. She didn't want to drop it onto the hard tile floor. All these years, she'd carted it around, carefully, but not overly so. The value had been sentimental, not monetary.

Now…

Izzy Poussard, a princess and a crown prince's wife?

No way.

Okay, some women—maybe many women—would be excited to discover they were a long lost princess from some faraway foreign land and married to a handsome prince. But not Izzy. Oh, sure, she wanted a happily ever after, but her fairy tale didn't involve enchanted castles, sparkling jewelry and Prince Charming. Her dream revolved around wearing a fire suit in team colors, working over the wall on a pit stop, becoming a crew chief and standing in the winner's circle with champagne being squirted everywhere.

The door to Rowdy's office opened. Niko, Jovan and her boss entered.

"It'll be just a few more minutes, Izzy," Rowdy said. "Duncan Moore is on his way."

"Thanks." Izzy had asked Rowdy to call one of their customers who was a big-name attorney in Charlotte. She needed to talk to a lawyer before Niko and Jovan tried to take the box from her. To her surprise, Niko had offered to cover all her legal expenses. Izzy hadn't wanted to accept the prince's charity. She hadn't relied on anyone since Uncle Frank's death. But she didn't have extra money lying around to cover surprise legal fees. Duncan Moore wasn't only one of the best lawyers, he was also one of the most high-priced attorneys in town. Being prideful was one thing. Being stupid was another. "And thank you, Niko, for covering my legal expenses."

"You're welcome," he said. "I am not here to cause you grief or unwanted expenditures."

Izzy wanted to believe him. The corners of her lips lifted into a closed-mouth smile.

He smiled back.

Butterflies flapped in her stomach. Uh-oh. She'd better watch it. Being attracted to a man claiming to be her husband would only complicate things and might lead to her losing ownership of the box.

"Duncan's here," Rowdy announced.

Thank goodness, Izzy thought.

Duncan Moore, bald, in his late fifties and on his third marriage, strutted into the office. On any other man a polka-dot bow tie would have looked ridiculous with a suit, but it worked well on the successful attorney.

"Sorry for the delay, everyone. Izzy." Duncan looked at Niko and bowed. "Your Royal Highness."

Niko acknowledged Duncan with a nod. "This is my aide and lawyer, Jovan Novak."

Jovan shook Duncan's hand.

Unease crept down Izzy's spine. The seriousness of the situation ratcheted up a notch with two lawyers present.

"We may proceed now," Niko said.

The tension in the office quadrupled. Izzy's legs shook so much the box on her lap jiggled up and down. She placed the box on Rowdy's desk and opened the lid. She removed the velvet-covered tray so the keyhole showed. "I didn't realize the tray came out or there was a keyhole until after Uncle Frank died. He allowed me to look at the box, but never touch it."

"Did your uncle say the box belonged to your mother?" Duncan asked.

"No, but I assumed so." Izzy hoped her words wouldn't give more credence to the prince's claims. "Uncle Frank just said it was important."

Niko held the key he'd worn around his neck. "Let us see how important."

His hand was as steady as a neurosurgeon's. If it had been her, she would be trembling. Who was she kidding? She was trembling.

He inserted the key in the hole.

Izzy was tempted to close her eyes. She held her breath instead. She wanted to know what was inside the bottom portion of the box, but she didn't want anything the prince had told her to be true.

He turned the key.

Click.

"The key fits," Niko announced.

The air whooshed from Izzy's lungs.

No, this can't be happening. It can't be true.

The bottom portion of the box slid out. A hidden drawer.

"Would ya look at that," Rowdy said with a hint of awe to his deep voice.

Even though she had been waiting for this moment for a few years now, she was afraid to look. All her curiosity had vanished, replaced by trepidation. She didn't care what was in the box. She only wanted things to go back to the way they'd been before Prince Niko arrived.

"It's the same tiara," Jovan said from across the office.

No. Isabel didn't want to see so she squeezed her eyes shut. Her chest constricted. She shuddered.

Someone touched her shoulder and squeezed gently. Rowdy. Both he and Boyd could be big old teddy bears. She opened her eyes, but saw Niko with his hand on her instead of her boss.

"Isabel." Concern filled Niko's voice. "Would you rather wait?"

The tenderness of his gaze brought tears to her eyes. The situation, she rationalized, not him. Still she appreciated his gesture of comfort, drew strength from it, too. "No."

Straightening, Izzy looked into the drawer past the small diamond tiara to find papers, photographs and jewelry. Her uncle Frank could have found the box or bought it at a garage sale or even stolen it in desperation. Maybe that was why she had no key.

No, she was just being silly now. None of those things would explain the prince knowing her mother's name or his key fitting the lock. Isabel needed to accept what was in front of her, except...

Niko reached into the drawer.

"Wait, sir," Duncan shouted.

The prince drew back his hand.

"May I please take a picture of the contents before they are disturbed?" Duncan asked with a camera in hand. "I would like to document everything. For both Izzy's and your sake."

"Certainly," Niko said.

The flash of the camera reminded Izzy of lightning and intensified the emotions warring inside her. She hated storms. Uncle Frank had died during a lightning storm. She swallowed back a tide of grief.

Duncan backed away. "Thank you, sir. Please proceed."

Niko didn't. Instead he looked at her. "At one time your parents had a key to the bride box. They placed these contents inside. Only you should remove them."

Anger flared. She loved Uncle Frank, but he had kept her past a secret. Why? Why hadn't he trusted her? She wanted to know why this had happened.

"Isabel—"

"I'll do it." She couldn't decide what to do about this until she knew more. "But only because I need to have all the facts."

Izzy felt four pairs of eyes staring at her. She was used to the attention. Not many people expected a female mechanic to fix their cars. This was different. Unsettling. But Uncle Frank had taught her to always hold her head high, no matter how uncertain she might feel inside. If only he were here now...

She scooted her chair closer to the desk. With a shaky hand, she raised the tiara from the box. "It's so tiny."

Niko nodded. "My parents had the tiara commissioned for you to wear at the wedding. The small diamonds represent all the towns and villages. The three larger diamonds symbolize you, me and Vernonia."

"It's hard to tell if it's exactly the same one in the photo," she said, knowing she was grasping at straws.

"It's the same one," Niko countered.

Izzy set the tiara on the desk. Next she removed foreign coins and dollar bills, a diamond pendant, an emerald bracelet and three stunning rings.

Those jewels would be worth a fortune if real. Maybe that was why Niko wanted the box back so badly. Money could make people do almost anything.

She picked up a photograph, a picture of a man and a woman.

"Those were your parents," Niko said softly.

Her parents. Izzy wasn't ready to believe it just yet. She stared at the handsome couple. They were smiling and holding hands. They looked happier than they did in the wedding photograph. "The woman is beautiful."

"You look like her," Rowdy said.

"I wish." Izzy's heart ached for some memory of the two people the prince claimed were her parents.

"You resemble your mother," Niko said. "But you have your father's eyes."

Izzy felt a rush of excitement. No one had ever seen a resemblance between her and Uncle Frank. She removed more photographs. Baby pictures, family portraits, casual snapshots, of people she didn't know taken in places she didn't recognize.

Next came an official looking piece of paper with foreign writing. "I don't know what it says."

"Allow me," Niko offered.

She handed it to him.

He glanced over the document. "It's your birth certificate. Evangaline Poussard Zvonimir is listed as your mother. Aleksander Nicholas Zvonimir is listed as your father. Your place of birth is Sachestia, Vernonia. That is in the northern part of the country."

Jovan placed the documents they'd shown her earlier on the desk. "In case you are concerned about the translation and wish to compare, ma'am."

"My name is Izzy," she corrected. "I would like to see a translation by an impartial person to confirm the document."

"How can you still not believe?" Niko asked.

"I'm simply being cautious," she admitted. "You've gone to a lot of trouble to find me. You could've just offered to buy the box and be done with it. And me."

"You are my wife," Niko said. "I cannot pretend you do not exist and be done with it or you."

Izzy grimaced. "Too bad there isn't some birthmark that would prove without a doubt that I'm royalty."

"Perhaps there is one." Wicked laughter lit Niko's eyes. "I would be happy to search for one."

Her cheeks warmed at the thought.

His faced reddened, too.

She hadn't been expecting that reaction from Niko, but his embarrassment made him seem less a dark, formal prince and more…human. That made Izzy feel a little more comfortable with him even if her heart pounded like a piston engine each time she noticed him staring at her.

She removed several pieces of paper stapled together. Again, the words were written in a language she couldn't read. She handed the pages to Niko.

He flipped through them. "This is your father's will naming you the sole beneficiary of his estate."

"I will need a copy of the will, sir," Duncan said.

"Of course." Niko handed it to the lawyer then turned his attention on Izzy. "Everyone believed you died with your parents so your father's estate went to—"

"You," she said without an ounce of doubt.

"As your husband, your inheritance passed directly to me."

"What kind of estate are we talking about, Your Highness?" Duncan asked.

Niko glanced at Jovan. "What is the approximate net worth?"

"Approximately twenty-five million euros," Jovan said.

She didn't know much about foreign currency, but she knew a lot of money was at stake here. "You're willing to give that to me for some box?"

"The box and an annulment," Niko clarified.

Rowdy whistled. "It's like winning the lottery, Izzy."

Yes, it was. She took a deep breath. That meant it was probably too good to be true.

"Let's not get too excited," Duncan cautioned. "We have no idea how the legal system works in Vernonia. Each country has its own laws for estates and inheritance. Something like this could be tied up in the court system for years."

"I would never keep anything that rightly belongs to Isabel," Niko stated firmly. "Vernonia might be a small country, but we have a parliamentarian government and a modern justice system. It will not take the High Court years to sort this matter out."

"Can't something like this be taken care of in the U.S?" Izzy asked.

"Your father's property is in Vernonia," Niko explained. "Besides, the High Court is private. There could be publicity if we used the court here in the United States."

She glanced at the lawyer. "Duncan?"

"I don't know anything about Vernonia's court system, but Prince Niko is correct about the publicity. America loves royalty. The press would have a field day if they found out you were an American princess."

Izzy frowned. "I'm not—"

"Come to Vernonia with me," Niko suggested. "We will appear in front of the High Court and have this matter resolved quickly."

Apprehension washed over her. She never went anywhere. "I don't have a passport."

"I can pull some strings," Niko said.

"Most definitely," Jovan agreed.

She bit her lip. "I don't know. Maybe I should take some time to think about it."

Silence filled the room. Outside in the garage bay an air compressor sounded. A horn honked. A car door slammed.

"There's a lot at stake, Izzy," Rowdy said. "Don't let that stubborn streak of yours get in the way."

Stubborn streak? She wasn't stubborn.

"Listen to Rowdy," Duncan advised. "Prince Niko believes you are Princess Isabel. He's willing to give you a multimillion dollar estate. What more do you need to think about?"

Her gaze bounced between Rowdy and Duncan. They made good points. Still she hesitated. Cautious. Nervous. Unsure.

"Something else is in the drawer, ma'am," Jovan said.

She glanced down and saw a note-size envelope tucked away in one corner. The word Isabel was written on the front. The cursive writing looked feminine.

As she picked up the small envelope, her hand trembled. The flap had been tucked inside, not sealed. Carefully Izzy removed sheets of paper and unfolded the pages. She was happy to see words written in English.

"Our Beloved Daughter." Tears pricked Izzy's eyes as she

read the words. No one had ever called her daughter. Not even Uncle Frank who she loved like a father.

She continued reading.

You are only a baby yet you are already a bride. Forgive us for sending you to America, but your father saw no other way to keep you safe. The marriage between you and Prince Nikola was supposed to protect you and keep peace among Vernonians. But that plan appears to have backfired and now you are in even worse danger. My greatest wish is that you never read this letter. I plan to destroy it when we arrive in the U.S. If you are reading this note now, then things did not go as your father and I planned. And for that, little princess, I am more sorry than you will ever know.

Your father is torn between the two sides wanting control of Vernonia. The Separatists first wanted to split into their own country, Sachestia, with your grandfather as king. Now they want to wrest full control from King Dmitar and take over the entire country, but your father would rather remain loyal to the throne and Vernonia. Your marriage, however, has unexpectedly antagonized both factions and made it impossible for him to support either side now. We must leave Vernonia as soon as possible. Your safety is our utmost concern. Once this craziness ends, we will happily return.

We do not dare leave the country together so we are sending you first. We are entrusting you to the care and protection of Franko Miroslav. He is your father's chauffeur, and our dearest and closest friend. He will do whatever is necessary to keep you from harm. We have arranged passage and paperwork so the two of you can escape to the U.S. We will follow the next day.

No one knows of our plan, including the king. He's a good man, but the fewer people who know your whereabouts the better. Your departure and location will remain a secret until it is safe.

Your father is telling me it's time for you to go. I must sign off now, Isabel.

We love you, our darling Izzy, and hope to be with you soon.

Love,

Mommy and Daddy

Izzy took several deep breaths as the words sunk in. She'd never felt anything toward the woman in the photo Uncle Frank had shown her, a woman who wasn't really her mother. But this letter written in her mother's own hand provided Izzy with a connection to the woman who gave birth to her. Something she'd longed for since she was little. Something she'd hoped to find by looking for the key.

"True." She sat back in the chair. The girl more comfortable in Shop class than Home Ec was a real-life princess with both a mother and a father. Everything the prince had said... "It's all true."

"I'm sorry," Niko said.

Izzy believed him. No one wanted to discover they were married to a stranger.

Married.

Her stomach roiled.

Marriage was only part of this. Everything she thought she knew about herself was wrong. Izzy wrapped her arms around her stomach. She wasn't who she thought she was. She had money. A title. A father.

Izzy recalled her parents' smiling faces from the wedding photograph. A mother and a father who had loved her. A mother and a father who had been killed before she could get to know them.

Emotion clogged Izzy's throat.

But it wasn't too late to fulfill one of their wishes. Her parents had planned on returning to Vernonia. That must have meant Uncle Frank planned on going back, too.

Come to Vernonia with me. We will appear in front of the High Court and have this matter resolved quickly.

Maybe seeing the place where she came from would help her figure out who she was and what her future held. She could get the marriage annulled and receive her inheritance. Forget going to pit crew school. She could buy her own racing team.

Izzy rose. "When do you want to leave for Vernonia?"

CHAPTER THREE

When do you want to leave for Vernonia?

Sooner rather than later. Niko sat at the table in the recreational vehicle, also known as an RV, where Isabel lived. His concern over the press discovering the reason behind his unannounced trip to the U.S. continued to grow. But Isabel still had to shower, dress and pack. That would take time. They would be leaving later whether he liked it or not.

Isabel stood in front of the small refrigerator still wearing her bulky, stained coveralls. She rubbed her hands together as if nervous. "Would you like something to drink or eat?"

He appreciated her hospitality. Twenty-three years away from Vernonia hadn't erased centuries of innate good breeding. "No, thank you."

With a hesitant expression, she glanced toward the back of the RV. "It won't take me more than a few minutes to get ready."

A lump on the faded brown-and-orange plaid cushion behind his back made him shift positions. "The plane will not take off without us."

As she closed a partition that separated the back portion of the motor home from the front section, Niko surveyed the interior with dismay. Warped wood veneer. Cracked cabinet and cupboard doors. Frayed carpeting. Cramped space. The RV had to be as old as Isabel.

What had Franko been thinking? Yes, the chauffeur needed to keep her safe, but why had he never contacted the king for assistance? Why had Franko allowed it to come to this?

Niko exhaled on a sigh.

Isabel was no damsel in distress. She'd impressed him with the way she'd dealt with her world being turned inside out. She hadn't been blinded by his title or money. She wouldn't accept his word as the truth without concrete evidence. Surprising, given she lived in near poverty in a shabby motor home with no family or resources. A princess of Vernonia deserved better than a life spent working long hours bent over a car engine and coming home to half a dozen barking, trembling Chihuahuas who lived next door.

She wouldn't be his wife for much longer, but he wanted Isabel to have the kind of life her parents intended for her to have. She belonged in a castle.

The partition jiggled like it was stuck.

"Isabel?" Niko asked, wondering if she needed assistance.

"I'm almost finished," she said from behind the thin wall.

He checked his watch. Five minutes. That had to be a world record. Then again, Isabel didn't seem to be a woman who primped or even cared about her appearance.

The partition jerked open.

As she walked out of the back toward him, he did a double-take. Her faded blue jeans fit like a second skin, clinging in all the right places, accentuating her feminine curves and long legs. The fabric of her T-shirt stretched across her chest. Her high, round breasts jiggled. Her shiny brown hair swung back and forth below her shoulders.

He met her gaze, captivated by her warm, brown eyes. An appealing mix of intelligence and caring shone in their depths.

This was his…wife?

"I'm ready to go," Isabel announced.

So was he. Niko was ready to follow wherever she wanted to go.

"I don't own a lot of clothes." Isabel motioned to the worn purple duffel bag she carried behind her. The bride box with all its original contents was in the limousine with Jovan. "What I have probably isn't nice enough to wear to court."

"I will make arrangements for you to go shopping once we

arrive." He would head off any of her financial concerns. "Do not worry about the cost."

"You're already paying for a lot."

"I don't mind." Niko would enjoy seeing her in designer gowns with jewels adorning her graceful neck. He would enjoy removing those things from her, too. Too bad that would never happen. "You are my wife."

"Only until the annulment," she reminded.

"Yes, but until then it is my responsibility to take care of you."

Isabel pushed her chin forward almost defiantly. "I can take care of myself."

"I know that." He still wouldn't mind a turn. Most women wanted him to take care of them. It felt odd that Isabel didn't. He bowed his head in apology. "A poor choice of words on my part. I promise to make it up to you."

"No need."

As she brushed past him, an appealing mix of vanilla and jasmine filled his nostrils. The smell was a significant improvement over the motor oil one earlier. "I want to."

"That's okay." Her smile nearly knocked him off his seat. "I've already forgiven you."

Niko didn't want her forgiveness. He wanted...her.

Damn. The attraction to Isabel was unexpected and unwelcome. His duties and responsibilities always took priority. Niko was practically engaged to Julianna. He shouldn't be attracted to any woman.

Not even your wife? a voice mocked.

He balled his hands to gain control. His father had taught him to keep emotion reined in. Otherwise it became a weakness, one that others, particularly adversaries, would use to their advantage.

Niko focused his gaze on Isabel's pretty face. Maybe it would be better to concentrate on her forehead. "Is there anything else you need to pack for the trip?"

"No. I won't be in Vernonia that long."

"You might like it there."

She shrugged. "This has been my home since I was six."

He couldn't believe she'd lived like this for the past seventeen years. "That's a long time."

"When Uncle Frank bought the RV, he said we would never have to leave home again. We could always take it with us." She removed a carton of milk from the refrigerator and poured it down the sink. "I wonder if he was thinking about Vernonia when he said that."

"Possibly." Niko glanced around her hovel. "There are many other places to live than here."

"I know." Isabel rinsed the carton in the small sink. "This motor home is nothing more than an old metal shed compared to a lot of other places, but I've been happy here. A little lonely since Uncle Frank died, but it's hard to leave the good memories behind."

"You will make new memories."

"I need to come to peace with the old ones first." She stared off into the distance. "So many things about Uncle Frank are making more sense now. The lack of photographs. Wanting me to study martial arts. Keeping such a low profile. Being so protective. Even if he wasn't related to me by blood he's still family. The only I ever knew."

Niko nodded. "We shall honor Franko for the sacrifices he made by keeping you safe."

"Thank you." Gratitude shone her eyes. "Vernonia must have meant a lot to him or he would have never given up so much for me. I always thought he was satisfied living like this, and I'd be the one to leave someday. Now I know he didn't plan on living here forever, either. He would have returned…home."

Isabel's words eased some of Niko's concerns about her future. "Your father's estate will enable you to live wherever and however you want."

She sighed. "The thought of so many choices is intimidating."

"Think of only one choice at a time. It won't seem so… overwhelming."

"Good advice," she said. "Thanks."

Helping her pleased him. "Is there anything else you need?"

Isabel glanced around. "Boyd is going to check on the RV while I'm away so everything should be okay."

Niko remembered the tall man who had driven her and Jovan to retrieve the box. The same man had come out to check on her and watched her from the garage. A woman as attractive as Isabel was sure to have men after her. One who worked with her would have an advantage. "Is Boyd your boyfriend?"

"Boyd?" She scrunched her nose. "He's like a brother. Some people think we're a couple, but we're just friends."

The news brought an unfamiliar sense of relief. But Boyd wasn't the only man in Charlotte. "Do you have a boyfriend?"

"No boyfriend."

"But you date."

"Not nearly as much as I probably should. I work too much overtime to have a serious relationship. And the boys at the garage can be a little overprotective when guys do drop by."

The news pleased Niko more than it should have.

"What about you?" she asked.

"No boyfriend."

She grinned. "Any girlfriends?"

He used to have girlfriends. He'd dated models to princesses. Julianna wasn't his girlfriend per se, yet she was the woman he planned to marry. Better to keep things simple than give Isabel too complicated an explanation. "Yes, I have a girlfriend."

"What's her name?"

"Julianna. We are planning to marry."

"Congratulations, Niko." Isabel locked a window latch. "I hope the two of you are very happy together."

Her enthusiasm surprised him. "You do?"

"Of course I do," she admitted. "Why wouldn't I? I may be your wife, but that was a choice neither of us made or would choose today."

Niko winced. Her words stung. He might not choose her, but he didn't see why she wouldn't choose him. He was a prince and quite eligible according to the tabloids and magazines. "Who would you choose to marry?"

"No one."

"You do not wish to marry?"

"I have a few things I want to do first."

"Tell me about these things."

"I'm planning to enroll in pit crew school, work on a pit crew and eventually be a crew chief."

Those were unusual goals for a woman. Unthinkable for a female in Vernonia let alone a princess. "You like racing."

"I love racing. Open-wheel, stock car, go-kart, it doesn't matter as long as there's a checkered flag at the end."

The passion in her voice matched the light in her eyes and reminded him of Julianna when she sailed. Perhaps the two women had more in common than Niko had thought. "Your inheritance will allow you to do almost anything you want in racing."

"Yeah, I guess focusing on going to pit crew school now is like a Lotto winner who plans to keep their job." Isabel swung the strap of a blue backpack over her shoulder. She opened the door. "Ready to roll, Highness."

Then again, maybe she didn't have that much in common with Princess Julianna after all.

Across the tarmac at the Charlotte Douglas International Airport, jet engines roared.

This was unreal. Izzy stood on the landing at the top of the portable aircraft staircase with a gorgeous prince who happened to be her husband. She still couldn't believe what was happening.

Each beat of her heart slammed against her ribs. She'd never once dreamed of traveling to a far off destination except to attend a race. But here she was about to board a private plane and fly off to another continent…

An airplane sped down the runway.

She shivered. Soon that would be her plane.

Some might call this an exciting adventure, but not Izzy. Her misgivings were increasing by the minute.

Another aircraft taxied by. The silver, red and blue color-

scheme seemed almost festive compared to Vernonia's solid
white airplane with only an aircraft numbers, letters and a small
coat of arms for markings.

A royal coat of arms.

A chill ran down her spine.

She could never have imagined this happening to anyone let
alone her. A grease monkey who cared more about the Winston
Cup standings than the lines of succession for European thrones
was now a princess?

Below her at the bottom of the stairs, a local security detail
stood watch. A custom agent checked paperwork with the security liaison officer who wore a uniform and seemed to be part
of the flight crew.

The shock of discovery still had her reeling. Denial battled
acceptance. In spite of the physical evidence, Izzy still found
the truth hard to accept. Would she ever feel like Princess Isabel
Poussard Zvonimir Kresimir? She doubted it.

Facing the open doorway, Izzy sensed rather than felt Niko
standing behind her. She clutched the strap of her backpack.

"It's time to board," he whispered from behind her. His warm
breath fanned her neck.

Awareness shot through Izzy. Her uneasiness quadrupled.

Hold it together.

She straightened, not wanting to appear weak. "I know."

Yet the open doorway loomed in front of her like a mysterious
black hole. Her heart pounded so fast, Izzy thought her chest
might explode.

All she had to do was step across the threshold and board
the plane. Too bad her feet felt as if they'd been permanently
attached to the staircase. But they knew what Izzy kept trying
to forget.

This wasn't only about never having flown before. She had
absolutely no idea what waited for her on the other side. Of the
doorway or when she arrived in Vernonia.

She'd never had to face the unknown alone. Uncle Frank had
always been there to pave the way. Even after his death, she'd
continued working at Rowdy's, living in the RV and following

the plan they'd dreamed up together. But now she found herself on a new, uncertain path with all her plans swept away.

Worse, there was no turning back.

Her life was irrevocably changed whether she boarded the plane or stayed in Charlotte. The realization made her light-headed.

The prince moved closer, crowding her from behind. He emanated strength and warmth. Her pulse skittered.

Uh-oh. Izzy needed to put a little distance between them. Not that she had much room to go anywhere. She shifted to the side until her backpack and hip hit the staircase railing. "Give me a minute."

Niko gently placed his hand on the curve of her back.

Izzy stiffened. The slight touch made her more apprehensive.

"You will have plenty of time once we board," he said.

She was losing control of this situation, of her life. "Things are happening too fast. I need everything to slow down."

"Everything will slow down when we are in the air. We have a long flight ahead of us."

A long flight that would carry her away from everything familiar. Nerves smacked into her like a rogue wave. Her stomach churned.

"Isabel," Niko said.

Another plane took off. The roar louder than any engine she'd ever heard at the racetrack. Goose bumps prickled her skin.

"I told you I needed a minute." The words came out harsher than she intended.

"It's been an eventful day," Niko said.

"You think?" She swallowed around the crown-jewel-size lump in her throat. "I doubt anyone else has ever had a day like today. I wish it were all a dream. But it's not. And now I'm stuck."

"Stuck?"

"Having to go to Vernonia to annul the marriage and get my inheritance," she admitted. "Unfortunately I have no idea what's going to happen once we arrive. I may have been born there, but it might as well be Mars."

Niko's assessing gaze made her feel like one of Cinderella's ugly stepsisters. "Vernonia is different from what you are used to. Some would call the country old-fashioned. Others antiquated. Especially when it comes to gender roles."

Izzy half laughed with a mix of desperation and fear. "If you're trying to make me feel better, it's not working."

"I will not lie to you, Isabel," he said. "Your life has changed. But you will not have to deal with any of this on your own."

A sense of inadequacy swept through her. Izzy was used to handling everything on her own, but she was completely out of her comfort zone here and practically shaking in her held-together-with-super-glue tennis shoes.

"It will be my pleasure to help you," he offered.

Niko made a dashing knight in shining armor, but Izzy didn't like being cast in the role of damsel in distress. She didn't want or need his help. "Thanks, but I can do this on my own."

Please let me be able to do this on my own.

With a deep breath, Izzy stood and stepped through the doorway of the plane.

"Welcome aboard, Your Royal Highness," a male flight attendant with a crew cut and navy blue uniform greeted. "We have a seven course dinner for you as well as movies for your entertainment."

It took Izzy a minute to realize the man was addressing her. "Thank you," she muttered, wondering how he knew who she was.

The flight attendant smiled at her. "Would you like me to escort you to your seat, ma'am?"

"Thank you, Luka, but I will show Princess Isabel the way," Niko said before Izzy could answer.

Luka bowed. "Enjoy your flight, ma'am, sir."

"I thought you wanted to keep my identity a secret to avoid publicity," she whispered to Niko as she moved away from Luka.

"Only until after we appear before the High Court," he explained quietly.

As his male scent surrounded her, heat rushed through her veins. She hoped the High Court would be their first stop after they landed.

"Do not worry," he continued. "The crew is part of the Vernonian Air Force. They can be trusted with the information. As can the palace staff."

That seemed like a lot of people in on the secret, but he was the prince. "If you say so."

"I do."

Izzy made her way down the aisle, holding her backpack in front of her. The interior, a mix of warm beiges, browns and blues, created a welcoming environment. Couches and tables filled the first section of the cabin.

"This is the lounge area," Niko explained. "Feel free to come up here if you want to stretch your legs."

"I doubt I'll unfasten my seat belt during the flight."

The corners of his mouth lifted. "That may get uncomfortable if you have to use the facilities."

Her cheeks warmed. She hadn't considered that.

The second section of the cabin contained rows of seats. The wide leather seats looked comfortable and luxurious, not narrow and cramped and squished together as her high school classmates had described after their graduation trip to the Caribbean. Izzy hadn't been able to afford the trip, so had stayed home and worked at Rowdy's garage.

Times sure had changed. Mechanic Izzy Poussard was now Princess Isabel, the wife of the crown prince of Vernonia. She nearly laughed at the absurdity of it.

"This is where we sit for takeoff and landing, or, if you choose," Niko said, "the entire flight."

Izzy passed the row where Jovan sat. A few other seats were taken by people she hadn't seen before. She continued to the last row of empty seats before a divider.

Before she could sit, a female flight attendant rushed from the rear of the plane. The young woman wore a navy jacket and skirt. Her blond hair was neatly braided into a bun. "Good evening. Allow me to hold your backpack for you, Your Royal Highness."

Before Izzy could say a word, the backpack strap was lifted out of her hand. Every one of her muscles tensed, bunching into tight balls. She wasn't used to being catered to. It was disconcerting because she didn't feel like royalty.

She sat in the window seat and buckled her seat belt.

The flight attendant handed the backpack to Izzy. "Would you care for something to drink or eat, ma'am?"

"No, thanks." Izzy didn't want to upset her stomach any more than it already was. Her nerves were getting the best of her. Over the flight, over Vernonia, over Niko. Maybe if she distracted herself…

She pressed a button that turned on the overhead light. She twisted a knob that regulated the airflow nozzle.

Niko sat next to her. "Are you certain you do not want anything?"

Izzy wanted this to be over with. "No, thanks, Your Highness."

"Call me Niko."

"I'm not sure I should get in the habit of calling you by your first name. As soon as our marriage is annulled I doubt you'd want to be on such familiar terms with a commoner."

"You are not a commoner," he said. "You are a princess by birth. Royal Sachestian blood flows through your veins."

"That may be true, but I was raised American. Royalty is something other countries have."

"Americans have unofficial royalty. The Kennedys, the Rockefellers, the Hiltons."

"I suppose, but a princess isn't something I aspired to be beyond the age of four or five. Wearing a tiara has never been a dream of mine."

"You may feel like an American, but you are a Vernonian." He spoke as if her being a Vernonian was the most important thing she could be. No one had ever spoken to her that way. Not even Uncle Frank. "You will be amazed by the history of your family."

Intrigued, she leaned toward him. "I have a family history?"

"Your lineage goes back centuries. Your father's family played an integral role in the formation of our country, when Sachestia in the north merged with the south to form what we now call Vernonia." He fastened his seat belt. "If you have questions about anything, please ask."

"I—" The lights in the cabin flickered. She clutched the seat armrests until her knuckles turned white. "What's that?"

"The APU, auxiliary power unit, coming on," he explained. "It powers the lights and air system while we are in flight."

"Oh, yeah. I should have remembered that."

The plane moved backward.

Oh boy, oh boy, oh boy.

"Do not worry." Niko covered her hand with his large one. His skin was warm, but not soft. Scars and calluses covered his hand and fingers. "The plane is being moved so the pilot can taxi to the runway."

Forget about the plane. His touch disturbed her more than it comforted. She tried to slip her hand from beneath his, but couldn't. "I'm sorry if I've acted like a wimp, but I'm okay now."

"You've handled everything remarkably well, Isabel. You should be proud of yourself."

He wouldn't let Izzy remove her hand from his, but his words made her sit taller. She wanted to be brave for him, but mostly herself. That was what Uncle Frank would have wanted her to be.

The engines roared to life. She sucked in a breath.

Nothing to worry about. Nothing to worry about.

The words became a mantra.

The plane taxied to the runway. Out the window, she saw the airport lights shining in the darkness. Pretty, but she would rather be at home watching a television show than sitting on a luxurious private jet holding hands with a handsome prince.

Too late to back out now.

Izzy pressed her feet against the floor of the plane.

"We will be in the air shortly," Niko said.

All she could do was nod.

The jet lurched to a stop. The engines whined, the sound growing louder. She was too nervous to appreciate the speed of the rotor. The cabin shook like the crowd at Daytona when cars went three wide. Izzy held her breath.

Suddenly the jet speeded down the runway.

She glanced out the window at the world passing by her.

"Remember to breathe," he said.

She did.

Nikola squeezed her hand.

This time his touch reassured her. She met his eyes. Her gaze dropped to his mouth. She thought about kissing him until she couldn't think straight, but that seemed a little extreme. Maybe burying her face against his chest until this was over would be better. She closed her eyes instead.

"Look at me, Isabel."

She forced her eyes open. Her gaze locked with his intense green eyes.

"You are safe," he said. "As long as you are with me, you will always be safe."

The confidence and strength he exuded made her almost believe his words. But she knew *safe* didn't really exist. If it did her parents would be alive. Uncle Frank, too.

The vibrations increased until she thought the plane might break apart. The forward momentum pushed her back against her seat. Niko laced his fingers with hers.

The plane lifted off the ground.

The lights below grew smaller and smaller until they disappeared altogether. The plane climbed at a steep angle, as if it were a fighter jet not a passenger plane.

The aircraft jolted. She sucked in another breath.

"A patch of turbulence," Niko said. "Normal."

None of this was normal. Not the takeoff, not the prince sitting next to her. And certainly not this life-altering adventure she was embarking on.

After what seemed like forever, the plane leveled.

"We've reached cruising altitude." Niko kept his hand on hers. "Not too bad."

It wasn't a question.

"No," she admitted. "But we still have to land."

The corners of his mouth lifted. "Landing will be easier."

"Really?" she asked.

He nodded. "You'll be tired due to the time change. You may even be asleep when the wheels touch ground."

"I'm not sure I'll be sleeping after everything that's gone on. My mind's a big jumble right now."

"You should try to sleep," he encouraged her. "Tomorrow will be a big day."

"Are we going straight to the court?" she asked.

"The High Court is not in session on Saturday. We will go to the castle."

"Castle?"

"My parents want to meet you."

"I've never met a king or a queen."

"You have, but you don't remember."

"What's your father like?" Izzy asked.

"He's very…kingly."

"That's intimidating," she admitted. "I'm glad I don't remember meeting him or I might be more nervous than I already am."

"He only wants to reassure himself you are alive and well." Niko squeezed her hand. "You have nothing to worry about."

This time Izzy knew the prince was wrong. Dead wrong.

She had lots to worry about, starting with the tingles shooting up her arm as he touched her. But even worse was the realization that she didn't want him to let go of her hand.

Not now.

Not when they landed in Vernonia.

Not…ever.

CHAPTER FOUR

As THE plane cruised at thirty-three thousand feet, the interior cabin lights dimmed. The engines droned, but unlike the white noise device Niko usually traveled with, the sound did not soothe him. He couldn't sleep. Too many things weighed on his mind. But a busy day did lie ahead. He should at least try to rest.

Niko pressed the button on the armrest. The leather seat reclined into a comfortable position. He closed his eyes but couldn't stop the continuous stream of information flowing through his brain. Thoughts about Vernonia, Julianna, his father and most especially the woman sitting in the seat next to him.

Isabel.

Opening his eyes, he turned toward her.

She sat with her seat reclined and her head resting against a pillow. She'd fallen asleep after struggling against her heavy, drooping eyelids and drawn-out yawns for almost an hour.

Isabel's unwillingness to give in to her tiredness without a fight made him wonder if she turned everything she did into a battle. Her actions today suggested as much. But the political peace that came with her lineage could be good for the country.

Yes, Isabel seemed like a fighter. No doubt the Vernonian in her. Niko smiled at the thought that she would likely disagree with him. No matter, he would want her on his side. If he had a side. Thankfully those days were over. No one would be forced to choose who to support or who to fight again.

Once he and Julianna said the words "I do," Niko would

have the financial resources and international support to bring his country into the modern age and, in time, the European Union.

Nothing could stand in his way now.

Not an antiquated custom. Not a childhood bride.

Niko's gaze focused on Isabel once again.

He'd been married to her for the past twenty-three years, almost all of her entire life and over three-quarters of his. If not for the missing bride box, he would have never known she existed. Things would have been less complicated for him that way. But once she received her inheritance her circumstance would improve dramatically. A better life was waiting for Isabel. The life her parents would have wanted for her. That made what he was going through more acceptable.

He worried what responsibilities would be thrust on Isabel's shoulders once she arrived in Vernonia. People would judge her. She would need training to be a princess. Stylish clothes and makeup lessons would improve her appearance. A manicure would help with her dirty, chipped nails though not much could rid her hands of the calluses, cuts and scars. Perhaps she could start a new fashion trend by wearing gloves.

In spite of Isabel's faults and disregard for etiquette and style, she was a refreshing change from the other royals he'd encountered over the years. She was not caught up in the tangled web of tradition. Even Julianna, as perfect as she was, came from a kingdom more out-of-date than Vernonia.

He admired Isabel for working on cars. He remembered what being a soldier was like. Living day-to-day, sometimes hour-to-hour. It was the closest thing to an ordinary existence he'd had. Even after she put her mechanic days behind her, she could relate to the people at their level.

Isabel might not know how to be a princess yet, but at least she was a contemporary woman, something rarely found in his country. He could use that to his advantage as he moved forward with his plans. Though right now she looked more like a schoolgirl than a woman with the cashmere blanket tucked around her shoulders.

The cover rose and fell with each of her breaths. Her hair fanned across the pillow, the brown strands contrasting with the white fabric. The slender column of her neck contradicted the stiff backbone she'd shown earlier. The curve of her cheek and fullness of her lips weren't diminished by the lack of makeup and lip-gloss on her face. She possessed a natural beauty.

Although Niko appreciated her spirit and self-reliance, he couldn't deny the appeal of this softer side. The defiant set of her chin and tight jaw had relaxed. The result of sleep, but she looked so peaceful and serene. He wondered if she ever looked this way awake. He doubted it.

With her lips slightly parted, she almost appeared to be smiling. The result of a pleasant dream? A dream about him?

No. Her dreams were none of his business. Isabel might be his wife, but he should think of her like a sister. Anything else would be…inappropriate given his intention to marry Julianna.

Isabel shifted in her seat. The way she stretched reminded him of one of the feral cats who lived in the stable. As she settled into a new position, the top half of her blanket fell from her shoulders and pooled on her lap.

He could see the rise and fall of her chest better now. The V-neck collar gave a tantalizing view of creamy skin and lace. The fabric of her shirt stretched across her breasts. The cool cabin temperature beaded her nipples.

Niko covered her with the blanket and tucked the edge around her shoulders.

"Sir," Jovan said, standing in the aisle.

Niko jerked his hands away from Isabel, feeling as if the palace's renowned pastry chef had caught him sneaking a *tulumbe* from a batch soaking in syrup overnight.

"It is late." Jovan handed him a blanket. "There is nothing more to be done until we arrive in Vernonia. Please rest, sir."

Niko knew sleep was futile, but he placed the blanket on his lap. Jovan was only trying to do his job. "The shopping arrangements…"

"Have been taken care of, sir. Princess Julianna has offered her assistance and expertise."

The future wife helping the soon-to-be former one? The thought of the two women, so very different, made Niko's temples throb. "That will be...interesting."

"Princess Julianna's sense of duty is matched only by your own," Jovan said. "She simply wants to help you, sir."

Niko only hoped Isabel accepted the help. That independent streak of hers might get in the way. "Julianna will make a fine queen."

Jovan nodded. "She will also be an excellent role model for Princess Isabel to emulate, sir."

"Yes." Niko glanced at Isabel to see if she was still asleep. He lowered his voice. "She will need all the help she can get."

Jovan smiled at the sleeping woman. "Princess Isabel is not what I expected, but she has...spirit. She puts on no airs. Plays no games."

"She is different and has a certain down-to-earth charm," Niko agreed. "In time she could become a role model herself."

Jovan's brows furrowed. "I do not think she intends to stay long enough for that to happen, sir."

"Once Isabel sees all Vernonia has to offer, she will want to stay. We can have her things shipped over."

"You sound certain, sir."

"I am," Niko stated. "You saw the hovel she calls home. Her life in the United States leaves much to be desired."

"She doesn't seem to mind that life, sir," Jovan said. "And with her inheritance..."

"Perhaps she does not know any better."

Niko's gaze returned to Isabel's face. Her full lips still appeared to be smiling. He wouldn't mind a taste of them. A kiss.

No. He couldn't allow himself to go there, even if he was... tempted.

He focused his attention on his aide. "Staying in Vernonia is best for Isabel."

Just as Julianna was best for Vernonia, thus best for him.

"I wonder what Princess Isabel will have to say about that, sir," Jovan said.

"She may not have an Ivy League education, but she is intelligent. It won't take her long to realize where her future lies."

"If she disagrees, I suppose we can finally make use of the tower, sir," Jovan joked.

Niko laughed. "You've been spending too much time around my father."

"Isabel."

A man was calling Izzy's name, but she didn't open her eyes. Her alarm clock hadn't buzzed yet. That meant this must still be part of her dream, an odd mix of fairy tale and nightmare with a brooding, handsome prince holding her captive in a tower.

"Isabel," the man said again.

She liked the way the three syllables rolled off his tongue. I-sa-bel. She snuggled against the pillow, wanting more sleep and more of him.

The bed lurched, as if she were riding on a flying carpet that had come to a sudden stop.

"Welcome to Vernonia," the male voice continued.

Where? And then she realized.

Izzy wasn't in bed dreaming. She forced her heavy eyelids open. Bright sunlight streamed through the window. She blinked. The plane had not only landed, but also parked. A small turboprop taxied by.

Every single one of her muscles tensed. Yesterday had been real. The box. Her parents. The prince.

She clutched the armrests.

"Good morning, Isabel," Niko said from the seat next to her.

Izzy saw nothing good about this morning. She was tired, surrounded by strangers and far away from home. She turned toward Niko to tell him as much, but her mouth went dry at the sight of him.

Hello, Prince Hottie. Heat pulsed through her veins.

The stubble on Niko's face made him look sexier, dangerous. Especially with his scar. A real bad boy. His clothes remained unwrinkled, as if he'd just stepped away from a photo shoot, not spent the night flying across an ocean and a continent.

"You didn't eat much dinner last night," he said. "Are you hungry?"

She wouldn't mind a bite of him.

Strike that. A serving of prince sunny side up wasn't on the menu this morning. Or any morning, Izzy reminded herself. This wasn't just some guy. He was her husband. At least for another couple of days until the High Court was back in session.

Izzy toyed with the edge of the blanket covering her lap. "No, thanks. I'm not hungry."

"I will have a meal delivered to your room in case you are hungry later."

Room service? She wiggled her toes with anticipation. She'd never stayed at a nice hotel that offered room service. Maybe this trip would have some bright spots. "Thanks, but please don't go to any trouble. I can order my own food."

"It is no trouble," he said.

But it was for her. "I prefer to do things myself."

"Luka already came by with the warm towels," Niko continued as if she hadn't spoken. "If you would like one—"

"No, thanks. I'm good."

Tired, but good. Izzy yawned, hoping she wasn't breaking some princess protocol. She needed more sleep. A shower wouldn't hurt. Once she arrived at the hotel...

"Ready to see your homeland?" Niko asked.

Vernonia might be her place of birth, but she would never call it her homeland. "I suppose I can't stay on the plane all day."

"You could."

"Really?"

"You're a princess," he said, as if she knew all the rules about being royalty. "But you might get bored."

"I don't do well being bored."

"That doesn't surprise me."

She stood and placed the shoulder strap of her backpack over her shoulder.

"The crew will carry your backpack," Niko said.

"I don't mind."

"The crew does. They consider it an honor to serve you."

"I'm, uh, not really comfortable with that. My wallet and ID are in it."

"It looks strange for a princess to be hauling around a backpack."

"It's my purse," she countered. "Besides I don't care what other people think of me."

A muscle flicked at his jaw. "You've made that quite obvious."

Niko pressed his lips together. The same way he'd done in Charlotte. He wasn't happy with her. He'd probably better get used to it for as long as she was in town.

"Just so you know," she said. "It bugs me when people try to tell me what I can or can't do."

She walked down the aisle before he could say anything else to annoy her.

The other passengers, who had been introduced by job titles, not names during the flight, had already deplaned. The flight crew, including the pilots, stood in a line at the front of the plane. Izzy thanked them and exited.

At the top of the portable staircase, she took a deep breath. The crisp air refreshed her.

The airport wasn't as large as the one in Charlotte and seemed to be built on a plateau. Everything from the control tower to the runways looked brand-new. Beyond the runways the flat landscape gave way to foothills and rocky mountains beyond that.

Niko joined her on the landing. He motioned to a black limousine at the bottom of the stairs. "Our chariot awaits."

Attached to the front of the car were two small blue and white flags with yellow emblems in the center. They fluttered in the cool breeze. Uniformed guards with large guns stood nearby. A man in a black suit unloaded the luggage from a cart. He carefully placed her battered duffel bag into the trunk as if it contained fragile Fabergé eggs, not thrift store bargain buys.

Feelings of inadequacy swept through her. Izzy was

completely out of her league here. She clutched the metal hand-rail like a lifeline.

Niko extended his arm. "I'm only offering because you must be tired."

His gesture of chivalry brought tears to her eyes. Uncle Frank used to do the same thing before escorting her across the street or down a parking lot staircase. Izzy wiped her eyes with her hand.

Boy, she must really be jet-lagged to get so sentimental. But Niko was right. Her legs were stiff from the flight. Her shoes fit tighter, making her wonder if her feet had swollen. She couldn't pretend she wasn't feeling more tired by the minute.

Falling down the stairs was a distinct possibility in her current condition and would not be a good start to her visit to Vernonia. Forget making a faux pas. The stage was set for an epic fail. She couldn't let that happen.

Better safe than sorry. Izzy wrapped her arm around Niko's. "Thanks."

Together, they descended the stairs. He went slowly, short-ening his long stride. For her sake, Izzy realized. Her thoughts about him being a knight in shining armor weren't too far off. Still she wasn't comfortable needing his assistance. She'd been standing on her own two feet for the last five years, ever since Uncle Frank died. Leaning on someone else felt odd and unnatu-ral, even if it was only for the length of the portable staircase.

"You are not merely tired." His gazed remained focused straight ahead, never straying her way. A slight breeze ruffled the ends of his hair. Even the scar on his face suited him. He wasn't a perfect prince, but he wasn't that bad. "You are exhausted."

"Yeah." She struggled not to yawn. "Though I'm not sure why since I slept most of the flight."

"Jet lag. It's the middle of the night in Charlotte," he ex-plained. "You need time to adjust. You can rest soon. Though not too long or your body clock will be thrown off even more."

"A short nap is all I need."

"A short nap you shall have."

His grin made her breath catch in her throat. Izzy wouldn't mind if he tucked her in and kissed her good-night.

Her foot missed a step. As if in slow motion, she fell backward. Her right hand clutched the railing. Her left hand gripped Niko's arm. Somehow he caught her before her bottom hit the staircase.

"Are you okay?" he asked.

His strong arms righted her so she was standing upright. "Yes," she said grateful. "Thanks to you."

"Only a few more steps."

Thank goodness. Her entire body trembled. Not because of the near fall, but because of Niko. Looks aside, his compelling presence drew her in like a tow truck's winch. She needed to get away from him.

As soon as Izzy reached the tarmac, she slid her arm from his. The chauffeur opened the back door. She climbed inside. Leaning back against the leather seat, she stretched out her legs, relieved to be away from Niko.

He slid into the limousine and sat next to her even though the rest of the seats were empty. Darn the man. Didn't he understand the concept of personal space?

His thigh pressed against hers. Not on purpose, she thought. Still her temperature rose.

The prince might be a hottie, but he was off-limits. He was her husband, but he planned on marrying someone else. His heart wasn't on the open market. She couldn't allow herself to be attracted to him.

Izzy scooted away. She needed something to defuse her growing awareness to him. "Where's Jovan?"

"In the front with the driver." Niko pressed a button and lowered the dark glass separating the back of the limousine from the front. "Jovan is making sure everything will be ready for you to shop today."

"I don't have to go shopping today."

"I know you are tired. I wish you could have more time to adjust, but my parents expect you to attend dinner tonight."

"Tonight?" Her voice cracked. "That's, um, nice of them, but dinner isn't really necessary. I mean, in a few days, we won't even be married."

"Our parents were friends. They orchestrated our wedding," Niko explained. "You are and always will be a princess of Vernonia and should consider us family."

Family.

Izzy felt a pang in her heart.

The word family brought up all kinds of strange emotions. Ones she'd tried to ignore while growing up. She'd never had any family except Uncle Frank. "That's a generous offer, but I feel more like a serf than a royal."

"A royal serf," Niko said. "An oxymoron."

"How about a royal waif?" she suggested.

Laughter danced in his warm eyes. "Serf, waif or princess, you'll find acceptance here, Isabel."

The only people who had ever accepted her were back at Rowdy's garage, but she appreciated Niko trying to make her feel better. She stifled a yawn.

"After you rest, you will shop. Someone will help you select and organize the various outfits you'll need."

"Um, thanks." Izzy didn't know whether to be offended or grateful he was providing her help. She didn't care about what was in style or not, but she wasn't colorblind. "I don't need a lot."

"Most women like having several different outfits."

"I'm not like most women."

His gaze raked over her. "No, you are not."

She didn't think he intended that to be a compliment, but she wasn't offended. His words reaffirmed what she already knew. Izzy Poussard wasn't princess material. She didn't belong in Vernonia. She needed to take care of business, learn about her family and return home to Charlotte.

As the limo left the airport, Niko pointed out the window toward a town up ahead. "We're entering the capital city."

Izzy was surprised to see a city smaller and more compact than Charlotte with narrower roads. But the commotion on the streets suggested a busy, bustling town.

A crane lifted steel girders while men in yellow hard hats guided them onto the fourth floor of a construction site. Next door, scaffolding covered the front of a new office building and men painted. Across the street, a woman in a multicolored skirt, boots and long sweater pushed a baby stroller. Two teenagers kicked a soccer ball back and forth as they hurried past the woman and child. A man in a business suit glanced at the limousine before hurrying into a newer five-story building made of steel and glass.

"What do you think?" Niko asked.

"It's very modern for a country that allowed children to marry."

"I told you, that is against the law now."

"Yes, you did." She didn't see any garbage or graffiti anywhere. That was quite an achievement. "Everything is so new and clean. Even the streets."

"This part of town was demolished by bombing," he explained. "Rebuilding takes time and money. Projects are being spread out to best utilize our resources."

The limousine drove into another part of town. This section consisted of smaller stone and brick rectangular buildings each painted a different color. Some were new, but many were older. Several had window boxes, but no flowers. "Is this a residential area?"

"Yes."

Izzy noticed one similarity among the colorful homes. Holes on almost every structure. Bullet pocks? she wondered.

A memorial sign hung on a pole. Flowers and pictures were attached. She shuddered.

"I can't imagine what living through a war must be like. Just watching the television coverage of 9/11 was difficult. Granted I was a teenager, but this…" A weight pressed down on her chest. "I hope this never happens again."

"I intend to make sure it doesn't," Niko stated firmly. "War is never pleasant, but fighting amongst your own is particularly brutal. Friend against friend. Brother against brother. Both the Loyalists and the Separatists accepted the treaty unanimously.

Our postconflict elections have gone well. We are fortunate to have not faced some of the problems that have plagued other Balkan countries. I am determined to see that peace is upheld and good triumphs for all Vernonians. No matter what side they supported in the conflict."

Her respect for him rose. "Good luck."

"Thank you."

The limousine left the town behind and traveled up a steep hill. Tall trees lined both sides of the road and cast shadows on the pavement. As the car crested a bump, she saw a castle in the distance.

Her heart beat triple time.

A fairy-tale castle, so perfect it appeared to have been painted on a canvas of blue. Turrets jutted into the sky. Leaded glass windows sparkled. Silver roof tiles gleamed beneath the morning sun. She'd never seen anything so beautiful in her life.

"Wow."

"We are fortunate the castle remained in such good shape given the battles fought here," Niko said. "The wall took several mortar hits, but that was the worst of the damage."

"Thank goodness." Jovan turned around from the front seat. "The royal family stayed in residence during the conflict."

"When we weren't fighting," Niko said.

Izzy was surprised a royal would be out on the front line. "You fought in the war?"

"Yes." The one word spoke volumes. "Stefan and I fought with the loyalists to preserve the boundaries and traditions of all people."

Izzy could imagine Niko as a warrior, fierce and hard, defending his people to the death. That took courage and strength. She pointed to the jagged scar on his cheek. "Did you get that fighting?"

"Yes, we are all marked in some way by the conflict," he said. "Some scars are physical. Others are not."

Did Niko have other scars? Hidden ones? Izzy wanted to know, but didn't know him well enough to ask. She wanted to see if there was more to this seemingly in-control prince than met the eye. Curiosity about the man her parents had married her off to, she rationalized.

As the limousine approached the castle, the immense structure loomed in front of her. Was that a moat?

She peered out the window. Yes, it was. A river flowed underneath a bridge flanked by armed guards. One waved the limousine across.

Two minutes later, the car stopped in front of tall, wooden doors. A uniformed man stepped outside. His white dress shirt, creased pants and sharp jacket made Izzy feel totally underdressed in her faded jeans, T-shirt and ratty sneakers. No wonder the prince was so keen on her shopping.

"Your bag will be delivered to your room, ma'am," Jovan said before exiting the limousine.

"Wait a minute." Izzy's gaze locked with Niko's. "I thought I was staying at a hotel."

"You are legally my wife," Niko said. "You will stay here at the castle until the annulment has been granted."

"I want to stay at a hotel."

"No."

Darn the man. He hadn't listened to her before. If he had, he wouldn't be telling her what to do. "But—"

"The castle is the most suitable place for you to stay."

Izzy could rattle off a hundred reasons why she shouldn't stay here with him, the queen and the king. She settled on one. "I'd be more comfortable in a hotel."

"You will be more comfortable here," Niko countered. "Your every whim will be catered to by the castle's staff."

"I don't have any whims that need catering."

He set his jaw. "No hotel."

Her eyelids felt heavy. She needed to sit down. "I really—"

"This isn't up for negotiation."

Her tiredness was putting her at a disadvantage. She couldn't think fast enough. "Please."

"You will sleep better here than anywhere. Trust me."

Izzy didn't trust him. She couldn't.

"It's also better for you to stay at the castle for security reasons."

Okay, that she could accept.

"Fine. I'll concede on that point." She stared down her nose. "But just so you know, as soon as we get the annulment, I'm outta here."

I'm outta here.

Niko had one parting thought before he handed Isabel off to a maid.

Good riddance.

He kept the thought to himself, balling his hands into fists instead. He would not lower himself to *her* level.

The woman was ill-mannered and brash. She had no idea how she was supposed to act. A month locked in the tower with only etiquette and protocol books might actually help her learn to be a princess. The room in the tower would be better for her than the rusty aluminum can she called home. Though she would probably miss the grease from the garage.

The sharp click from his heels against the wood floor as he strode through the hall echoed his irritation.

"Niko."

He stopped and flexed his fingers. He did not want his annoyance at his "wife" to affect his soon-to-be new wife.

Julianna stood in the doorway of the library. Her designer skirt and short-fitted jacket complemented her figure the same way her deftly applied makeup accentuated her features. Her long, blond hair gleamed under the lights. "Welcome home."

One word came to mind as he stared at her—perfection. He couldn't have found a better princess to be Vernonia's queen. Her beauty was matched by her intelligence. She spoke four languages fluently—German, French, Italian and English. She was an Olympic-caliber sailor and an excellent spokesperson. She had the necessary family connections and wealth, but her sense of duty set her above many of the other unmarried royals he'd met over the past few years. She knew what her country expected of her, and she fulfilled her duty without question. One hundred and eighty degrees different from Isabel.

"It's good to see you, Julianna."

"And you." She sounded genuinely pleased to him. That would bode well for their future together, if only he could stop thinking about…his current wife. "I hope your trip went well," Julianna added.

The hallway was empty, but that didn't mean people weren't listening. He didn't want to take any chance of someone over-hearing him.

"Let's talk in the library where we will not be disturbed." Niko led her past floor-to-ceiling bookcases to a small meeting room in the back. He closed the door.

Julianna ran her fingers along the polished walnut desk. "I had no idea this room was even here."

Memories of pestering his older brother, Stefan, while he attempted to study surfaced. Niko pushed them and the pang of grief aside. "Thank you for offering to help Isabel with her shopping."

Julianna smiled softly. "It's the least I can do for you."

Niko had always put Vernonia first. He dated, but had never had a true partner to confide in or ask for help. Perhaps that would change soon. "Thank you."

"You're welcome, but it's not a hardship. I love to shop."

He wasn't about to criticize his current wife to his future spouse, but he didn't want Julianna blindsided, either. "You may find Isabel a reluctant shopper."

"I'm sure I can convince her a shopping spree is in order."

"It could be a challenge," Niko admitted. "Isabel does not want to be a princess."

Julianna smiled knowingly. "Every woman wants to be a princess, even if they would never dare admit it aloud."

"Not Isabel." His blood pressure rose thinking about her. "I've never met a woman who tried so hard not to be female."

Julianna furrowed her finely arched brows. "Isabel wants to be a man?"

"No, but she is a car mechanic. She works hard not to look

like a woman. No makeup. Baggy coveralls. Very casual clothing. No dresses or high heels."

"You sound exasperated."

"She is exasperating."

"First impressions can be deceiving," Julianna counseled, making Niko wonder if this was how she spoke to her younger brothers. "Isabel must be in shock."

"The news has shocked her, but I don't believe my impression of her is far off." Niko thought about her parting words to him. "Isabel is young. She speaks without thinking. She has no sense of what it is to be royalty."

"She sounds refreshing."

"I thought so yesterday, but today we keep…clashing," he admitted. "She slept so peacefully last night, but when she awoke this morning she was more beast than beauty."

Julianna's mouth quirked. "Isabel is a beauty?"

"Not exactly," he backtracked. "Some men might find her attractive."

"Do you?"

"She's my wife. I don't think of her in that way."

Amusement gleamed in Julianna's eyes. "I see."

"There's nothing to see," he countered. "Fortunately Isabel agrees an annulment is the only option. She was excited to hear about our getting married."

Julianna sighed. No doubt relieved the upcoming royal engagement and nuptials faced no more obstacles. "We can add her to the wedding party. A royal wedding can never have too many attendants."

"That is thoughtful of you." Her thoughtfulness was another reason why Julianna was perfect for his country. "I doubt Isabel will want to remain in Vernonia that long."

"You must convince her to stay," Julianna insisted.

"You haven't met her."

"It doesn't matter," Julianna countered. "Isabel has a duty to fulfill here in Vernonia."

"I understand what you are saying, but Isabel is very—" he

searched for a somewhat complimentary adjective "—independent. I don't think she is the type to fulfill her duty."

"She needs training," Julianna said. "I can help her."

"You don't know what you're offering to take on."

"Come now, you make her sound like an ogre."

"Not an ogre," he admitted. "Ornery."

"I have four younger brothers. I can handle ornery."

"See how shopping goes, then you can decide if you want to continue helping her or not."

"I can't wait to see what you think of her with a brand-new wardrobe complete with coordinating accessories, shoes and makeup."

Niko's shoulders tensed. No way would Isabel agree to a total makeover. "Just get her into a dress by dinnertime, and I'll be much obliged."

"Obliged enough for another sail tomorrow?" Julianna challenged.

The jaunt to America had wreaked havoc with his schedule. Niko had little to no free time right now. He appreciated Julianna's help because that meant he didn't have to deal with Isabel himself. The woman didn't need only a fashion makeover, she needed a complete personality transplant. Niko doubted even the capable Aliestle princess could do much with Isabel by dinnertime. But if Julianna was willing to try…

"If you can make her presentable to my parents, I'll gladly find the time to go sailing with you tomorrow."

CHAPTER FIVE

Izzy didn't want to like it here. She wasn't going to fit in no matter what she did. The less attached she got to anyone or anything during her short visit the better. But right this minute she wouldn't want to be anywhere else but Vernonia.

Nothing could beat floating on this cloud.

Okay, she was lying on a four-poster queen-size bed, but the mattress was truly fit for a king. Or a princess. No lumps, bumps or peas to be found. The feather pillow conformed to the shape of her head and supported it exactly right. The luxurious sheets cocooned her. She sighed in delight.

Best nap ever.

She never knew a bed could be so comfortable or sheets could feel so soft.

Izzy kept her eyes closed, wanting to linger on the cloud a little longer. But not too long. She didn't want to throw her body clock any more as Niko had mentioned earlier.

Niko.

He hadn't looked happy when he'd handed her off to a maid named Mare. Izzy hadn't been as polite as she could have been. Being tired had contributed, but she didn't like being bossed around. She wasn't one of Niko's subjects. He seemed to forget she was an American. He couldn't tell her what to do.

The image of his ruggedly handsome face formed in her mind. Those to-die-for blue-green eyes. That dark mane of hair. His killer...

What was she doing thinking about him? Izzy opened her eyes.

Darkness filled the room. That was weird. Some natural light had been filtering in through the large windows when she lay down.

Oh, no. Panic spurted through her. Had she slept too long?

Bolting upright, she glanced at the digital clock on the nightstand. Only two and a half hours had passed.

Relief washed over her. But why was the room so dark?

She glanced around, allowing her eyes to adjust. Her gaze rested on the closed yellow damask drapes. They'd been open before she fell asleep.

Izzy squirmed with uneasiness. She had lived alone for the last five years and wasn't used to anyone being around when she slept. A good thing she wouldn't be here long.

She tossed back the covers and slid from the bed. Her bare feet sunk into a thick, colorful rug covering the hardwood floors.

Talk about living large. The grandeur of the interior exceeded the castle's fairy-tale exterior. She felt as if she were staying in a museum with antique furniture, famous paintings and exquisite tapestries. Everything looked so expensive she didn't want to touch anything she could break.

Inside the expansive bathroom, Izzy found her toiletry kit sitting on the gold-veined marble countertop. Someone must have removed it from her duffel bag. Having people do everything for you was really weird.

A thick, plush white robe hung on a gold hook. She ran her fingertips over the soft fabric. The robe was nicer than any of the clothing she had brought with her. A good thing she was going shopping.

Izzy brushed her teeth in the gold sink. Everything was gold, from the faucets to the gold seals on the pretty soap wrappers. Even the fluffy white towels had gold embroidery on the bottom portion. Uncle Frank would have gotten a kick out of this big gold bathroom.

She felt a familiar tug at her heart.

Then again, he hadn't been a simple car mechanic. He would have been used to castles and bathrooms like this. Living in a motor home had been the opposite extreme. Had he been hiding her? Or maybe Uncle Frank had wanted to give her as normal a life as possible, not one with gold sinks. Izzy believed he'd kept the past a secret and raised her the way he did for a reason.

Aleksander and Evangaline Zvonimir might have been her birth parents, but Frank Miroslav had been Izzy's father. He had wiped her tears when she hurt herself, boosted her self-confidence when the kids at school teased her for being different, and taught her everything she knew and loved about cars. He'd saved her life by leaving his own family to raise her in another country. She was only beginning to comprehend what he'd given up for her. It was too late to say thank-you, but Izzy wanted to make it up to him somehow. Maybe she could find his relatives and tell them how wonderful he'd been to her.

Emotion clogged her throat. She shook it off. The way she'd learned to do these last five years.

A shower would make her feel better. She turned on the water. As she undressed, steam filled the bathroom. She stepped into the large shower.

Hot water pulsed down on her as if she were standing in a heated waterfall. She nearly sighed at the decadence of the oversize showerhead.

Okay, Izzy grinned, comfy beds and amazing showers were definitely perks to being a princess. She could even forgive the invasion of privacy while she slept. A shower like this could make her forgive and forget most everything.

Normally she finished showering in a couple of minutes due to the size of the RV's tiny water heater. This time, Izzy stayed in until her fingertips shriveled like raisins.

Best shower ever.

She turned off the water, dried off with a towel, slipped into the luxurious robe and combed her hair.

Out in the bedroom, she padded to her duffel bag. It wasn't where she'd left it.

Izzy looked around. Her backpack sat on the table, but her

duffel bag was nowhere to be seen. That was odd. The purple would be hard to miss against the yellow and gold decor.

Maybe whoever placed her toiletry bag in the bathroom had put the duffel bag away. Izzy checked inside the gilded armoire. Empty hangers hung on the rack. She slid out the two drawers. No bag or clothing. She checked under the bed. Nothing there, either.

This wasn't good. She wanted to get dressed.

Izzy had the clothes she'd worn on the flight, but she didn't relish the thought of putting them on again. They were dirty, and she was clean.

Her cell phone was no use. Anyone she could call was half a world away and asleep. They couldn't tell her where to find her duffel bag.

She thought for a moment. Only one explanation made sense. Someone must have taken her bag. To wash the clothes, iron them, who knew why?

A castle this size had to have a large staff. She would flag someone down and ask how to contact Mare.

Izzy poked her head out of her room. The wide hallway was empty. Waiting for someone to appear, she shoved her hands into the deep pockets of the robe. No one came.

"Is anyone out there?" she half whispered.

No reply.

Come on. Izzy grew impatient. This was a castle for goodness' sake. Maids and butlers should be running around. She would have to find someone herself.

She tightened the belt of her robe

Stepping into the hallway, Izzy left the door to her room open. She wanted to remember which room was hers.

The farther she moved away from her room, the more antsy Izzy became. Walking around with wet hair, barefoot and wearing nothing but a robe was not exactly princesslike. A castle probably had rules. Ones she would know. Maybe she should go back.

She was about to turn around when a white-haired man exited a room. The older gentleman was tall, wore a nice suit and walked with a slight limp. On closer look, she noticed he had a prosthetic leg.

No matter what side you were on, we are all marked in some way by the conflict. Some scars are visible. Others are not.

Niko hadn't been kidding. Izzy couldn't believe an old man had to fight in the war. Maybe he'd been a soldier at the beginning. Unless he'd just been a casualty. Thinking about what these people had endured made her heart ache.

He headed in a different direction.

She ran up to him. "Excuse me."

The man stopped. His eyes widened when he saw her.

"Do you work here?" she asked.

He blinked. "I do."

"Finally."

He studied her with probing green eyes. "Who might you be?"

"I'm Izzy. I arrived this morning from the United States."

"Welcome, Izzy." His smile deepened the lines on his face. "I'm Dee."

"Nice to meet you, Dee." In spite of all the wrinkles, he was still attractive. He must have been really handsome when he was younger. She couldn't help but think of Niko. "I'm in a bind. My bag with my clothing has disappeared. I searched the room, but can't find it."

"Oh, dear, that is quite a predicament."

She nodded. "I don't imagine trickster ghosts haunt this place?"

"No, though we do have our share of skeletons in the closet."

"That's what I figured." She felt more comfortable with the staff than royalty. One more reason she wasn't cut out to be a princess. "I'm sure you have work to do, but would you please tell me how I might locate Mare? She was assigned to help me, and I'm wondering if she knows where my bag might be."

"Part of my job is making sure everything runs the way it is supposed to around here."

"Oh, you're the castle manager."

"Something like that." He sounded amused. "I don't know where Mare is, but I know where we can find your clothes."

"Great."

Dee extended his arm. "Allow me to escort you."

She took his arm. "Thanks."

He walked with a steady stride. His leg didn't slow him down. "What do you think of Vernonia so far, Izzy?"

"I didn't see much during the drive from the airport, but this castle—" she looked up at a fresco painted on the ceiling "—it's straight out of a fairy tale."

"I hope the accommodations are to your liking."

"They are lovely. Thank you," she said. "I wanted to stay at a hotel, but Prince Niko wanted me to stay here. He said I would be more comfortable."

"I hope you are comfortable."

"I've only been here a few hours, but I've already had a nice nap and a wonderful shower."

"An excellent start," Dee said.

Izzy nodded. She wondered if Niko would agree. Earlier he couldn't wait to get away from her. No doubt he wanted her visit to be a short one. At least they agreed on something.

"I believe what you seek is inside here." Dee stopped in front of a pair of wide double doors and opened one of them. "These ballroom doors are heavier than they look."

She peered inside and gasped. This wasn't a ballroom. This was a clothing store.

Mannequins, decked out in elaborate outfits with matching accessories, fought for space on the parquet floor between racks of clothing and shoes. Stylishly dressed women bustled about in short skirts and high heels, carrying purses, lingerie and shoes. A mix of perfumes lingered in the air.

The room looked to be a pumped up, steroid-version of *What Not to Wear*. This was so not the kind of shopping Izzy had in mind. She struggled to breathe.

Some women might tingle with excitement at the thought of being let loose among all these clothes and shoes, but the sight filled Izzy with dread. Fashion didn't interest her in the slightest.

She was into comfort, not style. Worse, these women had gone to all this trouble for her. Niko and Jovan, too.

Near a three-paneled mirror, she noticed a man who looked out of place among all the feminine finery.

Not just a man. Niko.

He'd showered, shaved and changed suits. He looked like he had at the garage—hot. She wasn't the only one who thought so. A few of the other women kept stealing glances.

Niko didn't seem to notice. He was engaged in a conversation with a gorgeous blonde supermodel. Feeling more out of place than before, Izzy crossed her arms over her stomach.

Dee cleared his throat.

Conversations stopped. Women froze in place. Heads bowed. Eyes lowered.

"What's happening?" she whispered and moved closer to Dee.

"Do not worry." He smiled down at her. "Everything is fine, Izzy."

Niko stared intently at her, making her question the fine part. "What are you—"

"Izzy's bag with her clothing disappeared from her room," Dee said, rather bravely Izzy thought considering the fierce expression on Niko's face. "I offered her my assistance."

"The women needed her sizes so they borrowed her bag, Father."

Realization hit Izzy between the eyes. She inhaled sharply. "Dee as in Dmitar."

"Yes, my dear," Dee said.

"Oh, no." Her cheeks burned. She pulled the robe tighter as if she could somehow disappear into its folds. "You're the king, the one who emailed me about the box, and I'm an idiot."

"Father—"

King Dmitar held up his hand the way Niko had done with Jovan.

Niko remained silent. Izzy had forgotten about that trick, but made a note to remember it for later.

"You're not an idiot, Izzy," King Dmitar said kindly. "You are delightful. I see the best of your parents in you."

Emotion tightened her throat. "Thank you, Your Majesty."

"As for my son…" King Dmitar turned his attention to Niko. "Izzy does not know our ways. She should not be left on her own and forced to figure out where her clothing disappeared to."

Niko bowed his head. "Yes, sir."

King Dmitar turned his attention back to her. "And a suggestion, Izzy."

"Yes, Dee." She cringed at her lapse. "I mean, Your Majesty."

"Queen Beatrice does not like the color pink. You may wish to keep that in mind while shopping."

"Thanks for the tip, sir." Izzy smiled, trying to make the best of the situation. "I'm not much into pink myself."

"Excellent." The king eyed the racks of dresses. "The queen does like the color purple. As do I."

"I'll remember that, sir. Thank you."

He focused on each person in the room until his gaze came to rest on the stunning blonde who had been talking with Niko. The king pressed his lips together for a moment. "I see you are in good hands. I will leave you to your shopping."

With that, the king departed.

As soon as the doors closed, the women went back to carrying accessories to the mannequins. The blonde, who had been speaking with Niko, supervised them.

Izzy blew out a puff of air. "I can't believe that was your father."

Niko stood next to her with an irritated look in his eyes. "Who did you think he was?"

"The castle manager."

The irritation vanished. Niko laughed. "I suppose that is one of his job responsibilities."

"You're not helping."

Niko raised a brow. "I didn't think you needed anyone's help."

Izzy made a face at him.

"You may have trouble finding an outfit to go with that expression," he teased.

"I'm sure I can find an outfit to match every expression as well as one to wear each hour of the day. I thought I was going shopping at a store or a mall." She motioned to all the clothing. "It's a bit…much, don't you think?"

"Not for a princess," Niko said. "There will be dinners, outings, appearances at the High Court."

"I won't be here that long."

"Long enough."

Izzy tried to take it all in. Tried and failed. "I think I'm beginning to understand what Cinderella might have gone through."

"Except in your case the shoe already fits."

"But we want to get it off as soon as possible."

"That is the plan."

He sounded excited. Izzy set her chin. "You know, dude, I want the annulment just as badly as you do."

Before he could reply, the supermodel hurried over, walking on high heels as if she were wearing tennis shoes. She probably taught Pilates, cooked like a gourmet chef and rescued orphans from third-world countries in her spare time. The woman smiled, showing off two rows of perfectly spaced white teeth. The boys at the garage would be comatose in her presence. "You must be Princess Isabel."

"Isabel," Niko said. "This is Her Royal Highness Princess Julianna Von Schneckel of Aliestle."

Julianna. Niko's girlfriend and future wife. She was also a princess. No wonder he couldn't wait to annul the marriage and marry a woman who exuded so much confidence and beauty even a *Sports Illustrated* swimsuit model would be intimidated.

Izzy was out of her element in every possible way. She forced her foot to stop tapping.

Julianna extended her arm. Everything about the princess was perfect right down to her manicured and polished fingernails. "It's wonderful to meet you, Isabel."

She shook her hand. Julianna's grip was firm and her hands rougher than Izzy expected them to be. "And you."

Niko watched them with interest. No doubt comparing his current wife to his future one.

A chilling thought inched its way down Izzy's spine. She hoped he wasn't planning to stay while she tried on clothing. This was going to be difficult enough without him here watching or, worse, providing commentary.

"Thanks for arranging all this, Niko." Izzy tried to sound as cheerful as she could. "But I'm sure you have better things to do with your time so don't feel you have to stick around. As your father said, I'm in good hands."

"You're in excellent hands," Niko said. "But I have a few minutes before my meeting."

Bummer, Izzy thought.

"You keep Isabel company, Niko," Julianna said. "I want to get everyone in their places."

People had places? Izzy took a deep breath and exhaled slowly.

"It won't be that bad," Niko said, as soon as Julianna was out of earshot.

"Want to trade places?" Izzy asked.

"My legs weren't meant for dresses."

"Mine, either. I mean, I haven't worn a dress since…" Uncle Frank's funeral, she realized. "It's been a long time."

"You'll look fine."

She shrugged. "New clothing isn't going to turn me into a princess."

"Whether you wear a pair of coveralls or a dress by Chanel, you are already a princess," he said. "But new clothing might help you feel more comfortable here."

She stared at the large crystal chandeliers hanging from the ballroom ceiling. "I don't think that's possible."

"You only just arrived."

"I'm not like her."

"Her?"

"Your girlfriend. Princess Julianna."

"I never thought you were like Julianna," Niko said. "You said you needed clothing so I arranged for you to go shopping."

"I should learn to keep my mouth shut."

"Perhaps." He sounded amused. "But this is a gift, Isabel. I appreciate you coming all this way to settle matters. Please indulge yourself shopping. Even if you never plan on wearing the clothing once you leave, you can always donate the clothes to a worthy cause."

That was some gift, Izzy realized. Royalty really were different than normal folk. "You're wasting a lot of money doing this."

"The expense is irrelevant."

"Maybe for you." Her gaze locked with his. "But for me, this would buy a lot of car."

A knowing smiled played at the corner of his mouth. "Noted."

Something held them connected. Izzy didn't know what, but she couldn't look away. Truth was, she didn't want to. She had no idea how long they stood like that, but it felt like forever.

"Are you two finished sparring so we can shop?" Julianna asked playfully.

As Niko looked away, Izzy felt an odd sense of rejection from the broken connection. It must be jet lag.

He focused his gaze on his future bride. "Yes."

"Then off with you." Julianna waved her hand toward the doors. "Your presence will make Isabel uncomfortable."

He nodded once. "Enjoy the shopping, ladies."

Izzy watched as Niko exited the room. "You need to teach me how to do that."

"I am going to teach you many things. How to handle a prince is only one of them."

"I don't think I could ever handle Niko like that."

"I believe you already have." Julianna smiled mischievously. "Ready to shop till you drop?"

"Not really." Izzy wondered what the princess had meant by her first sentence. Then again, maybe she was reading too much into things. "I'm not big on shopping and clothes and things like that."

Julianna's grin widened. "Then it's good you have me."

CHAPTER SIX

THAT evening, Niko stood in the dining room with Julianna, waiting for his parents and Isabel to arrive. Servants scurried about like mice only instead of carrying crumbs and cheese they carried pitchers of water and platters.

Anticipation filled the air. Even Niko felt himself caught up in it. Everyone wanted a glimpse of Princess Isabel. Unfortunately she was far from the princess they expected to see. She might be here by birthright, but she was clearly unhappy and didn't want to stay. The thought of her leaving brought a strange pang. Even if a wrench belonged in her hand, not a scepter.

He glanced at his watch. "Isabel is late."

"Isabel is not late." Julianna swirled her champagne flute. She looked lovely in a green cocktail dress and silver heels. Isabel could never pull off such an outfit. "A princess needs to make an entrance. Anxious to see her?"

"Anxious to know how much damage control I'll need to do tonight. Perhaps she has decided not to attend."

"Oh, believe me, she'll be here." Julianna smiled, as if she knew a secret. "By the way, the wind should be lovely for a sail tomorrow."

"I'll believe it when I see it."

"The wind? Or your wife?"

Niko liked Julianna. There might not be any chemistry between them, but a friendship was growing. Friendship would be a good foundation for a marriage. Perhaps, in time, passion would enter into the relationship. Then again, passion never lasted, so perhaps friendship would be enough. "That role will soon be…"

Footsteps sounded outside the dining room. He glanced across the large room to the wide doorway.

A stunning woman wearing a lavender dress stood with a hesitant smile on her gorgeous face.

His heart rate kicked up a notch.

What a beauty. He gaze was immediately drawn to her expressive eyes. The rest of her was as appealing. Her brown hair was piled on the top of her head, secured by an invisible clip of some sort. Soft tendrils framed her oval face. But her eyes continued to mesmerize him.

"So what time should we leave on our sail tomorrow?"

"Time?" he asked yet couldn't take his eyes off the vision in the doorway.

Julianna laughed. "The makeover definitely worked."

Niko did a double take. "Isabel?"

"She cleans up quite well, don't you think?"

He'd seen her cleaned up, but not like this. All he could do was stare captivated. Isabel was…stunning.

"I can't believe you said she reminded you of a man," Julianna continued quietly. "She may not like the color pink and prefer motor oil to moisturizer, but she's quite feminine."

"I see that."

He liked what he saw. The above the knee hem of her dress showed off Isabel's long legs. He hoped she would be wearing more dresses. Legs like hers needed to be shown off, not hidden beneath coveralls, jeans and bathrobes.

"Though I will admit the rest of her princess transformation may take a lot more time," Julianna said. "Isabel says whatever is on her mind. That must stop or the media will take advantage of her."

"I have no doubt in your abilities now."

"I had fun. Izzy may not be a typical princess, but she's a charming young woman."

"Izzy?"

"That's what her friends call her," Julianna said.

Isabel had mentioned she liked being called Izzy, but he preferred her full name, liked the way it rolled off his tongue. Izzy sounded too...pedestrian. But there was nothing dull or unimaginative about her now. The lavender complemented her pale complexion. The style flattered her figure. She looked like a princess. "I doubt any of her friends would recognize her."

"You didn't."

"Shock."

"Nothing more?" Julianna asked.

Attraction, desire, lust. But he knew better than to tell his future wife those things. "Nothing else."

"Be a dear, Niko, and escort her into the dining room." Julianna sounded genuinely pleased with his reaction. "She's still trying to master the art of walking in high heels. I'd hate to see her make a mistake and berate herself over it."

He wasn't going to have to be asked twice. He smiled at Julianna, who looked almost smug with satisfaction. "I will be right back with your work of art."

As he approached Isabel, Niko was even more impressed by her transformation. The expert makeup application complemented her high cheekbones. Her glossed lips sparkled. Flecks of gold danced in her eyes. A complete change from the way she'd looked asleep on the airplane. Julianna had outdone herself. "You look lovely, Isabel."

"Thanks."

Niko caught a whiff of her vanilla and jasmine scent. That was the one thing that hadn't changed.

"I feel like a fraud," she whispered.

He didn't understand the agitation in her voice. She should be happy with the makeover. "Why a fraud?"

"I'm still me. Only the outer packaging has changed," she explained. "With all this makeup on, I feel like a clown. I'm sure in this dress and high heels, I must look like a corner hooker."

Niko winced. "No one would mistake you for anything but a princess."

Too bad she didn't act or speak like one.

"I appreciate that," she said. "Even if it's not one hundred percent true."

He extended his arm. "May I?"

"Royalty is big on escorting."

"It is part of our prince training."

"Is princess training available?" she asked.

"Yours has already started."

She pursed her glossed lips. "I was kidding."

He raised a brow. "I'm not."

She eyed his arm warily then placed her hand over his.

Niko felt a jolt of awareness. Perhaps it was just a shock from static electricity.

"Just so you know, I'm only doing this so I don't end up spread-eagled on the floor with my new lace thong showing."

Niko's gaze drifted to her round, delectable bottom and lingered for a second.

What the hell was he doing?

Abruptly he forced himself to look into her eyes. Anywhere else was unacceptable. He really would have preferred not knowing what type of lingerie she wore underneath her dress. The erotic image plastered across his brain would take time to erase. "I will make sure that doesn't happen."

For both their sakes.

Isabel took a step, teetering on her heels. "I don't know why anyone would choose to strap these torture devices to their feet."

"Why did you?"

"Because Princess Julianna told me I had to. A closet full of shoes seems to be a prerequisite for being a princess. But it seems as if none of them are allowed to be comfortable."

He smiled at the exasperation in her voice and led her into the dining room with nary a stumble or peek at her panties.

She glanced around the room. "Wow."

Niko understood her look of awe. The room was quite impressive with its marble fireplace, the gold damask-covered walls, chandeliers and the long, rectangular table set with fine china, sparkling crystal, freshly cut flowers and a candelabra full of lit candles.

"No wonder you dress for dinner around here," she added. "Black tie not optional."

Julianna joined them halfway across the room. "Good evening, Izzy."

"Hey, Jules."

Niko noticed and liked the familiarity between the two women. Shopping must quicken the bonds of feminine friendship. Perhaps Jovan had been correct about Julianna being Isabel's role model.

"You look lovely," Julianna said.

Isabel smiled. "Thanks to you."

A waiter appeared with the tray of champagne flutes. Niko took one and handed the glass to Isabel.

"No, thanks." She waved him off. "Tonight's going to be hard enough without adding alcohol to the mix. I doubt your parents would appreciate me dancing on the table."

No, but Niko wouldn't mind too much. He did, however, approve of her good judgment in refusing to drink.

Isabel studied one of the place settings. "I might have better luck dancing than trying to figure out what silverware and glass to use when."

"Go from the outside in," he said, remembering all the etiquette lessons forced on him even during the war.

"Watch what we do," Julianna added. "You'll do fine."

Two little lines appeared above Isabel's nose. She rubbed her hands together as if nervous. "Maybe I should get a plate to go."

A flurry of noise sounded in the doorway. Niko stiffened. "My parents have arrived."

"Don't worry." Julianna touched Isabel's shoulder. "Just remember what I told you earlier."

Isabel nodded, but she bit her lower lip. Uncertainty filled her eyes.

He almost felt sorry for her.

His father entered the dining room with a rare smile. He

acknowledged Niko and Julianna before turning his full attention on Isabel. "What a lovely dress, Izzy."

Niko appreciated the way his father was trying to make her
feel comfortable by using her nickname. King Dmitar could
intimidate even the most seasoned statesman.

She curtsied. "Thank you, King Dmitar."

"I would like to introduce you to my wife, Her Royal Majesty
Queen Beatrice." Dmitar presented his mother, who wore a floor-
length ball gown, a diamond necklace and matching tiara. No
one would mistake her for anything but the queen. "Beatrice,
this is Isabel, but her friends call her Izzy."

Niko bit back a laugh. His mother would never call Isabel by
anything other than her given name.

"We are delighted to have you back in Vernonia, Izzy,"
Beatrice said.

What? Niko stared in disbelief.

"It's a pleasure to meet you, Your Royal Majesty." Isabel
curtsied again only this time she swayed on her heels like a tree
in a windstorm. A soft gasp escaped her lips. Panic flashed in
her eyes.

Niko grabbed her elbow so she wouldn't tip over.

She mouthed the word "thanks," and shrugged off his hand.
She didn't look any steadier on her feet so he kept hold of her.
"Isabel is still recovering from the long flight. I'm sure she
would like to sit down."

"Of course." Dmitar motioned everyone to the table. "We
have much to discuss."

"Yes, we do." Beatrice sat, and a waiter handed her a napkin.
"But now that I've seen Izzy myself I agree with you, Dee. We
won't have any trouble."

Isabel was seated across the table from him. She shot a questioning gaze to him and Julianna.

"Trouble, Mother?" Niko asked, curious what his parents
had been discussing.

"Your father and I have been discussing Izzy's future,"
Beatrice said.

His mother's words set off an alarm in Niko's head. Waiters

brought out the first course and set the bowls of soup on the table at the exact same time.

"That's really nice of you all." Izzy's smile looked forced. "But it's not necessary, Your Highnesses."

"But it is," King Dmitar countered. "All this must still be a shock to you, Izzy, but we are your family now. We don't have much time. We must make plans for what is to happen next."

"An annulment comes next, Father," Niko said. "We will go to the High Court first thing Monday morning."

Izzy nodded. "You don't need to waste your time planning anything, sir. My future is set."

"I appreciate your concern over my time." Dmitar's expression was earnest. "But I think it's time for a little history lesson."

Niko took a sip of his chilled eggplant soup. His father's lessons usually lasted until the wee hours of the morning.

Dmitar continued. "You, Izzy, are the last of the royal Sachestian bloodline that ruled the northern region for years before joining with the southern portion of the country to form Vernonia. For centuries, the Separatists have asked that your bloodline rule the north again. But the Loyalists have wanted the Kresimir bloodline to rule over all the land. The two groups hotly disagreed and fights would break out."

"A little like the Montagues and the Capulets?" Izzy asked.

"Only not so romantic," Niko said.

"But still quite Shakespearean," Beatrice said.

Julianna nodded. "History has shown a marriage between rival sides can ease strife and lead to peace."

"Excellent point, Julianna." Dmitar took a sip of water. "Over time, the arguments between the Separatists and the Loyalists intensified, Izzy. An official petition to separate the Northern portion of Vernonia circulated in the late 1980s. Civil war seemed imminent. Your father believed that a union between the two royal families would appease the Separatists and avoid war. His goal, our goal really, was to unite Vernonia once and for all with your marriage. But the civil unrest turned violent with terrorist acts. The people remained divided, and war broke out."

Silence enveloped the room.

Isabel toyed with her napkin. She hadn't tasted the soup yet. "It must have been a horrible time, Your Majesty."

"Horrible does not begin to describe it, my dear. Our country has been at peace for the last five years," Dmitar said. "But that was after the last of the Sachestian bloodline was killed during the conflict. The Separatists believed, they still believe, no Sachestian descendents remain. But now that you have returned like a Phoenix from the ashes—"

"So let's not tell them I'm back. No one has to know about me," Izzy interrupted. "I'm sorry for butting in, sir, but your country has been through enough. I don't want to cause any problems here. The truth is I really don't want to be a princess. Let's get the marriage annulled. If you can't transfer my father's estate we can figure something else out so I can disappear from Vernonia forever."

"That sounds like an excellent plan." Niko was proud of her for speaking up and succinctly saying what needed to be said. That was one positive to Isabel's lack of princess skills. Julianna would have never said anything.

"I wish it were that simple," Dmitar said with regret. "We cannot pretend the Separatists do not exist or that their desire is not real."

"Julianna's father supported the Separatists during the war," Niko countered. "They support my marriage to her?"

"Yes, but they do not know about Isabel."

"Father—"

"Imagine you are a Separatist," Dmitar interrupted. "You have agreed per the peace accord to be a part of a new united Vernonia. You believe all the members of your royal family are dead, but suddenly discover one young princess lives. Oh, the joy. But then you learn the crown prince of your country has annulled his marriage to your princess so he can wed a different princess from another country. How do you think that will go over in this so-called united land?"

"You make it sound like I'm being slighted or something, sir,"

Isabel said. "I want the annulment. I don't want to be married to Niko."

Her firm tone left no doubt that she wanted out of the marriage as much as he did. She'd said that, but still the rejection surprisingly stung. Niko wasn't used to women not wanting to be with him. "Our marriage was only to avoid a civil war, Father. The war is over. There is no reason for us to remain married."

"Perception can be as strong a motivator as reality," Dmitar said. "Vernonians have quick tempers. Our loyalty is our strength, but our biggest weakness. We will cling to our causes until the bitter end. Whether right or wrong."

Niko stiffened in shock. "I hope you are not suggesting we remain married, sir."

Isabel's mouth formed another perfect O. Clearly she was aghast at the idea.

Julianna leaned forward with interest. Niko couldn't believe she was sitting here with their engagement on the line without saying a word.

Dmitar stared at him. "You have made it clear that is not an option."

Isabel's shoulders dropped. Her features relaxed. A smile tugged on the corners of her mouth.

Julianna leaned back against her chair, but her lips were pressed together.

Niko would have expected her to be happier. Perhaps she was nervous about his father's intentions. Niko would put her at ease. "Marrying Julianna is best for Vernonia. No offence, Isabel."

"None taken," she said.

"So you've said over and over again." Dmitar's gaze went from Julianna to Isabel to Niko. "That leaves me no choice but to find Isabel another husband. One she must marry the minute the annulment is granted."

"What?" Isabel shrieked.

"Why?" Julianna asked, sounding taken aback.

"Father." Niko had brought Isabel here. He didn't want the American to be forced into an arranged marriage. "You can't be serious."

"I'm very serious," Dmitar explained. "If Izzy is married, the Separatists can be upset about the turn of events, but can do nothing to change the situation. If she remains single…"

Dread pulsed through Niko's veins. "They could demand we remarry or use her to rally against you."

"Yes," Dmitar said.

Niko thought he'd considered every angle. He believed the Separatists were content with their coalition in the government, that they were comfortable with his family as heads of state. He was so focused on modernizing that he never thought they would demand a marriage alliance in the face of improved economic development. But apparently he had been wrong. Because of that, Isabel would be the one to pay. She did not deserve to have her life plans derailed any more than they already had been.

"No." Isabel's face paled. "There has to be another way. Anything…"

He respected the way she stood up for herself. "Let us have time to think of an alternative, Father."

"The High Court convenes on Monday," Dmitar said. "You have one day to think of an alternative that will maintain peace. Otherwise Izzy must get married."

"Who do you plan to marry her off to?" Niko couldn't think of anyone in the kingdom that would be a match. The thought of some other man with her…whoa, he needed to reel in his thoughts.

"I've been working on that, dear." Beatrice stared at Izzy with interest. "Here's the list of eligible royals I've come up with so far…"

Talk about a living nightmare. Izzy's future was at stake. She had to think of something and fast.

Izzy lay in bed wide-awake. Her mind raced fast enough to capture the pole position at Darlington Raceway. Unable to sleep, she glanced at the clock. 2:04. No way she could sleep. Not with the conversations from dinner replaying through her mind like reruns of a TV show.

She imagined a show called *The Royal Kresimirs*. The

preview would consist of shots of each of them. King Dmitar saying she needed to marry. Queen Beatrice rattling off a list of potential husbands. Prince Niko interjecting his opinion on each name his mother read. Princess Julianna smiling as she attempted to keep the peace. Izzy racking her brain to find a way out of being forced to marry.

But this was too far-fetched to be a television show. Something like this should never happen. Not in the twenty-first century. Not to an American citizen.

That gave Izzy an idea.

She could call the Embassy. Surely the State Department would help her out.

No, that would only solve her problem, not…Vernonia's.

Izzy wasn't attached to this strange country. Until yesterday she'd only heard of the place in the news, but Vernonia had meant something to her parents and to Uncle Frank. She wasn't selfish enough to ignore the war fought here or pretend another one couldn't happen again.

Her stomach growled.

She'd been so upset she couldn't eat dinner. She'd even turned down a slice of chocolate torte served for dessert. That had been dumb. Chocolate always made her feel better. Maybe a leftover slice was in the kitchen. That would raise her spirits.

She crawled out of bed, shrugged on the white bathrobe and stepped into the hallway. Still not sure which room was hers, she left the door open.

A few minutes and a couple wrong turns later, Izzy sat in the castle's deserted kitchen poking at a slice of chocolate torte with her fork. Her appetite was still missing in spite of her tummy's grumblings. She couldn't muster enough enthusiasm to take a bite of chocolate.

Pathetic.

"Here you are." Niko's voice cut through the silence and startled her. "I wondered where you had disappeared to."

"How did you know I was gone?"

"The door to your room was open." He walked toward her,

past the wall of stainless steel refrigerators and around the massive commercial stoves.

"All the doors look alike." She noticed he wore the same dress shirt and pants as earlier, but he'd ditched the jacket and tie. He'd also unbuttoned the collar and rolled up the sleeves. The casual style looked good and made Niko seem approachable, more like a normal guy than a crown prince. "I left mine open so I wouldn't walk into the wrong room."

"Smart move. I called your name, but you didn't answer." He sat in the chair next to her. "I thought you might have run away."

"Running away was the first thing I thought of doing." Izzy stared at the uneaten torte. "But I crossed it off the list."

"You have a list?"

"Well, yeah." She stabbed the fork into the torte and left it there. "I know this doesn't really affect you, but we're talking about my future. I'm not going to grab a splash of gas and hope I can make it to the end of the race. I need a full tank before I take an alternative to your father."

"What happens to you does affect me, Isabel." Niko's lips thinned. "Why do you think I'm still awake?"

She shrugged. "Just heading back to your own room for the rest of the night?"

"No." His jaw tightened. "I've been trying to come up with a solution myself. If I had thought this would happen, I would have never brought you back to Vernonia."

Izzy felt lower than pond scum. She'd accused him of having a midnight tryst while he'd been playing knight in shining armor trying to save her butt. "Sorry."

"No need to apologize. We need to find a way out of this."

We. Izzy didn't feel so alone. She didn't like needing help, but she liked having Niko with her now. She wasn't getting very far on her own.

He eyed her torte suspiciously. "Are you going to eat that?"

"No."

"May I?"

She pushed the plate toward him. "It's all yours."

"Thank you." He raised the fork. "What stopped you from running away?"

"Logistics," she admitted. "I can't get back home without a U.S. passport or cash."

"Ah, yes. You only have the temporary Vernonian passport Jovan arranged for you."

Izzy nodded. "But I don't have it. Jovan does."

"If you want it—"

"If I ran away, you wouldn't be able to get an annulment. That means you couldn't marry Jules without committing bigamy."

"Thank you for sticking around. I'm much obliged, as will Julianna be." He scooped up a forkful of torte. "I did think of one possibility. It's a bit extreme."

"I'm open to anything at the moment. Including extreme."

"How about faking your death?"

She stared at him in disbelief. "That's on my list."

The edges of his mouth curved. "Great minds think alike."

"It's a good idea," Izzy said. "I don't want to die, but if people thought I was dead, there would be no issues with the Separatists. No one would complain if you married Julianna. I would be free to live my life however I wanted."

"The logistics would be more complicated than running away."

She nodded. "There can't be a body."

"That limits the ways a person can die."

"I know."

"Fire," Niko suggested.

"Wouldn't bones and teeth be left?" she asked.

"Unless it was an inferno of some sort, but that might be dangerous."

"I wouldn't want anyone to get hurt."

"Of course not." He rubbed his chin. That sexy razor stubble had reappeared. "Drowning."

"Bodies disappear at sea never to be seen again."

Niko nodded. "Julianna is a world-class sailor. You could fall overboard."

"I like the drowning part, but do you really want to involve your future wife in something like this? I mean it's probably illegal."

"No, she should not be involved."

That meant it was just the two of them. Izzy felt like Niko was her partner in crime. "I could still fall into the sea somehow. Off a boat or a cliff."

"You will have to be prepared to say goodbye to Isabel Poussard forever."

Izzy thought about her life, of the people she'd come in contact with, known and loved. "You're right. I wouldn't be six foot under dead, but I would be dead to everyone who knew me."

"There would be no going back."

No going back. She would never be able to do anything racing related. But it was more than her dream she'd be losing. She thought of her friends back in Charlotte, of Rowdy and Boyd and the rest of the boys at the garage. Her chest tightened.

If she got married and had to stay in Vernonia or another nearby country, her life would be different, but at least she could visit her friends. Faking her death would mean never talking to them again. "Honestly, I don't think I could lie to my friends about dying. Not after the hurt and grief we all went through when Uncle Frank died."

"I would rather not have to lie or break any laws, either."

She slumped in the chair. "We're right back where we started."

"We will think of something else."

Niko sounded confident, but a strange sensation settled in the pit of her stomach, one having nothing to do with not eating dinner. She had no way out of this mess. The reality of the situation seemed…undeniable. "I'm not sure there is anything else."

He set his fork on the plate. "Isabel—"

"Think about it." She fought the rising panic. "We've both been up half the night trying to figure this out. Faking my death is the best we came up with."

"We just need time."

"It's already Sunday." A lump formed in her throat. "We don't have much longer."

"That means…"

Tears stung her eyes. "I know what it means."

"You don't want to get married."

"No. But when I think what might happen if I don't…" This wasn't a debate about differences between two political parties and their views on the issues. People were willing to kill for what they wanted. Her parents had been murdered and her uncle Frank had given up his entire life because of the conflict between the Separatists and the Loyalists. Izzy had wanted to do something for her family. Maybe this was it. She blinked to keep the tears at bay. "I don't think I have any choice."

CHAPTER SEVEN

NIKO covered Izzy's hand with his. The warm touch was a harsh reminder to her that another man, a stranger, would soon call himself her husband and be the one touching her. Hot tears spilled down her cheeks.

She turned away so Niko wouldn't see her cry.

He cupped her chin and turned her face toward him. Gently he wiped the tears from her cheeks with his fingers. "I will not allow you to be forced into a marriage you do not want."

"Thanks, but this is bigger than you and me. People have suffered too much already. My parents and Uncle Frank sacrificed their lives. I won't be the catalyst for more violence and pain."

"I did not believe you had what it takes to be a princess, but you do," Niko said. "My apologies, Isabel."

The sincerity in his voice brought another round of tears. She would miss hearing him say her name.

"Thanks." Izzy sniffled. "I'm usually not so girly about things."

"I'm glad you're a girl," he said. "Or I couldn't do this."

Niko gathered her into his arms.

Izzy stiffened. She didn't need him, but she had no desire to back out of his embrace. The loneliness in her heart made her relax and lean toward him so he could pull her closer.

Pressing her cheek against his hard chest, she felt the beat of his heart, steady and strong. Invisible warmth enveloped her. For the first time in years, she felt safe. All the emotion she'd been holding in poured out.

Niko didn't try to soothe her with platitudes. He simply held her, rubbing her back. It was more than she had expected from him. It was all she needed at the moment.

She didn't know how long Niko kept his arms around her, but slowly her breathing settled. Her tears stopped. Izzy found the strength she needed in his arms. "I know what I have to do. It's just…I can't imagine having to spend the rest of my life married to someone who was forced to be my husband. It seems so wrong to me."

He brushed his hand through her hair. "You are not used to the concept. But arranged marriages aren't all bad. There's friendship, companionship, having a common purpose."

His closeness comforted her. Izzy could almost believe things would be better. "I only wish…"

"Tell me."

Izzy hesitated, but Niko had been so caring, so kind she had to tell him. "I wish instead of marrying some random royal with a fancy title I could marry for love. But at this point I'd settle for being able to choose who I married."

Niko continued to comb his fingers through her hair. "Whom would you choose?"

The thought of him popped into her mind then quickly vanished. The emotion of the situation, his compassion, was making her feel closer to him.

"Tell me who," he pressed.

None of her dates liked cars or racing the way she did. The guy she spent the most time with was Boyd. Building go-carts together, working at dirt tracks on pit crews, watching races. They shared the same interests and the same dreams. They just weren't…romantic. "Boyd," she decided.

"Your coworker?" Niko drew back to stare into her eyes. "You said he wasn't your boyfriend."

"He's not, but he's one of my closest friends. He wouldn't expect us to have, um, a real marriage."

"You mean sex."

Her cheeks burned. She shouldn't have said anything. "Yes."

"You would be satisfied with a marriage in name only?"

"It isn't about being, um, satisfied," she said. "We wouldn't have to be married for decades. Only a few years. Long enough for things to stabilize in Vernonia and for you and Jules to have a couple of heirs. Then we could divorce."

Izzy heard something that sounded like a gasp. She peered over Niko's shoulder. "What was that noise?"

"I didn't hear anything," he said.

She looked back again, but didn't see anyone. Must have been the refrigerator or something. "Do you think your father would allow me to marry Boyd?"

"We can ask him," Niko said. "Would Boyd go along with the idea?"

"Probably. A lot of people have assumed we're a couple. We know each other pretty well." She pictured her coworker and friend. Boyd was an all-American, beef-fed Southerner. Down home and down to earth. Strong and rugged, but kindhearted like Niko. Not model handsome, but a lot of women found Boyd easy enough on the eyes. "I think he'd say yes because of our friendship, but if I told him I wanted to start a race team together that would most likely seal the deal. He's more car crazy than I am."

Niko's mouth twisted. "Would you be happy married to Boyd?"

"Marriage has never been on my radar screen, but…" She thought about her parents and Uncle Frank. Marrying a man she loved like a brother was nothing compared to the sacrifices they had made. She would do this for them. "If Vernonia remains at peace, then yes. I would be happy married to Boyd."

Niko let go of her. "We shall take this alternative to my father in the morning."

"That's only a few hours away." Izzy felt cold without his arms around her. She fought the urge to wrap her arms around herself to warm up. "Fingers crossed he says yes."

"Vernonia is indebted to you, Isabel." Niko's gaze met hers, and her heart bumped. "And so am I."

She didn't care about Vernonia, but him… His face was so

close to hers. Something—passion, perhaps?—flashed in his eyes, and heated her blood. He tilted his head.

Niko was going to kiss her.

Izzy's pulse rate skyrocketed. Her mouth went dry.

Heaven help her, she wanted him to kiss her.

She parted her lips in anticipation.

Niko held her hand, raised it to her mouth and kissed it. The brush of his lips was soft, a caress. She nearly sighed.

He lowered her hand. "If there is anything you ever need…"

She needed him to kiss her. Not her hand, but her lips.

Here. Now.

Niko released her hand.

Disappointment shot through her. No matter how much she wanted this moment to mean something more than one person comforting another, it didn't.

It couldn't.

Izzy might want her lips to be crushed by his, but it would never happen. Niko was too honorable. He would never hold her passionately. He would never share his dreams with her. He would never whisper words of endearment into her ears.

Those were things he would do with…Jules.

Niko was going to marry the pretty princess from Aliestle. And if the king said yes, Izzy would marry Boyd. She would return to the United States with a husband and a partner. They would join the world of racing, not as members of a pit crew, but as the owners of a new racing team.

Izzy would have everything she wanted. And so would Niko.

A happy ending for everyone involved, including Vernonia. There was just one problem. Why didn't she feel happier?

The next morning, Niko sat next to Isabel on a settee in the king's private drawing room. His father stood across from them with a stern look on his face as he considered their request. The tension in the room was palpable. The silence increased Niko's discomfort level. He would rather be elsewhere, but he didn't want Isabel to have to go through this alone. She deserved his support for what she was willing to do for him and Vernonia.

Isabel rested her clasped hands on her lap. She wore a lime-green skirt and matching jacket. The heels on her shoes weren't as high as last night, making it easier for her to walk. She looked very much like a princess.

The only clue anything was wrong were the dark circles beneath her eyes. But he'd still place his money on her. The defiant tilt of her chin told Niko she was ready for a fight.

His father had no idea who he was dealing with. As Niko had learned last night in the kitchen, neither did he. Isabel was a strong and amazing woman. Beautiful and so much more than he imagined she could be.

Thoughts of her had kept Niko awake most of the night. Each time he'd closed his eyes he remembered the scent of her hair, the taste of her skin, the warmth in her heart. He never imagined feeling this way about her. Attraction explained part of it, but there was also his respect and admiration for her willingness to do what was best for Vernonia. All three were combining to a potent mix of affection.

Niko should be having these feelings about Julianna, not Isabel. He was anxious to get this matter resolved so he could refocus and not allow unwanted and unwarranted feelings for the American to cloud his thoughts.

Dmitar paced back and forth. "There is much to consider here."

Isabel's lower lip trembled. Only slightly, but the vulnerability Niko saw in that moment pressed down on him like a two tonne weight. She'd been uncomfortable crying in front of him. She liked handling things on her own. But he couldn't sit and do nothing now.

He reached out, covered her hand with his and squeezed.

The edges of her mouth lifted in a close mouthed smile.

His heart beat faster. He smiled back.

The lines on Dmitar's forehead deepened. Niko's shoulder muscles tensed until he realized the reason behind the change in his father's facial expression. He was staring at Niko's hand on top of Isabel's.

Niko pulled his hand away. Not that he should feel guilty. It wasn't as if he'd just kissed Isabel. He may have thought about kissing her last night, but today he'd simply offered a gesture of comfort. The fact he enjoyed touching her and holding her last night was of no consequence.

Gratitude, he rationalized. That was what Niko felt for Isabel. Appreciation for the sacrifice she was willing to make. Nothing...more.

"You are satisfied with this alternative, Izzy," Dmitar said finally.

"Satisfied is a relative term, Father," Niko answered. "This marriage is being forced upon Isabel."

Dmitar glared at him. "Your name is not Izzy."

Niko pressed his lips together.

"I admit I'd rather not have to marry at all, sir," Isabel answered honestly with her head held high. "But I will be more satisfied with this option than what was proposed at dinner."

Dmitar rubbed his chin. He usually made up his mind quickly. The decision wasn't that complicated yet was taking longer than it should.

That worried Niko. Isabel hadn't eaten breakfast. She looked as if she hadn't slept. She needed the situation to be resolved.

"Father," Niko said. "This alternative is the best option for Isabel. The choice of a husband should be hers."

"What's best for Isabel may not be what's best for Vernonia," Dmitar countered.

"Like Niko said, I believe this is the best option for Vernonia," Isabel said without any hesitation. "I've known Boyd for years. We like the same things. People we know won't think it's weird if we eloped. They will believe we're married, not trying to pull the wool over someone's eyes."

"That means the Separatists would believe it, too," Dmitar said.

She nodded. "If they thought it was a ruse, we'd be right back where we started."

"Plausibility is important," his father agreed.

Finally, Niko thought. Progress. "So you agree, sir."

"Are you in love with this Boyd fellow?" Dmitar asked.

"This is ridiculous." Niko stood, irritated and frustrated. "Love has nothing to do with it, Father. Please do not make this any harder on Isabel than it already has been."

Dmitar frowned. "I will not tolerate any more outbursts from you."

"I will stop when you cease toying with Isabel."

"Thanks, Niko." She smiled up at him, and his pulse quickened. "I appreciate you standing up for me, but I don't mind answering your father's question."

She sounded sincere. Niko sat.

"I love Boyd, sir."

Isabel's words hit Niko like a left jab. He felt an instant, squeezing pain. Something he'd never felt before. Surprise. That was what it must be. She had not mentioned this last night.

"Boyd is one of my closest friends," she continued. "He's like a brother. There are no, um, romantic feelings between us. The marriage would be in name only with the intention of divorcing when it was safe."

The tightness in Niko's chest eased with her clarification, but a small part of him envied Boyd for having such a relationship with Isabel. Niko had never had a close friendship with a man let alone a woman. At least not since the death of Stefan who had been big brother and best friend rolled into one. Now Niko's duty to Vernonia always took precedence over everything and everyone else. Including long-term romantic relationships. Short-term ones, too.

"That is quite a sacrifice you are willing to make," his father said.

Isabel shrugged. "Not really if you look at what my parents and Uncle Frank did. They gave their lives. I still get to be involved in car racing so I wouldn't call what I'm doing a sacrifice, sir."

Dmitar beamed. "You've thought this through, Izzy. Well done."

Niko's admiration for her grew. "I agree."

She looked up at him.

Isabel's hazel eyes appeared greener. It must be her jacket bringing out the color. He could still see the same gold flecks he noticed last night. Very pretty.

Dmitar cleared his throat.

Niko looked at his father.

"I accept this alternative," Dmitar proclaimed. "Isabel may marry Boyd."

"Yes!" Isabel pumped her fist. "Thanks, Dee. I mean, Your Highness. Majesty. Sir."

Not quite the perfect princess, but she was the perfect Isabel. Niko smiled.

"We will delay your appointment with the High Court until Tuesday to give Boyd time to arrive," Dmitar said. "Have Jovan prepare the necessary paperwork for the annulment, transfer of Aleksander's estate and a marriage license."

"He's already working on them, Father," Niko said.

Dmitar raised a brow. "Confident I would say yes?"

"Hopeful," Niko admitted. That and he hadn't been able to sleep knowing how negatively all this was affecting Isabel.

"Then we're all set," Dmitar said.

"Not quite, sir." Izzy stood, and Niko rose to his feet. "I still have to see if Boyd will marry me."

Dmitar chuckled. "He's a fool if he doesn't want to be your husband."

"Not only a fool." Niko liked the blush on Isabel's cheeks. "A complete idiot."

"Well, I hope Boyd is neither of those things, but I'd better find out." She curtsied. "If you'll excuse me, sir."

Dmitar dismissed her. As soon as she exited, he grinned wryly. "I never thought there would come a day when I'd hear you admit to being not only a fool, but also an idiot."

"I didn't."

"Not directly," his father said. "But you are married to Izzy and don't want to be her husband."

"It's not the same situation," Niko protested. "Julianna brings a large dowry, one bigger than Isabel's inheritance, Aliestlian trade support and investors, a royal pedigree that will provide alliances with other European kingdoms and the knowledge necessary to be queen. Even the Separatists support her. Isabel is an American, a mechanic. She doesn't know the first thing about being a princess or Vernonia. She has no qualifications to be queen."

"Isabel is honest, loyal, smart and has royal blood running through her veins," Dmitar said. "You say she has no qualifications yet this American mechanic is willing to marry someone she doesn't love for a country she hadn't stepped foot in until twenty-four hours ago."

Each word stabbed at Niko like one of the soldier's bayonets on display at the National Museum. He stared at the ground.

"You may want to redefine what makes a queen, my son," his father counseled. "Not only for your own sake, but your wife's. Otherwise you really will look foolish."

"Come on." Izzy checked the reception bars on her cell phone. Nothing. She shook the phone. "What's a girl gotta do to get coverage around here?"

The castle wasn't that far from town. There had to be a cell tower somewhere. She'd tried using one of the phones inside the castle, but couldn't figure out how to get a dial tone. If only Niko were here...

Strike that. She didn't need his help or those blue-green eyes of his to make her heart go pitter-pat.

Izzy walked past the garden and down three steps.

Her eyes burned from exhaustion. The stone path hurt the bottom of her feet. Her fault. She'd ditched her shoes ten minutes ago. But she couldn't give up.

The king had given his approval. Now she needed Boyd's.

Time was ticking. Izzy needed to make this call. She checked the display. No bars. "I bet this place still uses dial-up internet connections."

"A few villages in the mountains rely on dial-up, but the castle has a wireless network," Niko said from behind her.

"What are you doing out here?" She was surprised to see him. It was as if her thoughts had conjured him up like some magic wish. "I thought you had stuff to do."

"I do, but I thought I'd see if you had reached Boyd."

"Not yet." She held up her lousy excuse for a cell phone. "No service."

His smile turned to a laugh. "So that's why you were threatening to feed your phone to the fish."

"I—" Okay, she had said that, but he hadn't been there. "How did you know that?"

"A gardener warned the staff about a barefoot American screaming at her cell phone." Amusement danced in Niko's eyes. "I had a feeling it might be you."

Heat stole into her cheeks. "Jules said when you're royalty someone is always watching even if you can't see them."

"Yes."

"But I wasn't screaming," Izzy defended herself. "At least not that loudly."

Grinning, he punched in a couple of numbers and handed his cell phone to her. "It's a satellite phone. I put in the country code for America. You're all set."

"Thanks." She appreciated Niko's help. It wasn't only the phone. He'd stuck up for her with his father this morning. If only Niko could make the call…

Nerves battered at her stomach. She swallowed, her mouth suddenly full of cotton. This was her future, so much depended on the outcome of this one call. She stared at the phone in her hand.

He rocked back on his heels. "I can give you some privacy."

"It's up to you."

"I'll stay."

Izzy figured he would. Niko took his responsibilities seriously. That included her, even if she was his wife in name only. She punched in Boyd's number and held the phone to her ear.

Niko watched her intently.

Izzy focused on the phone ringing. Once, twice, three times.

"Hey." Boyd sounded sleepy, as if she'd woken him up, but his voice came across strong and clear.

"It's Izzy."

"Good to hear from you, Iz. Is that prince dude treating you nice?" Boyd asked.

Her gaze met Niko's, and her pulse skittered. "I'm, uh, calling you on his phone."

"I don't like the way he looks at you."

Izzy glanced over at Niko, taking in his broad shoulders and athletic physique that his suit couldn't hide. His appreciative gaze traveled the length of her. She liked how he looked at her very much. "Don't worry about that, but…"

"What is it?" Boyd's voice sharpened.

She gripped the phone tighter. "I'm in a bit of a jam and need your help."

"You want my help?"

"You don't have to sound so surprised."

"Okay, but I am," Boyd said. "Doesn't matter, though. Whatever you need, my answer is yes."

"You might want to wait to hear what I have to ask you." As she smiled, her gaze met Niko's again. He gave her a conspiratorial wink. This time her heart stuttered. "It, um, might change your answer."

She needed to focus. Something she found hard to do with Niko around. But this was too important to let a pretty face distract her.

As Izzy studied a leaf on the ground, she explained to Boyd what had happened between the Separatists and the Loyalists in the past, what could happen in the future and how she had become drawn into the mess.

"So what do you need from me?" Boyd asked.

"I know it's a lot to ask, but I need a husband. Not forever. Just a few years." She took a deep breath. "Will you marry me, Boyd?"

* * *

Niko watched Isabel as she waited for Boyd's answer. Her toes wiggled. She kept readjusting the phone at her ear.

The man was a fool for making Isabel wait so long.

All of a sudden, a smile brightened her face. "Thanks, Boyd. You don't know what this means to me."

She laughed, a delightful sound that floated on the air. "Okay, you're on."

On what? Niko wondered. He would have liked to hear both sides of the conversation.

Izzy flashed him the thumbs-up sign. She was happy. Good. But he should be feeling relief, not the regret and disappointment playing ping-pong inside him.

"I'll have Jovan call you with all the details." She bounced from foot to foot. "Yeah, I know. I'll see you soon. Bye."

Izzy disconnected the call. She ran to Niko and threw her arms around him. "I don't have to marry a total stranger. Boyd said yes!"

Her soft curves molded against Niko. Heat pounded through his veins.

She hugged him tightly. "Thanks."

Niko wasn't sure what he'd done to earn this reaction. He didn't really care. He wrapped his arms around her. She fit perfectly against him.

"We did it," she said.

"Yes." The scent of her hair filled his nostrils. "We did."

He stared down at her face. She looked up at him.

Isabel's mouth was so close. Her lips were parted. An invitation?

He wanted to kiss her, more than he'd ever wanted to kiss a woman before. He wanted to know what her kiss tasted like. Sweet or tangy?

So tempting.

Longing filled her eyes. With each breath she took, each beat of her heart, it became clear. She wanted him to kiss her.

Yet he hesitated.

Julianna was ready to marry Niko.

Isabel was his wife, but another man had just accepted her

proposal to marry her. Anything they did would be wrong. Illicit. Hurtful to the two people they'd agreed to marry.

Niko lowered his arms and stepped out of her embrace.

Disappointment pinched her face. Her smile faltered, but only for a moment. She handed him his phone. "I'm sorry for getting carried away with my celebrating."

"You do not need to apologize."

Izzy glanced around. "If someone saw…"

"You are my wife. We hugged. That is not a crime."

"Yeah, a hug." She sounded disappointed. "No big deal."

"Right." Though it had felt like a bigger deal to him. He missed her body touching his. Her warmth. The feel of her moist breath.

"Jules wants to work with me today." Isabel wouldn't meet his eyes. "Princess lessons."

He couldn't deny the chemistry between them, but that was a complication he couldn't afford. Whatever he was feeling was strictly physical. He hardly knew Isabel. "I have things to take care of myself."

"I'd better get going. I need to remember where I took off my shoes."

"If you can't find them…" He was about to offer to help her, but he couldn't. He needed to limit his time with her. "Ask one of the staff to assist you."

Izzy nodded. "See you later?"

She was a fair princess. And he didn't want her anywhere near him.

The words of—it might have been Shakespeare—swirled through Niko's head.

"Perhaps." Unless he could convince Julianna to join him for dinner after they went sailing. He needed her to take his mind off Isabel. "Otherwise, I'll see you tomorrow at breakfast."

Two hours later, Izzy walked through the library with a book on her head. Okay, "through" was a slight exaggeration. She only made it three steps before the book fell off and landed on the wood floor with a thump.

"I don't see why I need to do this." Izzy blamed her lack of concentration on not sleeping last night, but the real reason was Niko. She couldn't stop thinking about hugging him and wanting to kiss him. "It's not like anyone will ever be watching how I walk."

"Princesses need to have perfect postures," Jules said.

"But I'm not going to be a princess." Izzy stared at the etiquette book she'd been balancing on her head. None of this stuff Jules was trying to teach her mattered. Not now anyway. "I'm going to marry my friend Boyd and go back to Charlotte. As long as I put my napkin in my lap at mealtime, I'll be good."

"Being good isn't enough. You must be the best. People have certain expectations," Julianna said, proving once again why Niko wanted to marry her. "You are a princess no matter where you live."

"Yeah, but if someone ever calls me by my title I might have to deck them."

Jules cringed. "Izzy…"

"I know." Izzy sighed. "Princesses don't punch."

"You are allowed to fight back if attacked."

What defined an attack? Since arriving in Vernonia, she felt as if she'd gone nine rounds. She was exhausted, confused and frustrated. Not to mention attracted to her soon-to-be-ex-husband and the soon-to-be-husband of her new friend. "I just want to go home."

"I'm so sorry, Izzy." Compassion filled Jules's eyes. "I know exactly how you feel."

The beautiful princess who would marry the handsome prince and live happily ever after as they ruled Vernonia had no idea how Izzy felt. No one could. Still she didn't want to be rude. That went against princess protocol. "Thanks."

Jules started to say something, but pressed her lips together. Niko and King Dmitar used the same gesture. Maybe it was a royal thing, stiff upper lip and all that.

"I'm good. Really," Izzy added. "At least I get to pick who I marry, right?"

"Yes. You are quite fortunate in that regard." Jules removed a

heavier book from one of the shelves. "Try again. Remember…
shoulders back, chin up and smile as you walk."

Izzy placed the book on her head. "I'm going to have the best
posture of any mechanic east of the Mississippi."

"That's the spirit." Jules checked her watch. "I'm going sailing with Niko. Would you like to come along?"

Izzy remembered the "faking her death by drowning" suggestion, and a smile tugged at her lips. She would like to go, but
she didn't want to be a third wheel. Jules was the closest thing
to a girlfriend Izzy had here, yet she had wanted to kiss Niko.
That went against princess protocol as well as the friendship
code. She needed to distance herself from the prince. "Thanks,
but I need to practice. Then I want to take a nap."

"You could sleep on the boat," Jules offered. "We'll be going
out to dinner afterward. It should be fun."

"Sounds like it, but no thanks."

"You're sure?"

Was there a hint of disappointment in Jules's tone? No, Izzy
had to be mistaken. The lovely princess was just clarifying her
position.

You are allowed to fight back if attacked.

She remembered Jules's firm handshake. Izzy had a feeling
the princess could hold her own in a fight especially when it
came to another woman hitting on Niko. Not that Izzy would,
but she didn't want to put Jules or herself in an awkward position
by intruding on their evening. "I'm absolutely positive."

And maybe if Izzy repeated the words enough times, she
might actually believe them.

CHAPTER EIGHT

The next day, Izzy ate breakfast alone in the morning area. That was what she called the smaller dining room because the only time she ever saw it being used was in the morning. At least for the two she'd been here.

Izzy took a bite of the cheese blintzes covered with a raspberry sauce and swallowed. Delicious.

Add yummy food to the list of princess perks.

Jules entered and sat opposite Izzy. The princess looked stylish in a polka-dot, short-sleeve dress with her hair worn loose.

"Good morning, Izzy." A server filled Jules's cup with coffee. "You look more rested today."

"I am." Izzy had woken feeling a little more like herself. She'd realized her attraction to Niko was nothing more than a crush. Yes, he was gorgeous and had come to her rescue, so to speak. That had been fine with her world imploding yesterday, but she saw things more clearly this morning. "A little sleep can go a long way."

Or maybe it was common sense kicking in. She didn't want a man to see her as anything but an equal. Niko came from a totally different world and viewpoint. She would never want to even try to be his equal. So why spend any more time thinking about almost-kisses or dreamy blue-green eyes?

Izzy sipped her freshly squeezed orange juice. "I hope you had a nice sail and dinner."

She squelched the pinprick of jealousy. She'd tried hard last night not to think of the two together out on the water. And she'd mostly succeeded.

She had more important things to think about. Boyd arrived today. Tomorrow her marriage to Niko would be annulled. She would receive her inheritance and marry her coworker and friend. She would return to Charlotte with more than she ever imagined. Perhaps not the same happily-ever-after Jules and Niko would share, but a good one just the same.

"I did. It was very enjoyable. Thank you." Another server placed a plate in front of Jules. "I love sailing. There's nothing I'd rather do."

"That's how I feel about car racing."

"We have more in common than you realize." The sincerity in Jules's voice wrapped around Izzy like a hug. "I hope you enjoyed your evening."

"I had dinner with the king and queen."

"And?"

Izzy recalled the conversation. Well, inquisition. "It was… interesting."

"How so?"

Her head and throat hurt thinking about all the talking she'd done. "They asked me so many questions I felt like a game show contestant."

Jules sipped her coffee. "What did they want to know?"

"Everything and anything."

"Intriguing."

"They may have been wanting to make me feel more comfortable," Izzy admitted. "I had a couple mishaps at dinner."

"Oh, dear."

She smiled. "That's exactly what the queen said. After my third mistake, Queen Bea was laughing along with King Dee and wondering if she was using the correct fork or not."

"Laughter makes everything better."

Niko stormed into the room with a stack of newspapers in his hands. His lips were pressed together, his eyes dark. "We have a problem."

Izzy had no idea what sort of problems could put so much worry on a prince's face, but it couldn't be good.

Jules set her fork on the plate. "What has happened?"

Niko opened one of the papers and showed them the front page headline written in English.

Princess Isabel Zvonimir Kresimir Lives!

Jules gasped. She covered her mouth with her hands.

Izzy stared at her name with a strange sense of detachment. It almost seemed surreal to see herself called a princess and her first name paired with two different last names. "What does the article say?"

"It's a complete biography of you, including your return to Vernonia." He handed the paper to Izzy. "Whoever leaked this information to the press will pay."

"It'll be okay." Izzy wanted to put a positive spin on things. They had a plan. They didn't need to get distracted. "We knew my identity would come out at some point."

"We wanted to control when that happened." Niko tossed the rest of the papers on the table. "Read the article."

Izzy did. Each time she read the words wife or bride, she squirmed. The details in the story made the knot in the pit of her stomach grow. "Whoever leaked the information must have overheard my conversation with your parents last night."

Niko frowned. "We have never had any problems with the staff before."

"Some of the article is word for word what I said. It's also kind of strange." Izzy scanned the article once more. "There's very little about my life before I arrived in Vernonia. Your parents and I discussed my job, but nothing is mentioned. This article makes it sound like I was living the life of an exiled royal hiding out in North Carolina, not a mechanic working at a garage to make ends meet."

"That is good," Jules said. "People will only see you as a princess."

Izzy straightened. "There's nothing wrong with being a mechanic."

"No," Jules admitted. "But as King Dmitar said the other night, there's a perception."

Niko's frown seemed permanently etched on his face. "I would have rather they called you a grease monkey than my wife or princess bride."

Izzy winced. Okay, that hurt. "Why don't we head to the High Court now, then you won't ever have to hear that about me again."

Jules shot her a compassionate look. "I don't think Niko intended his words in that way."

His hard gaze met Izzy's and softened. His cheeks reddened. "No, I...I did not. I apologize. But the wording, especially the usage of husband and wife, suggests a closer, more intimate relationship than what we have."

"The article is slanted that way," Izzy agreed. "But once the annulment—"

"Jovan is at the royal offices in town," Niko interrupted. "People are assembling. The Separatist colors are flying in support of you. The people want you to be the next queen."

Her mouth gaped. "The people just found out about me."

His jaw thrust forward. "Word travels fast."

"You need to talk to them." Her eyes implored him. "Tell them Jules is going to be your wife. Explain how I'm engaged to Boyd."

Jules's gaze met Niko's. Some unspoken communication passed between them. "I cannot," he said.

The sudden silence increased the tension in the room tenfold. Izzy felt clueless. She struggled to put the pieces together.

The Separatists have wanted your bloodline to rule their portion of Vernonia.

Your father believed that a union between the two royal families would appease the Separatists and avoid war. His goal, our goal really, was to unite Vernonia with your marriage.

History has shown a marriage between rival sides can ease the strife and lead to peace.

I hope you aren't suggesting we remain married, sir.

Something clicked in Izzy's brain. The shocking realization

made it hard for her to breathe. The weight of a people, a country, pressed down on her chest, on her heart.

She wanted to believe she was wrong. She had to be wrong. "There isn't going to be an annulment, is there?"

A muscle flicked at Niko's jaw. "The response by the Separatists this morning is similar to how the conflict began twenty-odd years ago."

Conflict. She heard the anguish in his voice. What he really meant was war. A bloody civil war that had killed her parents and caused a nation to suffer.

"The High Court and my father will not allow an annulment now," he added.

Vernonians have quick tempers. Our loyalty is our strength, but our biggest weakness. We will cling to our causes until the bitter end. Whether right or wrong.

Izzy trembled. She couldn't give in to the emotions raging through her. "You mean, for now."

Regret shone in his eyes. "I mean, ever."

Niko's words snuffed out her spark of hope.

No annulment. Niko would remain her husband. She would remain…here. Her life, her dreams…

She stared at the table, struggling not to lose it completely. And then she remembered she wasn't the only one affected by this.

Guilt at her selfishness coated her mouth. Her gaze bounced between Niko and Jules. "What about the two of you?"

"A dowry can't stop a war. Only you can, Isabel," Niko said as if he were already resigned to his fate. "None of us want this, but for the sake of Vernonia, will you consider remaining my wife?"

That was romantic. Not.

"This is crazy. Our marriage didn't stop the war twenty-three years ago." The words poured from her lips like steam from an overheated engine. "We don't know that it will work this time or if it will even come to that. We shouldn't be forced to give up our dreams for a what-if."

Niko's eyes sharpened with disdain. Tight lines bracketed his mouth. "I will not risk my country and my people so you can return to America to play with race cars."

The abrupt change in him unnerved her, but she met his accusing eyes without flinching. "I was talking about you and Jules."

"I'm okay with this, Izzy." Jules sounded encouraging, but that was her nature. The princess wouldn't show how she really felt.

"Well, I'm not." Fighting her emotions, she stood. "The two of you are perfect together. You're in love. You should be able to get married."

"Isabel," Niko said. "You should know—"

"I know enough." The desperation in her voice matched the way Izzy felt inside. She might be attracted to Niko, but that wasn't enough reason to marry a man who didn't love her, a man who wanted to marry someone else. "This country is completely whacked. I want nothing to do with it. Nothing at all."

She pushed back her chair, not caring that it clattered to the floor, and ran out of the room.

Izzy disappeared from sight before Niko could stop her.

Regrets assailed him. He had hoped she would eagerly do what was required of her, not get emotional and run away. He needed to make her understand what was at stake. "That did not go well."

"She is young. An American." Julianna stared into her coffee cup. "All this is foreign to her."

"I'll go after her."

"Give her a little time."

"Isabel is upset. She shouldn't be alone." He'd hurt her thinking she was being selfish. He needed to explain about his relationship to Julianna, too. "It's my responsibility."

Julianna sighed. "Izzy is not a responsibility. She's a person. Your wife. A woman can tell if you're there because you want to be or because you feel obligated."

"I do feel obligated." Frustration tightened the muscles in his neck and shoulders. "Isabel is not prepared to fulfill this role. Not the way you are."

"Isabel is not a typical princess, but her heart is in the right place."

"She does not want to be my wife."

"She is upset and frightened. Your behavior only served to make her more so."

His jaw tensed. He didn't like being called out on his behavior. "Isabel's feelings about arranged marriages are very clear."

"I will stay and help her adjust," Julianna said. "Perhaps if I do not return home, my father won't try to make another match for me right away."

Niko studied Julianna's face. Her eyes looked brighter. Her complexion had more color. "You're happy things turned out this way."

"Not happy. I would never wish this upon dear, sweet Izzy. But I am…relieved," Julianna admitted. "No one should be forced to marry someone they do not love. No offense."

"None taken." This side of her surprised him. "Yet you agreed to the marriage."

He cringed. His words sounded a lot like his father's.

She lifted her shoulder in a delicate shrug. "I was only doing what my father told me to do. What was expected of me. As I have always done my entire life."

Her words sounded similar to what Niko had said in the past. "I have done the same thing."

She raised a finely arched brow. "Are you certain about that?"

Her question offended him. He squared his shoulders. "Everything I have done has been for Vernonia."

"If that's the case, why would your parents go to the press about Izzy?"

"My parents would never—"

"They were the only ones who could have done this," Julianna interrupted. "While you and I were at dinner, they quizzed Izzy about her past. Her answers appear in the article. Isn't it strange that only positive information was published about her? The press rarely works that way."

I may not be a stickler for tradition, Father, but I will always do what is best for the country.

As will I.

Niko's stomach knotted. "I need to speak with my father."

Julianna rose. "I'll find Izzy."

He appreciated her help and her friendship. "You would have made a fine queen."

"Thank you." She bowed her head. "I have no doubt you will be an excellent king, especially with Izzy by your side."

If only he believed that could be true...

As if on autopilot, Izzy followed the directions given to her by a butler. The stone path should lead her to the garage. That was the only place she could think of at the castle where she might not feel so out of place, the only spot that reminded her a little of home.

The tower loomed above Izzy, as if mocking her. The castle no longer seemed part of a romantic fairy tale. It belonged in a terrifying Gothic novel.

Would she ever be allowed to go back to Charlotte? If only to visit? Or would she be forced to stay in Vernonia forever, married to a man who didn't want her for his wife?

Izzy's insides twisted. She might have found Niko attractive. She might have wanted to kiss him. She might have even dreamed about him, too. But Izzy couldn't fathom spending the rest of her life married to a husband she didn't love, a husband who didn't love her.

She stumbled on a rock. Stupid heels. Somehow she managed to catch herself before falling flat on her face. Surprising since she felt as if she were carrying two tires—the hopes and dreams of Vernonia—on her shoulders. She was about to collapse from the load.

Izzy kicked her shoes off to keep from falling again.

Up ahead, she saw a rectangular brick building. That had to be the garage.

Welcome relief flowed through her. She quickened her step and entered through the side door.

The smell of motor oil greeted her like a long-lost friend. Tears pricked her eyes, but she wasn't going to cry. If she started, she might not be able to stop.

Izzy surveyed the interior: tools, tires, air compressor, an old truck and a limousine. She leaned against a wall and slid to the cement floor.

Her shoulders slumped. She closed her eyes.

Izzy had no idea how long she sat there. She didn't care. Here in the garage, she belonged. She couldn't say that about any other place in the castle, not even the bedroom where she slept.

A door on the opposite side opened. The sharp staccato of heels echoed through the garage until Jules stopped in front of Izzy. "Rough morning."

Without looking up, she nodded.

Jules sat next to her on the ground.

Izzy shot her a sideways glance. "You're going to get dirty."

"That'll make two of us."

"I don't mean to be rude, but I don't feel like talking."

Jules wrapped her hands around her bended knees. "Then you can listen."

Izzy stared at the puddle of oil under the truck. Somebody needed to fix that leak.

"Niko and I aren't in love."

She looked at Jules. "What?"

"It was an arranged match. My third, actually," Jules explained. "Arranged marriages are the tradition in Aliestle, whether you are a royal or a commoner. My first match was made when I was seven, but he was later deemed unacceptable. Too bad because I really…liked him. My second was made when I was twenty-five. My marriage to Prince Richard of San Montico would have realigned our two countries after one hundred and thirty-nine years of feuds, but he was in love with someone else and married her. And then came Niko. He's honorable. Respectful. Attractive. But I'm not in love with him."

Izzy couldn't believe what she was hearing. "The two of you get along so well."

"We agreed to the match. We have common goals and a similar sense of duty."

"Duty?"

"I am a princess of Aliestle. My duty is to do what is best for my country," Jules said. "I am sure my father will make a fourth match for me as soon as he learns what has happened here."

"I had no idea, Jules. I'm so sorry." Compassion made Izzy reach out to her friend. "If I were you I would have run away by now."

Jules laughed. "I imagine you would have, but this is how I've been raised. Aliestle is more archaic than Vernonia when it comes to customs. But the land is rich with natural resources so we can afford to be...eccentric and backward with some of our traditions."

"But to marry someone you don't love..."

"I have dreamed about marrying for love since I was a little girl." Jules sighed. "The reality is an arranged marriage to best suit the needs of my country."

"That seems to be my new reality as a royal, and it sucks."

"Yes, sometimes it does," Jules admitted. "Duty and country first. But I'll tell you a secret. Even though I've always known I would be told who to marry, I've never given up hope that somehow I'd be able to marry for love. However remote the possibility."

"I hope it works out for you."

"Thanks, but I'm not holding my breath," she said.

"I know it won't happen for me now."

"No, but Vernonia needs you, Izzy."

"Vernonia isn't my country."

"It was your parents' country and your uncle Frank's."

Izzy hadn't been thinking about them this morning. Only herself. That wasn't the way to honor the three people who had loved her so much and given up so much for her.

Guilt over her selfishness seared her heart. She needed to focus on what they would have wanted her to do in this situation, even if it wasn't what she wanted. "I only wish it didn't feel so wrong. I wish…I loved Niko."

"But you have feelings for him, yes?"

"It's been like a roller-coaster ride since I met Niko in Charlotte. I don't know what I feel for him."

"Remember, just because you don't love someone at the beginning doesn't mean you won't love them in the end. Love can grow over time."

"Do you really believe that?"

Jules smiled wryly. "Well, every time my father proposes another match I hope it's true."

Izzy couldn't ignore the bigger part in all this—Vernonia. People here, like people everywhere, deserved to live in peace. That was what her parents had wanted. That was what she believed her uncle Frank had wanted, too. Izzy's dreams of car racing seemed almost childish in comparison. Even if the High Court would grant her an annulment, she might be needed here in Vernonia. "I guess I'll have to hope it's true, too."

Niko stood in the king's office. Sweat beaded on his forehead and dampened the back of his shirt. He clenched his hands, struggling to control his temper. It wasn't working. "I can't believe you would betray me like this, Father."

"I didn't betray you, Niko. I spoke to the press for one reason and one reason only. To protect Vernonia. The Separatists want Izzy to be the next queen. We can't join the EU if we're having another civil war." Dmitar's lips thinned. "One day you'll understand the difficult decisions a ruler must make."

"If I am to rule, you need to treat me like the crown prince, not a pawn."

His father frowned, looking affronted. "I haven't—"

"You could have been honest about what needed to be done and explained your reasons. Not manipulate the situation the way you have." The words rushed out full of emotion and guilt at what his father's actions had done to two innocent women. "You have forced Isabel into a corner and hurt Julianna. Vernonia desperately needs the alliance with Aliestle. It's more than the dowry. The trade support and the influx of investment capital will enable us to modernize and join the European Union."

"Julianna is wealthy and beautiful, and even though her country has Separatist ties, she cannot unite the people the way Izzy will."

"Unite the people?" Niko stared at his father in disgust. "Have you not seen the gathering this morning? The Separatists' colors are already flying. It's history repeating itself. Isabel should be taken from Vernonia immediately."

"So you can marry Julianna."

"So Isabel will be safe. I fear for her safety. As should you."

Dmitar gave him a speculative look. "You like her."

"Excuse me?"

"Izzy." Amusement gleamed in his father's eyes. "I saw the way you touched her yesterday. The way you stared into her eyes."

Uncomfortable, Niko shifted his weight between his feet. He may like her, but that didn't mean they should remain married. "I hardly know her. I appreciate her sacrifice. I'm concerned about her well-being due to your underhanded tactics. The protests—"

"Izzy is safe," Dmitar interrupted. "These gatherings are different from the ones before. These are celebrations, my son. Unity. Finally."

Satisfaction sang in his tone.

Something more was going on here. Niko could feel it in his bones. Going to the press had only been one part of this. "You never planned on allowing Isabel to marry Boyd."

"I never planned on allowing you to annul the marriage in the first place."

Niko took a step forward. "How dare you?"

"I am the king. I do what is necessary."

"Necessary?"

"As soon as I saw the picture of the box and discovered Izzy was alive, I saw a real chance at lasting peace for Vernonia. A united country, all regions, all people. That is what Prince Aleksander and I hoped would happen twenty-three years ago with your marriage. I doubted you would go along so I used the annulment as bait to get your cooperation."

Fury infused Niko. "You can't play with lives this way."

"You were fine marrying Julianna."

"It was my choice. I've always been willing to marry without any preconceived notions of love," Niko said through clenched teeth. "But you've dragged Isabel into this with your machinations and lies."

His father shrugged. "The end is worth the means."

"No, Father. It is not." Niko squared his shoulders. "I have tried to fulfill Stefan's role. I've tried to live up to being crown prince and sacrifice for Vernonia, but you cannot continue to scheme and coerce a young woman into marriage. This type of action must stop. Now."

"A ruler must—"

Niko held up his hand, cutting off his father. "Be honorable in both thoughts and deeds. That is what you taught me. If Isabel refuses to remain married to me, I will support her decision, despite the dangers."

Panic flashed in Dmitar's eyes. "You must convince her. Vernonia needs an heir as soon as possible. A baby with both royal bloodlines."

"A baby?" Niko nearly choked. "Isabel doesn't want to be my wife. I doubt she will go willingly into my bed."

"Your duty—"

"I know my duty, sir," Niko said. "I've always known what is expected of me. I will talk with Isabel, but unlike you, Father, I will not manipulate her into marriage. The choice will be hers. And hers alone."

CHAPTER NINE

JULES headed back to the castle, but Izzy stayed in the garage. She wanted to repair the oil leak on the truck. She found tools and drained the remaining oil.

"You need a pair of coveralls so you don't ruin your outfit."

Izzy's heart lurched at the sound of Niko's voice. Pathetic. She hated the way she responded to him. He was only being nice because Vernonia needed her. She focused on the engine. "A little grease on my clothes won't hurt anything."

"I wonder what Tom Ford, Marc Jacobs and Stella McCartney would say about that."

She recognized the names of the famous fashion designers only because she now owned some of their clothing. "You mean Henry Ford."

Niko gave a short laugh. "I believe these belong to you."

His words forced her to glance his way. He looked out of place in the garage dressed so proper in a blue suit, white dress shirt and yellow silk tie. Her shoes dangled from the crook of his fingers. Out of place, but as sexy as a model in a magazine.

She wouldn't deny his physical appeal, but that didn't mean she would fall in love with him. Worse, what if she fell in love with him and he didn't fall in love with her?

She forced her gaze back to the truck and bent over the engine.

"I found one shoe in a bush and the other embedded heel down on the grass," he said.

"Keep 'em."

"They are not my size."

A smile tugged at her lips. She couldn't help it. "I'm sure you can find someone else they fit."

"They fit you, Isabel." He set them on the cement floor next to her. "Perfectly."

Izzy bit back a sigh. He was making an effort. The least she could do was meet him halfway. She straightened and stuck her foot in one of the shoes.

Niko kneeled to help her.

"I've got it," she said.

He stood, letting her do it herself.

She slipped on the other shoe.

"I am sorry for what I said earlier. For all of this," Niko apologized, his expression contrite.

She fought the urge to reach out to him. Self-preservation, not the grease on her hands, kept her from doing so. "Me, too. I shouldn't have run out like that."

"You had every right," Niko said. "We have been pawns in my father's game. His agreeing to let you marry Boyd was simply his own ruse to put his plans into action. He is the one who leaked the information about you to the press. He never intended to allow us to annul the marriage."

Dee had been so nice to her. The queen, too. "Why would he do that?"

"To unite Vernonia. That has been his goal as king. It's the same goal he shared with your father when they married us off."

Her father. Izzy's chest tightened.

"What do you want to do?" Niko asked.

"There's a choice?" She'd been trying to resign herself to her fate since talking with Jules.

His eyes darkened. "I hate what my father has done. I won't force you into…"

"Marriage."

He nodded. "I told you the first day I wouldn't lie to you. I don't want to coerce you into remaining my wife."

Izzy appreciated that. "I'm not what you wanted for Vernonia."

"No." His word, though honest and expected, jabbed her heart like a knife. "But it's what the country needs. Part of being a princess or a prince is putting your people first."

Niko believed that wholeheartedly. Jules, too. Izzy understood the necessity of peace, but not this duty they kept talking about.

That made her uneasy. Especially when she thought about the future.

How would Izzy know if Niko came to care about her or if he was simply doing his duty, the way he had been doing since the first day they met? The question left her as unsettled as the thought of unrequited love.

Still she appreciated his leaving it up to her. Too bad she really didn't have a choice.

"I don't like what your father did, but I will remain your wife. For Vernonia," she clarified, not wanting him to get the wrong idea.

"Thank you." He sounded relieved. "I know what you are giving up."

"Keeping peace is the most important thing. I couldn't live with myself if I was the reason for people being hurt." She fiddled with the engine to keep her hands busy. "I just hope your father is more honest and open in the future. Otherwise it will make things...difficult."

"I spoke with him about that." Niko seemed hesitant, uncertain.

"What?"

"My father believes Vernonia needs an heir. He wants one as soon as possible."

Her stomach knotted. "This will be a, um, real marriage?"

"I am the crown prince." A small smile played at the corners of Niko's lips, drawing her gaze. He had such a well-formed mouth, so inviting... "An heir and a spare are the minimum for any royal marriage. Real or not."

She blinked and forced herself to look away as heat crept up her neck. "Can't a person get used to one thing before having something else thrown at her?"

He placed his hands on her shoulders.

Warmth, delicious and oh, so inviting, emanated from the point of contact and flowed through Izzy. The entire dynamics of the situation seemed to change with the one touch. She focused on the word seemed. This was still an arranged marriage with a total stranger, who cared more about duty and country than anything else.

"This is not the kind of marriage you planned on having with Boyd," Niko said. "But we can make this work."

"How?" Izzy wished she shared his confidence. "It's not as if we're going to fall madly in love with each other."

"No, this isn't a love match, but that doesn't mean we can't have a successful union."

"Successful?"

"Providing the necessary heirs."

"So it's all about the baby making."

"That is a large part of it."

"I appreciate your honesty, but maybe you could sugarcoat it a little."

"You need to know what you're getting into," Niko said, as if he were an employer offering her a job, not a husband speaking about their relationship.

"Do we live together?" she asked. "I'm not sure how this kind of marriage will work."

"We have two options. A state marriage. That is living as husband and wife until we have the required number of heirs, then we live our separate lives, only appearing together at state functions or for our children's sake."

Izzy wasn't expecting a fairy-tale ending, but she hadn't been prepared for something so…calculated. "Would I be able to return home to live? To Charlotte, I mean."

He hesitated. "Possibly, but you must understand a divorce would never be allowed and custody arrangements might be tricky."

Niko was talking about children yet they'd never kissed. "What's the other option?"

"We live as husband and wife until death do us part."

"A together forever kind of thing?" she asked.

"As close to that as we could manage," he said. "In the old days, arranged marriages were quite successful. Why shouldn't ours be? We like each other, right? Besides, contemporary marriages based on love don't come with guarantees. Many people end up separating. Every marriage takes work if it's going to last."

"What kind of work?" she asked honestly. "I've never had a serious relationship before."

"Me, either," he admitted. "We will have to figure out what it takes together."

Izzy rested the palms of her hands on the car. A marriage based on respect and honesty wouldn't be bad. She was attracted to him. "If we can't figure it out, we can always just live apart."

A vein throbbed at his jaw. "If the marriage does work…"

"Then we'll owe your father a big thank-you."

Niko rocked back on his heels. "So it's settled."

"Not yet." Izzy straightened. "I don't see how we can begin to make a marriage work when I don't feel married."

"We are married."

"I know we got married, I saw the photograph and the marriage certificate, but I don't remember getting married. Maybe if we had a wedding ceremony, one we both remembered, I'd feel like your wife."

His gaze searched her face. "This is important to you."

"To feel married. Yeah, especially if we're going to, um…"

Amusement twinkled in his eyes. "Have sex."

This was *so* not what she wanted to be talking about with him. "Provide Vernonia with an heir."

"Do you enjoy sex, Isabel?"

Oh, man, he assumed she'd had sex. What was she going to say?

"I…" She looked around as if the answer would pop up on

the hood or headlight for her to see. Of course, it didn't. Where was an enchanted castle when you needed one? "I don't know. I've never…"

She couldn't finish the sentence. He might be her husband, but that somehow made it more embarrassing.

"Never?" he repeated, sounding intrigued.

"Never." She felt self-conscious under his gaze. "I had the chance, more than once, but I always thought having sex after the first or second, even the third date was selling myself short. Uncle Frank said it should be an expression of love and commitment, not a way to cap off dinner or a movie."

Niko didn't say anything.

She flushed. "I'm a total freak, aren't I? I don't know how to be a princess. And I have no clue how to, you know."

"You are not a freak." He reached out to tuck a strand of hair behind her ear. "You're beautiful."

She shivered at the light touch. If only she felt beautiful.

"Do not worry. We have not known each other long, but there is a chemistry between us," he said in a husky tone.

Okay, at least he'd felt it, too. That had to count for something.

He moved closer. "I didn't pursue it because of Julianna."

"That was honorable of you."

Wicked laughter gleamed in his eyes. "But now that it is the two of us and you are my wife…"

Izzy stepped back until she hit the truck's bumper. "Look, I wanted to kiss you in the kitchen two nights ago. Outside near the garden yesterday. But now I don't want to do anything until I feel married."

He raised a brow. "Not even kiss?"

Temptation flared. A touch made her feel all tingly. A kiss might send her right over the edge. "No."

"We will have a wedding." His smile crinkled the corners of his eyes, and her heart beat like a drum. "We shall have a royal wedding complete with a fanfare of bugles, a packed cathedral and a horse-drawn carriage that would make Cinderella envious."

"That sounds so elaborate." And overwhelming. "I was thinking more along the lines as a quick trip to the courthouse."

"You need to think bigger," he said. "In fact, a wedding isn't enough. We will also go on a honeymoon."

Every single nerve ending stood at attention. She balled her hands so tightly her nails poked into her palms. A honeymoon implied romance, intimacy, sex. "That really isn't necessary."

"It is if we are to get to know each other and start our marriage right."

And, she realized with a sinking feeling in her stomach, conceive an heir. If that was all Niko wanted, their marriage really didn't stand a chance.

At precisely one o'clock in the afternoon the following Saturday, a flourish of trumpets announced the royal wedding procession. As fifteen hundred guests sat in the intricately carved wooden pews, the ancient stone cathedral's walls swallowed the music. An omen or poor acoustics?

Izzy shivered with apprehension.

The first of twelve bridal attendants, all wearing ice-blue strapless silk gowns, strolled out of the vestibule and into the church. She'd barely met any of the women, but at least Jules was her maid of honor.

Even though I've always known I would be told who to marry, I've never given up hope that somehow I'd be able to marry for love. However remote the possibility.

Jules had received another reprieve from the altar. She'd also convinced her father to support trade and offer investment capital to assist Vernonia's rebuilding efforts. Izzy hoped the princess's generosity would be rewarded and she would be allowed to marry for love.

It was too late for Izzy, but things were improving between her and Niko. She'd been on her best behavior trying to learn all she could about being a princess from Jules. Niko seemed to be trying, too.

Would trying be enough to make a marriage work?

Izzy hoped so. She clung to the idea that love could grow

over time. That they could have a forever kind of marriage, not a state one.

Music continued to play. Izzy recognized the song. Soon it would be her turn to walk down the aisle.

She remembered her princess instructions.

Shoulders back. Chin up. Smile.

Izzy could do this. She was a princess of Vernonia, even if she felt like a mechanic from Charlotte. She was doing this for her new country. For her parents. For Uncle Frank.

And Niko.

Her chest tightened at the thought of him.

He was waiting for her at the front of the church. Boyd, acting as his best man, would stand next to him. When she'd explained to her friend that marrying Niko was her choice and she liked him, Boyd had given her a strange smile and a shrug. Whatever sting he might have felt disappeared when the king offered to buy Boyd a new truck for his troubles.

Izzy took a deep breath and exhaled slowly.

Through her lace veil, she watched another attendant, the youngest daughter of a former Separatist leader, enter the church through the massive arched doorway. The oohs and aahs of the crowd floated on the air as they did during a fireworks display. The flashing of the camera bulbs and the web of electrical cords from the television crews made it seem more like a sports event than a wedding. Selling the television rights to the royal nuptials of the crown prince to the half-American princess had brought in more money than anyone had expected.

Rowdy, her former boss, cleared his throat. He stood next to her in the vestibule ready to walk her down the aisle. Sweat beaded on his forehead. He looked uncomfortable in the tuxedo. "You sure about this, Izzy?"

No. But she thought about Niko. He'd been honest about his reasons for marrying her. He'd been open about the need for heirs and the types of marriages they could have. But she'd also noticed the tenderness in his eyes when she caught him looking at her, the way he'd helped her since arriving and the love he had for his country. All those things told her he was a good, honorable man. "I'm sure."

Rowdy's eyes gleamed. "All your uncle wanted was for you to be safe and happy."

"I am. Honest."

"Then we're good to go." Her ex-boss sniffled. "You are a beautiful bride."

"Thanks, Rowdy." Izzy felt pretty, even though she'd had plenty of help to look so good. Since early this morning, she'd been fussed over, primped and pampered with a massage, manicure, pedicure and expert makeup application. Everything had been overseen and supervised by Jules. Three hairdressers had spent over an hour sweeping her hair up and through the diamond tiara that secured the cathedral-length veil. The last of the crystals and pearls had been hand-sewn on the bodice of her wedding gown only an hour ago by a dress designer named Delia.

Yes, the crew of wedding experts had transformed Izzy into a fairy-tale princess bride even though she'd been the prince's wife for the last twenty-three years. A happily-ever-after wasn't waiting for her after the exchange of "I dos." The birth of heirs would classify the match as a success or a failure, but would the union be full of love or loveless? That was the big question. One that wouldn't be answered for...years.

Two more attendants made the long walk down the aisle. In the vestibule, the remaining bridesmaids and six flower girls moved forward. Izzy had been introduced to all of them five days ago at a luncheon thrown by the wives of Parliament members.

Nerves escalating, Izzy gripped her all-white rose bouquet. She focused on the flowers' sweet fragrance.

Three more attendants made their way down the aisle. The folds of their gowns swished like flags in the wind.

Shoulders back. Chin up. Smile.

Jules flashed her a smile and a thumbs-up before stepping into the church. The six flower girls, dressed in layers of white ruffles, played with the white rose petals in their baskets. One of them, the youngest daughter of a duke, giggled.

The tight-faced, headpiece-wearing wedding coordinator shushed her. "Quiet. It's almost your turn."

And then it would be Izzy's turn.

Her pulse rate doubled. She took a calming breath. Another. And another. But it didn't help.

In the old days, arranged marriages were quite successful. Why shouldn't ours be?

She clung to Niko's words, holding out the hope that they could spend the rest of their years together, not apart and married in name only.

The flower girls skipped into the church.

"It's almost time, ma'am," the wedding coordinator said.

Izzy's heart slammed against her chest. Each fierce beat reminded her of the cannon being shot off during the royal orchestra's performance of Tchaikovsky's *1812 Overture* at the Royal Hall on Tuesday night.

Another flourish of trumpets sounded. Rather, bugles, as Niko had called them. The signal. Her signal.

"Ready?" Rowdy asked.

Izzy would never be ready for this.

She glanced behind her at the massive wooden church doors. Two royal guards flanked either side. The instinct to run had never been stronger. But where would she go? What would she do? And who would clean up the mess she left behind?

She might not be a fairy-tale princess locked in a tower, but she was a prisoner of circumstance as was Niko. The two of them were stuck with each other. Better just make the best of it.

Shoulders back. Chin up. Smile. "I'm ready."

Rowdy kissed the top of her hand. "You're the daughter I never had. I'm proud of you. I know Frank would be, too."

Tears stung her eyes. Rowdy's words filled her with warmth. "Thank you. Thank you so much."

She took hold of his arm. Somehow she managed to lift her

heavy feet and step into the church without tripping on her gown and falling on her face.

Dignitaries, royalty, even movie stars stood to watch her, but the faces blurred. She focused on the altar.

Her step faltered, but thanks to Rowdy's strong arm no one realized her lapse.

Shoulders back. Chin up. Smile. And breathe.

Izzy needed to breathe or she was going to faint.

She neared the altar. Boyd wore a tuxedo and stood to the right in front of the pew where the king and queen sat.

Rowdy removed his arm from hers.

A tidal wave of doubt and apprehension surged down her spine. Izzy clutched the bouquet's handle so hard it bent.

Rowdy gave her other hand a squeeze. The gesture reassured her. Then he placed her hand into Niko's.

She stared at his neatly trimmed nails, smooth skin, strong hand. A husband's hand. The father of her children's hand.

His fingers clasped around hers. Tingles shot up her arm.

Breathe. Just breathe.

Slowly her gaze traveled to his sleeve—a gold braided cuff against black—and up his arm. He wasn't wearing a tuxedo, but a uniform with gold braiding at the shoulders and a light blue sash, one of the colors from the Vernonian flag, worn diagonally across his chest. A thin row of white from his shirt collar could be seen at the top of the jacket. Ribbons and medals decorated the left side. He wore a thin gold belt around his waist.

He looked like a prince from the movies. Long, thick lashes framed familiar blue-green eyes. His straight nose complemented high cheekbones. Full lips contrasted with the sculpted planes of his face. A mane of brown hair fell to his wide shoulders.

He smiled, and his rugged features softened. Even his scar.

Tingles formed in her stomach.

Niko was almost too beautiful for a man, for a mere mortal. Yet here he stood, as if crafted by the angels in Heaven especially for her. Her heart sighed.

And that was when Izzy knew.

There was only one reason she'd agreed to remain married

to Niko. He might not be Prince Charming, but that didn't matter.

This might not be a love match for Niko, but it was turning into one for her.

She was already falling for her husband. And falling hard.

Niko stared at the woman standing next to him at the altar. Isabel wasn't beautiful; she was stunning. With her light brown hair artfully arranged around a diamond tiara, she was the epitome of what a princess should look like. Her elegant white gown accentuated her curves and ivory complexion.

He should be happy. His people had rallied around this young American, but she wasn't the princess bride he'd been expecting. Wanted. All his hopes and dreams for modernizing Vernonia had rested on his marriage to Julianna. Thanks to his father, Niko could forget about gaining entry into the European Union for years, if ever. His most important duty now was to impregnate Isabel.

Not that he would mind the task, but the rest...

We will have to figure out what type of work it takes. Together.

Niko had no idea what working together with Isabel would be like. He'd never had the same girlfriend for more than a couple of months, and even then he hadn't had a lot of free time. His best friend and closest partner had been his older brother, Stefan, who had kept Niko out of trouble and saved his life on at least two occasions. He didn't know how to create a new relationship. Having seen his parents' arranged marriage would help, but Isabel...

He glanced down at her.

She stared up at him as if he were the sun, moon and stars rolled into one. He could barely breathe. No one had ever looked at him that way.

It had to be the emotion of the moment. Or her makeup.

Isabel came to this marriage out of duty, the same as him. She already had an escape route planned.

If we can't figure it out, we can always just live apart.

He hoped things didn't come to that, even though that was the way many of his peers lived once they had secured the necessary heirs.

The archbishop spoke.

Niko focused his attention on the celebrant, concentrating on the words of the opening prayer. He'd been too young to remember his first wedding ceremony. He should pay attention to this one. Unlike Izzy, he doubted an exchange of vows would make him feel more married. Only time and possibly a child would do that.

But no matter how he felt, Niko would put Vernonia first. He could still do his duty, as a prince and as a husband. And he would.

Even though Izzy was a continent away from home, the gestures and words of the ceremony were similar to weddings she'd attended back in Charlotte. That gave her an unexpected sense of familiarity. Comfort. The last things she'd expected to feel today.

Staring at Niko's handsome face, Izzy concentrated on the archbishop's words—love, honor, until death do you part.

"I do," she said when he'd finished speaking.

Niko released a quick breath.

Relief, she hoped. Not regret.

She knew exactly what she wanted. A real marriage. The together forever kind. But in order for that to happen Niko had to fall for her the way she was falling for him.

"Do you have the rings?" the archbishop asked.

As the ring ceremony continued, Niko repeated the necessary words. Izzy prayed they would come true. He slid a beautiful wide diamond and ruby encrusted gold band on her ring finger. A perfect fit.

She ran her fingertip along the gold band she would give him. The royal historian claimed the diamond, ruby, emerald and sapphire cross heirloom ring not only provided protection, but also brought truth to light. Those two things had made choosing this wedding band from the royal family collection an easy one.

She gripped it hard, afraid she might drop it. "I give this ring as a token of my love and fidelity."

With only the slightest tremble, she slid the ring onto his finger. Once again, a perfect fit.

The archbishop declared them husband and wife. He smiled. "You may kiss your bride."

Their first kiss. Izzy tensed due to a mix of nerves and anticipation. And the thousands of onlookers.

As Niko lowered his mouth to hers, she closed her eyes.

His lips brushed hers and disappeared.

That was it? Izzy pushed aside her disappointment and opened her eyes. She thought Niko had wanted to kiss her.

Suddenly his mouth returned, pressing against her lips. Hard, demanding, as if seeking her very soul. The urgency and need in his kiss frightened yet excited Izzy. She'd never been kissed like this.

It took every ounce of willpower not to cling to him, but she couldn't forget where she was. And who was watching. Not only the guests sitting in the pews, but a television audience watching at home.

Niko drew back, but only far enough to whisper in her ear. "I cannot wait for tonight."

Anticipation buzzed through her. Izzy moistened her thoroughly kissed lips and glanced at the shimmering diamond ring on her finger.

She couldn't wait for tonight, either.

The reception passed in a blur. The guests seemed to be enjoying themselves with the free-flowing champagne and mouthwatering food. Or cuisine as the queen called it.

Unbelievably Izzy felt like a princess. She floated across the dance floor, whirling and twirling to the orchestra, with Niko's strong arms around her. He stayed at her side the entire time, introducing her to so many diplomats and dignitaries she couldn't begin to remember their names. Rarely did he let go of her hand. She felt special, cherished, and that eased some of her nerves about what would happen later tonight.

Their wedding night.

She was excited, but a little worried about the two of them alone. Together. In bed.

After cutting the cake, Izzy stood at the railing of the landing between two sets of curved staircases for the bouquet toss. She held onto the handle of her white rose bouquet. Anticipation filled the eyes of the women standing below her.

"Is something wrong?" Niko asked in a low voice that seeped through her like warm caramel sauce.

"No." She remembered being one of the single ladies called to the dance floor at a friend's wedding last summer. No matter their station in life, royal or commoner, women wanted to catch the bouquet. "Just taking it all in."

"Savor the moment," Niko whispered. "But you may want to put the women out of their misery sooner rather than later."

With a smile, Isabel turned her back to the railing. On three, she let the flowers soar into the air behind her. She whipped around.

Women reached for flowers. A few missed by mere inches. The petals grazed another's fingertips. The bouquet landed in Jules's hands. The lovely princess stared down at the roses in wide-eyed dismay and promptly dropped them.

Izzy laughed, but no one else seemed amused.

The wedding coordinator rushed to Jules's side, scooped up the bouquet and placed them in the stunned princess's hands. The royal photographer corralled Jules for a picture with the bride.

Izzy stared at the camera. "You're smiling, but your eyes don't look happy."

"Catching the bouquet might be a sign," Jules admitted. "I fear I may find myself matched to another royal in need of a wife before I return home to Aliestle."

The camera flash made Izzy blink. They struck a different pose for the photographer. "Stay here."

Jules sighed. "I wish I could."

"I'm serious," Izzy said. "We're spending tonight at the castle, but then we leave on our honeymoon. The king and queen won't mind. They like having guests."

"My father might mind."

"At least think about it," Izzy urged.

"I will," Jules said. "Thank you."

Hours later in the suite that would be the bedroom Izzy shared with her husband, servants helped her out of her wedding gown. All the while, she wondered why Niko wasn't doing this. Wasn't a husband supposed to undress his wife on their wedding night?

Mare combed out her hair. Another woman ran a warm bath. A third lay out Izzy's peignoir set. The lovely confection of thin white fabric, lace and ribbon had been a gift from Jules.

Izzy appreciated the women's efforts. They were just trying to do their jobs, but what was next? A mug of warm milk and a plate of cookies?

All this pampering felt odd. Off. The most important part of tonight was missing. Where could Niko be? The future of their marriage didn't bode well when a husband blew off his wife on their wedding night.

Izzy dismissed the women. She didn't need anyone to add to her growing anxiety. She could put on her own nightgown. But after bathing and re-tying the satin ribbon on the robe for the third time, she wondered if she'd made the right decision. The bow was still lopsided.

Not that Niko would probably even notice.

Izzy paced barefoot across the large room. She noticed a television set inside an armoire and a bookshelf full of books. But she was not in the mood to watch TV or read.

She glanced at the clock.

I cannot wait for tonight.

His words during the ceremony had made her think of what would be happening when they were alone, not at their reception.

The flames of the lit candles flickered. Shadows danced on the wall. He was coming to their room, wasn't he?

Izzy walked to the French doors, opened them and stepped

onto the balcony. Stars twinkled in the inky sky. A breeze, carrying the scent of roses from the garden below, ruffled her hair and nightgown.

This was her new home.

She wanted to be with her new husband.

She just wished he'd get his butt up here.

CHAPTER TEN

NIKO entered the suite with the bride box in his hands. He placed the wedding gift on the table next to two crystal flutes and a bottle of champagne chilling in a silver bucket. The box belonged to Isabel once again. The archaic custom had been fulfilled. He only hoped she felt like his wife now. If not, he would do his best to make sure she did by morning.

He was prepared. The kiss during the ceremony had only whetted his appetite and made him want to skip the reception. The room appeared ready, too.

Soft music played from an iPod docking sound system. Flickering candles provided a romantic atmosphere. The duvet and sheets had been turned down, ready for him to carry his virgin princess bride to their bed.

All he needed was Isabel.

Desire carried him to the bathroom in search of her. She wasn't there. Niko took the time to remove his belt, sash and jacket. He also kicked off his shoes and pulled off his socks.

Out in the bedroom area, he still didn't see her. She wasn't the kind of woman to cower in the closet. That left…

Niko strode to the balcony doors with a sense of purpose that belied anything he'd felt about her, about any woman, before. Isabel consumed his thoughts. She invaded his dreams. Maybe once he had her that would stop. He hoped so. He didn't like being so distracted.

He opened one of the doors quietly.

She stood on the balcony facing away from him. Niko had

no idea what she was looking at in the darkness. Niko only knew what he saw—a vision in white with a starry sky as her backdrop.

His heart beat a rapid tattoo.

The breeze toyed with the ends of her hair the way his fingers longed to do. The fragile fabric of her long robe and matching nightgown ruffled around her legs, hinting at the treasures hidden beneath. Treasures that would soon belong to him, and him alone.

Niko would show Isabel one of the perks of their forced union. He wanted to make this night, their wedding night, special for her. They might have been married for twenty-three years, but tonight they would unite as husband and wife. He wanted her to enjoy the physical side of their marriage, not see it as an obligation to provide heirs to the kingdom. That could go a long way in making their marriage successful.

He stepped onto the balcony. "Wishing on a star or reconsidering faking your death?"

"I must admit drowning isn't looking too bad, but now that my wish has come true I might have to stick around a little longer." She turned with an expectant look on her face. "What took you so long, Highness?"

Niko wanted to take her right there. But he inclined his head instead. "I was forced to play polite with too many heads of state. I apologize for my delay, Highness."

She stared down her nose at him, but even though she was ten feet away from him the desire in her eyes was unmistakable.

Anticipation sizzled. His blood heated and thrummed through his veins.

"I assume you will make it up to me," she said coquettishly.

Her unexpected playfulness hinted at the fun they would have tonight. "I won't stop until you are satisfied."

She walked toward him, but not close enough to touch.

The breeze lifted the ends of her hair again, brushing several strands across her face. His fingers itched to tuck the wayward strands behind her ear. To touch her.

Isabel's bare feet carried her closer until she was bathed in the soft light from the room. The silhouette of her breasts could be seen through the sheer fabric. His groin tightened.

"Promises, promises," she teased.

"I promise you will have no complaints, milady."

His words earned him a breathtaking smile. She reached for the satin ties on her gown. Her fingers fumbled. Not as cool and collected as she appeared to be. That endeared her even more to him.

He longed to undress her, to see her standing naked before him, but he would give her a little more time.

"Allow me." Niko tied the two pieces of ribbon into a neat bow. "There."

Her confused eyes stared up at him through her thick lashes. "Aren't you supposed to untie it?"

"I didn't know we were in such a hurry."

She flushed.

"Impatient?" he asked.

"Well, yeah." Isabel tilted her chin. "Given you're only wearing your shirt and not the full uniform, I figured you were ready for the green flag so we could start the race."

"You want to race through tonight?"

"No, I mean—"

Smiling, he swept her into his arms and cradled her snugly. Her eyes widened. "What are you doing?"

Soft, feminine curves pressed against him. His body tingled with awareness. "Carrying you over the threshold."

"I didn't think you were a big fan of traditions and customs."

"A few have their place." As he carried her to the door, his gaze rested on her mouth. "Especially on a wedding night."

She trembled. "Okay, the nerves are starting to really kick in."

He held her tighter. "Better?"

"Actually, yes." Isabel ran her fingertip along the scar on his cheek. She shifted against him, stretching until she pressed her lips against the side of his face, against his scar. "So beautiful."

"Not as beautiful as you."

"I had help."

"With or without help, you're still beautiful."

He didn't want to rush, but he wasn't that patient, either. Unable to resist the temptation in his arms any longer, he lowered his mouth to hers. She arched to meet his kiss.

With no archbishop, no audience and no cameras watching, Niko could do what he had wanted to do at the cathedral—take his time. No racing to the finish line tonight.

He wanted to savor the kiss, to linger and enjoy. She tasted sweet and warm with a hint of chocolate, like fondue. The castle chef used to make the rich chocolate fudge sauce for Niko's birthday. Just as he had done when he was younger, he soaked up the taste.

As he pushed open the door with his shoulder, Isabel's eager lips pressed against his. Testing, tasting, hungry. Her arms circled around him. One hand combed through his hair. The other splayed against his back, between his shoulder blades, pressing him forward.

Nothing else mattered but Isabel. Sensation swirled through Niko.

She wanted this. Wanted him.

Heat flared.

Her tongue darted into his mouth to tangle with hers.

Exploded.

Niko moved toward the bed, never letting his lips leave hers. He couldn't get enough of her kiss, of her. But he had to stop, for just a moment. He lifted his mouth from hers.

Isabel's eyes opened, her gaze hot and languid, intense and soft. A mass of contradictions. Just like her, his mechanic, his princess.

His wife.

He struggled to remain in control. He wanted to dispense with the niceties, abandon decorum and push up the hem of her gown and take her. But, this was her first time. She deserved better. He needed to go slow, not overwhelm her with tangled limbs and sweaty skin and breathless sex.

Carefully, gently, he lowered her to the foot of the bed so she was sitting on the edge. He stood in front of her, watching her. Waiting for her to look away in shyness.

Her gaze never wavered from his.

Talk about a turn-on.

His chest tightened. His control slipped a notch. Maybe three.

Niko tugged on one of the ribbon ends to undo the bow he'd tied on the balcony. He pushed the chiffon robe off her shoulders and down her arms until it fell over her hands and onto the bed.

He bent over her, kissing her bare shoulder and showering more kisses along her neck and jaw.

Izzy leaned back her head, giving him better access to her graceful neck. He continued kissing her. He loved the smell and taste of her skin. Finally his mouth grazed her earlobe.

A soft moan escaped her lips.

She was ready for more. So was he.

Niko wanted to make her his wife in every sense of the word. He touched the thin straps on both sides of her nightgown, noticing the softness of her skin beneath the rough pads of his fingertips.

She pushed his hands away. "Not yet."

He stared down at her, confused.

Before he could say anything, Isabel kneeled on the bed. She reached for a button on his shirt. "It's my turn."

Kneeling in front of Niko, Izzy's insides quivered with anticipation as she worked with trembling hands to remove his shirt. Through the cotton, she felt the heat of his skin, the rise and fall of his chest. His breathing was no steadier than hers.

That made her feel better and quieted some of her nerves.

Izzy hadn't done this before, but she'd overheard the guys at work. She knew what was supposed to happen. She wasn't about to let Niko do all the work tonight. No way. No how. She wanted him to enjoy tonight, too.

Her fingers shook as she slid another button from its hole.

"It's taking a long time," he said.

She moved on to the next button. "We're still on the warm-up lap."

"My tires are warm. I'm ready to start the race."

Izzy placed her palm over his heart. "Not yet."

His muscles rippled beneath the fabric. So athletic. So strong. He made her feel cherished, special. His. It was all she could do not to sigh.

Was this how a wife was supposed to feel?

She wanted to be his, but she also wanted him to be hers.

Izzy's fingers fumbled as she undid the last button. She brushed his shirt open, her hands grazing his warm skin. Tingles pulsed up her arms.

A key on a silver chain hung around his neck. The key to the bride box.

Izzy fingered it. "You're still wearing it."

"Not anymore." He pulled the chain over his head and gave her the necklace. "The bride box is on the table next to the champagne. It belongs to you, my wife, once again."

She held the key. The bride box and its missing key had enabled Dee to force them together. But she didn't want to think about those things right now. "Thank you."

"You're welcome." His gaze practically caressed. "Now toss the key on the floor so we can get back to what we were doing."

Izzy did.

Inching closer on her knees, she pushed the shirt over his broad shoulders and down his strong arms, arms that had carried her so effortlessly across the threshold as if she weighed nothing.

Her pulse skittered.

Izzy stared at his bare chest and tight abs in awe and admiration. She wanted to memorize everything about him. His arms, chest and back showed the scars of war from his time as a soldier. Like the ribbons and medals he'd worn earlier, these were his badges of honor. He'd fought to protect Vernonia. She had no doubt he would fight to protect her. A dizzying current of desire traveled through her.

She touched his chest, tracing the length of a scar running from his shoulder to his waist. At the end of it, she opened her palm over his ribs, her thumb rubbing another, smaller scar under his sternum.

He drew in a sharp breath.

She pulled her hand back. "Sorry."

"No, it's fine."

"I'm not sure what I'm supposed to do next."

"You don't have to worry about that. It's my turn." Niko raised her hand to his mouth and kissed each of her fingers. "You're overdressed."

He reached for the strap of her nightgown.

"The lights?"

With a swoop of his arms, Niko lifted her off the foot of the bed and carried her toward the head of the bed. He set her on her feet so she was standing right in front of him.

He bent over and pressed a button on the nightstand. The lights went off, but the candles around the room provided a romantic glow. "More comfortable now?"

Izzy nodded, feeling shy. She was not like the other women in his life, the polished, beautiful princesses and models he must have dated.

He pushed the straps of her nightgown off her shoulders and down her arms. Izzy's cheeks warmed. The gown fell to the floor, leaving her exposed to his view.

Slowly his gaze raked over her. Appreciative. Seductive. Possessive.

Her heart jolted.

"You are stunning. Enchanting." His hands moved over her body. Shivers of delight followed his touch. "Captivating."

His words melted her insides.

He ran his finger along the curve of her hip. "No lacy thong."

"I thought it, um, might get in the way."

"Fast learner."

"When it comes to some things." She winked, feeling more brazen. "Kiss me."

His lips captured hers again. This time with urgency and need. He needed her. The realization made Izzy's heart sing. She returned his kisses with reckless abandon.

There was no turning back. She wanted him.

As they kissed, he placed her hands on the waistband of his pants.

Excited, nervous, her fingers undid the hook, but fumbled with the button the same way they had with his shirt. Finally she got it and his zipper. He stepped out of his pants and briefs.

Izzy cast her gaze downward. Oh, my. She swallowed. Hard.

Her fingers reached out and gently touched him.

He inhaled sharply again. Captured her hand before easing her onto the mattress. Her head rested against a pillow.

He climbed onto the bed, the mattress dipping under his weight. As he lay over her, his hair fell forward, the long ends teasing her skin like a feather. The tantalizing scent of him surrounded her. He lowered his head until his lips brushed hers.

Each touch, each kiss, each brush of his body sent shivers of pleasure radiating outward. He made her feel so desired, so sexy. She wanted to make him feel the same.

Boldly Isabel explored his body with her hands again. A low sound emerged from Niko's throat. She had no idea what she was doing, but his response gave her the courage to continue.

"We just started the race," Niko said. "But if you keep that up, I might have to black flag you."

His use of a racing term made her stomach tingle. "Why would you want to send me to the pits?"

Sweat dampened his forehead. "Breaking the rules."

"Forget the black flag. You can't penalize me for not knowing the rules." Her confidence spiraled. She continued touching him. "We have way too many laps to go to finish the race."

"Yellow then."

"Caution?"

He placed his hand over hers. "Slow down. Otherwise you won't be able to avoid the debris on the track."

She ran her hands over his hips and up his chest. "Better."

A flash of humor crossed his face. "For you."

She laughed. "What's it going to take to get the green flag again?"

"Ready to race?"

She nodded enthusiastically. "You?"

"I think you can answer that question." He drew a line along her jawline. "I don't want to hurt you, but since it's your first time…"

If she had done this before, she would be more comfortable, confident. She would be more like the women he was used to. But in spite of her nerves she was happy she had waited until tonight. Until him.

Her hand was still on his chest. She felt the beating of his heart beneath her palm. "I trust you."

Something flashed in his eyes. "I lapped you. Let's get you caught up."

Niko kissed her again until she thought her pounding heart might burst out of her chest. But he didn't stop there. It was his turn to touch her. His fingers sent pulsations of pleasure radiating outward.

A fire ignited inside her, and she arched toward him. She wanted more, so much more.

Her heart swelled with happiness and something she'd never felt before. She pulled back enough to look into Niko's eyes. "Just so you know, the bride box is now mine and so are you."

He slid between her legs, and her body, awash in sensation, welcomed him.

Niko was the only man Izzy wanted. The only man she would ever need. The only husband she could ever imagine having.

Lying in bed the next morning, Niko stared at Isabel asleep. She curled against him, her legs wrapped around his. He needed to untangle himself so he could get out of bed, but he didn't want to wake her.

If Isabel woke, she would want to know where he was going. Niko had no idea. He only knew he wanted—needed—to get away from her to think.

He pulled one of his legs out from under hers.

The sex had been great. Better than he expected. Isabel's curiosity and eagerness had made up for any lack of experience. He'd been powerless to resist her. She'd left him satisfied, spent and wanting more.

Wind blew into the room from an open balcony door.

Damn. He had been in such a hurry to get Isabel to bed he hadn't thought to close the door. Privacy was always an issue here at the castle. He was usually more careful. But with Isabel, he lost all control during the kiss at the ceremony.

Niko couldn't remember the last time he had allowed that to happen. He didn't like how losing control felt. He had wanted to make Isabel his wife, but she'd made him her husband. He wanted her again this morning. His body ached for her and his heart…

He raked his hand through his hair.

No. His heart needed to remain immune to his wife's charms, her humor, her beauty, her seduction. Diving into the marriage *heart* first would not be a smart idea.

Niko understood how falling in love with a woman he had to be married to made sense, but he wasn't ready to be in love. He didn't know when he'd be ready.

Isabel may have come willingly to his bed last night, but their marriage was a direct result of his father's underhanded tactics. Niko was not going to lie to her about his feelings, but would she be as straightforward with him?

He had no idea if Isabel was committed to this marriage or not. Loving his wife wouldn't harm Vernonia, but she'd had no qualms about divorcing Boyd once their in-name-only marriage had served its purpose. She might feel the same way about this marriage. About him.

Niko wasn't ready to risk that.

He needed to keep an emotional distance and not become

too attached. Losing Stefan had been difficult enough. Having Isabel walk away…

Niko would not put himself through that again, no matter how physically attracted he was to his wife. He had done his duty and married her. He would continue to do his duty and get her pregnant. He would do whatever it took to make their marriage successful.

But emotions had no place in this marriage right now. No place at all.

Izzy didn't want to open her eyes. She was sore and tired, but she wanted to spend the rest of the day in bed with her husband.

Her husband.

Heat rose as Izzy remembered how she'd responded to Niko's kiss, his touch, him. Ready for more, she reached toward Niko, but her hand found only empty space. She opened her eyes. He wasn't there. "Niko?"

No answer.

She hadn't expected to wake up alone this morning. She wrapped herself in the sheet and checked the bathroom and the balcony. Not there, either.

A knock sounded.

Why would Niko knock to enter his own room? Izzy exchanged the sheet for her robe and opened the door. Mare stood with a tea cart containing breakfast. "Good morning, ma'am. The chef has prepared breakfast for you."

A breakfast for one based on the tray and silverware, Izzy noted. That added to her unease. "Have you seen Prince Niko?"

"Yes, ma'am." Mare wheeled the cart into the room. "He's in his office."

Working, Izzy realized with relief. She shouldn't have been surprised given they were leaving on their honeymoon today. Niko must have wanted to get a few things done before they left. How responsible of him. Another trait she liked about her husband.

Izzy enjoyed her meal on the balcony. The scent of the roses from the garden smelled fresher. The sun in the sky shone brighter. The smile on her face felt wider.

And her heart…

She closed her eyes and looked up so the sun's rays kissed her face. The heat against her skin reminded Izzy of Niko. He cared about Vernonia with a fierce loyalty and love. She hoped he would come to care the same way about her. And she intended to do whatever she could to make that happen.

Two hours later, Izzy walked next to Niko toward the helipad. She cast a sideways glance at him. This was the first time she'd seen him all morning. He looked stylishly casual in his polo shirt, khakis and leather loafers. The man always looked good whether in formal attire or his birthday suit. She smiled at the image that brought to mind. "Where are we spending our honeymoon?"

"You'll see soon enough."

"I hope I packed the right clothes."

His brows furrowed. "Mare should have packed for you."

Izzy shrugged. "I like doing it myself."

"You must embrace your role as a princess of Vernonia, Isabel."

Niko didn't sound upset, but he wasn't smiling. Maybe she could fix that. "I'd rather embrace Vernonia's crown prince."

He didn't smile, but his eyes no longer looked so serious. "You must embrace both."

The helicopter traveled north. A majestic mountain range with snowcapped peaks rose sharply into the clear blue sky. The terrain, rugged and etched, reminded her of Niko. A feeling of warmth welled inside her. Her husband shared so many similarities with this land he loved. "It's beautiful."

"Yes." Staring out the window, he seemed preoccupied. Eager to make a connection like the one she'd felt last night while in his arms, Izzy placed her hand on top of his.

He turned toward her though the smile on his face didn't reach his eyes.

She smiled back, sure she was mistaken.

But he didn't lace his fingers with hers and hold her hand.

That was…weird. After last night, she expected them to be closer, but he seemed almost ambivalent.

"Is something wrong?" she asked.

"No."

"Too much work you didn't get to?"

"No."

"Tired?"

"I am fine," he said stiffly.

"You don't seem fine." His aloofness annoyed her and set off alarms in her head. "You're acting different."

His jaw thrust forward. "I am the same as I always am."

No, he wasn't. He'd been nicer, friendlier the day they met than he was right now. She pulled her hand away. He didn't even seem to notice. Hurt burrowed in deep.

Was the honeymoon already over before it began?

Apprehensive, Izzy stared out the window and told herself to give him more time. She concentrated on the scenery. Villages dotted the landscape both in the mountains and foothills and valley floor as beautiful as a painting.

She glimpsed a castle in the distance. Smaller than the one the royal family lived in, but just as fairy tale worthy with a tower and spires jutting into the sky.

As the helicopter traveled toward the castle, the structure came into clearer view. Her breath caught in her throat. A wall made of stones surrounded the grounds. Paths crisscrossed a carpet of lush green grass. Tall trees surrounded a crystal blue lake.

Izzy pressed her forehead against the window for a better look. "I love that castle."

"It's yours," Niko said.

She looked his way. "Mine?"

"That is where you lived with your parents," he clarified. "It's your family home."

Her home? Izzy stared out the window in disbelief. "This is where we're going?"

"Yes," he said. "Not quite as warm as the beach."

"It's a million times better than the beach." Maybe she was

overanalyzing Niko's words and actions. He'd obviously put some thought into where to spend their honeymoon. "It's perfect. Thanks."

The castle turned out to be even more spectacular in person with more bedrooms than she could count, an obliging staff—many of whom were related to Uncle Frank—and a large six bay garage that had the potential to be a mechanic's dream hangout.

As the days passed, Izzy and Niko explored the property, toured various villages and visited with residents. She was enjoying herself, but she continued to sense a difference in Niko. Oh, he was polite, even solicitous, but he acted more like her friend than her husband no matter how hard she tried to initiate a deeper emotional connection.

Maybe that was how marriage was supposed to be, except...

When they were in bed, Niko couldn't seem to get enough of her. He gave her a taste of the intimacy she desired; a glimpse of how wonderful all parts of their marriage could be not just the physical side. They spent their nights and mornings learning about each other and sharing themselves. It whetted her desire for more. But once they left the bedroom, the closeness vanished as if an invisible wall had been erected between them.

"You like it here," Niko said three days later as they strolled through the grounds.

"I do," she admitted. "I love it here. The castle. The people. The villages."

You.

Izzy wanted to lose herself and her heart in Niko, but was too afraid to tell him how she felt. He'd told her he wouldn't lie to her. She wasn't prepared for that kind of honesty. Not on their honeymoon. But she could be honest about other things.

"This place—" she inhaled the fresh mountain air, trying to quell her uneasiness "—it feels like..."

"Tell me."

"Home."

"That's because Sachestia is your home," Niko said. "You can return whenever you wish."

You, not we. The one word changed everything she had convinced herself could happen. Maybe not today or tomorrow, but someday. Disappointment squeezed her heart.

The hope of love blossoming in her marriage was withering. The promise of "until death do us part" was turning into nothing more than a dull ache. Izzy might want more, but she resigned herself to not needing more than the physical intimacy Niko offered. She had a feeling that nothing would make him love her. Not even time.

The next day Niko rowed Isabel across the lake in a small boat. The days they spent together seemed to drag compared to the nights that were over much too quickly. He remembered the swing of her hips and the look in her eyes this morning. All her enthusiasm and energy seemed to have disappeared out here in the light of day. "You look…tired."

"I'm…not."

Niko waited for her to say more. She didn't.

That was his fault. His trying to distance himself from her was finally working. At first she wouldn't let him push her away, but lately she no longer seemed to care if they talked or remained silent. Except when they were having sex. Then everything between them worked perfectly. If not for the security detail watching from shore, he would take her now. "You're not very talkative today."

Isabel shrugged. "We only have a couple of days left here."

A bird flew overhead. Somewhere nearby a frog croaked.

The smell of freshly mowed grass from the lush lawns bordering the lake hung in the air, but Niko would rather inhale her vanilla and jasmine scent. "It's too bad we can't stay longer."

She perked up. "Really?"

"Yes." He wasn't sure about marriage yet, but he liked being on a honeymoon and spending time with her. "I haven't relaxed this much since…I can't remember when."

Her shoulders sagged again. "Me, either."

He didn't like seeing her this way. "You don't look relaxed."

"I'm worried about what things will be like after we leave."

Niko could kiss away her worry, but he wanted to be honest with her. "Things will be different when we return home."

She trailed the tips of fingers in the water. "No more great sex?"

"I promise the great sex will continue no matter where we are." He shook the rowboat. "This seems sturdy enough."

Isabel gave him a resigned smile, but he saw no invitation in her eyes.

"Once we are back, we won't spend the same amount of time together as we have here." An unexpected look of relief crossed her features. A look Niko didn't understand nor like. "You'll be expected to assume your role as a princess of Vernonia."

"Right away?"

"How does tomorrow sound?" Perhaps if Isabel had something more to do she would be happier. "Regional officials have requested our presence at a village celebration. This will be a perfect introduction to the duties you'll have when we return home."

She shook her head. "We're on...vacation."

"Yes, but they only want us to participate in the parade. It shouldn't take long."

"I'm not sure I'm ready for that."

"All you have to do is smile and wave. The parade will be an excellent way for people who remember your parents to see you as their princess."

She wrung her hands. "What if I fall on my face?"

"You'll be sitting in a carriage."

Isabel stuck out her tongue at him.

He grinned, relieved her playfulness had returned. "If you fall, I'll catch you."

She stared at him with an unreadable expression in her beautiful eyes. He wished they would twinkle the way they had earlier in the week. "I guess it would be okay."

He'd hoped for more enthusiasm, but at least she was taking her place as a Vernonian princess seriously. That pleased him. "Thank you, Isabel."

Her gaze grew serious. "Is this what my life will be like when we return? Parades and whatnot?"

"You will be expected to take a public role making appearances, going on outings, attending openings. You'll get used to the routine after a few times."

Her gaze cut away. "Sounds like a lot of fluff. Princess waving and cutting ribbons."

She made the tasks sound so trivial. "There is some fluff involved, but participating in events is expected by the people and an important part of our duties."

"Duty or not, I'm not a fluff person," she said. "I prefer to do a task. Help people. Accomplish something. That's one reason I like being a mechanic."

"What's another reason?"

"Cars are awesome." She splashed him. "Which you would know if you ever drove one instead of being chauffeured around all the time."

Niko splashed her back. He'd missed this side of their relationship. He might not want things too serious between them, but that didn't have to take away all their fun. "You will be able to accomplish many things and help people with your solo agenda."

Her arms dropped to her sides. "My what?"

"Good Works," he clarified. "The social issues, charities and causes you want to focus your energies on apart from the ones we work on together."

"Are these Good Works another one of my duties?" she asked.

He nodded. "The entire country will follow what you choose to do."

She stared off into the horizon. The twinkle returned to her eyes and loosened the knot in his stomach. "I could bring a Formula 1 race to Vernonia."

Niko dug the oars into the water to take a deeper stroke. He needed to steer her away from that idea. "Grand Prix is an interesting thought, but I'm sure you will come up with something else."

"Think about it." Two little lines formed above her nose. "A race sponsored by a long lost American princess would give Vernonia lots of good press and tourist dollars."

"Most princesses work on things like education or health issues. That's why they call them Good Works."

She slid him a furtive glance. "I'm not like other princesses."

"I know, but you're working on that, right?" he half teased.

She didn't look amused. "Cars and racing are my things. Why can't I combine those with Good Works?"

"Having your own interests is fine, but you are still Her Royal Highness Crown Princess Isabel of Vernonia," Niko explained. "You will become a role model."

Isabel frowned. "So you don't think I can be a role model now."

"You'll be a stronger role model if you take your contemporary outlook and make it more appealing to the masses."

Isabel crossed her arms over her chest. "So I'm not appealing, either."

"That is not what I meant."

"What do you mean?" Her voice rose and not in a good way. "You talk about wanting to modernize Vernonia yet you cling to all these outdated stereotypes. You should show Vernonians that things are changing."

"Show, yes, but we cannot shock people into progress."

"My working as a mechanic is not shocking. Neither is bringing an F1 race to Vernonia. It's a pretty darn good idea actually. You shouldn't dismiss it without at least considering it."

"Change takes time." Niko knew Izzy had a stubborn side. He didn't want her to dig in her heels about this. "Before you become too attached to this race idea, consider what Julianna might do if she were in your shoes."

Isabel winced. "You want me to be like Jules?"

"She would be an excellent role model for you to emulate when it comes to the choice of Good Works."

Anger flared in Isabel's eyes. "I don't know what Jules might choose to do, but I know something she wouldn't do."

"What?" he asked.

Isabel grabbed one of the oars and threw it into the water on the starboard side of the rowboat.

Forget stubborn. Now she was being ungracious. Niko reached for it. "You're not being nice."

Isabel stood. "I'm only getting started."

He didn't know what she had in mind, but her voice had an edge to it he hadn't heard before. "Sit down before you fall overboard."

She leaned over toward one side. The boat tipped.

"Isa—"

Niko splashed into the cold water. Isabel, too.

He tried to reach her so he could help her back into the rowboat, but she dodged his arm. "Come here," he shouted.

She lay on her back and kicked, putting more distance between them. "Jules is my friend, but I don't want to be like her. I want to be me."

With that, Isabel swam toward shore. Each long, graceful stroke took her farther and farther away from him. The security detail on shore scrambled into the water.

Niko gathered the oars, climbed back into the rowboat and watched her with a sinking feeling in his gut.

The honeymoon wasn't scheduled to end for two more days, but it was definitely over now. Niko rowed back to shore. He had no idea what this meant long-term. He wasn't sure he wanted to know.

CHAPTER ELEVEN

THE next day, an overcast sky hid the afternoon sun. Emil, the castle butler and Uncle Frank's cousin, predicted rain would fall on the parade. The weather wasn't ideal for the village's celebration, but it matched Izzy's mood perfectly.

She had barely spoken ten words to Niko since the incident on the lake. He'd slept in another room last night. He'd skipped breakfast this morning. She hadn't seen him until an hour ago when they left the castle for the village.

An icy silence filled the limousine during the drive. Izzy didn't know what to say to Niko. If she had ever had a disagreement with a guy she dated, she just never went out with him again. Fighting seemed like such a waste of time and energy. But that meant she'd never learned how to deal with conflict.

"Ready?" Niko asked as they took their seats in a horse drawn carriage decorated with fresh, colorful wildflowers.

The space on the bench seat between her and Niko felt as wide as the infield at the Indy 500. She forced a smile for the villagers' benefit. "No, but I think it's too late for them to cancel the parade. Unless Emil is right about a rainstorm."

"The people would be disappointed," Niko said flatly.

Villagers lined the narrow street, waving every imaginable size of Vernonian flags. "It reminds me of the Fourth of July parades back home except there isn't any red, white and blue."

"Each of the colors in the Vernonian flag has meaning. The light blue represents the sky, that our country may be as tranquil as the heavens above. The white stands for purity of heart and action. The yellow crest is the color of the sun, as it faithfully raises each day we pledge our loyalty to remain faithful to one another."

"That's beautiful," she said. "I don't know whether the story behind the colors of the U.S. flag is fact or fiction."

"If this was the Fourth of July, you would be eating hot dogs and hamburgers."

"Yeah, but the grilled spiced meat with onions cooking in that booth over there smell pretty good." She motioned to her designer skirt, cropped jacket, hat, gloves and high heels. "Though I would never be dressed like this. I'd have on jeans or shorts and a T-shirt."

"People came to see a princess today."

A Sachestian princess. The future queen. Anxiety fluttered. "I know."

She didn't want to disappoint them which was why she'd worn the clothing the maid had put out this morning. But even though she wore fancy clothing and answered to Her Royal Highness or ma'am, she was still the same Izzy inside. Nothing would change that.

Not a new wardrobe.

Not princess lessons.

Not a prince for a husband.

If only Niko understood that and could accept her as she was. Then their marriage might stand a chance. As it was…

Izzy adjusted her white gloves and focused on the people. The friendly smiles and waves from the villagers lessened her apprehension.

Ahead of their carriage, a pickup truck pulled a float carrying folk dancers dressed in traditional costumes. Music played by the marching band behind them filled the air. The boom of the bass drum matched the beat of her heart, a combination of the anxiety over the parade and her marriage.

She waved and smiled, as did Niko. But once again, his smile didn't reach his eyes. He remained silent, as did she. The villagers didn't seem to notice the strain between them. For that, Izzy was thankful.

The carriage came to a sudden stop. The driver set the brake. The two horses whinnied and pawed at the ground.

She noticed the float in front of them had stopped, too.

A local official rushed up to the carriage.

"What is happening?" Niko asked.

"The truck pulling the dancers' float has broken down, Your Royal Highness. We are summoning a mechanic."

Finally, Izzy thought, a chance to be useful. She hopped out of the carriage without any assistance from the security.

Niko followed her off. He stood next to her on the street. "What are you doing?"

She straightened her skirt. "They need a mechanic."

"You are a princess."

"Why can't I be both?" Izzy kept her voice low and a smile on her face. Jules would be so proud.

"It's inappropriate," Niko said, under his breath. "Unacceptable."

She removed her white gloves. "The parade must go on."

"Don't do this, Isabel. The people—"

"I am more like these people than you."

"No, you are not. Do not do this. There will be consequences."

"You're overreacting." Izzy thought about Princess Diana, who had been known as the People's Princess. Diana hadn't been given that title by sitting around and waiting for others to take charge. "I know what I'm doing."

He pressed his lips together.

Annoyance flared. "Would you please stop with that royal stiff upper lip thing you always do?"

His eyes darkened. "I don't know what you're talking about."

As Izzy hurried past the float with the dancers, she tucked her gloves into a pocket on her jacket.

An official fell into step with her. "How may I be of assistance, Your Royal Highness?"

"I'm going to see if I can fix the truck."

The man gasped. "We need a mechanic, ma'am."

Izzy raised her chin. "I am a mechanic."

And a damn good one, she thought.

The hood of the truck was already opened. Several people stood there contemplating the inner working of the vehicle.

"The engine didn't die," the truck driver said, scratching his balding head. "But the truck won't move."

"Excuse me," Izzy said, nudging her way through several festively clad dancers.

The group parted for her like the Red Sea. The scent of motor oil from the engine smelled better than perfume, but the truck had to be older than her. She climbed on the grill to look inside. It even had a carburetor. She checked the hoses and the fan belt. Grease dirtied her hands. One of her fingernails chipped. For the truck to just stop moving, something must have broken or come undone. And that was when she saw it. "A-ha. A broken throttle linkage to the carburetor."

Izzy sensed rather than felt Niko move right behind her.

He whispered, "Let someone else fix it."

"I know how to do it." She looked at those standing around. No one was smiling. "I need a pair of glasses. Sunglasses would work, too. Wire rimmed ones would probably be easiest. I promise to replace them."

One of the officials stepped forward. Disapproval filled his eyes, but he handed her a pair of glasses.

"Thank you." Izzy broke off one of the earpieces. She threaded the piece through the linkage and twisted the ends together. She lowered the hood and stepped out of the way. "That should do it."

The truck driver shifted into gear. The truck rolled forward. "It worked."

The crowd was so quiet. No one cheered or waved flags. The people stared with a look of shock and disappointment in their eyes. She didn't understand. The parade could continue, but the only ones smiling at her were the children.

There will be consequences.

An old man shook his head. Two men frowned. A group of women whispered and motioned to her.

Izzy hurried back to the carriage and climbed aboard. She brushed her dirty hands together, wishing for a wet wipe. Grease stained her skirt.

A crisp white handkerchief appeared at the end of Niko's extended arm. His tight jaw and narrowed lips told her he wasn't happy. He could join the club.

Izzy took it and wiped her hands. "I don't see why everyone is so upset."

The carriage lurched forward.

"People came expecting to see a princess, someone special not like themselves." Niko snatched the handkerchief from her and wiped her chin. "But instead they see a woman who doesn't care enough to keep her clothes clean for them. Your hands are dirty. Your fingernails chipped. They feel cheated and disrespected."

Heat burned her cheeks. "I wanted to win the people over by helping."

"You could have accomplished that by walking out to the crowd and visiting with them while the truck was repaired. You could have told someone what to fix instead of insisting you do it yourself."

Humiliation flowed through her veins. She glanced down at her still dirty hands and put on her gloves. "You never told me."

"You never gave me a chance, but can you honestly say you would have listened to me?"

She stiffened with shame, but she continued to wave and smile at the villagers along the parade route. The people, however, didn't return the gesture. "This is who I am," she said quietly.

"You are not a commoner, Isabel." Niko waved at a small girl holding a green balloon. "You are the special woman willing to sacrifice your future, your dreams for her country. You are Royal Highness Crown Princess Isabel of Vernonia. It's time you started acting like her."

As she blew a kiss to a little boy sitting on his father's shoulders and holding a small American flag, Niko's words sunk in.

A horrible realization washed over her. "You're never going to accept Izzy Poussard, mechanic and race car fanatic."

"It is time for you to leave the past behind and move on," he said.

"The way you want Vernonia to move on without changing your own outdated views."

"I told you change takes time." His gaze met hers. "I know what Vernonia needs."

My father believes Vernonia needs an heir. He wants one as soon as possible.

Her worst fear was turning out to be true. Niko hadn't wanted to go on a honeymoon to start the marriage off right. He'd only wanted her to get pregnant. No wonder things were so great in the bedroom, but not anywhere else.

This marriage had been a sham from the very beginning.

"You never really wanted a wife." Her insides twisted. "The only thing you want is a baby. You said you'd be honest, but you're no different than your father."

The silent ride from the village seemed to push Isabel farther away from Niko. He longed to reach out to her, but he couldn't. Not when he was so on edge. He'd never been in a situation like this. Anger, frustration, hurt and something unfamiliar he couldn't define swirled inside him. He needed to keep the emotions in check so he wouldn't lose control.

The limousine stopped in front of the castle. Niko stepped out. Isabel followed. Without a look back, she marched into the castle like a soldier on a mission.

Niko felt the same way. He followed her up to their bedroom and closed the door.

She took a deep breath. "This was all a big mistake."

Relief washed over him. She understood that she had let him down—and had let herself down. That explained her outburst. "Send a formal apology to the village. Tell them you're sorry for your lapse in judgment and inappropriate behavior during the parade today."

Her mouth gaped. "I'm not talking about the parade. I'm talking about our marriage."

All the emotion he'd been holding in exploded like a volcano. Anger surged. "You mean the marriage I was trapped into?"

"It's not like I wanted to marry you!" she lashed back. Her eyes glistened, but she didn't cry. "I want to be in an equal partnership with someone who will accept me, love me for who I am, not for who they want me to be. I want to be a wife, not a duty or obligation that has to be juggled with a bunch of other responsibilities. I don't want to be married to a man who keeps me at arm's length and only wants to have sex with me because he needs an heir."

Each of her emotionally charged words jabbed at him like pummeling fists. Niko could barely think above the uproar in his head. He didn't know if he could give her what she wanted. He resented her for wanting more already. "We just got married. We've only known each other a few weeks. This was never supposed to be a starry-eyed romance or a love match."

Her mouth twisted. "You've made it quite clear that's not what you want."

"Would you rather I lie and tell you what you want to hear?"

"I want you to be honest, Niko."

"I have been honest!" His voice sounded harsh, raw. He didn't know how to handle all this emotion. "I've tried to be honest with you since we met."

"It's my turn to be honest." Her gaze bored into him. "I'm not sure I can do this state marriage the way I thought I could. I just don't get this whole duty thing. I'm not sure I ever will."

His heart skipped a beat. "Isabel—"

She held up her hand, and he stopped talking.

"I'm never going to be the perfect princess you want for Vernonia." Her voice cracked. "I don't want to be a royal broodmare, either. I need time to think, to figure out what I want to do."

His lungs constricted. He struggled to breathe. "Do?"

"Whether I remain in Vernonia or return home to Charlotte."

Her words stunned him. Whatever difficulties had come between them, Niko knew Isabel had a large heart. She must really be hurting to consider returning to the U.S. "We agreed to figure things out together."

"The only place we're really together is in bed. Sex won't solve anything." The pain in her pretty eyes was undeniable. "We need to figure things out on our own before we can do anything together."

"No."

"It's time for you to go."

Unfamiliar panic flared. He didn't want to leave her. Lose her.

Feelings overwhelmed him, overcame his tentative control. In a swift move, he pulled her to him and crushed his lips against hers in a brutal kiss. Isabel didn't back away, but kissed him back. He didn't know the right words to express how he felt, didn't even understand how he felt, but he could show her. Niko poured all his emotions, all his feelings into the kiss until she clung to him.

Finally, regretfully, he drew back. He saw the same passion, the same confusion in her eyes that he felt. "I'll leave you now."

The weeks passed. Izzy remained at her family's castle. The only contact with Niko had been a month ago when a package of documents arrived transferring her father's estate, including ownership of the castle, to her. He hadn't emailed, texted or called her.

Maybe that was why she'd felt so tired and crummy lately. A broken heart. She hoped not.

Izzy hadn't figured out what she should do or where she should go. She couldn't stop thinking about that kiss Niko had left her with. His desperation had been so real, palpable, but if that was the case, if that was how he felt, why hadn't he contacted her?

She decided to stay in Sachestia a little longer to learn more about her father's family. She spent her days visiting the various villages in the area, meeting the people and even working the land as a harvest came around. Not exactly princess behavior, but slowly she began making some inroads with the villagers after the parade fiasco.

The older generation seemed to have fixed ideas like Niko about what royalty should do, but the teenagers and children didn't. They accepted her as she was. They wanted to know more about cars so she offered to teach them about basic car repairs. Fifteen children showed up. The village official had told her to expect five.

During the class, she felt light-headed and had to sit down. One of the students, the daughter of the village's doctor, insisted Izzy see her father right away. Before she could say a word, the children were escorting her across the street to a small medical clinic.

The doctor turned out to be in his mid-forties, very nice and quite thorough with the tests he ran. She sat in the exam room alone waiting for the results.

"I have good news, ma'am," he said on his return.

"I'm healthy?"

"Yes, but you're also pregnant."

Pregnant. With Niko's child. She sat frozen, too stunned to feel anything.

"How…?" She'd been so overwhelmed and stressed that she hadn't thought about her period. It had never been very regular before, but still… "I mean, I know how, but how far along?"

"I'd like to do an ultrasound so we can figure that out."

Izzy nodded, unable to speak. She could easily narrow down the dates to the week, the only week they'd spent together as husband and wife. That would make her seven, possibly eight weeks pregnant.

The royal broodmare had fulfilled her duty without even trying. Izzy didn't know whether to laugh or cry.

A baby.

A surge of love, strong and protective, flowed through her. She hugged her stomach. If only Niko were…

But he wasn't.

Would you rather I lie and tell you what you want to hear?

No, but still Izzy's heart splintered. The baby she carried was as much his as hers. Keeping the news from him would be cruel and unforgivable.

As soon as the ultrasound was completed, she would call him with the news. Even if he were the last person she wanted to talk to.

Niko sat behind his desk in his office. The words on the monitor blurred. He rubbed his eyes.

The long hours were starting to catch up with him. But work was the only thing that had filled the void these past weeks.

Not void, he corrected. The empty space next to him in bed. But work couldn't touch the empty space in his heart.

Niko's forehead throbbed. He massaged his temples to stave off another headache.

In the outer office where Jovan worked, a phone rang.

Niko looked up, stretching the cords of muscles in his neck. When he finished he saw his aide standing in front of his desk.

"There is a call for you, sir," Jovan said.

"You deal with it."

"It's Princess Isa—"

Niko grabbed the receiver off his desk. "Isabel."

His aide walked out of the office with a smile and closed the door.

"Hey, Niko."

Hearing the sound of her voice for the first time in seven weeks filled him with an odd mixture of relief and regret. "You received the estate transfer paperwork."

"Yes, thank you."

Uncomfortable silence filled the line.

He'd always known what to say, especially when it came to women, but Isabel left him as tongue-tied as a schoolboy with a crush on his teacher, instead of a crown prince who had dated some of the most beautiful women in the world. But only one woman haunted his dreams now.

"I—"

"I didn't call about that," she said at the same time.

"Excuse me," he said. "Tell me why you phoned."

"I—I'm pregnant. With twins."

Her news stunned him. "Twins."

"Yes," she said. "An heir and a spare."

He would have laughed except for the serious edge to her voice.

"I hope you are happy," she said, her voice devoid of any emotion.

"I'm thrilled." And he was. The pregnancy would get them back on track. "I'll be there tomorrow to bring you home."

"This doesn't change anything."

"But you're pregnant."

"Pregnant, Niko, not sick," she said. "At least not yet. The doctor warned me morning sickness could happen."

"You need to be seen by a physician at the university hospital."

"I'm satisfied and happy with the village doctor."

"But—"

"I'm staying here, but I thought you should know about the babies."

At least she was in Sachestia and hadn't returned to the United States. For that he was grateful. She sounded different, more mature. The pregnancy? he wondered. "Thank you."

"I'd rather the news remain within the family and close members of the staff until the first trimester, just in case I miscarry. You never know what might happen this early."

His chest ached. He wanted to be with her. "Is the doctor concerned?"

"No, but I'd rather not have to deal with something like that publicly."

Good thinking. "I understand."

"Thanks." She cleared her voice. Perhaps she wasn't so

unaffected by this as she sounded. "My next appointment is in a couple of weeks if you want to come."

"Yes," he said without hesitation, thankful for the invitation. "I will make sure my calendar is clear that day."

"I'll send the information to Jovan."

To Jovan. Niko's insides twisted. He hated this wall between them. "Fine."

"Okay, then."

He wasn't ready to let her go. "If you need anything…"

"Goodbye, Niko. See you at the appointment."

She hung up before he could reply.

Emotion roiling through him, Niko rose from his desk, exited his office and made the familiar walk to the king's office.

His father's assistant looked up from his computer monitor. "The king—"

"Will see me now." Niko walked past the royal guards, opened the door himself and entered his father's office.

King Dmitar hung up the phone. "Niko—"

"Isabel is pregnant with twins."

"Even better than I hoped for." A wide grin lit up Dmitar's face. "When does she arrive home?"

"She is staying in Sachestia. She must still be trying to figure things out."

"Have you figured anything out?" his father asked, as if remembering what Niko had told him when he returned alone from the honeymoon.

"I don't like fighting the way we did. I want to be with her, but she may not want what I can offer her."

"You have a duty—"

"To Vernonia."

"You also have a duty to your wife and your children." Dmitar rose and walked around to the front of his desk. "I know I've told you to control your emotions and do what is best for Vernonia, but I'm not sure that is the advice I want to give my grandchildren."

"What?" Niko stared, sure he hadn't heard his father correctly.

"A united Vernonia has been the goal of kings for centuries, but united at what cost? Stefan's life? All the other sons and daughters and mothers and fathers who died during the conflict?" Regret filled Dmitar's voice and darkened his eyes. "I wouldn't allow my own feelings to influence my decision-making. I kept telling myself what my father had told me. Emotion is a weakness. So I brushed aside my concerns over you and Stefan. Your mother's worries, too. Now every time I look at the damn map of Vernonia on the wall over there, I wonder."

"Wonder what?" Niko asked, barely able to breathe.

"If I'd let the Separatists go, would Stefan still be alive today?"

Niko had never heard his father like this before. He stepped forward, unsure what to do. "Father—"

"That's why I had no choice but to see this through to the end and make sure you and Izzy remained married. I have to know if a united Vernonia is worth all the sacrifices made. Especially your mother's broken and grief-filled heart."

"It will be, Father."

"I regret losing Stefan, but you are a good ruler, Niko. You will be a fine king."

He stood taller. "Thank you."

"But I am concerned," Dmitar admitted. "You speak of modernizing the country, yet you hold a few old-fashioned notions. Especially your ideas of what a princess should be."

Isabel had said something similar. Uncomfortable, Niko shifted his weight between his feet.

His father continued. "Izzy might not be a clone of every other princess out there, but she can still be who she is and the love of your life. The two are not mutually exclusive even if your marriage was an arranged match."

Niko considered his father's words. "The people—"

"She's more than made up for the lapse at the parade. The people have forgiven her. They love her."

"You've been spying on her."

Dmitar raised a brow. "And you haven't?"

"I may have sent a couple royal guards north to Sachestia on a brief...scouting trip."

"Thought so." Dmitar laughed. "You've always done whatever was asked of you, but it's time you were selfish. Forget everything else. Save your marriage and keep Izzy in Vernonia, not through manipulation as I attempted, but through love and loyalty freely given."

"You want me to go after her."

"That's your decision, not mine," Dmitar said. "But if you have any feelings for her, do not allow anything to keep you apart."

Niko had never allowed himself to be vulnerable with anyone before Izzy. He'd opened up with her, but she wanted him to be vulnerable beyond the bedroom, to trust her in a way he'd never trusted anyone before. He didn't know if he could do that. "What if I still don't know how I feel?"

"Figure it out. Fast." His father's gaze rested on a photograph of Stefan that hung on the wall. "Life can change in an instant, Niko. You don't want to have to live with that regret. Trust me."

CHAPTER TWELVE

Figure it out. Fast.

His father's words replayed in Niko's mind the rest of the day and evening. He wanted to figure it out. *Had* to figure it out.

Later that night, he tossed and turned, drifting in and out of sleep. Images of Isabel, twins, his father and Stefan collided into a half-awake, half-dreamlike state. The bed lurched, as if someone had shaken the entire wooden frame. Or bumped into it in the dark.

Could it be Isabel had figured things out herself and returned on her own? Hope mushroomed in his chest like a nuclear blast.

Niko bolted upright, instantly awake. He glanced to the spot on his left. Still empty.

Disappointment squeezed his heart. So far the only thing Niko had figured out was that he missed her. He missed her smile, her laughter, her kisses, her warmth. He even missed the grease under her nails. He missed every fiber of her being, especially the twin babies she now carried.

Wait. He looked around the room. If Isabel hadn't shaken the bed… Something else must have caused it.

As if on cue, a knock sounded on his door.

"Enter," Niko said.

Jovan in a dark navy robe and slippers rushed into the room, concern etched on his face. "There was an earthquake. They believe 6.8 on the Richter scale. The epicenter is in the north in Sachestia."

Niko's gut knotted with fear. "Isabel?"

"We cannot contact the castle. All communications in the area are down."

He jumped out of bed and rushed to his closet. "I must go."

"The helicopter will be here in forty minutes."

"Too long." He changed out of his pajama bottoms and into clothing. "Activate the emergency plan."

"Notifications went out as soon as confirmation of the earthquake was received."

His emergency response project was working properly, but he didn't care. All his thoughts were focused on Isabel. On her well-being. Her safety. She had to be all right. And the babies. He buttoned his long-sleeved shirt. "I am going to see my father. I will meet you at the helipad."

He ran through the hallway toward his parents' suite.

Niko's stomach churned with fear and worry. Isabel could be lying in the rubble of the castle, injured and alone. If anything happened to her...

Life can change in an instant, Niko. You don't want to have to live with that regret. Trust me.

No regrets. Niko understood that part. He only hoped he wasn't too late.

He didn't know if he could give Isabel the kind of marriage she wanted, but he would give all he could, and love her. He hoped, if she were safe and gave him the chance, what he offered would be enough for her.

"Fill the truck with food, water and blankets," Izzy instructed her staff, who bustled to and fro from the castle carrying supplies. Some were dressed. Others wore their pajamas and robes. A chill hung in the night air. The sun wouldn't rise for at least two more hours. She zipped up her jacket. "Hurry. We need to get up to the village ASAP."

"ASAP?" Emil asked.

"As soon as possible." She bent over to pick up a case of water. "I want to leave in five minutes."

"No, ma'am," Emil took the case from her hands and placed

it into the back of a truck. "I will see that the supplies arrive safely. You must stay here."

He sounded so much like Uncle Frank.

"I'm pregnant, not sick." Isabel had told a handful of the staff members what was going on in confidence. She patted her tummy. "The twins are safe and warm in there. I know what I can and can't do."

Emil eyed her warily. "The doctor—"

"Said I could continue all my normal activities. Helping others in need is a normal activity."

Worry creased Emil's brow. "Prince Niko would not agree."

"Then it's good he's not here." Just hearing his name made the emotions swirl inside Izzy. Her eyes implored Emil. "I'm sure supplies and help will be coming, but we're the closest to the village. We must go."

Emil nodded, respect gleaming in his eyes. "Your father and Franko would be proud of you, ma'am. I believe Prince Niko would be, too."

She doubted the latter, but appreciated Emil's words anyway. "Thanks."

Duty was important to her husband. He seemed afraid to let himself go and lose control, or rather had been afraid until their fight after the parade. Izzy couldn't forget the kiss he'd left her with. Full of emotion, brutal and punishing, the kiss seemed to betray the way he was also so strict with himself as prince. She was beginning to wonder if he'd held back his affection from her for that reason. Heaven knew she'd held herself back. She'd never told Niko she loved him. A mix of fear, pride and stubbornness had kept her from declaring her feelings.

There's a lot at stake, Izzy. Don't let that stubborn streak of yours get in the way.

Maybe she had been too stubborn. But there wasn't time for that now. She jumped into the truck. "Let's go."

Isabel's castle was deserted. No vehicles remained. It looked as if a tornado had ripped through the pantry and linen closets.

Broken vases, glasses and sculptures. Tipped over bookcases and display cabinets. But no bodies. No blood.

Relief flowed over Niko.

Isabel must have evacuated and taken the staff with her, but where?

There were so many villages he couldn't begin to guess where she might be. He prayed she would remain safe wherever she was.

Hours later, Niko stepped through the rubble of one mountain village with a two-year-old child in his arms. The boy had cuts and bruises, but thankfully no broken bones.

The boy cried. "Mama."

Niko didn't know what to say to the distraught child, who had been sleeping under his bed when the earthquake hit. A neighbor had heard the boy's screams and pulled him from the rubble. They were still searching for the rest of his family. "They are looking for your mama."

The big, fat tears stopped rolling down the child's face. He stared up at Niko. "Papa?"

"They are looking for him, too."

Gratitude filled the child's eyes. He rested his head against Niko's chest.

Niko swallowed around the lump of emotion in his throat.

A nurse appeared in sweat-stained surgical scrubs. "I'll take him, sir."

Reluctantly he handed the injured boy to the nurse. "His family is missing. Please…"

Don't lose him was what Niko wanted to say given the number of people needing help and the chaos around here.

She nodded in understanding. "We will take good care of him, sir."

With that the nurse hurried into a hospital tent that had just been erected next to the medical clinic.

Help continued to arrive. The sound of helicopters and heavy machinery filled the air.

His father was in another village helping, but Niko hoped the king saw what he saw. A united Vernonia.

Whether Separatist or Loyalist during the conflict, people worked side by side in this mountain village, searching for survivors in the rubble and helping those that had been injured. Differences in point of view no longer mattered; they were all fellow Vernonians. Niko couldn't be more proud of the people.

If only he knew where Isabel was... That she was safe...

He noticed a familiar looking man up ahead. "Emil!"

The man turned and bowed. He had a can of oil in his hand. "Sir."

"Where is Isabel?"

Emil glanced around, looking uncomfortable. "She is safe, sir."

Safe wasn't good enough. Niko wanted his wife to be with him. He felt like a better man when he was with her. The past no longer mattered. The future seemed brighter. "Take me to her. Now."

The butler led Niko back toward the medical tent. "Princess Izzy is attempting to fix the medical clinic's generator, sir. I tried to stop—"

Niko raised his hand. "I've learned nothing can stop my wife once she sets her mind upon something."

She wanted him to trust her, to let her figure out how to be a princess herself, but he hadn't known how to do that. He was ready to try now.

Emil grinned. "A true Vernonian."

"Yes, she is." And the love of my life.

Years of dirt and grime coated the clinic's generator Izzy had found in the destroyed storage area in the back of the clinic. Villagers had carried it into an open area, eager for her to fix it with the tools they'd cobbled together. Izzy doubted if the generator had run in years or if it would have run under the best of circumstances. Her determination faltered, a combination of futility and frustration. Not to mention fatigue.

No. Izzy pursed her lips. The people were counting on her. She had to do this.

Kneeling, she checked a fuel line. "Come on. Show Izzy what's not right."

"Isabel."

The sound of Niko's voice washed over her like a ray of sunshine after a morning thunderstorm. She wasn't surprised to see him here. He was the crown prince. He should be here. But the vise grip on her heart wouldn't allow Izzy to even peek in his direction. She kept focused on the motor.

"You shouldn't be here," he said firmly.

Still telling her what to do. Well, she always knew Niko wasn't Prince Charming. Izzy blew out a puff of air.

"Don't worry, your heir and spare are safe." Her voice came out harsher than she intended. "I would never do anything to risk the babies."

Izzy knew he cared about the babies. She wished he cared about her. The hurt stabbing her heart was beyond tears.

The sounds of banging, shovels and axes surrounded them.

Izzy tightened a loose coil. On the next try, the generator started. Thank goodness. She stood and wiped her hands on the coveralls that Boyd had sent her with an embroidered name tag that said Princess Izzy in cursive writing. A way of saying thanks. Boyd really liked his new truck.

"I know you would never intentionally put our children at risk," Niko said.

Izzy could see his feet walking toward her, and she hated that her pulse quickened.

Niko stopped. "But I cannot stand the thought of anything happening to you."

"Me?" Hope flared, but she tapped it down. She wouldn't be swayed by charm-laced words or his pretty face or his wide shoulders or blue-green… "You only married me because you had to."

"I could say the same thing about you."

At least he admitted it. She tucked the thought away and marched past him. "Come on."

He followed her as she negotiated her way around the rubble.

She picked up two shovels and handed him one. "Know how to use one of these, Highness?"

"I do."

Izzy forced herself not to look at him. With so much work to be done, she needed to remain detached. She gestured with her own shovel. "Clear the rubble from the clinic's door."

"I want to talk to you."

She shut out any awareness of him. She couldn't afford the distraction. "Not now."

"What are you doing here?" He took her elbow with one hand.

"I'm doing what we're supposed to be doing." She shrugged away from him. "Helping our people."

With that she walked away, forcing herself not to look back.

Hours passed. Izzy worked, clearing, comforting and repairing. She even managed to get another generator started.

Taking a break, she rubbed her lower back. All the bending and kneeling had taken its toll.

The sun was starting to set. It looked as if a bomb had exploded in the village square. Only a few buildings had survived intact. Most had walls missing. Some had collapsed to the ground in a heap of rubble. But help kept arriving from every direction. More survivors continued to be rescued.

Niko handed her a bottle of water. "Drink."

She thought of the children in the hospital tent. "Someone else might need it."

"You need it." He shoved the bottle into her hands. "More supplies are on the way. Aliestle, San Montico and the U.S. are sending assistance. Vernonia is not on our own. We have help, and we will recover."

"The people will need to hear you say that." She sipped from the bottle. The refreshing water slid down her dry throat. "Okay, I did need that."

"You've worked hard, Highness."

"So have you."

Izzy glanced Niko's way. His pants and jacket were ripped

and dusty. Drops of red—blood?—were spattered on his sleeve. Stubble covered his dirty face. His hair was tangled.

He'd never looked more like a prince than he did now.

She swallowed a sigh and drank more water.

When she finished, Niko took her grease-covered, dirty hands in his. Her heart hammered. "You look so much like the mechanic who walked out of that garage in Charlotte and stole my heart."

Her breath caught in her throat. "What?"

His eyes shone with affection. "You are the most perfect princess I could hope to find."

"Yeah, right. I look nothing like a princess."

He gave her a lopsided grin. "Exactly."

She stared at him confused. "Huh?"

"Isabel, Izzy, Princess, Your Highness, my wife. Your name doesn't matter." Niko pointed to her heart. "What matters is here. You have the heart of a princess."

Izzy was both excited and aggravated. "So why didn't you tell me this sooner?"

"I didn't know. Maybe I wasn't ready to admit it until today," he said. "I wanted to be honest with you, but I wasn't honest with myself. I thought I knew what I was doing with my life. I had everything mapped out, and then this strange, kind, determined woman was thrust into my way and turned everything upside down."

"Strange?"

"Strange and beautiful." His smile sent tingles shooting through her. "You changed everything and left me uncertain how to act. Until now. I realize what a tremendous gift you are."

"When Uncle Frank died I holed myself up and stuck with what was comfortable." She stared up at Niko. "You thrust me into this whole new world and I've been trying to forge a path."

Niko squeezed her hand. "You won't have to forge it alone."

Izzy looked around at the devastation, but amid the rubble

she saw signs of life, of love. "I know what Vernonia means to you. The land. These people. I'm here now because I understand this duty you are so attached to."

His gaze met hers. "A duty you are attached to also."

She nodded.

"Our duty isn't only to Vernonia. It's to each other and our children." Niko's words made her heart sing. "I want you with me, Isabel. Always. I offer all that I have and all that I am. I hope that is enough."

The choice was hers. She could take what he was offering or leave it.

Izzy stared at the man in front of her. Her heart overflowed with love. "I miss you, Niko. I let my fears and pride get in the way of us being together, but no longer. I love you. I've loved you since our wedding day. I'm not sure what my role is supposed to be, but I'm ready to embrace it. With your help, maybe I won't fall flat on my butt."

"You won't. I won't let you fall."

Niko gathered her into his arms. She went willingly, eager for his touch and his warmth. He lowered his mouth to hers, reclaiming her with a slow, hot kiss.

Her heart danced, dipping and twirling as if on a ballroom floor and not a disaster zone.

"You are the only woman I want," he said, his voice so full of love she could barely breathe. "The only one I need. I love you. I want to marry you."

Izzy sunk into his embrace. "We've already married. Twice."

"This time I want to marry you out of love, not duty or obligation. Nothing fancy. Just us." He placed his hand over her stomach with an almost reverent touch. "And these two."

"Yes! I'd like that very much." Laughter spilled from her lips. "Maybe the third time we'll get it right."

"If not, we'll try again until we do." He looked her straight in the eye. "Just so you know, I'm never letting you go, High-ness."

"You can't even if you want to, Highness." She grinned. "In case you forgot, your bridal box, the key and you are mine."

EPILOGUE

Izzy cradled His Royal Highness Aleksander, the future heir
to the Vernonian throne, in her arms. Contentment and peace
flowed through her. The baby slept with a serene expression
on his beautiful face, a face that reminded Izzy of her beloved
husband. She kissed her son's tiny forehead, inhaling the baby
scent she never imagined could smell so good.

Niko carefully adjusted a little blue cap on His Royal Highness
Franko's head.

Her heart overflowed at the sight of her loving husband and
two healthy sons. Izzy exhaled on a sigh. Life couldn't get much
better.

This was only the beginning, but she understood what happily
ever after meant. She was living the fairy tale and felt blessed
by all she'd been given from Vernonia, her people and Niko.

"Franko is asleep," Niko said quietly, as he stared lovingly
at the child in his arms.

She glanced down. "So is Alek."

Their eyes met in unspoken understanding. Between all the
nursing and diapering, getting both babies to sleep at the same
time was quite a coup.

Niko's gaze clouded with concern. "The noise—"

"The pediatrician assured me that we're high enough from
the crowd that the decibel level won't be a problem."

"I was more worried about them waking them up."

"They eventually will need to get used to noise and the attention," she said.

"The boys are lucky to have such a knowledgeable princess as their mother." Niko's smile made her heart leap. "And I am the most fortunate man in the world to be able to call you my wife."

She winked. "Just so you know, the feeling's mutual, Highness."

Desire gleamed in his eyes. "If only we didn't have to—"

"But we do. Duty calls." She walked toward the arched balcony doors of the Parliament building. "It's time to introduce Vernonia to their new princes."

Niko smiled mischievously. "You know what I'd rather do."

He eyed her like a man lost in the desert would look at a glass of water, leaving no doubt in Izzy's mind what he wanted to do. Even with the extra weight from the babies and breasts that leaked milk at the most inopportune times, Niko desired her. But her doctor said they needed to wait two more weeks. "It won't be much longer."

Niko's gaze went to each of their sons then rested on her. "Definitely worth the wait."

"Good answer."

"I'm learning."

"Yes, you are. You can swaddle and diaper like a pro now."

"As can my father."

Dee and Bea both wanted to take active roles in the twins' daily lives. The castle had never been so busy. Izzy couldn't imagine what it would be like when the boys started walking.

"What do you think of having some princesses or some more princes in the future?" Niko asked.

She pursed her lips. "I suppose you can never have too many spares."

Niko kissed her, as she had wanted him to do. A quick brush of the lips, but it would do. For now. His blue-green eyes gazed deeply into hers. No way would she ever doubt his love for her. Not for a second.

Izzy smiled up at him. "And I know you can never have too much family."

TO DANCE WITH A PRINCE

BY
CARA COLTER

First published in Great Britain 2011
Harlequin Mills & Boon Limited,
Eton House, 18-24 Paradise Road, Richmond, Surrey TW9 1SR

© Cara Colter 2011

ISBN: 978 0 263 88866 9

23-0311

Harlequin Mills & Boon policy is to use papers that are natural, renewable and recyclable products and made from wood grown in sustainable forests. The logging and manufacturing processes conform to the legal environmental regulations of the country of origin.

Printed and bound in Spain
by Litografia Rosés S.A., Barcelona

Dear Reader,

It is such an incredible time of year here in British Columbia. The scent of lilacs fills the air, the flower buds are full and round, and the horses are kicking up their heels in lush green pasture. Spring is such a gorgeous time of renewal and hope, and yet…weeding needs to be done. The lawnmower breaks. A family member is sick. An unexpected bill comes in. A grandchild is going through a heart-wrenching challenge.

That is what I love about a good book. It provides that moment to pause, to plump up the pillows on the bed, crawl in, and be whisked away to a wonderful fantasy world.

So I hope you'll regard the book in your hands as an invitation. Slip away. Come play. Take a mini-vacation with me to the Isle of Chatam, meet the man who will be king, and the ordinary woman who can see through his armor to his heart.

And I promise when you come back from this storybook holiday you'll have felt the triumph of love, and you'll be so much more ready to tackle whatever challenges your life holds today. I'm honored, as always, to be part of your journey.

With love,

Cara

Cara Colter lives on an acreage in British Columbia with her partner, Rob, and eleven horses. She has three grown children and a grandson. She is a recent recipient of the *Romantic Times* Career Achievement Award in the 'Love and Laughter' category. Cara loves to hear from readers, and you can contact her or learn more about her through her website: www.cara-colter.com

To Rose and Bill Pastorek
with heartfelt thanks for creating such an incredible
garden, a "mini-vacation" for everyone
who experiences it.

CHAPTER ONE

THE HOWL OF PURE PAIN sent icicles down Prince Kiernan of Chatam's spine. He shot through the door of the palace infirmary, and came to a halt when he saw his cousin, Prince Adrian, lying on a cot, holding his knee and squirming in obvious agony.

"I told you that horse was too much for you!" Kiernan growled.

"Nice to see you, too," Adrian gasped. "Naturally, the moment you told me the horse was too much for me, my fate was sealed."

Kiernan shook his head, knowing it was all too true. His cousin, seven years his junior, was twenty-one, reckless, but usually easily able to deflect the consequences of his recklessness with his abundance of charm.

A fact Adrian proved by smiling bravely at a young nurse. Satisfied that the girl was close to swooning, he turned his attention back to Kiernan.

"Look, if you could spare me the lecture," Adrian said, "I am in desperate need of a favor. I'm supposed to be somewhere."

First of all, his cousin was never desperate. Secondly, Adrian rarely worried about where he was supposed to be.

"DH—that's short for Dragon-heart—is going to kill

me if I'm not there. Honestly, Kiernan, I've met the most fearsome woman who ever walked."

And thirdly, as far as Kiernan knew his cousin had never met a woman, fearsome or not, he could not slay with his devil-may-care grin.

"Do you think you could stand in for me?" Adrian pleaded. "Just this once?" The nurse probed his alarmingly swollen knee, and Adrian howled again.

What Kiernan was having trouble fathoming was how Adrian, who would be the first to admit he was entirely self-focused, was managing to think about *anything* at this particular moment besides his injury.

"Just cancel," Kiernan suggested.

"She'll think I did it on purpose," Adrian said through clenched teeth.

"Nobody would think you had an accident on purpose to inconvenience them."

"*She* would. DH, aka Meredith Whitmore. She snorts fire." An almost dreamy look pierced Adrian's pain. "Though her breath is actually more like mint."

Kiernan was beginning to wonder what his cousin had been given for pain.

"The fact is," Adrian said sadly, " DH eats adorable little princes like me for her lunch. Barbecued. She must have the mint after."

"What on earth are you talking about?"

"You remember Sergeant Major Henderson?"

"Hard to forget," Kiernan said dryly of the man in charge of taking youthful princes and turning them into disciplined, rock-hard warriors, capable of taking commands as well as giving them.

"Meredith Whitmore is him. The Sergeant Major. Times ten," Adrian said, and then whimpered when his knee was probed again.

"You're exaggerating. You must be."

"Would you just stand in for me? Please?"

"What would make me agree to stand in for you with a woman who likes her princes barbecued and who makes Sergeant Major Henderson look like a Girl Scout leader? I don't even know what I'm standing in *for*."

"It was a mistake," Adrian admitted sadly. "I thought it was going to be a lark. It sounded like so much more fun than some of the other official *lesser prince* options for Chatam Blossom Week."

Blossom Week was the Isle of Chatam's annual celebration of spring. Dating back to medieval times, it was a week-long festival that started with a fund-raising gala and ended with a royal ball. Opening night was a little over a week away.

Adrian continued, "I could have given out awards to the preschool percussion band, given the Blossom Week rah-rah speech *or* done a little dance. Which would you have picked?"

"Probably the speech," Kiernan said. "Have you given him something?"

"Not yet," the nurse said pleasantly, "but I'm about to."

"Lucky you," Adrian said, batting his eyes at her, "because I have the cutest little royal backside—ouch! Was that unnecessarily rough?"

"Don't be a baby, Your Highness."

Adrian watched her walk away. "Anyway, I said I'd learn a dance. I was going to perform with an up-and-coming troupe at the fund-raising evening. It's a talent show this year. My suggestion to call the fund-raiser *Raise a Little Hell* was vetoed. Naturally. It's going to be called *An Evening to Remember*, which I think is *totally* forgettable."

"I'm not taking your place for a dance number! We both know I can't dance. Prince of Heartaches causes Foot Aches, Too." It was a direct quote from a newspaper headline, with a very unflattering picture of Kiernan crushing some poor girl's foot at her debutante ball.

"Ah, the press is hard on you, Kiernan. They never nickname me. But in the past ten years you've been the Playboy Prince—"

That had been when Kiernan was eighteen, fresh out of an all-boys private school, one summer of freedom before his military training. He had been, unfortunately, like a kid let out in a candy shop!

"Then, the Prince of Heartaches."

At the age of twenty-three, Prince Kiernan had become engaged to one of his oldest and dearest friends, Francine Lacourte. Not even Adrian knew the full truth behind their split and her total disappearance from public life. But, given a history that the press was eager not to let him shake, it was assumed Prince Kiernan was to blame.

"Now," Adrian continued, "since Tiff, you've graduated to Prince Heartbreaker. Tut-tut. It would all lead one to believe you are so much more exciting than you are."

Kiernan scowled warningly at his cousin.

"Don't give me that look," Adrian said, whatever the nurse had given him relaxing the grimace on his face to a decidedly goofy grin. "Your tiff with Tiff."

While the press *loved* the high-spirited high jinks of Adrian, Kiernan was seen as too stern, and too serious. Particularly since two broken engagements to two very popular women he was seen as coldly remote.

He knew the title Prince Heartbreaker was probably going to be his mantle to bear forever, even if he lived out the rest of his days as a monk, which, after what he'd been through, didn't seem entirely unappealing!

After all, the future of his island nation rested solidly and solely on Kiernan's shoulders, as he was the immediate successor to his mother, Queen Aleda's, throne. That kind of responsibility was enough for one man to bear without throwing in the caprice of romance.

Adrian was fourth in line, a position he found deliciously relaxing.

"You should have thrown that Tiffany Wells under a bus," Adrian said with a sigh. "She deserved it. Imagine tricking you into thinking she was pregnant. And then do you let the world know the true reason for the broken engagement? Oh, no, a man of honor—"

"We're not talking about this," Kiernan said fiercely. Then, hoping to get back on one topic and off the other, "Look, Adrian, about the dancing thing, I don't see how I could help—"

"I don't ask much of you, Kiern."

That was true. The whole world came to Kiernan, asking, begging, requesting, pleading causes. Adrian never did.

"Do this, okay?" Adrian said, his words beginning to slur around the edges. "It'll be good for you. Even if you make a fool of yourself, it'll make you seem human."

"I don't seem human?" He pretended to be affronted.

His cousin ignored him. "A little soft shoe, charm the crowd, get a little good press for a change. It bugs the hell out of me that you're constantly portrayed as a coldhearted snob."

"Coldhearted? A snob?" He pretended to be wounded.

Again, he was ignored. "That's if you can survive the fire-breather. Who, by the way, doesn't like tardiness.

And you…" his unfocused eyes shifted to the clock, and he squinted thoughtfully at it "…are twenty-two minutes late. She's waiting in the Ballroom."

The smart thing to do, Kiernan knew, as he left his cousin, would be to send someone to tell the fire-breather Adrian was hurt.

But the truth was he had yet to see a woman who had managed to intimidate Adrian. Because if Kiernan was legendary for his remoteness, his cousin was just as legendary for his charm.

The press loved Prince Adrian. He played Prince Charming to his darker cousin's Prince Heartbreaker. And, oh, how women loved Prince Adrian.

Kiernan just had to see the one who did not.

Kiernan decided to go have a look at Adrian's nemesis before giving Adrian's excuses and dismissing her. In his most warmhearted and non-snobby fashion.

Meredith glared at the clock.

"He's late," she muttered to herself. The truth? She couldn't believe it! It was the second time Prince Adrian had been tardy!

She'd been intimidated by the young prince and his status for all of about ten seconds at their first meeting at her upscale downtown Chatam dance and fitness studio.

And then she'd seen he was like a puppy—using the fact he was totally adorable to have his way! Including being late. Meredith was so beyond being charmed by a man, even one as cute as him.

So, she'd laid down the law with him. And she'd been certain he wouldn't dare be late again, especially since she had conceded to changing their meeting place to the Chatam Palace Great Ballroom as a convenience to him.

Which just showed how wrong she could be when it came to men, even while she thought she was totally immune to sexy good looks and impossible charm!

Meredith glanced around the grandeur of the room and tried not to be overly awed at finding herself here.

She breathed in the familiar scents of her childhood. Her mother, a single woman, had been a cleaning lady. Meredith recognized the aromas of freshly shined floors, furniture wax, glass cleaners, silver polish.

Her mother would have been as awed by this room as Meredith was. Her mother had dreamed such big dreams for her daughter.

Ballet will open doors to worlds we can hardly imagine, Merry.

Worlds just like this one, Meredith thought gazing around the room. Wouldn't her mother be thrilled to know she was here?

Because every door that ballet could have opened for Meredith—and her mother—had slammed shut when Meredith had found herself pregnant at sixteen.

Morning sunshine streamed in the twelve floor-to-ceiling arched windows that were so clean they looked like they contained no glass. The light glinted across the Italian marble of the floors, and sparked in the thousands of Swarovski crystals of the three huge chandeliers that dangled from the frescoed ceiling.

Meredith glanced again at the clock.

Prince Adrian was half an hour late. He wasn't coming. Meredith had had her doubts about this whole scheme, but been persuaded by the wild enthusiasm of the girls.

Crazy to let the teenage girls, the ones she mentored

and loved and taught to dance, younger versions of herself, believe in fairy-tale dreams.

She, of all people, should know better.

Still, looking around this room, something stirred in her. She was going to dance here, prince or no prince.

In fact, that would be very in keeping with the charity she had founded, that gave her reason to go on, when all of her life had crashed down around her.

Meredith taught upbeat modern dancing as part of the program No Princes, which targeted the needs of underprivileged inner city female adolescents.

"You don't need a prince to dance," Meredith said firmly. In fact, that would make a good motto for the group. Perhaps she should consider adding it to their letterhead.

She closed her eyes. In her imagination, she could hear music begin to play. She had broken with ballet years ago, not just because her scholarship had been canceled. When she finally returned to dance, the only place that could ease the hurt of a heart snapped in two, she had found she could not handle the rigidity of ballet. She needed a place where her emotion could come out.

But even so, Meredith found herself doing the famous entrée of Princess Aurora in the Petipa/Tchaikovsky ballet, *The Sleeping Beauty*.

But then, she let the music take her, and she seamlessly joined the *allegro* movements of ballet with the modern dance that had become her specialty. She melded different styles of dance together, creating something brand new, feeling herself being taken to the only place where she was not haunted by memories.

Meredith covered the floor on increasingly light feet,

twirling, twisting, leaping, part controlled, part wild, wholly uninhibited.

She became aware that dancing in this great room felt like a final gift to the mother she had managed to disappoint so terribly.

The music that played in her head stopped and she became still, but for a moment she did not open her eyes, just savored the feeling of having been with her mother for a moment, embraced by her, all that had gone sour between them made right.

And then Meredith could have sworn she heard a baby laugh.

She spun around just as the complete silence of the room was broken by a single pair of hands clapping.

"How dare you?" she said, feeling as if Prince Adrian had spied on her in a very private moment.

And then Meredith realized it was the wrong prince!

It was not Adrian, eager and clumsily enthusiastic, like a playful St. Bernard, but the man who would be king.

Prince Heartbreaker.

Prince Kiernan of Chatam had slipped inside the door, and stood with his back braced lazily against the richness of the walnut. The crinkle of amusement around the deep azure of his eyes disappeared at her reprimand.

"How dare I? Excuse me. I thought I was in my own home." He looked astonished, rather than annoyed, by her reprimand.

"I'm sorry, Your Highness," she stammered. "I was taken off guard. That dance was never intended for anyone to see."

"More's the pity," he said mildly.

Meredith saw, instantly, that the many pictures of him printed by papers and tabloids did not begin to do him justice. And she saw why he was called Prince Heartbreaker.

Such astonishing good looks should be illegal. Paired with his station in life, it seemed quite possible he could break hearts with a glance!

Prince Kiernan was more than gorgeous, he was stunning. Tall and exquisitely fit, his perfectly groomed hair was crisp and dark, his face chiseled masculine perfection, from the cut of high cheekbones to the jut of a perfectly clefted chin.

Though he was dressed casually—it looked like he had been riding, the tan-colored jodhpurs hugging the cut of the muscle of his thigh—nothing could hide the supreme confidence of his bearing.

He was a man who had been born to great wealth and privilege and it showed in every single thing about him. But an underlying strength—around the stern line of his mouth, the way he held his broad shoulders—also showed.

And Meredith Whitmore was, suddenly, not an accomplished dancer and a successful businesswoman, but the cleaning lady's daughter, who had been trained to be invisible in front of her "betters," who had stupidly thrown her life away on a dream that had ended more badly than she ever could have imagined.

She thought of the unleashed sensuousness of that dance, and felt a fire burn up her cheeks. She prayed—desperately—for the floor to open up and swallow her.

But she, of all people, should know by now that the desperation of a prayer in no way led to its answer.

"Your Royal Highness," she said, and all her grace fled her as she did a clumsy curtsy.

"You can't be Meredith Whitmore," the prince said, clearly astounded.

"I can't?"

Even his voice—cultured, deep, melodic, masculine—was unfairly attractive, as sensual as a touch.

It was no wonder she was questioning her own identity!

Meredith *begged* the confident, career-oriented woman she had become to push the embarrassed servant's daughter off center stage. She begged the vulnerability that the memory of Carly's laugh had brought to the surface to go away.

"Why can't I be Meredith Whitmore?" Despite her effort to speak with careless confidence, she thought she sounded like a rejected actress who had been refused a coveted role.

"From what Adrian said, I was expecting, um, a female version of Attila the Hun."

"Flattering."

A hint of a smile raced across the firm line of those stern lips and then was gone.

It was definitely a smile that could break hearts. Meredith reminded herself, firmly, she hadn't one to break!

"You did give me a hard time for standing inside my own door," he said thoughtfully. "Adrian said, er, that you were something of a taskmaster."

The hesitation said it all. Meredith guessed that Prince Adrian had not worded it that politely. The fact that the two princes had discussed her—in unflattering terms—made her wish for the floor to open up redouble.

"I was actually about to leave," she said with the

haughtiness of a woman who was not the least vulnerable to him, and whose time was extremely valuable—which it was! "He's very late."

"I'm afraid he's not coming. He sent me with the message."

Meredith felt a shiver of apprehension. "Is it just for today? That Prince Adrian isn't coming?"

But somehow she already knew the answer. And it was her fault. She had driven him too hard. She had overstepped herself. He didn't want to do it anymore. She had obviously been too bossy, too intense, too driven to perfection.

A female version of Attila the Hun.

"I'm sorry. He's been injured in an accident."

"Badly?" Meredith asked. The prince, puppylike in his eagerness to please, had been hurt, and all she was thinking about was that she was being inconvenienced by his tardiness?

"He's been in a riding accident. When I left him his knee was the approximate size and shape of a basketball."

Meredith marshaled herself, not wanting him to see her flinch from the blow to her plans, to her girls.

"Well, as terrible as that is," she said with all the composure she could muster, "the show must go on. I'm sure with a little resourcefulness we can rewrite the part. We aren't called No Princes for nothing."

"No Princes? Is that the name of your dance troupe, then?"

"It is actually more than a dance troupe."

"All right," he conceded. "I'm intrigued. Tell me more."

To her surprise, the prince looked authentically interested. Despite not wanting to be vulnerable to him in any way, Meredith took a deep breath, knowing she could not pass up this opportunity to tell someone so influential about her group.

"No Princes is an organization that targets girls from the tough neighborhoods of the inner city of Chatam. At fifteen and sixteen and seventeen a frightening number of these girls, still children really, are much too eager to leave school, and have babies, instead of getting their education."

Her story, *exactly*, but there was no reason to tell him that part.

"We try to give them a desire to learn, marketable skills, and a strong sense of self-reliance and self-sufficiency. We hope to influence them so they do not feel they need rescuing from their circumstances by the first boy they perceive as a prince!"

Michael Morgan had been that prince for her. He had been new to the neighborhood, drifted in from somewhere with a sexy Australian accent. She was fatherless, craving male attention, susceptible.

And thanks to him, she would never be that vulnerable again. Though the man who stood before her would certainly be a test of any woman's resolve to not believe in fairy tales.

"And where do you fit into that vision, my gypsy ballerina?"

So, the prince *had* seen something. *His* gypsy ballerina? Some terrible awareness of him tingled along her spine, but she kept her tone entirely professional when she answered him. She, of all people, knew that tingle to be a warning sign.

"I'm afraid all work and no play is a poor equation for anyone, never mind these girls. As well as looking after a lot of paperwork for No Princes, I get to do the *fun* part. I teach the girls how to dance."

"Prince Adrian didn't seem to think it was fun," he said dryly.

"I may have pushed him a little hard," she admitted.

Prince Kiernan actually laughed, and it changed everything. Did the papers deliberately capture him looking grim and humorless?

Because in that spontaneous shout of laughter Meredith had an unfortunate glimpse of the kind of man every woman hoped would ride in on his white charger to rescue her from her life.

Even a woman such as herself, soured on romance, could feel the pull of his smile. She steeled herself against that traitorous flutter in her breast and reminded herself a man did not get the name Prince Heartbreaker because he was in the market for a princess!

In fact, before he'd been called Prince Heartbreaker, hadn't he been called the Playboy Prince? And something else? Oh, yes, the Prince of Heartaches. He was a dangerous, dangerous man.

"Kudos to you if you *could* push him hard," Prince Kiernan said wryly. "How did Adrian come to be a part of all this?"

It was a relief to hide behind words! They provided the veneer of rational, civilized thought, when something rebellious in her was reacting to him in a very upsettingly primal way!

"One of our girls, Erin Fisher, wrote a dance number that really tells the whole story of what No Princes does. It's quite a remarkable piece. It takes girls from hanging out on street corners flirting with boys, going nowhere, to a place of remarkable strength and admirable ambition. The piece has a dream sequence in it that shows a girl dancing with a prince.

"Unbeknownst to any of us, Erin sent it to the palace, along with a video of the girls dancing, as a performance suggestion for *An Evening to Remember*, the fund-raiser that will open Blossom Week. She very boldly suggested Prince Adrian for the part in the dream sequence. The girls have been delirious since he accepted."

Meredith was shocked by the sudden emotion that clawed at her throat. She shouldn't have a favorite, but of all the girls, Erin was so much like her, so bright, so full of potential. And so sensitive. So easily hurt and discouraged.

"I'm sorry for their disappointment," Prince Kiernan said, making Meredith realize, uneasily, he was reading her own disappointment with way too much accuracy.

Prince Kiernan was larger than life. He was *better* than the pictures. His voice was as sexy as a piece of raw silk scraped along the nape of a neck. He was a *real* prince.

But still, she represented No Princes. She *taught* young women not to get swept away, not to believe in fairy tales. She rescued the vulnerable from throwing their lives away on fantasies, as she had, no matter how appealing the illusion.

The abundance of tabloid pictures of actress Tiffany Wells' tearstained face since her broken engagement with this man underscored Meredith's determination not to be vulnerable in any way, to any man, ever again.

Her days of vulnerability were over.

"A little disappointment does nothing but build character," she said crisply.

He regarded her thoughtfully. She thrust her chin up and folded her arms over her chest.

"Again, I'm sorry."

"It's quite all right," she said, forcing her voice to be firm. "Things happen that are out of our control."

She would have snatched those words back without speaking them if she knew that they would swing the door of memory wide open on the event in her life that had been most out of her control.

Meredith slammed the door shut again, blinking hard and swallowing.

The prince was looking at her way too closely, again, as if he could see things she would not have him see. That she would not have anyone see.

"Goodbye," Meredith managed to squeak out. "Thank you for coming personally, Your Highness. I'll let the girls know. We'll figure something out. It's not a big deal."

She was babbling, trying to outrun the quiver in her voice and failing. She kept talking.

"The girls will get over it. In fact, they're used to it. They're used to disappointment. As I said, we can rewrite the part Prince Adrian was going to play. Anybody can play a prince."

Though she might have believed that much more strongly before standing in the damnably charismatic presence of a real one!

"Goodbye," she said, more strongly, a hint for him to go. The quiver was out of her voice, but she had not slammed the door on her worst memory as completely as she had hoped. She could feel tears sparking behind her eyes.

But Prince Kiernan wasn't moving. It was probably somewhere in that stuffy royal protocol book she'd been given that she wasn't supposed to turn her back on him first, that she wasn't to dismiss *him*, but she had to. She had to escape him gazing at her so piercingly, as if her whole life story was playing in her eyes and he could see it. It would only be worse if she cried.

She turned swiftly and began pack up the music equipment she had brought in preparation for her session with Adrian.

She waited for the sound of footfalls, the whisper of the door opening and shutting.

But it didn't come.

CHAPTER TWO

MEREDITH DREW TWO OR THREE steadying breaths. Only when she was sure no tears would fall did she turn back. Prince Kiernan still stood there.

She almost yearned for a lecture about protocol, but there was no recrimination in his eyes.

"It meant a lot to them, didn't it?" he asked quietly, his voice rich with sympathy, "And especially to you."

She had to steel herself against how accurately he had read her emotion, but at least he didn't have a clue as to why she was really feeling so deeply.

It felt like her survival depended on not letting on that it was a personal pain that had touched her off emotionally. So, again, she tried to hide behind words. Meredith launched into a speech she had given a thousand times to raise funds for No Princes.

"You have to understand how marginalized these girls feel. Invisible. Lacking in value. Most of them are from single-parent families, and that parent is a mother. It's part of what makes them so vulnerable when the first boy winks at them and tells them they're beautiful.

"So when a prince, when a real live prince, one of the biggest celebrities on our island recognized what they were doing as having worth, it was incredible. I think it made them have hope that their dreams really could come true. That's a hard sell in Wentworth. Hope is a dangerous thing in that world."

Kiernan's face registered Wentworth. He *knew* the name of the worst neighborhood on his island. She had successfully diverted him from her own moment of intense vulnerability.

But before she could finish congratulating herself, Prince Kiernan took a deep breath, ran a hand through the crisp silk of his dark hair.

"Hope shouldn't be a dangerous thing," he said softly, finally looking back at her. "Not in anyone's world."

Honestly, the man could make you melt if you weren't on guard. Thankfully, Meredith's life had made her stronger than that! She had seen lives—including her own—ruined by weakness, by that single moment of giving in to temptation.

And this man was a temptation!

Well, not really. Not realistically. He was a prince, and she was a servant's daughter. Some things did not mix, even in this liberated age. Her roots were in the poorest part of his kingdom. She was not an unsullied virgin. She had known tragedy beyond her years. It had taken away her ability to dream, to believe.

The only thing she believed in was her girls at No Princes. The only thing that gave her reprieve from her pain was dancing.

No, there were no fairy tales for her.

She did not rely on anyone but herself, and certainly not a man, not even a prince. That was why she had been so immune to Prince Adrian's charms.

Merry, Merry, Merry, she could almost hear her mother's weary, bitter voice, *when in all your life has a man ever done the right thing?*

Her mother had been so right.

So Prince Kiernan shocked Meredith now. By being the one man willing to do the right thing.

"I'll do it," he said with a certain grim resolve, like a man volunteering to face the firing squad. "I'll take Prince Adrian's place."

Meredith felt her mouth open, and then snapped shut again. There was no joy in the prince's offer, only a sense of obligation.

Naturally I'll marry you, Michael had lied to her when Meredith had told him about the coming baby.

Oh, darlin', pigs will fly before that man's going to marry you. You're dreaming, girl.

Meredith had a feeling the prince would *never* run out on his obligations. Still, she had to discourage him.

Teaching Prince Adrian the steps to the dream sequence dance had been one thing. Despite his royal status, working with the young prince had been something like dealing with a slightly unruly younger brother.

This man was not like that.

There were things a whole lot more dangerous than hope.

And Prince Kiernan of Chatam, the Playboy Prince, the Prince of Heartaches, Prince Heartbreaker, was one of them.

"It's not a good idea," Meredith said. "Thank you, anyway, but no."

The prince looked shocked that anyone could turn down such a generous offer. And then downright annoyed.

"You just have no idea how much work is involved," Meredith said, a last ditch effort to somehow save herself. "Prince Adrian had committed to several hours a day. We have just over a week left until *An Evening to Remember.* I don't see how we could get you caught up. Really." He didn't seem to be hearing her, so she repeated, "Thanks, but no."

Prince Kiernan crossed the room to her. Closer, she could see his great height. The man towered over her. His scent was drugging.

But not as much as the light in those amazing blue eyes. Still cool, there was something powerful there. His gaze locked on her face and held her fast in a spell.

"Do I look like a man who is afraid of work?" he asked, softly, challengingly.

The truth? He didn't have a clue what work was. He wouldn't know it probably took a team of people hours on their hands and knees to polish these floors, to clean the windows, to make the crystals on the chandeliers sparkle like diamonds.

But she didn't say that because when she looked into his face she saw raw strength beneath the sophisticated surface. She saw resolve.

And Meredith saw exactly what he was offering. He was *saving* the dreams of all the girls. As much as she did not want to be exposed to all this raw masculine energy every single day for the next week, was this really her choice to make?

Ever since Prince Adrian had agreed to dance in *her* production, Erin had dreamed bigger. Her marks at school had become astonishing. She had mentioned, shyly, to Meredith, she might think of becoming a doctor.

Meredith couldn't throw away the astonishing gift Prince Kiernan was offering her girls because she felt threatened, vulnerable.

Still, her eyes fastened on the sensuous curve of his full lower lip.

God? Don't do this to me.

But she already knew she was not on the list of those who had their prayers answered.

The prince surprised her by smiling, though it only intensified her thought, of *don't do this to me.*

"I'm afraid," he said, "it's probably you who doesn't know how much work will be involved. I have been called the Prince of Foot Aches. And you have only a short time to turn that around? Poor girl."

His smile heightened her sense of danger, of something spinning out of her control. Meredith wanted, with a kind of desperation, to tell him this could not possibly work.

Dance with him every day? Touch him, and look at him, and somehow not be sucked into all the romantic longings a close association to such a dynamic and handsome man was bound to stir up?

But she had all her pain to keep her strong, a fortress of grief whose walls she could hide behind.

And she thought of Erin Fisher, and the girl she herself used to be. Meredith thought about hopes and dreams, and the excited delirium of the dance troupe.

"Thank you, Your Highness," she said formally. "When would you be able to begin?"

Prince Kiernan had jumped out of airplanes, participated in live-round military exercises, flown a helicopter.

He had ridden highly strung ponies on polo fields and jumped horses over the big timbers of steeplechases.

He had sailed solo in rough water, ocean kayaked and done deep-sea dives. The truth was he did not lead a life devoid of excitement and, in fact, had confronted fear often.

What came as a rather unpleasant surprise to him

was the amount of trepidation he felt about *dancing*, of all things.

He knew at least part of that trepidation was due to the fact he had made the offer to help the No Princes dance troupe on an impulse. His plan, he recalled, had been to see the Dragon-heart with his own eyes, make Prince Adrian's excuses, and then dismiss the dance instructor.

One thing Prince Kiernan of Chatam was not, was impulsive. He did not often veer from the plan. It was the one luxury he could not afford.

That eighteenth summer, his year of restless energy, heady lack of restraint, and impulsive self-indulgence had taught him that for him, spontaneity was always going to have a price.

The military had given him an outlet for all that pent-up energy and replaced impulsiveness with discipline.

Those years after his eighteenth birthday had reinforced his knowledge that his life did not really belong to him. Every decision was weighed and measured cautiously in terms, not of his well-being, but the well-being of his small island nation. There was little room for spontaneity in a world that was highly structured and carefully planned. His schedule of appointments and royal obligations sometimes stretched years in advance.

Aware he was *always* watched and judged, Kiernan had become a man who was calm and cool, absolutely controlled in every situation. His life was public, his demeanor was always circumspect. Unlike his cousin, he did not have the luxury of emotional outbursts when things did not go his way. Unlike his cousin, he could not pull pranks, be late, forget appointments.

He was rigidly *correct*, and if his training and inborn sense of propriety did not exactly inspire warm fuzziness, it did inspire confidence. People knew they could trust him and trust his leadership. Even after Francine, the whispers of what had happened to her, people seemed to give him the benefit of the doubt and trust him, still.

But then his relationship with Tiffany Wells, an exception to the amount of control he exerted over his life, seemed to have damaged that trust. His reputation had escalated from that of a man who was coolly remote to a man who was a heartless love-rat.

There would be no more losses of control.

And while it was not high on his list of priorities to be popular, he did see performing the dance as an opportunity to repair a battered image. His and Tiffany's breakup was a year ago. It was time for people to see him as capable of having a bit of fun, relaxing, being human.

Was that why he'd said yes? A public relations move? An opportunity to polish a tarnished image, as Adrian had suggested?

No.

Was it because of the girls, then? He had been moved by Miss Whitmore's description of the goals of No Princes. Kiernan had felt a very real surge of compassion for underprivileged young women who wanted someone they perceived as important to value them, to recognize what they were doing as having merit.

But had that been the reason he had said yes? The reason he had been swayed to this unlikely cause that was certainly going to require more of him than signing a cheque, or giving a speech or just showing up and shaking a few hands? Was that the reason he'd said yes to a cause that had his staff running in circles trying to rearrange his appointments around his new schedule? Again, *no*.

So, was it her, then? Was Meredith Whitmore the reason he had said *yes* to something so far out of his comfort zone?

Kiernan let his mind go to her. She had astounding hazel eyes, that hinted at fire, unconsciously pouty lips, a smattering of light freckles and a wild tangle of auburn locks, the exact kind of hair that made a man's hands itch to touch.

Add to that the lithe dancer's body dressed in a leotard that clung to long, lean legs, and a too-large T-shirt that hinted at, rather than revealed, luscious curves. There was simply no denying she was attractive, but not in the way one might expect of a dancer. She was at odds with the dance he had witnessed, because she seemed more uptight than Bohemian, more Sergeant Major than free-spirited gypsy.

Beautiful? Undoubtedly. But the truth was he was wary of beauty, rather than enchanted by it, particularly after Tiffany. The face of an angel had hidden a twisted heart, capable of deception that had rattled his world.

Meredith Whitmore did not look capable of deception, but there was something about her he didn't get. She was young, and yet her eyes were shadowed, cool, measuring.

Not exactly cold, but Kiernan could understand why Adrian had called her Dragon-heart, like something fierce burned at her core that you would get close to at your own peril.

So, he had said yes, not because it would be a good public relations move, which it would be, not wholly on the grounds of compassion, though it was that, and not because of Meredith's beauty or mystery. It was not even her very obvious emotional reaction to her disappointment and her valiant effort to hide that from him.

No, he thought frowning, the answer to his agreeing to this was somewhere in those first moments when she had been dancing, unaware of his presence. But what *exactly* it was that had been so compelling as to overcome his characteristic aversion to spontaneity eluded him.

So, the astounding fact was that Prince Kiernan, the most precise of men, could not pinpoint precisely what had made him agree to do this. And the fact that he could not decipher his own motivations was deeply disturbing to him.

Now, he paused at the doorway of the ballroom, took a deep breath, put back his shoulders, and strode in.

He hoped to find her dancing, knowing the answer was in that, but she was not to be caught off guard twice.

Meredith was fiddling with electronic equipment in one corner of the huge ballroom, her tongue caught between her teeth, her brow drawn down in a scowl. She looked up and saw him, straightened.

"Miss Whitmore," he said.

She was wearing purple tights today, rumpled leg warmers, and a hairband of an equally hideous shade of purple held auburn curls off her face. She didn't have on a speck of makeup. She did have on an oversized lime green T-shirt that said, *Don't kiss any frogs.*

He was used to people trying to impress him, at least a little bit, but she was obviously dressed only for comfort and for the work ahead. He wasn't quite sure if he was charmed or annoyed by her lack of effort to look appealing.

And he wasn't quite sure if he felt charmed or annoyed that she looked appealing anyway!

"Prince Kiernan," she said, a certain coolness in her tone, which was mirrored in the amazing green gold of those eyes, "thank you for rearranging your schedule for this."

"I did as much as I could. I may have to take the occasional official phone call."

"Understandable. Thank you for being on time."

"I'm always on time." He could see why she intimidated Adrian. No greeting, no polite *how are you today?* There was a no-nonsense tone to her voice that reminded him of a palace tutor. He could certainly hear a hint of Dragon-heart in there!

"Brilliant," she said, and then stood back, folded her arms over her chest, and inspected him. Now he could also see a hint of Sergeant Henderson as her brows lowered in disapproval! He felt like he had showed up for a military exercise in full dress uniform when the dress of the day was combat attire.

"Do those slacks have some give to them? I brought some dance pants, just in case."

Dance pants? He disliked that uncharacteristic moment of spontaneity that had made him say yes to this whole idea more by the second. He wasn't going to ask her what dance pants were, exactly. He was fairly certain he could guess.

"I'm sure these will be fine," he said stiffly, in a voice that let her know a prince did not discuss his *pants* with a maiden, no matter how fair.

She looked doubtful, but shrugged and turned to the electronics. "I have this video I want you to watch, if you don't mind, Your Highness."

As he came and stood beside her, the scent of lemons

tickled his nostrils. She flicked a switch on a bright pink laptop. The light from the chandeliers danced in her hair, making the red threads in it spark like fire.

"This has had twelve million hits," she said, accessing a video-sharing website.

He focused on a somewhat grainy video of a wedding celebration. A large room had a crowd standing around the edges of it, a space cleared in the center of it for a youthful-looking bride and groom.

"And now for the first dance," a voice announced.

The groom took one of his bride's hands, placed his other with a certain likeable awkwardness on her silk-clad waist.

"This is the bridal waltz," Meredith told him, "and it's a very traditional three-step waltz."

The young groom began to shuffle around the dance floor.

Kiernan felt relieved. The groom danced just like him. "Nothing to learn," he pronounced, "I can already do that." He looked at his watch. "Maybe I can squeeze in a ride before lunch."

"I've already lost one prince to riding," she said without looking up from the screen. "No riding until we're done the performance."

Kiernan felt a shiver of pure astonishment, and looked at Meredith Whitmore again, harder. She didn't appear to notice.

She tacked on a *"Your Highness"* as if that made bossing him around perfectly acceptable. Well, it wasn't as if Adrian hadn't warned him.

"Excuse me, but I really didn't sign up to have you run my—"

Meredith shushed him as if he was a schoolboy. "This part's important."

He was so startled that he thought he might laugh out loud. No one, but no one, talked to him like that. He slid her a look as if he was seeing her for the first time. She *was* bossy. And what's worse, she was *cute* when she was bossy.

Not that he would let her know that. He reached by her, and clicked on the pause button on the screen.

It was her turn to be startled, but he had her full attention. And he was not falling under the spell of those haunting gold-green eyes.

"I am already giving you two hours a day of practice time that I can barely afford," he told her sternly. "You will not tell me what to do with the rest of my time. Are we clear?"

Rather than looking clear, she looked mutinous.

"I've set aside a certain amount of my time for you, not given you run of my life." There. That should remind her a little gratitude would not be out of order.

But she did not look grateful, or cowed, either. In fact, Meredith Whitmore looked downright peeved.

"I've set aside a certain amount of time for you, also," she announced haughtily. "I'm not investing more of my time to have you end up out of commission, too! We're on a very limited schedule because of Prince Adrian's horse mishap."

Prince Kiernan looked at Meredith closely. Right behind the annoyance in her gorgeous eyes was something else.

"You're deathly afraid of horses," he said softly.

Meredith stared up into the sapphire eyes of the prince. The truth was she was not deathly afraid of horses.

But she was deathly afraid of a world out of her control.

The fact that he had got the *deathly afraid* part of her with such accuracy made her feel off balance, as if she was a wide open book to him.

She felt like she needed to slam that book shut, and quickly, before he read too much of it. Let him think she was afraid of horses!

It wasn't without truth, and it would be so much better than the full truth. That Meredith Whitmore was afraid of the caprice of life.

"Of course I'm afraid of horses," she said. "They are an uncommon occurrence in the streets of Wentworth. My closest encounter was at a Blossom Festival parade, where a huge beast went out of control, plunged into the crowd and knocked over spectators."

"You're from Wentworth, then?" he asked, still watching her way too closely.

He seemed more interested in that than her horse encounter. Well, good. That alone should erect the walls between them. "Yes," she said, tilting her chin proudly, "I am."

But instead of feeling as if the barrier went up higher, their stations in life now clearly defined, when he nodded slowly, she felt as if she had revealed way too much of herself! She turned from the prince swiftly, and clicked on the Play button on the screen, anxious to outrun the intensity in his eyes.

She focused, furiously, on the video. As the groom looked at his new wife, something melted in that young man's face. It was like watching a boy transform into a man, his look became so electric, so filled with tenderness.

Too aware of the prince standing beside her, Meredith scrambled to find sanctuary in the familiar.

"If you listen," she said, all business, all dance

instructor, "the music is changing, so are the steps. The dance has a more *salsa* feel to it now. Salsa originated in Cuba, though if you watch you'll see the influences are quite a unique blend of European and African."

"This really is your world, isn't it?" Kiernan commented.

"It is," she said, and she prayed to find refuge in it as she always had. It was just way too easy to feel something, especially as the dance they watched became more sensual. It felt as if the heat was being turned up in this room. Prince Kiernan was standing so close to her, she could feel the warmth radiating off his shoulder.

On the video, the young groom's whole posture changed, became sure and sexy, his stance possessive, as he guided his new bride around the room to the quickening tempo of the music.

"Here's another transition," Meredith said, "He's moving into a toned down hip-hop now, what I'd call a new school or street version rather than the original urban break dancing version."

A man's voice, an exquisite tenor soared above the dancing couple. *I never had a clue, until I met you, all that I could be—*

And the man let go of his wife's hand and waist and began to dance by himself. He danced as if his new bride alone watched him. Gone was the uncertain shuffle, and in its place was a performance that was nothing short of sizzling, every move choreographed to show a love story unfolding: passion, strength, devotion, a man growing more sure of himself with each passing second.

"You'll see this is very sporty," Meredith said, "and these kind of moves require amazing upper body strength, as well as flexibility and good balance.

It's part music, part dance, but mostly guts and pure athleticism."

She cast him a look. The prince certainly would have the upper body strength. And she had not a doubt about his guts and athleticism.

What she was doubting was her ability to keep any form of detachment while she worked with him trying to perfect such an intimate performance.

The dancer on the computer screen catapulted up onto one hand, froze there for a moment, came back down, and then did the very same move on his other side. He came up to his feet, tossed off his jacket, and loosened his tie.

"If he takes anything else off I'm leaving," Kiernan said. "It's like a striptease."

She shot him a look. Now this was unexpected. Prince Kiernan a prude? Where was the man of *Playboy Prince* fame?

They watched together as the groom's feet and hips and arms all moved in an amazing show of coordinated sensuality. The bride moved back to the edges of the crowd, who had gone wild. They were clapping, and calling their approval.

As the final notes of the music died the young groom took a run back toward his bride, fell to his knees and his momentum carried him a good ten feet across the floor. He caught his wife around her waist and gazed up at her with a look on his face that made Meredith want to melt.

The young groom's face mirrored the final words of the song, *I have found every treasure I ever looked for.*

There was something so astoundingly intimate about the video that in the stillness that followed, Meredith found herself almost embarrassed to look at Kiernan, as if they had seen something meant to be private between a man and a woman.

She pulled herself together. It was dancing. It was theater. There was nothing personal about it.

"What did you think?"

"I thought watching that was very uncomfortable," Kiernan bit out.

So, he'd picked up on the intimacy, too.

"It was like watching a mating dance," he continued.

"I see we have a bit of prudishness to overcome," she said, as if the discomfort was his alone.

But when his eyes went to her lips, Meredith had the feeling that the prince had a way of persuading her he was anything but a prude.

Something sizzled in the air between them, but she refused to allow him to see she was intimidated by it. And a little thrilled by it, too!

Meredith put her hands on her hips and studied him as if he was an interesting specimen who had found his way under her microscope.

"You didn't see the romance in it?" she demanded. "The delight of entering a new life? The hope for the future? His love for her? His willingness to do anything for her?"

"Up to and including making a fool of himself in front of—how many did you say—twelve million people? Every male in the world whose bride-to-be has insisted they look at this video is throwing darts at a target with his face on it!"

"He didn't look foolish! He looked enraptured. Every woman dreams of seeing *that* look on their beloved's face."

"Do they?" He was watching her again, with that look in his eyes. Too stripping, too knowing. "Do you?"

Did she? Did some little scrap of weakness still exist in her that wanted desperately to believe? That did want to see a look like the one on that young groom's face directed at her?

"I'm all done with romantic nonsense," she said, not sure whom she was trying to convince. Prince Kiernan? Or herself?

"Are you?" he asked softly.

"Yes!" Before he asked *why*, before those sapphire eyes pierced the darkest secrets of a broken heart, she rushed on.

"Prince Kiernan, the truth is I am an exception to the rule. People generally *love* romantic nonsense. Romance is the ultimate in entertainment," Meredith continued. "It has that feel-good quality to it, it promises a happy ending."

"Which it doesn't always deliver," he said sourly.

The ugly parts of his life had been splashed all over the papers for everyone to read about. He was, after all, Prince Heartbreaker.

But Meredith was stunned that what she felt for him, in that moment, was sympathy. For a moment, there was an unguarded pain in his eyes that made him an open book to her.

Which was the last thing she needed.

"All I'm saying," Meredith said, a little more gently, "is that if you can do a dance somewhat similar to that, it will bring down the house. What do you think?"

"How about I'm not doing anything similar to that? Not even if the entertainment value is unquestionable."

"Well, of course not that dance precisely, but that

video captures the spirit of what we want to do with this portion of the dance piece."

"It's too personal," he said firmly.

"It's for a dream sequence, Your Highness. This kind of dancing is very much like acting."

"Could we *act* more reserved?"

"I suppose we could. But where's the fun in that? And the delicious surprise? You know, you do have a reputation of being somewhat, um, stodgy. This would turn that on its head."

"Stodgy?" he sputtered. "Stern, remote, unapproach-able, even snobby I can handle. But stodgy? Isn't stodgy just another word for prudish?"

He looked at her lips again, and again his eyes were an open book to her.

Meredith had to keep herself from gasping at what she saw there, something primitive in its intensity, a desire to tangle his hands in her hair, yank her to him, and find out who was really the prude, who was really stodgy.

But he shoved his hands deep in his pockets, in-stead.

Was she relieved? Or disappointed by his control?

Relieved, she told herself, but it sounded like a lie even in her own mind.

"We'll modify the routine to your comfort level," she said. "Now, let's just see where you're at right now. We can try and tweak the routine after that."

She turned her back to him, gathering herself, trying to regain her sense of professionalism. She fiddled with her equipment and the "bridal waltz" came on again.

She turned back to him and held out her hand. "Your Highness?"

It was the moment of truth. She had a sudden sense,

almost of premonition. If he accepted the invitation of her hand *everything* was going to change.

He must have felt it, too, because he hesitated.

Meredith took a deep breath.

"Your Highness?"

He took her hand.

And Meredith felt the sizzle of it all the way to her elbow.

CHAPTER THREE

"THIS IS HOW WE WOULD open the number," Meredith said, "with a simple three-step waltz, just like the one in the video."

Prince Kiernan moved forward, trying not to think of how her hand fit so perfectly into his, or about the softness of her delicately curved waist.

He was also trying not to look at her lips! The temptation to show Miss Meredith Whitmore he was no prude, and not stodgy, either, was overwhelming. And since he didn't appear to be convincing her with his stellar dance moves, her lips were becoming more a temptation by the minute.

"Hmm," she said, "Not bad *exactly*. I mean obviously you know a simple three-step waltz. You just aren't, how can I say this? Fluid! Mind you, that might just work at the beginning of the number. It would be great to start off with a certain stand-offishness, an armor that protects you from your discomfort with closeness."

Was she talking about the theatrics of the damned dance or could she seriously read his personality that well from a few steps? The urge to either kiss her or bolt strengthened.

He couldn't kiss her. It would be entirely inappropriate, even if it was to make a point.

And he didn't have to bolt. He was the prince. He could just say he'd changed his mind, bow out of his participation in the dance.

"But right here," she said, cocking her head at the music, "listen for the transition, we could have you loosen up. Maybe we could try that now."

Instead of saying he'd changed his mind, he subtly rolled his shoulders and loosened his grip on her hand. He wasn't quite sure what to do with the hand on her waist, so he flexed his fingers slightly.

"Prince Kiernan, this isn't a military march."

Oh, there were definitely shades of Dragon-heart in that tone!

He tried again. He used the same method he would use before trying to take a difficult shot with the rifle. He took a deep breath, held it, let it out slowly.

"No, that's tighter. I can feel the tension in your hand. Think of something you enjoy doing that makes you feel relaxed. What would that be?"

"Reading a book?"

She sighed as if it was just beginning to occur to her he might, indeed, be her first hopeless case. "Maybe something a bit more physical that you feel relaxed doing."

He thought of nothing he could offer—everything he could think of that he did that was physical required control, a certain wide-awake awareness that was not exactly relaxing, though it was not unenjoyable.

"Riding a bicycle!" she suggested enthusiastically. "Yes, picture that, riding your bike down a quiet tree-lined country lane with thatched roofed cottages and black-and-white cows munching grass in fields, your picnic lunch in your basket."

He changed his grip on her hand. If he wasn't mistaken

his palm was beginning to sweat, he was trying so hard to relax.

She glanced up at him, reading his silence. "Picnic lunch in the basket of a bicycle is not part of your world, is it?"

"Not really. I'm relaxed on horseback. But then that's not part of your world."

"And," she reminded him, a touch crankily, "horses are the reason why you're in this position in the first place."

Again, he felt that odd little shiver about being spoken to like that. It could have been seen as insolent.

But it wasn't. Adrian had warned him, after all. But what he couldn't have warned him was that he would find it somewhat refreshing to have someone just state their opinion so honestly to him, to speak to him so directly.

"In the pictures of you in the paper," she went on, "your horses seem absolutely terrifying—wild-eyed and frothy-mouthed." She shuddered.

"Don't be fooled by the pictures you see in the papers," he said. "The press delights in catching me at the worst possible moments. It helps with the villain-of-the-week theme they have going."

"I think it's 'villain-of-the-month'," she said.

"Or the year."

And unexpectedly they enjoyed a little chuckle together.

"So, you've seriously never ridden a bike?"

"Oh, sure, I have, but it's not a favorite pastime. I was probably on my first pony about the same time most children are given their first bicycles. Am I missing something extraordinary?"

"Not extraordinary, but so *normal*. The wind in your

hair, the exhilaration of sweeping down a big hill, racing through puddles. I just can't imagine anyone not having those lovely garden variety experiences."

He was taken aback by the genuine sympathy in her tone. "You feel sorry for me because I've rarely ridden a bike down a country lane? And never with a picnic lunch in the basket?"

"I didn't say I felt sorry for you!"

"I can hear it in your voice."

"Okay," she admitted, "I feel sorry for you."

"Well, don't," he snapped. "Nobody ever has before, and I don't see that it should start now. I occupy a place of unusual privilege and power. I am not a man who inspires sympathy, nor one who wants it, either."

"There's no need to be so touchy. It just struck me as sad. And it occurred to me that if you've never done that, you've probably never played in a mud puddle and felt the exquisite pleasure of mud squishing between your toes. You've probably never had a few drinks and thrown some darts. You've probably never known the absolute anticipation of having to save your money for a Triple Widgie Hot Fudge Sundae from Lawrence's."

"I fail to see your point."

"It's no wonder you can't dance! You've missed almost everything that's important. But what's to feel sorry about?"

He was silent. Finally, he said, "I didn't know my life had been so bereft."

She shrugged. "Somebody had to tell you."

And then he chuckled. And so did she. He realized she had succeeded in making just a little of the tension leave him. But at the same time, they had just shared something that took a little brick out of the wall of both their defenses.

"Well," he said dryly. "Imagine doing a bike ride with an entourage of security people, and members of the press jumping out in front of you to get that perfect picture. Kind of takes the country lane serenity out of the picture, doesn't it?"

"The peaceful feeling is leaving me," she admitted. "Is it a hard way to live?"

"I don't have a hard life," he said. "The opposite is probably true. Everyone envies me. And this life-style."

"That's not what I asked," she said quietly. "I wondered about the price, of not knowing if people like you for you or your title, of having to be on guard against the wrong photo being taken, the wrong word being uttered."

For an astounding moment it felt as if she had invaded very private territory. It annoyed him that the one brick coming out of the wall seemed to be paving the way for its total collapse.

For a moment he glimpsed something about himself being reflected back in her eyes.

He was alone. And she knew it. She saw what others had not seen.

He reminded himself that he *liked* being alone.

He allowed the moment to pass and instead of telling her anything remotely personal, he said, "How about fly-fishing a quiet stream? For my relaxing thing that I think about?"

Ah, he was shoving bricks back in the wall. Thank goodness!

"Perfect," she said. The perfect picture. Impersonal. "That kind of fishing even has a rhythm, doesn't it? See? Hold that picture in your head, because the way you are moving right now is much better."

Of course the minute she said that, it wasn't!

"I've fished on occasion," she said. "Nothing as fancy as fly-fishing. A pole and a bobber on a placid pond on a hot day."

"Really? I've always found women make scenes when they catch fish."

She rapped him with sharp playfulness on his shoulder. He was so startled by the familiarity of the move he stumbled.

"What a terrible stereotype," she reprimanded him. "I can't stand that fragile, helpless, squeals-at-a-fish stereotype."

"So, you're not a squealer?" he said, something like a smile grazing his lips.

She blushed, and it was her turn to stumble. "Good God, I didn't mean it like that."

He studied her face, and his smile deepened with satisfaction. He drew her closer and whispered in her ear, "Now who's the prude?"

But he didn't quite pull it off. Because she was blushing. He was blushing. And suddenly a very different kind of tension hissed in the air between them. He narrowly missed her toe.

With a sigh, she let go of him, moved a few steps away, regarded him thoughtfully.

"Adrian, I mean Prince Adrian, did not have these kinds of inhibitions."

"Adrian could use a few inhibitions in my opinion."

She sighed again. She was exasperated already and they'd been at this for all of fifteen minutes. "Are you going to be difficult every step of the way, Your Highness?"

"I'm afraid so."

"I'm up for a challenge," she told him stubbornly.

"I'm afraid of that, too." He said it lightly, but he was aware he was not kidding. Not even a little bit.

Meredith marshaled herself.

"Okay, let's start again." She moved closer to him, held up her hand. He took it.

"Deep breath, slide your foot, forward, one, two, right, one, two…slide, Your Highness, not goose-step! Look right into my eyes, not at your feet. Ouch!"

"That won't happen if I look at my feet," he said darkly.

"It's an occupational hazard. Don't worry about my feet. Or yours. Look into my eyes. Not like that! I feel as if you're looking at something unpleasant that got stuck to your shoe."

He scowled.

"And now as if you are looking at a badly behaved hound."

He tried to neutralize his expression.

"Bored, reviewing the troops," she pronounced.

"I am not bored when I'm reviewing the troops!"

She sighed. "Your Highness?"

"Yes?"

"Pretend you love me."

"Oh, boy," he muttered under his breath.

"Ouch," she said as her foot crunched under his toe. Well, it wasn't really his fault. What a shocking thing to say to a prince.

Pretend you love me.

Oh, God, what had made her say that? As if the tension in the air between them wasn't palpable enough!

Thankfully, the prince had no gift for pretense. He was glaring at her with a kind of pained intensity, as if she was posed over him with a dentist's drill. It was making her want to laugh, but not a happy laugh.

The nervous laugh of one who might just have to admit defeat.

Meredith had never met anyone she couldn't teach to dance. But then, of course, anyone who showed up at her studio *wanted* to learn.

And the truth?

She'd never been quite so intimidated before.

And not solely by the fact that Kiernan was a prince, either.

It was that he was the most masculine of men. He oozed a certain potent male energy that made her feel exquisitely, helplessly feminine in his presence. Her skin was practically vibrating with awareness of him, and she was on guard trying to hide that. Twice she had caught him staring at her lips with enough heat to sizzle a steak!

Unfortunately her job was to unleash all that potent male energy, to harness the surprising but undeniable chemistry between them, so that it showed in dance form. If she could manage that, she knew her prediction—that he would bring down the house—was entirely correct.

But Kiernan seemed as invested in keeping control as she was in breaking through it to that indefinable something that lurked beneath the surface of control.

"Maybe that's enough for the first day," she conceded after another painful half hour of trying to get him to relax while waltzing.

He broke his death grip on her hand with relief that was all too obvious.

"Same time tomorrow," she said, packing her gear. "I think we'll forget the waltz, and work on the next section tomorrow. I think you may find you like it. Some of the moves are amazingly athletic."

He didn't look even remotely convinced.

And an hour into their session the next morning neither was she!

"Your Highness! You have to move your hips! Just a smidgen! Please!"

"My hips are moving!"

"In lock step!"

Prince Kiernan glared at her.

Meredith sighed. "You want them to move more like this." She demonstrated, exaggerating the movement she wanted, a touch of a Tahitian fire dance. She turned and looked back at him.

The smoldering look she had wanted to see in his eyes while they were dancing yesterday was in them now.

It fell solidly into *the be careful what you wish for* category.

"Your turn," she said briskly. "Try it. I want to practically hear those hips *swishing*."

"Enough," he said, folding his arms over the solidness of his chest. "I've had enough."

"But—"

"No. Not one more word from you, Miss Whitmore."

His expression was formidable. And his tone left absolutely no doubt who the prince was.

Prince Kiernan was a beautifully made man, perfectly proportioned, long legs, flat hips and stomach, enormously broad shoulders.

But the way he moved!

"I'm just trying to say that while your bearing is very proud and military, it's a terrible posture for dancing!"

"I said not one more word. What part of that don't you

understand?" His tone was warning. "I need a break. And so do you."

He turned his back on her, took a cell phone from his pocket and made a call.

She stared at his broad back, fuming, but the truth was she was intimidated enough not to interrupt him.

When he turned back from his call, his face was set in lines that reminded her he would command this entire nation one day. He already shouldered responsibility for much of it.

"Come with me," he said.

Don't go anywhere with him, a voice inside her protested. It told her to stand her ground. It told her she had only days left to teach him to dance! They had no time to waste. Not a single second.

But Prince Kiernan expected to be obeyed and there was something in his tone that did not brook argument.

Meredith was ridiculously relieved that he didn't seem to need a break from *her*, only from dancing. He had already turned and walked away from her, holding open the ballroom door.

And Meredith was shocked to find herself passing meekly through it, actually anticipating seeing some of his palace home. She had always entered the palace grounds, and the ballroom directly through service entrances.

He went down the hallway with every expectation that she would follow him.

She ordered herself to rebel. To say that one more word that he had ordered her not to say.

But for what purpose? Why not follow him? Things were going badly. They certainly couldn't get any worse.

They hadn't even shared a chuckle this morning. Everything was way too grim, and he was way too up-tight. Except for the *warrior about to ravish maiden* look she'd received after demonstrating how hips were supposed to move, the prince's guard was way up!

As it turned out, all she saw of the interior was that hallway. Still, it was luxurious: Italian marble floors, vases spilling over with fresh flowers set in recessed alcoves, light flooding in from arched windows, a painting she recognized, awed, as an original Monet. She had a cheap reproduction of that same painting in her own humble apartment.

The prince led her out a double French-paned glass door to a courtyard, and despite the freshness of the insult of being ordered not to say another word, something in Meredith sighed with delight.

The courtyard was exquisite, a walled paradise of ancient stone walls, vines climbing them. A lion's head set deep in one wall burbled out a stream of clear water. Butterflies glided in and out of early spring blooms and the warm spring air was perfumed with lilacs.

A small wrought iron table set with fine white linen was ready for tea. It was laid out for two, with cut hydrangeas as a centerpiece. A side table held a crystal pitcher, beaded with condensation from the chilled lemonade inside it. A three-tiered platter, silver, held a treasure trove of delicate pastries.

"Did you order this?" she asked, astounded. She barely refrained from adding *for me?* She felt stunned by the loveliness of it, and aware she felt her guard was being stormed.

As an only child she had dreamed tea parties, acted them out with her broken crockery, castoffs from houses her mother had cleaned. Only her companion then had been a favorite teddy bear, Beardly, ink stained by some disdainful rich child who'd had so many teddy bears to choose from that this vandalized one had made its way to the cleaning lady's daughter.

This time her companion was not nearly so sympathetic or safe!

"Sit down," he told her. Not an invitation.

The delight of the garden, and the table set for tea, had stolen her ability to protest. She sat. So did he. He poured lemonade in crystal goblets.

She took a tentative sip, and bit back a comment that it was fresh, not powder. As if he would know that lemonade could be made from a pouch!

"Have a pastry," he said.

Pride wanted to make her refuse the delicacies presented to her, but the deprived child she'd been eyed the plate greedily, and coveted a taste of every single treat on it. In her childhood she had had to pretend soda crackers and margarine were tea pastries. She selected a cream puff that looked like a swan. She wanted to look at it longer, appreciate the effort and the art that went into it.

And at the same time she did not want to let on how overawed she was. She took a delicate bite.

She was pretty sure Prince Kiernan had deliberately waited until she was under its influence before he spoke.

"Now," he said sternly, "we will discuss *swishing*."

The cream puff completely undermined her defenses, because she said nothing at all. She made no defense for swishing. None. In fact, she licked a little dollop of pure white cream off the swan's icing-sugar-dusted feathers.

For a moment, he seemed distracted, then he blinked and looked away.

But there was less sternness in his tone when he spoke.

"I am not swishing my hips," he told her. "Not today, not tomorrow, not ever."

The sting was taken out of it completely by the fact he glanced back at her just as she was using her tongue to capture a stray piece of whipped cream from her lips and seemed to lose his train of thought entirely.

"I think," she said reverently, "that's about the best thing I've ever tasted. Sorry. What were you saying?"

He passed the tray to her again. "I don't remember."

She was sure a more sophisticated person would be content with the cream puff, but the little girl in her who had eaten soda crackers howled inwardly at her attempt to be disciplined.

She mollified her inner child by choosing a little confection of chocolate and flaky pastry. He was doing this on purpose. Using the exquisiteness of the treats to bribe her, to sway her into seeing things his way.

"It was something about swishing," she decided. The pastry was so fragile it threatened to disintegrate under her touch. She bit it in half, closed her eyes, and suppressed a moan.

"Was it?" he growled, the sound of a man tormented.

"I think it was." She opened her eyes, licked the edge of the pastry, and a place where chocolate had melted on her hand. "That was fantastic. You have to try that one."

He grabbed the chocolate confection in question and

chomped on it with much less finesse than she would
have expected from a prince. He seemed rattled.

"Do these have drugs in them?" she asked.

"I was just about to ask myself the same thing.
Because I can't seem to keep my mind on—"

"Swishing," she filled in for him, eyeing the tray.
"Never mind. It's not as important as I thought. We'll
figure out something you're comfortable with."

He smiled, at first she thought because he had been
granted reprieve from swishing. Then she realized
he was smiling at her. "You have a sweet tooth. One
wouldn't know to look at you."

Between his smile and the confections, and the fact
he *looked* at her, she didn't have a chance.

"Yes," Meredith conceded, "let's forget swishing. It
would have been fun. There's no doubt about that. The
audience would have gone wild, but it's not really *you*
if you know what I mean."

"Why don't you try that one?"

He was rewarding her for the fact he had gotten his
way. She could not allow herself to be bribed. "Which
one?"

"The one you are staring at."

"I couldn't possibly," she said wistfully.

"I'd be disappointed if you didn't."

"In that case," she said blissfully and took the tiny
chocolate-dipped cherry from the tray. "Do you eat like
this every day?"

"No," he said a trifle hoarsely, "I must say I don't."

"A pity."

Outside the delightful cloister of the garden, she
heard the distinctive clop of hooves on cobblestone.

"Ah," he said with a bit too much eagerness, getting

up. "There's my ride. Please feel free to stay and enjoy the garden as long as you like. Tomorrow, then."

Again, it was not a suggestion or a question. No, she had just been given a royal dictate. He was done dancing for the day, whether she was or not.

He strode away from her, opened an arched doorway of heavy wood embedded in the rock wall and went out it.

Do something, Meredith commanded herself. So she did. She took a butter tart and popped the entire thing in her mouth. Then, ashamed of her lack of spunk, she leapt from her chair and followed him out the gate. She had to let the prince know that time was of the essence now. If he rode today they would have to work harder tomorrow. She'd made one concession, but she couldn't allow him to think that made her a pushover, a weakling so bowled over by his smile and tea in the garden that he could get away with anything.

She burst out of the small courtyard and found herself in the front courtyard of the castle. She stood there for a moment, delighted and shocked by the opulence of the main entrance courtyard in front of the palace.

The fountain at its center shot geysers of water over the life-size bronze of Prince Kiernan's grandfather riding a rearing warhorse. The courtyard was fragrant, edged as it was with formal gardens that were bright with exotic flowering trees.

The palace sat on top of Chatam's most prominent hill, and overlooked the gently rolling countryside of the island. In the near distance were farms and red-roofed farmhouses, freshly sown fields and lush pastures being grazed by ewes and newborn lambs.

In the far distance was the gray silhouette of the city of Chatam, nestled in the curves of the valley. Beyond that was the endless expanse of the sea.

Ancient oaks dappled the long driveway that curved up the hill to the palace with shade. At the bottom of that drive was a closed wrought iron and stone gate that guarded the palace entrance. To the left side of the gate was a tasteful stone sign, with bronze cursive letters, *Chatam Palace*, on the right, an enormous bed of roses, not yet in bloom.

Finding herself here, on this side of the gates, with the massive stone walls and turrets of the castle rising up behind her, was like being in a dream but Meredith tried to remind herself of the task at hand. She had to make her expectations for the rest of this week's practice sessions crystal-clear.

In front of the fountain, a groomsman in a palace stable uniform held a horse. Prince Kiernan had his back to her, his hand stroking one of those powerful shoulders as he took the reins from the groomsman and lifted a foot to the stirrup.

Meredith was not sure she had ever seen a man more in his element. The prince radiated the power, confidence and grace she had yet to see from him on the dance floor.

He looked like a man who owned the earth, and who was sure of his place in it.

The horse was magnificent. It was not one of the frightening horses she had seen in pictures, of that she was almost positive. Though large, and as shiny black as Lucifer, the horse stood quietly, and when he sensed her come out the gate he turned a gentle eye to her.

Except for nearly being trampled by that runaway

at the Blossom Festival parade all those years ago, Meredith had never been this close to a horse.

Instead of her planned lecture, she heard an awed *ooh* escape her lips.

Prince Kiernan glanced over his shoulder when he heard the small sound behind him.

And she, the one he thought he had successfully escaped, the one who could make eating a pastry look like something out of an X-rated film, stood there with round eyes and her mouth forming a little O.

He could leap on the horse and gallop away in a flurry of masculine showmanship. But there was something about the look on her face that stopped him.

He remembered she was afraid of horses.

He slipped his foot back out of the stirrup, and regarded Meredith Whitmore thoughtfully.

"Come say hello to Ben," he suggested quietly, dismissing his groomsman with a nod.

The debate raged in her face. Well, who could blame her? They had already crossed some sort of invisible line by having tea together. She was obviously debating the etiquette of the situation, wanting to be strictly professional.

And after watching her eat, he could certainly see the wisdom in that!

But he was aware of finding her reaction to the impromptu tea in the garden refreshing.

And he was aware of not being quite ready to gallop away.

And so what was the harm in having her meet his horse? He could tell she didn't want to, and that at the same time it was proving as irresistible to her as the crumpets had been. She moved forward as if she was being pulled on an invisible string. He could see her pulse racing in the hollow of her throat.

"Don't be afraid," Kiernan said.

She stopped well short of the horse. "He's gigantic," she whispered.

Prince Kiernan reached out, took her hand and tugged her closer.

They had been touching while they danced, but this was different. Everything about her was going to seem different after the semi-erotic experience of watching her devour teatime treats.

Still, he did not let her go, but pulled her closer, and then guiding her, he held her hand out to the horse.

"He wants to get your scent," he told her quietly.

The horse leaned his head toward her, flared his nostrils as he drew a deep breath, then breathed a puff of warm, moist air onto her hand where it was cupped in Kiernan's.

"Oh," she breathed, her eyes round and wide, a delighted smile tickling her lips. "Oh!"

"Touch him," Kiernan suggested. "Right there, between his mouth and his nose."

Tentatively, she touched, then closed her eyes, much as she had done when she decapitated the pastry swan with her lovely white teeth.

"It's exquisite," she said, savoring. "Like velvet, only softer."

"See? There's nothing to be afraid of."

But there was. And they both knew it.

She drew her hand away quickly from the horse's nose, and then out of the protection of Kiernan's cupped palm.

"Thank you," she said, and then rapidly, "I have to go."

He knew that was true, but he heard, not the words, but the fear, and frowned at it. The place where her heartbeat pulsed in her throat had gone crazy.

"Not yet," he said.

There was something in him that would not be refused. It went deeper than the station he had been born to, it went deeper than the fact he spoke and people listened.

There was something in him—a man prepared to lay down his life to protect those physically weaker than him—that challenged him to conquer her fear.

"Touch him here," he suggested, and ran his hand over the powerful shoulder muscle under the fringe of Ben's silky black mane.

She glanced toward the gate, but then made a choice. Hesitantly Meredith laid her hand where Kiernan's had been.

"I can feel his strength," she whispered, "the pure power of him."

Kiernan looked at where her hand lay just below the horse's wither, and felt a shattering urge to move her hand to his own chest, to see if she would feel his power, too, his strength.

Insane thoughts, quickly crushed. How was he supposed to dance with her if he followed this train of thought? And yet still, he did not let her go.

"If you put your nose to that place you just touched, you will smell a scent so sweet you will wonder how you lived without knowing it."

"I hope I'm not allergic," she said, trying for a light note, he suspected, desperately trying to break out of the spell that was being cast around them. But it didn't work. Meredith moved close to the horse, stood on tiptoe and drew in a deep breath.

She turned back to the prince, and he smiled with satisfaction at the transparent look of joyous discovery on her face.

"I told you," he said. "Do you want to sit on him?"

"No!" But the fear was gone. He saw her refusal, not as fright, but as an effort to fight the magic that was deepening around them.

"It's not dangerous," Kiernan said persuasively. "I promise I'll look after you."

He didn't know what he had said that was so wrong, but she suddenly went very still. The color drained from her face.

"Maybe another time," she said.

"You're trembling," Prince Kiernan said. "There's no need. There's nothing to be afraid of."

Meredith knew a different truth. There was so much to be afraid of people couldn't even imagine it.

But when she looked into Prince Kiernan's eyes, soft with unexpected concern, it felt as if the fear was taken from her. Which was ridiculous. The fact that she was inclined to trust him should make her feel more afraid, not less!

"Here, I'll help you up. Put your foot here, and your other hand here."

And she did. Even though she should have turned and run, she didn't. The temptation was too great to refuse.

She was a poor girl from Wentworth. And even though she had overcome her humble beginnings, she was still only a working woman.

This opportunity would never, ever come again.

To sit on a horse in the early spring sunshine on

the unspeakably gorgeous grounds of the Palace of Chatam.

With Prince Kiernan promising to protect her and keep her safe.

I promise I'll look after you. Those words were fair warning. She had heard those words, exactly those words, before.

When she had told Michael Morgan she was going to have his baby. And he had told her not to worry. He'd look after her. They would get married.

She could see the girl she had been standing on the city hall steps, waiting, her baby just a tiny bulge under her sweater. Waiting for an hour and then two. Thinking something terrible must have happened. Michael must have been in an accident. He must be lying somewhere hurt. Dying.

Her mother, who had refused to attend the ceremony, had finally come when it was dark, when city hall was long closed, and collected Meredith, shivering, soaked from cold rain, from the steps.

That's where trust got you. It left you way too open to hurt.

But even knowing that, Meredith told herself it would be all right just to allow herself this moment.

She took Kiernan's instructions, put her foot in the stirrup and took the saddle with her other hand. Despite her dancer's litheness, Meredith felt as if she was scrambling to get on that horse's back. But then strong hands lifted her at the waist, gave her one final shove on her rump.

Despite how undignified that final shove was, she settled on the hard leather of the saddle with a sense of satisfaction.

For the first time—and probably the only time—in her life, Meredith was sitting on a horse.

"Should we go for a little stroll?"

She had come this far. To get off without really riding the horse seemed like it would be something of a shame. She nodded, grabbed the front of the saddle firmly.

With the reins in his hands, Kiernan moved to the front of the horse. Instead of taking her for a short loop around the fountain, or down the driveway to the closed main gate, he led the horse off the paved area and onto the grass that surrounded the palace.

The whole time, his voice soothing, he talked to her.

"That's it. Just relax. Think of yourself as a blanket floating over him." He glanced back at her. "That's good. You have really good balance, probably from the dancing. That's it exactly. Just relax and feel the rhythm of it. It goes side to side and then back and forth. Do you feel that?"

She nodded, delighting in the sensation, embracing the experience. She thought after a moment he would turn around and lead her back to the courtyard, but he didn't.

"You'll see the first of the three garden mazes on your left," he said. "I used to love trying to find my way out of it when I was a boy."

He amazed her by giving her a grand tour of parts of the palace grounds that were not open to the public. But even had they been, the public would never have known that was the place he rode his first pony, that was where he fell and broke his arm, that was the fountain he and Adrian had put dish detergent in.

With the sun streaming down around her, the scent of the horse tickling her nostrils, and Kiernan out in front of her, leading the horse with such easy confidence, glancing back at her to smile and encourage her, Meredith realized something.

Perhaps the scariest thing of all.

For the first time since the accident that had taken her baby six years ago, she felt the tiniest little niggle of something.

It was the most dangerous thing of all. It was happiness.

CHAPTER FOUR

WHEN KIERNAN GLANCED BACK at Meredith, he registered her delight. There was something about her that troubled him. She was too serious for one so young. Something he could not understand haunted the loveliness of the deep golds and greens of her eyes.

And yet looking at her now those ever-present shadows, the clouds, were completely gone from her eyes. It made her lovely in a way he could not have guessed. He turned away, focused on the path in front of him. Her radiance almost hurt.

"Oh," she said. "Kiernan! He's doing something!"

Kiernan turned to see the horse flicking his tail. He laughed at the expression on her face.

"Now, that's a *swish*," he said. "A bothersome fly, nothing more."

But some tension had come into her, and he was driven to get rid of it.

"On this whole matter of swishing," he said solemnly. "A hundred years ago I could have had you hauled off to the dungeon to straighten you out about who was the boss. Ten days of bread and water would have mended your ways."

He was rewarded with her laughter.

"And if it didn't, I could have added rats."

"Really, Kiernan," she laughed, "you've proven you can have your way for a pastry. Hold the rats."

Have his way? Having his way with her suddenly took on dangerous new meaning. He could practically feel her hair tangled in his hands, imagine what it would be to take the lushness of her lips with his own.

He risked a glance at her, and saw, guiltily, that her meaning had been innocent. He was entranced by her sunlit face, dancing with laughter.

Her laughter was a delicious sound, pure mountain water, gurgling over rock, everything he had hoped for when he had given in to a desire to chase the shadows from her eyes. More.

The laughter changed her. It *was* the sun coming out from behind clouds. Meredith went from being stern to playful, she went from being somewhat remote to eminently approachable, she went from being beautiful to being extraordinary.

He laughed, too, a reluctant chuckle at first, and then a real laugh. Their combined laughter rang off the ancient walls and suffused the day with a light it had not had before.

Kiernan knew it was the first time in a long, long time that he had laughed like this. It was as if his relationship with Tiffany had brought out something grim in him that he never quite put away.

But then the moment of exquisite lightness was over, and as he gazed up into the enjoyment on her face he realized that he was not fully prepared for what he saw there. Even though he had encouraged this moment, he did not feel ready for the bond of it. There was an utter openness between them that was astounding.

He felt like a man who had been set adrift on ice, who was nearly frozen, and who had suddenly glimpsed the promise of the warm golden light of a fire in the distance.

But his very longing made him feel weak. What had he been thinking? He needed to guard against moments like this, not encourage them.

Kiernan was not sure he had ever felt quite that vulnerable. Not riding a headstrong horse over slippery ground, not even when the press had decided to crucify him, first over Francine, ten times worse over the Tiffany affair.

He turned abruptly back toward the courtyard, but when they arrived, he stood gazing up at her, not wanting to help her off the horse.

To touch her now, with something in him so open, felt as if it guaranteed surrender. He was Adam leaning toward the apple; he was Sampson ignoring the scissors in Delilah's hand.

Hadn't Tiffany just taught him the treacherous unpredictability of human emotion?

Still, Meredith wasn't going to be able to get off that horse without his help.

"Bring that one leg over," he said gruffly, and then realized he hadn't been specific enough, because she brought her leg over but didn't twist and swing down into the stirrup, but sat on his horse, prettily side-saddle.

And then, without warning, she began to slide off.

And he had no choice but to reach out and catch her around her waist, and pull her to him to take the impact from her.

She stood there in the circle of his arms, her chin tilted back, looking into his face.

"Kiernan," she said softly, "I don't know how to thank you. That was a wonderful morning."

But that was the problem. The wonder of the morning

had encouraged this new form of familiarity. Barriers were down. She hadn't used his proper form of address.

She didn't even know she hadn't, she was so caught in the moment. And she never had to know how he had *liked* how his name had sounded coming off her lips.

But it was just one more barrier down, one more line of protection compromised. He should correct her. But he couldn't. He hated it that the moment seemed to be robbing him of his strength and his resolve, his sense of duty, his *knowing* what was right.

Aside from Adrian, who was this comfortable with him, there were few people in his world this able to be themselves around him, this able to bring out his sense of laughter.

Francine had. Tiffany never.

She did not back out of the circle of his arms, and he did not release her. The laughter was gone from her face. Completely. She swallowed hard.

The guard he had just put up felt as if it was going to crumple. *Completely*. And if it did, he would never, ever be able to build it back up as strong as it had been before, like a wall that had been weakened by a cannonball hit.

"Your Highness?"

Now, she remembered the correct form of address. Too late. Because now he longed to hear his name off her lips.

That's what he had to steel himself against.

"Yes?"

"Thank you for not letting me fall," she said.

But the truth? It felt as if they were falling, as if they were entering a land where neither of them had ever been, without knowing the language, without having a map.

"It's not if you fall that matters," he said quietly. "Everyone falls. It's how you get up that counts."

A part of him leaned toward her, wanting, almost desperately to explore what was happening between them. As if, in that new land he had glimpsed so briefly in her eyes, he would find not that he was lost.

But that he was found.

And that he was not alone on his journey.

Kiernan gave himself a mental shake. He couldn't allow himself to bask in that feeling that he had been *seen*, this morning, not as a prince, but for the man he really was. And he certainly couldn't allow her to see that her praise meant something to him.

Music suddenly spilled out an open window above them. She cocked her head toward it. "What on earth?' she asked. "What kind of magic is this?"

The whole morning had had that quality, of magic. Now, it seemed imperative that he deny the existence of such a thing.

"It's not magic!" he said, his tone suddenly curt. "The palace chamber quartet is practicing, that's all. It happens every Tuesday at precisely eleven o'clock."

He liked precise worlds. Predictable ones.

"Your Highness?"

He looked askance at her.

"Shall we?"

Of course he wasn't going to dance with her! He was too open to her, too aware of how the sun shone off her hair, of the light in her eyes, of the glossy puffiness of her lips. He had a horse that needed looking after. Her laughter and his had already made him feel quite vulnerable enough.

And yet this surprise invitation had that quality of delicious spontaneity to it that he found irresistible. Plus, to refuse might deepen her puzzlement, and if she studied the mystery long enough, would she figure it out?

That there was something about her he liked, and at the same time, he disliked liking it. Intensely.

But there was one other thing.

He had seen a light come on in her today. It still shone there, gently below the surface, chasing away a shadow he had realized had been ever-present until this morning.

He might want to protect himself.

But not enough to push her back into darkness.

And so he dropped the reins, uncharacteristically not caring if the horse bolted back to the stable. He felt like a warrior at war, not with her, but with himself. Wanting to see her light, but not at the expense of losing his power.

He felt as if he was walking straight toward his biggest foe. Because, of course, his biggest foe was the loss of control that she threatened in him.

Here was his chance to wrest it back, to take the challenge of her to the next level. He gazed down at her, and then took her hand, placed his other one on her waist.

There was something about the spontaneity of it, about the casualness of it, about the drift of the music over the spring garden, that did exactly what she had wanted all along.

Something in him *breathed*. He didn't feel rigid. Or stiff. He felt on fire. *A man who would prove he was in charge of himself.*

A man who could flirt with temptation and then just shrug it off and walk away.

A man who could see her light, and be pulled to it, and want it for her, but at the same time, not be a moth that would be pulled helplessly into the flame.

He danced her around the courtyard until she was breathless. Until she was his whole world. All he could see was the light in her. All he could feel was the sensuous touch of her fingertips resting ever so lightly on the place where his back met his hip. All that he could smell was her scent.

The last note of music spilled out the window, held, and then died. He became aware again of a world that was not Meredith. The horse stood, his head nodding, birds singing, sun shining, the scent of lilacs thick in the air.

Now, part two of the equation. He had danced with the temptation.

Walk away.

But she was finally looking at him with the approval a prince deserved. He steeled himself not to let it go straight to his head.

"That was fantastic," Meredith said softly.

"Thank you." With a certain chilly note, as if he didn't give a fig about her approval.

"I think you're ready to learn a few modern dance step moves tomorrow."

Tomorrow. He'd been so busy getting through the challenge of the moment that he'd managed to completely forget that.

There were more moments to this challenge. Many more.

Kiernan had known she would be that kind of girl.

The if you give an inch, she'll take a mile kind.

The kind where if you squeezed through one challenge she threw at you, by the skin of your teeth, only, another would be waiting. Harder.

And just to prove she had much harder challenges in

store for him, she stood on her tiptoes and brushed his cheek with her lips.

Then she stepped back from him, stunned.

But not as stunned as he was. That innocent touch of her lips on his cheek stirred a yearning in him that was devastating. Suddenly his whole life seemed to yawn ahead of him, filled to the brim with activities and obligations, but empty of the one thing that truly mattered.

It doesn't exist, he berated himself. He'd learned that, hadn't he?

For a moment, she looked so surprised at herself that he thought she might apologize. But then, she didn't. No, she crossed her arms over her chest, and met his gaze with challenge, daring him to say something, daring him to tell her how inappropriate it was to kiss a prince.

But he couldn't. And therein was the problem. She was challenging his ability to be in perfect control at all times, and he hated that.

Resisting an impulse to touch the place on his cheek that still tingled from the caress of her soft lips, Kiernan turned from her, and went to his horse. He put his leg in the stirrup and vaulted up onto Ben's back. Without looking back, he pressed the horse into a gallop, took a low stone wall, and raced away.

But even without looking, he knew she had watched him. And knew that he had wanted her to watch him and be impressed with his prowess.

Some kind of dance had begun between them. And it had nothing at all to do with the performance they would give at *An Evening to Remember.*

On the drive home from the palace, Meredith replayed her audacity. She'd kissed the prince!

"It wasn't really a kiss," she told herself firmly. "More like a buss. Yes, a buss."

Somehow she had needed to thank him for all the experiences he had given her that day.

"So," she asked herself, "what's wrong with thank you?"

Still, if she had it to do again? She would do the same thing. She could not regret touching her lips to the skin of his cheek, feeling the hint of rough stubble beneath the tenderness of her lips, standing back to see something flash through his eyes before it had been quickly veiled.

She parked her tiny car in the laneway behind her apartment, a walk-up located above her dance studio in Chatam. She owned the building as a result of an insurance settlement. The building, and No Princes, had been her only uses for the money.

Both things had given her a little bit of motivation to keep going on those dark days when it felt like she could live no more.

Tonight, when she opened the door to the apartment that had given her both solace and sanctuary, she was taken aback by how fresh her wounds suddenly felt.

It had been six years since it had happened.

A grandmother who had just picked up her grand-daughter from day care walking a stroller across a street. Who could know why Meredith's mother, Millicent, had not heard the sirens? Tired from working so hard? Mulling over the dreams that had been shattered? A stolen vehicle the police were chasing went through the crosswalk. Meredith's mother, Millicent, had died at the scene, after valiantly throwing her body in front of the stroller. Carly had succumbed to her injuries a few days later, God deaf to the pleas and prayers of Meredith.

Now, the apartment seemed extra empty and quiet tonight, no doubt because today, for the first time in so long, Meredith had allowed herself to feel connected to another human being.

Meredith set her bag inside the door, and went straight to the bookshelf, where there were so many pictures of her baby, Carly. She chose her favorite, took it to the couch, and traced the lines of her daughter's chubby cheeks with her fingertips.

With tears sliding down her cheeks, she fell asleep.

When she awoke she was clutching the photo to her breast. But instead of feeling the sadness she always felt when she awoke with a photo of her daughter, she remembered the laughter, and the happiness she had felt today.

And felt oddly guilty. How could she? She was not ready to be happy again. Nor could she trust it. Happiness came, and then when it went, as it inevitably did, the emptiness was nearly unbearable.

Meredith considered herself strong. But not strong enough to hope. Certainly not strong enough to sustain more loss. She was not going to embrace the happiness she had felt today. No, not at all. In fact, she was going to steel herself against it.

But the next morning she was aware she was not the only one who had steeled herself against what had happened yesterday.

If Meredith thought they had made a breakthrough yesterday when she had ridden the horse and Kiernan had danced in the courtyard with her, she now saw she was sadly mistaken.

He had arrived this morning in armor. And he danced

like it, too! Was the kiss what had done it? Or the whole day they had experienced together? No matter, he was as stiffly formal as though he had never placed his hand on her rump to sling her into the saddle of his horse, as if he had never walked in front of her, chatting about his childhood on the palace grounds.

Meredith tried to shrug her sense of loss at his aloofness away and focus on the job at hand.

She had put together a modified version of the newlyweds' dance from the internet and Prince Kiernan had reluctantly approved the routine for *An Evening to Remember*. She had hoped to have some startling, almost gymnastic, moves in it, which would show off the prince's amazing athletic ability.

But the prince, though quite capable of the moves, was resistant.

"Does the word *sexy* mean anything to you?"

Something burned through his eyes, a fire, but it was quickly snuffed. "I'm doing my best," he told her with cool reserve, not rattled in the least.

But he wasn't. Because she had glimpsed his best. This did not even seem like the same man she had danced with yesterday in the courtyard, so take-charge, so breathtakingly masculine, so sure.

The stern line of his lip was taking on a faintly rebellious downward curve. Pretty soon, he would announce *enough* and another day of practice would be lost.

Not that yesterday had been lost.

She sighed. "You know the steps. You know the rudiments of each move. But you're like a schoolboy reciting math tables by rote. Something in you holds back."

"That's my nature," he said. "I'm reserved. Something in me always holds back." His eyes fastened on her lips, just for a split second, and she felt her stomach do a loop-the-loop worthy of an acrobatic airplane.

If he didn't hold back, would he kiss her? What would his lips taste like? Feel like? Given her resolve to back away from all those delicious things she had felt yesterday, Meredith was shocked by how badly she wanted to know. She was shocked by the sudden temptation to throw herself at him and take those lips, to shock the sensuality out of him.

But she also needed for both of them to hold back if she was going to keep her professional distance. And she needed just as desperately for him to let go if she was going to feel professional pride in teaching him!

It was a quandary.

"Is it your nature to be reserved," she questioned him, "or your role in life?"

"In my case, those are inextricably intertwined."

He said that without apology.

"I understand that, but in dancing there is no holding back. You have to put everything into it, all that you were, all that you have been, all that you hope to be someday."

The question was, if he gave her all that, how was she going to walk away undamaged?

"This is a ten-minute performance at a fund-raiser," he reminded her, "not the final exam for getting into heaven."

But that's what she wanted him to experience, *exactly*. She realized for her it had become about more than their performance.

There was a place when you danced well, where you became part of something larger. It was an incredible feeling. It was a place where you rose above problems.

And tragedies. A place where you were free of your past and your heartaches. Yes, just like touching heaven.

But somehow she could not tell him that. It was too ambitious. He was right. It was a ten-minute performance for the fund-raiser opening of Blossom Week. Meredith was here to teach him a few dance steps, nothing more.

When had it become her quest to unlock him? To show him something of himself that he had never seen before? To want him to experience *that* feeling. Of heaven.

And that she was dying to see?

It had all become too personal. And she knew that. She had to get her own agenda straight in her head.

Teach him to do the routine, perform it well, and be satisfied if the final result was passable if not spectacular. The prince putting in a surprising appearance, making a game effort at the steps would be enough. The people of Chatam would *love* his performance, a chance to see him let his hair down, even if he was somewhat wooden.

Though, for her, to only accomplish a passable result would feel like a failure of monumental proportions. Especially since she had glimpsed yesterday what he could be.

Her eyes suddenly fell on two jackets that hung on pegs inside the coat check at the far end of the ballroom. They were the white jackets of the palace housekeeping staff.

As soon as she saw them, she knew exactly what she had to do.

And as she contemplated the audacity of her plan, she could have sworn she heard a baby laugh, as if it was *so* right.

It was a memory of laughter, nothing more, but she could see the face of the beautiful child who had been taken from her as clearly as though she still had the photo on her chest.

She was aware again, of something changing in her. Sweetly. Subtly. It wasn't that she wasn't sad. It was that the sadness was mixed with something else.

A great sense of gratitude for having known love so deeply and so completely.

Meredith was suddenly aware that her experience with love had to make her a better person.

It had to.

Her daughter's legacy to her had to be a beautiful one. That was all she had left to honor her with.

And if that meant taking a prince to a place where he was not so lonely and not so alone, even briefly, then that was what she had to do.

It wasn't about the dance they were doing at all.

It was about the kind of person she was going to choose to be.

And yes, it was going to take all her courage to choose it.

She moved past the prince to the coat check, plucked the jackets off the wall, and then turned back and took a deep breath.

Yesterday, spontaneity had brought them so much closer to the place they needed to be than all her carefully rehearsed plans and carefully choreographed dance steps.

Today, she hoped for magic.

CHAPTER FIVE

THE PRINCE BADLY WANTED his life back. He wanted *An Evening to Remember* to be over. He wanted the temptation of Meredith over; watching her demonstrate hip moves, taking her hand in his, touching her, looking at her and pretending to love her.

It was easily the most exhausting and challenging work he had ever done, and the performance couldn't come quickly enough in his opinion.

Though, somewhere in his mind, he acknowledged over would be over. No more rehearsals. No more bossy Meredith Whitmore. Who didn't respect his station, and was impertinent. Who was digging at him, trying to find the place in him he least wanted her to see, refusing to take no for an answer.

Who could make eating pastries look like an exercise in eroticism one minute, and look at a horse with the wide-eyed wonder of a child the next. Whose lips had felt like butterfly wings against his cheek.

Stop, Kiernan ordered himself.

She was aggravating. She was annoying. She was damnably sexy. But she was also *refreshing* in a way that was brand new to him. She was not afraid to tell him exactly what she thought, she was not afraid to make demands, she was not afraid of him, not awed by his station, not intimidated by his power.

And that, he reluctantly admitted, was what he was going to miss when it was all over. In so much of his life he was the master. What he said went. No questions. No arguments. No suggestions. No discussion.

How was it that in a dance instructor from Wentworth, he felt he had met his equal?

There was no doubt going to be a huge space in his life once she was gone. It seemed impossible she could have that kind of impact after only a few days. But he didn't plan to dwell on it.

Prince Kiernan was good at filling spaces in his life. He had more obligations than he had time, anyway, and many of those were stacking up as he frittered away hours and hours learning the dance routine he was coming to hate.

"We're going to go somewhere else today," Meredith announced, marching back over from the coat room with something stuffed under her arm. "I think the ballroom itself may be lending to the, er, stuffiness, we're experiencing. It's too big, too formal."

But he knew it wasn't the room she found stuffy. It was him.

"First stodgy, now stuffy," he muttered.

"Don't act insulted. You said yourself the role you play has made you that way."

"No, you suggested it was the role I played. I said I was born this way. And I never used the word stuffy. I think I said reserved."

"Okay, whatever," she said cheerfully. "We're going to do a little experiment today. With your reserve."

Oh-oh, this did not bode well for him. He was already hanging onto his control by the merest thread.

"Here," she said pleasantly, "put this on."

She handed him one of the white jackets she had stuffed under her arm. The one she handed him had the name *Andy* embroidered over one pocket in blue thread. He hesitated. What was the little minx up to?

Mischief. He could see it in the twinkle in her eye.

He should stop her before she got started, and he knew that. But despite the fact he had told himself he wasn't going to dwell on it, soon their time together would be over. Why not see what mischief she had planned? That spark in her eye was irresistible anyway, always reminding him that there was a shadow in her.

Like the unexpected delight of taking her for tea and then on that ride, this was part of the unexpected reprieve he'd been given from the stuffy stodginess of his life. He was aware he *wanted* to see what she had up her sleeve today.

So he slipped the white jacket over his shirt and did up the buttons. It was too tight across the chest, but she inspected him, and frowned. She went back to the coat check and reappeared with a white ball cap.

"There," she said, handing it to him. "Pull it low over your eyes. Perfect. All ready to smuggle you out of the palace." She shrugged into a white jacket of her own. It said *Molly* on the pocket.

"We can't smuggle me out of the palace," he said, but he was aware it was a token protest. Something in him was already taking wing, flying over the walls.

"Why not?"

"There are security concerns. I have responsibilities and obligations you can't even dream of. I can't just waltz out of here without letting anyone know where I'm going and why."

"To improve your waltz, I think you should. See?

There's that reserve again. Your Highness—no, make that Andy—have you ever broken the rules?"

"I don't have the luxury," he told her tightly.

She smiled at him. "Prince Kiernan of Chatam doesn't. Andy does. Let's go. It's just for a little while. Maybe an hour. In some ways, you're a prisoner of your life. Let's break out. Just this once."

He stood there for a moment, frozen. Again, he had a sense of her saying what no one else said.

And seeing what no one else saw.

She didn't see the prince. Not entirely. If she did, she would not have dared to touch his cheek with her lips yesterday. She saw a man first. The trappings of his status underwhelmed her. She saw straight through to the price he paid to be the prince.

And she wanted to rescue him. There was a kind of crazy courage in that that was as irresistible as the mischief in her eyes.

Of course he couldn't just go. It would be the most irresponsible thing he had ever done.

On the other hand, why not? The Isle of Chatam was easily the safest place in the world. He was supposed to be at dance class. No one would even miss him for a few hours.

Suddenly what she was offering him seemed as impossible to resist as the mischief that made her eyes spark more green than brown.

Freedom. Complete freedom, the one thing he had never ever known.

"Coming, Andy?" she said.

He sighed. "Molly, I hope you know what you're doing."

"Trust me," she said.

And Kiernan realized he was starting to. The one

thing he wanted to do least was trust a woman! And yet somehow she was wiggling her way past his defenses and entering that elite circle of people that he truly trusted.

He followed her outside to the staff parking lot. She led him to the tiniest car he had ever seen, a candy-apple-red Mini.

She got in, and he opened the passenger door and slid in beside her. His knees were in approximately the vicinity of his chin.

"They've gotten used to me at the service entrance," she said. "I'll just give them a wave and we'll breeze on through."

And that's exactly what happened.

In moments they were chugging along a narrow country road, he holding on for dear life. Kiernan had never ridden in a vehicle that was so...insubstantial. He felt as if they were inches above the ground, and as if every stone and bump on the road was jarring his bones. He actually hit his head on the roof of the tiny vehicle.

"Where are we going?" he asked.

"Remember I asked you about squishing mud up through your toes?"

"Yes, I do."

"That's where we're going."

"I don't want to squish mud up between my toes," he said, though he recognized his protest, once again, as being token. The moment they had driven through that back service gate to the palace something in him had opened.

He had made a decision to embrace whatever the day held.

"It doesn't matter if you want to or not. Andy does."

"But why does he?" he asked.

"Because he likes having *fun*."

"Oh, I see. There's nothing stuffy or stodgy about our man, Andy."

"Exactly," she said, and beamed at him with the delight of a teacher who had just helped a child solve a difficult problem. "Andy, you and I are about to give new meaning to *Dancing with Heaven*."

"I don't know the old meaning, Molly."

"You've never seen *Dancing with Heaven*? It's a movie. A classic romantic finding-your-true-self movie that has dance at its heart. It starred Kevin McConnell."

He didn't care for the dreamy way she said that name.

"I'll have to put watching *Dancing with Heaven* on your homework list."

"Andy doesn't like homework."

"That's true."

"He likes playing hooky. But when he's at school?"

"Yes?"

"He winks at the teacher and makes her blush."

"Oh-oh," she said.

"He likes motorcycles, and black leather, driving too fast, and breaking rules."

"My, my."

"He likes loud music and smoky bars, and girls in too-short skirts and low-cut tops who wiggle their hips when they dance."

"Oh, dear."

"He thumbs his nose at convention. He's cooled off in the town fountain on the Summer Day celebrations, disobeyed the Keep Off signs at Landers Rock, kept his hat on while they sing the national anthem."

"That's Andy, all right."

"He likes swimming in the sea. Naked. In the moon-light."

Unless he was mistaken, Meredith gulped a little before she said, "I've created a monster."

"You should be more careful who you run away with, Molly."

"I know."

"But they say every woman loves a bad boy."

Something in her face closed. She frowned at the road. Kiernan realized how very little he knew about her, which was strange because he felt as if he knew her deeply.

"Do you have a boyfriend?" He hadn't thought to ask her that before. There were no rings on her fingers, so he had assumed she was single. Now he wondered why he had assumed that, and wondered at why he was holding his breath waiting for her answer.

"I'm single." Her hands tightened on the wheel.

"I'm surprised." But ridiculously *relieved*. What was that about, since if ever there was a man sworn off love it was him? Why would he care about her marital status?

Only because, he assured himself, he didn't even want to think about her with a bad boy.

She hesitated, looked straight ahead. "I became preg-nant when I was sixteen. The father abandoned me. It has a way of souring a person on romance." He heard the hollowness in her voice, but he could hear something more.

Unbearable pain. And suddenly his concern for pro-tecting his own damaged heart evaporated.

"And the baby?" he asked quietly. Somehow he knew this woman could never have an abortion. Never.

And that adoption seemed unlikely, too. There was something about the fierce passion of that first dance he had witnessed her performing that let him know that. She would hold on to what she loved, no matter what the cost to her.

He glanced at her face. She was struggling for control. There was something she didn't want to tell him, and suddenly, with an intuition that surprised him, he knew it was about the shadow that he so often saw marring the light in her eyes.

He held his breath, again, wanting, no, *needing* to know that somehow she had come to trust him as much as he had come to trust her, even if it was with the same reluctance.

"It was a little girl. I kept her," she whispered. "Maybe a foolish thing to do. My mom and I had to work night and day cleaning houses to make ends meet. But I don't regret one second of it. Not one. All I regret is that I couldn't be with her more. With both of them more."

He felt a shiver go up and down his spine.

"My mom picked her up from day care for me on a particularly hectic day. They were crossing a street when a stolen car being chased by the police hit them."

Her voice was ragged with pain.

"I'm so sorry," he said, aware of how words were just not enough. "You seem much too young to have survived such a tragedy."

In a broken whisper she went on, "She wasn't even a year old yet."

Her shoulders were trembling. She refused to look at him, her eyes glued to the road.

He wanted to scream at her to pull over, because he needed to gather her in his arms and comfort her. But from the look on her face there were some things there was no comforting for.

"I'm so sorry," he said again, feeling horrible and helpless. He reached out and patted her shoulder, but she shrugged out from under his hand, her shoulder stiff with pride.

"It's a long time ago," she said, with forced brightness. "Today, let's just be Molly and Andy, okay?"

It couldn't be *that* long ago. She wasn't old enough for it to have been that long ago.

But she had trusted him with this piece of herself.

And her trust felt both fragile and precious. If he said the wrong thing it felt like this precious thing she had offered him would shatter.

Still, he could not quite let it go. He had to listen to the voice inside him that said, *ask her.*

"Could you tell me their names? Your baby's and your mother's?" he asked, softly, ever so softly. "Please?"

She was silent for so long that he thought she would refuse this request. When she answered, he felt deeply moved, as if she had handed him her heart.

"Carly," she whispered. "My baby's name was Carly. My mother's was Millicent, but everyone called her Millie."

"Carly," he said softly, feeling it on his tongue. "Millie."

And then he nodded, knowing there was nothing else to say, but holding those names to him like the sacred trust that they were.

There was something about the way he said her daughter and mother's names, with genuine sadness, and a simple reverence, that gave Meredith an unexpected sense of being comforted. Over the past days she had come to know Prince Kiernan in a way that made it easy to forget he was still the most powerful man in the land.

Something about the way he uttered those names made her understand his power in ways she had not before. His speaking Carly's name was oddly like a blessing.

Meredith felt tears at his gentleness sting her eyes, but she did not let them flow. Kiernan reached out, and loosed her hand from the gearshift, and gave it a hard squeeze before letting it go.

Why had she told him about Carly? And her mother? She could have just as easily left it at she was single.

Was it because she was asking him to let his guard down? And that request required more of her, too? Was it because some part of her had trusted he would handle it in just the right way?

Whatever it was, she waited for a sense of vulnerability to come, a sense that she had revealed too much of herself.

But it did not. Instead, she felt an unexpected sense of a burden that she had carried alone being, not lifted, but shared.

A prince sharing your burden, she scoffed at herself, but her scorn did not change the way she felt, lighter, more open.

But for now, she reminded herself, a newfound sense of awe of Kiernan would not forward her goal. He needed to be taken off his pedestal if she ever hoped to get him to dance as if he meant it.

So for today, Kiernan was not a prince, not the most wealthy, most influential, most powerful man in Chatam. Today he would be just Andy. And she was not a woman with an unbearable sadness in her past, just *Molly*, two palace housekeeping workers playing hooky from work for the day.

They arrived at the small unmarked pullout, the trail-head for what Meredith considered one of the greatest treasures of the Isle of Chatam, Chatam Hot Springs.

Meredith opened the boot of her small car, and loaded "Andy" down with bags and baskets to carry up the steep trail that wound through the sweetly scented giant cedar woods. She was enjoying this charade already. She would have never asked a prince to carry her bags!

Meredith was relieved to see, as they came around the final twist in the trail, there was not a single soul at Chatam Hot Springs. The natural springs were a favorite local haunt, but not this early in the day and not midweek. She had taken a chance that the hot springs would be empty, and they were.

Kiernan set down his cargo and gazed around. "What a remarkable place."

Puffs of mist rose above the turquoise waters that filled a pool edged by slabs of flat black slate rocks. Freshwater falls cascaded down a mossy outcropping at the far end of the pool. Lush ferns, and bunches of grass, sown with tiny purple and blue wildflowers, surrounded the rocks and the pool.

"You've never been here?"

"I've heard of it, and seen photographs of it many times. But to come here? When the royal entourage arrives, security would necessitate closing it to the people who enjoy it most. I have so many other pleasures at my disposal that it would seem unduly selfish to want this one, also."

She was already vulnerable to him because some-how the way he had reacted to her history had been so quietly *right*. Now she saw that despite the fact he lived in a position that could have easily bred arrogance, it had not. Kiernan clearly saw his position not as one of absolute power, but one of absolute service.

Still, the time for being too serious today was over.

"Oh, Andy," she chided him. "You're talking as if you think you're royalty!"

Still, she was delighted he had never been here before, pleased that she was the one who had brought him to something new, beautiful and unexpected.

"Oh, Molly," he said contritely. "You know me. Delusions of grandeur."

"I have a plan for bringing you down a few notches, Andy."

"I can barely wait."

And it actually sounded as if he meant that, as if he was embracing this experience with an unexpected eagerness.

"Well, then, kick off your shoes, and roll up your pants," Meredith suggested. "This is what I want to show you."

He didn't even argue with her.

Hidden in a tiny glade beside the hot springs, separated from the main pool by a dripping curtain of thick foliage, was a dip in the ground, approximately a quarter the size of the ballroom, that was filled with oozing, gray mud.

Meredith waded in. "Careful, it's—" just as she tried to warn him, one of her feet slipped. But before she even fully registered she was falling, Kiernan was beside her. He wrapped his arm around her waist, took her arm, and steadied her.

"Oh, Molly, you're a clumsy one. I'd give up those dreams of being a dancer if I were you."

She felt as if she could not get enough of the playful tone in his voice.

"I'll give up my dancer dreams if you'll give up yours of being a prince."

"Done," he said, with such genuine relief they both laughed.

"It's warm," he said, astounded, apparently unaware that even though he had let go of her waist, he still held her arm. "I've never felt anything quite like this."

And neither had she. Oh, the mud was exquisite; warm and thick, it oozed up through her toes, and then around her feet, and ankles, up her calves, but it was his hand, still steadying her arm, which she had never felt anything like.

They had been touching each other for days now.

But, except for that magical moment when the music had spilled over the courtyard, their dancing together had been basically all business. Their barriers had both been so firmly up. But that kiss she had planted on his cheek had taken the first chink out of those barriers, and now there were more chinks falling.

And so this outing and this experience wasn't all business even if she had cloaked her motivation in accomplishing a goal.

Meredith looked at Kiernan's face, dappled with sunshine coming through the feathery cedars that surrounded the pool, and something sighed within her. His face was exquisite, handsome and perfect, but she had never seen the expression she saw on it now.

Prince Kiernan's eyes were closed. He looked completely relaxed, and something like contentment had crept into the normally guarded lines of his face. He tilted his chin to the sun, and took a deep breath, sighed it out.

It was good.

But it wasn't enough.

She wanted, *needed* to see with a desperation not totally motivated by her end goal, the prince lose his inhibitions, that *restraint*, that was like an ever-present palace guard, surrounding him. Keeping others away from him. But also keeping him away from others.

She let go of his hand. She stooped, and buried her own hand in the mud, closed her fist around an oozing gob of goo. For a moment she hesitated.

It was true. Kiernan was just way too restrained. He could never reach his potential as a dancer while he carried that shield around him.

But this was probably still just about the worst idea she had ever had. She lived in a land still ruled by a very traditional monarchy. Schoolchildren and soldiers started their day by swearing their allegiance and obedience to this man's mother, Queen Aleda. But in time it would be him they stood and pledged their hearts to.

He had already shouldered much of the mantle of responsibility. Meredith knew, partly from the newspapers, and confirmed by the phone calls he sometimes had to take during dance practice, his interest in the economic health of the island was keen, that he had sharp business acumen, and that some of his initiatives had improved the standard of living for many people who lived here.

He promoted Chatam tirelessly abroad. He headed charities. He sat on hospital boards. He was the commander-in-chief of the military.

This man who stood with her, his pants rolled up to his knees, had influence over the lives of every single person in Chatam.

Really, it was no wonder he had trouble relaxing! So, this was probably one of the worst ideas Meredith had ever had. She *was* too cheeky. You did not, after all, in a land ruled by a monarchy, pick up a handful of oozing soft mud and hurl it at your liege!

But Meredith was committed to her course. Knowing somehow, in her heart, not her head, this was, absurdly, wonderfully, the *right* thing, she let fly with a handful of mud.

It caught him in the chest, and he staggered back a step, startled. He opened his eyes and stared down at the mud bullet that had exploded on his shirt.

His reaction would tell her a great deal about this man.

Furious anger?

Remote silence?

Complete retreat?

But, no, a smile tickled his lips, and when he looked up at her, she felt she might weep for what she had unmasked in his eyes.

"Disrespectful wench," he said. "I'd swear you are looking for a few nights in the dungeon."

There was a delightful playfulness in his tone.

"Andy! Are you in your prince delusion again? Dungeons, for pity sake! I suppose you'll be telling me about bread and water and rats next. Poor you. Tut-tut."

"Prince delusion? Oh, no, not at all. I'm in my warrior delusion, and you have just called me to battle. But I'm going to warn you, all prisoners go to the dungeon. If you please me, I might spare you the rats."

She giggled, a trifle nervously, because something

smoked in his eyes when he talked of making her his prisoner.

What had she started? And could she really handle it?

Kiernan stooped and came up with his big hand full of mud. He squinted at her thoughtfully, drew back his arm and took aim.

She began to run an awkward zigzag pattern through the sucking mud. The dark sludge he hurled whisked by her head.

"Ha-ha," she called over her shoulder. Meredith ducked, picked up her own mud ball and flung it back at him. But he'd had time to rearm, too.

Their mud balls crossed paths with each other, midair. His hit her solidly on the arm, with a warm, soft splat. It was like being hit with a dollop of just-out-of-the-oven pudding. Her missile wobbled through the air and went straight for his head.

Despite the fact he raised his arm in defense against the slow-flying projectile, it exploded against his raised bicep, and particles of it landed on his cheek, blossoming there like the petals of a mud flower. She drew her breath, shocked by her own unintentional audacity.

"I'm so sorry!" she called.

"Not nearly as sorry as you're going to be," he warned her.

He stopped, carefully wiped the muck off his cheekbone, and glared at her with mock fierceness. But Meredith saw there was nothing mock about the fact he did now look like a warrior! Of the barbaric variety that painted their faces before they went to battle.

He let out a cry worthy of that warrior and came after

her, stooping and hucking mud as fast as he could fill his hands with it.

In moments the glade rang with his shouts and her playful shrieking. They threw mud back and forth until they were both covered in dark blotches, until their hair was lost under ropy dreadlocks of sludge, their hands were like mud mitts at their sides, and their clothes had disappeared under layers of smelly black goo. Finally, only his teeth and the whites of his eyes still looked white. Andy's shirt was probably beyond repair.

The glade filled with the sounds of their laughter and playful insults, the sounds of them gasping for breath as they struggled to run through the sucking mud to escape each other's attacks.

"Take that, Molly!"

"You missed! Andy, you throw like a girl."

"*You* missed. *You* throw like a girl."

"But I am a girl!"

"A girl? A mud monster, risen from the deep! Take that!"

They were laughing so hard they were choking on it. It rang off the rocks around them, rode on the mist.

Despite the noise, the chaos, the hilarity, something quiet blossomed in Meredith. Something she had felt, ever so briefly on that horse yesterday, but other than that not for a long, long time.

Joy.

The quiet awareness of it knocked her off balance. With Kiernan hot on her heels, his raised hand full of mud rockets, she slipped. She went down in slow motion, somehow managing to twist so she wouldn't go into the muck face first. The mud cushioned her fall, and she fell on her back with a sucking *splat*.

She watched as Kiernan, too close, tried desperately

to stop, but his arms windmilled, and he fell right on top of her, saving her from the worst of his weight by bracing his arms around her.

She stared up into the face of her warrior prince. His eyes were alight with laughter, looking bluer than she had ever seen them look. His smile, against the backdrop of his muddy face, was brilliant, white as snow against a stone.

She had never felt anything quite so exquisite. She rested in a bed of warm mud, her skin slippery and sensuous with it. And Kiernan, equally as slippery, held himself off of her, but there were places their bodies met. His hard lines were pressed into the soft curves of her legs and her hips.

She touched him every day. But his guard had always been up.

Hers had been, too.

Only something, delicate and subtle, had shifted between them.

The laughter died in the air around them, and was replaced with a silence so profound that it vibrated with a growing tension, a deep awareness of each other.

He stared down at her, and some unguarded tenderness crept into his muddy, warrior's face.

Still holding most of his weight off her with one arm, he touched her lip with the hand he had just freed, scraped gently with his thumb.

Her joy escalated into exhilaration at the exquisite sense of being touched in such an intimate place, in such an intimate way.

"You have mud right here," he whispered, by way of excuse, but his voice hoarse.

For a splendid moment it felt as if every barrier was

down between them. Every one. As if her world was as wide open as it had ever been.

Everything became remarkable: the song of a bird nearby, the feel of the mud cushioning her, the smells that tickled her nostrils, the green of the fern plumes behind him.

Where his legs were sprawled across hers, the slide of their skin together where it made slight contact at their hips, the amazing light in his sapphire eyes, the scrape of his thumb against her lip, the slick muddiness of his hair, the sensual curve of his lips.

He was so close to her she could see the dark beginning of stubble on his cheeks, and his chin. He was so close to her his breath stirred across her cheek, featherlight, as intimate as his thumb which remained on her lips. He was so close to her she could smell the scent of him, wild and clean as the forest, over the scent of the minerals in the mud that covered them.

She closed her eyes against the delicious agony of wanting a moment to last forever.

To escalate.

"I warned you there would be consequences if I took you prisoner," he said, the words playful, while his tone was anything but.

Was he going to kiss her? Even as a rational part of her knew they could never pull back from that again, a less rational part of her wanted the taste of his lips on hers, wanted to feel them.

She took her hand, as if it didn't matter it was mud-covered, and traced a possessive line down the hard plane of his jaw. She touched it to the fullness of his lip.

As if it didn't matter to him that it was mud-covered, he teased her finger gently, nibbled it with his teeth.

She felt the featherlight touch of his lip against the skin of her finger. Was it possible to die of sensation?

If this—the merest touch of his lips to something as inconsequential as her finger—could cause this unbelievable rise of sensation within her, what would it be like if he took her lips with his own?

She felt as if it would be a death of sorts.

The death of all she had been before, the rising up of something new, the rising up within her of a spirit that was stronger and more resilient than she had ever imagined, similar to that spirit that rose in her when she danced.

A place that was without thought, and without history.

Heaven.

Brazen with wanting, she slipped her muddy hands around the column of his neck, and pulled him down to her.

His weight settled on her more fully, chest to the soft curve of breast, hard stomach to delicate swell, muscled legs to slender ones, fused.

A whisper of sanity called her back from the brink.

And then called louder, *stop*.

It reminded her of the price of such a heated moment, lives changed forever.

But in that moment, she didn't care if there was a price.

And apparently neither did he.

Because his lips touched hers. The fact they were both mud-slicked only increased the danger, the sensuality, the delicious sense of being swept away, of not caring about what happened next, of being pulled by forces greater than themselves.

His very essence was in the way he kissed her.

Kiernan tasted, not of mud, but of rain in a storm, pure, clean, elemental. His kiss was tender, welcoming, and yet the strength and leashed passion were sizzling just below the surface.

It had been so long since Meredith had allowed anything or anyone to touch her, emotionally or physically.

She had not even known the hunger grew in her, waiting for something, someone to touch it off, to show her she was ravenous.

She was ravenous, and Kiernan was a feast of sensation.

Everything about him swirled around her—the light in his sapphire eyes, the line of his hard body against hers, the taste of his lips, the hollow of his mouth—all those broken places within her were being touched by sensation that was fulfilling and healing and exhilarating.

It was madness. Exquisite, delicious, compelling madness.

And she had to stop it. She had to.

Except that she was powerless, in the grip of something so amazing and wondrous she could not have stopped it if her very life depended on it. She was just not that strong.

But he was.

He pulled back from her, she saw strength and temptation war in his eyes, and she was astounded—and saddened—when his strength won. He pulled himself away from her, hesitated, dropped back down and placed one more tiny kiss on the corner of her lip, and then pulled his weight completely off her and stood gazing down at her.

Meredith saw control replace the heat in his eyes.

She watched awareness dawn in his eyes, saw his reluctant acquiescence to the guard he always surrounded himself with.

She knew, with a desperate sadness, this moment was over.

CHAPTER SIX

KIERNAN COMPOSED HIMSELF, held his hand to her. She took it, and her body made an unattractive slurping sound as he tugged, and then yanked hard to free her from the mud.

If he said he was sorry, she felt she would die.

But he did not say that, and she felt a strange sense of relief that she could tell he was not sorry. Not even a little bit.

And neither was she, even though the consequences of what had just happened hung over her.

Neither of them spoke, looking at each other, aware with an awareness that could not be denied once it had been acknowledged.

He dropped her hand, but not her gaze.

"Thank you," he said softly.

She knew exactly what he meant. That moment of being so alive, so incredibly vibrantly alive had been a gift to both of them.

She had not even been aware how much she lived in a state of numbness until she had experienced this wonderful hour with him. It had been carefree, and laughter-filled, wondrous. Meredith felt as if she had been exquisitely and fully alive in a way she had not been for a long, long time.

If she ever had been that alive, that fully engaged, that spontaneous, that filled with wonder for the simple, unexpected miracle of life.

Still, leaving the utter and absolute magic of the moment, Meredith felt as if she was going to cry.

She covered the intensity of the moment by pasting a smile on her face. "You're welcome. People pay big money for the mud treatment at the spa."

"Yes," he said, watching her closely, as if he knew she was covering, as if he knew exactly how fake that smile was. "I know."

And of course he would know. Because that was his world. Spas and yachts and polo ponies.

His world. He had playfully said he would take her prisoner, but the truth was his world was a prison in many ways.

And he could not invite her into it.

She did not have the pedigree of a woman he would ever be allowed to love.

Love. How had that word, absolutely taboo in her relationship with him, slipped past all her guards and come into her mind?

But now that it had come, Meredith was so aware how this moment was going to have a tremendous cost to her. Because, she had ever so briefly glimpsed his heart. Because she had seen the coolness leave his eyes and be replaced with tenderness. Yes, this moment had come at a tremendous price to her. Because she had let her guard down, too.

For a moment she had wanted things she could not have. Ached for them.

Still, if she had this choice to make over, how would she do it? Would she play it safe and stay in the ballroom, tolerating his wooden performance, allowing his mask to remain impenetrable?

No, she would change nothing. She would forever be grateful she had risked so much to let him out of his world, and his prison. Even if it had only been a brief reprieve.

And in return, hadn't she been let out of hers?

He turned from her, but not before she caught the deeply thoughtful look on his face, as if every realization she was having was also occurring to him.

He walked back through the fern barrier, leapt into the hot springs completely clothed. She watched his easy strength, as he did a powerful crawl that carried him across the pool to the cascading water of the falls. She quelled the primitive awareness that tried to rise in her.

Instead, she dove into the pool, too. Her skin had never felt so open to sensation. He had climbed up on a ledge underneath the falls, and she saw the remnants of their day falling off of him as if it had never happened.

It was time to clean herself of the residue of the day, too. She swam across the pool and pulled herself up on the ledge beside him.

The fresh, cold water was shocking on her heated skin. It pummeled her, was nearly punishing in its intensity.

Though she and Kiernan stood side by side, Meredith was painfully aware some distance now separated them, keeping their worlds separate even in the glorious intimacy of the cascading water world that they shared.

She slid him a look and felt her breath catch in her throat.

His face was raised to the water, his eyes closed as

what was left of the mud melted out of his hair and dissolved off his face, revealing each perfect feature: the cut of high cheekbones, the straight line of his nose, the faint cleft of his chin.

The white of Andy's shirt had reemerged, but the shirt had turned transparent under the water, and clung to the hard lines of Kiernan's chest. She could see the dark pebble of his nipple, the slight indent of each rib, the hollow of a taut, hard belly. It made her mouth go dry with a powerful sense of craving.

To touch. To taste. To have. To hold.

Impossible thoughts. Ones that would only bring more grief to her if she allowed them any power at all. Hadn't her life held quite enough grief?

Was it the coldness of the water after all that heat, or her awareness of him that was making her quiver?

Meredith felt herself wanting to save this moment, to remember the absolute beauty of it—and of him—forever.

He finally turned and dove cleanly off the ledge, cutting the water with his body. With that same swift, sure stroke, Kiernan made his way back across the mineral pond to where he had set the baskets. How long ago? An hour? A little longer than an hour?

How could so much change in such a short amount of time?

She dove in, too, emerged from the pond, dripping, and flinging back the wetness of her hair. She saw, from the brief heat in his eyes before he turned away, that Molly's shirt must have become as transparent as Andy's.

She glanced down. And she had accused him of boring underwear? Her bra—a utilitarian sports model made for athletic support while dancing—showed clearly through the wet fabric. But from the look on his face you would have thought she was wearing a bra made out of silk and lace!

She shoved by him, and rummaged through the baskets, tucked a towel quickly around herself and then silently handed him a towel and a change of clothing.

Was there the faintest smirk on his face from how quickly she had wrapped herself up?

"You're prepared," he said.

Yes. And no. There were some things you could not prepare for. Like the fact you hoped a man would tease you about being a prude, like the fact it was so hard to let go of a perfect day.

But he didn't tease her, or linger. He ducked behind a rock on one side of the glade and she on the other. She did not want to think of him naked in a garden, but she knew the temptation of Eve in that moment, and fought it with her small amount of remaining strength.

The trip back was eerily silent, as if they were both contemplating what had happened and how to go forward—or back—from that place.

Meredith drove back through the same service entrance to Chatam Palace. On the way in she had to stop and show ID, and her palace pass. She did not miss the stunned look on the face of the guard as he recognized the prince squished in the seat beside her. He practically tossed her ID back through her window, drew himself to attention and saluted rigidly.

It could not have been a better reminder of who the man beside her *really* was.

And the look of shock on the guard's face to see the prince in such a humble vehicle with a member of the palace staff, could not have been a better reminder of who she really was, too.

He was not Andy. She was not Molly.

He was a prince, born to position, power and prestige. She was a servant's daughter, a woman who had given birth to an illegitimate child, a person with so much history and so much baggage.

She let the prince out, barely looking at him. He barely looked at her.

They did not say goodbye.

Meredith wondered if he would show up for their scheduled dance session tomorrow.

Would she?

The whole thing had become fraught with a danger that she did not know how to handle.

And yet, even that tingling sensation of danger as she drove away from the palace after dropping Kiernan off there, served as a reminder.

She was alive.

She was alive, and for the first time in a long, long time, she was aware of being deeply grateful that she was alive. The pain. The glory. The potential to be hurt. The potential to love. It was all part of the most incredible dance.

There was that word again.

Love.

"Forbidden to me," Meredith said. Because of who he was. Because of who she was, and especially because of where she had already been in the name of love.

But of course, what had more power than forbidden fruit?

When Prince Kiernan walked through the doors of the ballroom the next morning, Meredith did not know whether she was relieved he had come, or sorry that she had to be tested some more.

He was right on time as always.

They exchanged perfunctory greetings. She put on the music. He took her hand, placed his other with care on her waist.

The trip to the hot springs had obviously been an error in every way it was possible for something to be an error.

This was turning out to be just like the day she had ridden his horse and they had danced in the courtyard to the chamber music spilling out the palace windows.

Prince Kiernan's guard came down, but only temporarily!

And when it went back up, it went way up!

After half an hour of tolerating a wooden performance from him, Meredith was not tingling with awareness of being alive at all! She was tingling with frustration. Was he dancing this badly just to put her off? Maybe he was hoping she would cancel the whole thing. And maybe she should.

Except she couldn't. It was too late now to start over with someone else. The girls, rehearsing separately, at her studio, had practiced to perfection. They were there night and day, putting heart and soul into this.

She wasn't letting them down because Prince Kiernan was the most confoundedly stubborn man in the world.

But really, enough was enough!

"This is excruciating," she said, pulling away from him, folding her arms across her chest and glaring at him.

Somewhere under that cool, composed mask was the man who had chased her, laughter-filled, through the mud.

"I warned you I had no talent."

"Call somebody," she snapped at him. "It's like a

game show where you have a lifeline. Call somebody, and use your princely powers. Have them find us the movie *Dancing with Heaven*. And deliver it. Right here. Right now."

It was an impossible request. The movie was old. It would probably be extremely difficult if not impossible to find.

For a moment he looked like he might argue, but then he chose not to, probably because he wanted to do just about anything rather than dance.

With her.

With some new tension in the air between them. Harnessed, it would make for an absolutely electrical dance performance.

Resisted, it would make for a disastrous dance performance.

He took a cell phone out of his pocket, and placed a call.

"Tell them not to forget the popcorn," she said darkly. "And I'd like something to drink, too."

"You're being very bossy," he said. "As usual."

Within minutes his cell phone rang back. "It's set up in the theater room," he said.

"Can't we watch it here?"

"No, we can't. I'm not sitting on an icy cold floor to watch a movie. Not even for you."

Not even for you. She heard something there that she knew instantly he had not intended for her to hear. Something that implied he would do anything for her, up to and including going to the ends of the earth.

She deliberately quelled the beating of her heart and followed the prince to where he held open the ballroom doors for her.

It was the first time Meredith had been in the private

areas of the interior of the palace. The ballroom, along with the throne room, and a gallery of collected art was in the public wing of the palace, open to anyone who went there on a tour day.

Now, Prince Kiernan led her through an arched door flanked by two palace guards who saluted him smartly. The door led into the private family quarters of the palace.

They were in a grand entranceway, a formal living room on one side, a curving staircase on the other. The richness of it was startling: original old masters paintings, Persian rugs, priceless antiques, draperies and furniture upholstered in heavy brocaded silks. A chandelier that put the ones in the ballroom to shame spattered light over the staircase and entry.

Kiernan noticed none of it as he marched her up the wide stairs, under the portraits of his ancestors, many of whom looked just like him, and all of whom looked disapproving.

"What a happy looking lot," she muttered. "They have aloofness down to a fine art."

He glanced at the portraits. "Don't they?" With *approval*.

So *that's* where he got his rigidity!

"Maybe I'm wasting my time trying to break past something that has been bred into each Chatam for hundreds of years." And that they were proud of to *boot*.

"I've been trying to tell you."

And maybe if she hadn't been stupid enough to take him on that excursion yesterday, she would have believed him.

"This floor is where guests stay," he said, exiting the staircase that still spiraled magnificently upward. He led her down a wide corridor.

Bedroom doors were open along either side of the hallway and she peeked in without trying to appear too interested. The bedrooms, six in all, three on either side of the hallway were done in muted, tasteful colors. The décor had the flavor and feel of pictures Meredith had seen of very upscale boutique hotels.

It occurred to Meredith that princes and presidents, prime ministers, princesses and prima donnas had all walked down these corridors.

It reminded her who the man beside her *really* was, and she felt a whisper of awe. He opened the door to a room at the end of the long hallway.

Meredith tried not to gape. The "theater room" was really the most posh of private theaters. The walls were padded white leather panels with soft, muted light pouring out from behind them. The carpets were rich, dark gold with a raised crown pattern in yet darker gold. There were three tiers of theater style chairs in soft, buttery distressed leather. Each chair had a light underneath it that subtly illuminated the aisle. The chairs faced a screen as large as any Meredith had ever seen.

Two chairs were in front of all the others, and Kiernan gestured to one of them. Obviously she was sitting in a chair that would normally be slated for the most important of VIP's. She settled into the chair.

"Who's the last person who sat here?" She could not stop herself from asking.

If Kiernan thought the question odd he was polite enough not to let on. "I think it was the president of the United States. Nice man."

Never had she been more aware of who Kiernan really was.

And who she really was.

A man in a white jacket, very much like the one she

had borrowed from Andy, arrived with a steaming hot bowl of popcorn for each of them. He pushed a button on the side of her seat, and a tray emerged from the armrest.

"I was kidding about the popcorn," she hissed at Kiernan, but she took the bowl anyway.

"A drink, miss?"

Part of her was so intimidated by her surroundings, she wanted to just say no, to be that invisible girl who had accompanied her mother to work on occasion.

But another part of her thought she might never have on opportunity like this again, so, she was making the most of it. She decided to see how flummoxed the man would be if she ordered something completely exotic and off the wall—especially for ten o'clock in the morning. "Oh, sure. I'll have a virgin chi-chi."

The servant didn't even blink, just took the prince's order and glided away only to return a few minutes later.

"My apologies," he said quietly. "We didn't have the fresh coconut milk today."

She had to stifle a giggle. A desire to tease and say, *see that that doesn't happen again.* Instead, she met the man's eyes, and saw the warmth in them, and the lack of judgment.

"Can I get you anything else?"

"No, thank you for your kindness," she said. And she meant it.

She took a sip, and sighed. The drink, even without the fresh coconut milk was absolute ambrosia.

The movie came on. For the first few minutes Meredith was so self-conscious that Prince Kiernan was beside her. It felt as if she was on a first date, and they were afraid to hold hands.

Dancing with Heaven was dated and hokey, but the dance sequences were incredible, sizzling with tension and sensuality.

Though she had seen this movie a dozen times, Meredith was soon lost in the story of a spoiled self-centered young woman who walked by a dance studio called Heaven, peeked in the window, and was entranced by what she saw there. The dance instructor was a bitter older man whose career had been lost to an injury. He taught dance only for the money, because he had to.

Through what Meredith considered some the best dance sequences ever written, the young woman moved beyond her superficial and cynical attitude toward life and the instructor came to have hope again.

Wildly romantic, and sizzling with the sexual chemistry between the two, the instructor fought taking advantage of the young heiress's growing love for him, but in the end he succumbed to the love he had for her and the unlikely couple, united through dance, lived happily ever after.

What had made her insist the prince see this ridiculous and unrealistic piece of fluff?

When it was over, Meredith was aware of tears sliding down her face. She wiped at them quickly before the lights came up, set down her empty glass and her equally empty popcorn dish.

"Now you know what I expect of you. I'll see myself out. See you in the morning."

Kiernan saw that Meredith was not meeting his eyes. Something about the movie had upset her.

He ordered himself to let it go, especially after yesterday. Not that he wanted to think about yesterday.

He'd kissed her, and it hadn't been a little buss on

the cheek, either. No, it had been the kind of kiss that blew something wide open in a man, the kind of kiss that a man did not stop thinking about once it had happened.

It was the kind of kiss that made a man evaluate his own life and find it seemed empty, and without color.

The problem was they had been pretending to be ordinary.

And between an ordinary man and an ordinary woman maybe such things could happen without consequences.

But in his world? If he went where that kiss invited him to go, *begged* him to go, the world she knew would be over.

She had trusted him with her deepest secrets. How would she like those secrets to be exposed to the world? If he let his guard down again, if he allowed things to develop between them, Meredith would find her past at the center ring of a three-ring circus. Pictures of her baby would be dug up. Her mother's past would be investigated. Her ex would be found and asked for comments on her character.

So, even though the movie had upset her, it would be best to let her go.

And yet he couldn't.

He stepped in front of her.

"Are you upset?" he asked quietly.

She looked panicked. "No. I just need to go. I need to—"

"You're upset," he said. "Why? Did the movie upset you?"

"No, I—"

"Please don't lie to me," he said. "You've never done it before, and you have no talent for it."

She was silent.

He tipped her chin. "Did it remind you of your baby's father?" he asked softly. "Is that the way you felt about him?"

He remembered the sizzling sensuality between the on-screen couple, and he felt a little pang of, good grief, *envy.* But this wasn't about him. He could actually feel her trembling, trying to hold herself together.

"Talk to me, Meredith."

"It had a happy ending," she whispered. "I deplore happy endings! If it weren't for the dance sequences, I would have never asked you to watch such drivel!"

But he was stuck at the *I deplore happy endings* part. How could anyone so young and so vibrant have stopped believing in a happy ending for herself?

"My baby's father was older than me, twenty-two. He was new to the neighborhood, and all the girls were swooning over his curly hair and his suave way. I was thrilled that he singled me out for his attention. Thrilled."

Kiernan felt something like rage building in him at the man he had never met, the man who had used her so terribly, manipulated and fooled a young girl. But he said nothing, fearing that if he spoke, she would clam up.

And he sensed she needed to talk, she needed to say these things she had been holding inside. And he needed to be man enough to listen, without being distracted by her lips and the memory of their taste, without wanting *more* for himself. Without putting his needs ahead of her own.

"If I had married Michael, my baby's father, it would have been a disaster," she said. "I can see that now. As hard as it was for me and my mom to make ends meet, it would have only been harder with him. You want to know how bad my taste is in men? Do you want to know?"

He saw the regret in her eyes and the pain, and he wanted to know everything about her. Everything.

"He didn't even come to the funeral."

She began to sob.

And he did what he should have done yesterday in the car, what he had wanted to do.

He pulled her into his chest, and ran his hand up and down her back, soothing her, encouraging her. *Let it out.*

"I loved him, madly. I guess maybe I held on to this fantasy he was going to come to his senses, do the right thing, come back and rescue me. Prove to my mother she was wrong. Love us."

If he could have, he would have banished the shame from her face.

"Kiernan," she said softly, "he didn't care one fig about me. Not one. And I fooled myself into thinking he did. How can a person ever trust themselves after something like that? How?"

He loved that she had called him his name, no formal address. Wasn't that what was happening between them? And what he was fighting against?

Deepening trust. Friendship. Boundaries blurring. But as he let her cry against him, he knew it was more. Mere friendship was not something that would put his guard up so high. And mere friendship would never have him feeling a nameless fury at the man who had cruelly used her, walked away from his responsibilities, broken her heart as if it was nothing.

His fury at a man he had never met abated as he

became aware of Meredith pressed against him, felt the sacredness of her trust, and this moment.

He was not sure that he had ever felt as much a man as he did right now.

"You deserved so much better," he finally said.

"Did I?" She sounded skeptical.

He put her away from him, looked deep into the lovely green of her eyes. "Yes," he said furiously, "you did. As for trusting yourself? My God, cut yourself some slack. You were a child. Sixteen. Is that what you said?"

"Seventeen when Carly was born."

"A child," he repeated firmly. "Taken advantage of by an adult man. His behavior was despicable. To be honest? I'd like to track him down and give him a good thrashing!"

She actually giggled a little at that. "Maybe the dungeon?"

He felt relieved that she was coming around, that he saw a spark of light in her eyes. "Exactly! Extra rats!"

"Thank you," she said, quietly.

"I'm not finished. As for not trusting yourself? Meredith, you have taken these life experiences and made it your mission to change things for others. Do you remember what I said to you when you thanked me for not allowing you to fall off the horse?"

"Yes," she whispered, "You said it's not how you fall that matters. You said everyone falls. You said it was how you got up that counted."

He was intensely flattered that she had heard him so completely. He spoke quietly and firmly. "And how you are getting up counts, Meredith. Helping those Wentworth girls honors your baby. And your mother. And you."

She gave him a watery smile, pulled away from him,

not quite convinced. "Oh, God, look at me. A blithering idiot. In front of a prince, no less."

And she turned, he could tell she was going to flee, and so he caught her arm. "I'm not letting you go, not just yet. Let's have tea first."

Just in case he was beginning to think he was irresistible, she said, "Will it have the little cream puff swans?"

"Yes," he said. "It will."

He guided her out of the theater and to the elevator at the end of the hallway and took her to his private apartment.

"It's beautiful," she said, standing in the doorway, as if afraid to come in. And maybe he should have thought this out better.

Once she had been in here, would he ever be completely free of her? Or would he see her walking around, pausing in front of each painting like this, always?

"Is it you who loves Monet?" she asked.

He nodded.

"Me, too. I have several reproductions of his work."

"I understand," Kiernan said, "that he was near-sighted. That wonderful dreamy, hazy quality in his landscapes was not artistic license but how he actually saw the world. You know what I like about that?"

She looked at him.

"His handicap was his greatest gift. Your hardships, Meredith?"

She was looking at him as if he had a lifeline to throw her. And he hoped he did.

"Your hardships are what make you what you are. Amazingly strong, and yet good. Your goodness shines out of you like a light."

He turned away to look after tea. But not before he

saw that maybe he had said exactly the right thing after all, but maybe not enough of it. She did not look entirely convinced.

He had tea set up on the balcony that overlooked the palace grounds and the stunning views of Chatam.

"Instead of allowing your falls to break you," he insisted quietly, sitting her down, "you have found your strength."

"No, really I haven't."

Now he felt honor-bound not to let her go until she was convinced. Of her own goodness. Of her innate strength. Of the fact that she had to let go of all that shame. Of the fact she was earning her way, by the way she chose to live her life, to a new future.

"I want to know every single thing there is to know about you. I want to know how you've become the remarkable woman you are today." And he meant that.

She looked wildly toward the exit, but then she met his eyes. But just to keep him from feeling too powerful, then she looked at the tray of goodies a servant was bringing in.

"Oh," she said. "The cream puffs."

"I know how to get your secrets out of you, Meredith."

"There's nothing remarkable about me."

"Ah, well, let me decide."

She mulled that over, and then sighed. Almost surrender. He passed her the tray. She took a cream puff, and sighed again. When she bit into it and closed her eyes he knew her surrender was complete.

They talked for a long, long time. It was deep and it was true and it was real. He felt as if they could sit there and talk forever.

It was late in the afternoon before Meredith looked at her watch, gasped, and made her excuses. Within seconds she was gone. Kiernan was not sure he had ever felt he had connected with someone so deeply, had ever inspired trust such as he had just experienced from her.

Kiernan sat for a long time in a suite that felt suddenly cold and empty for all the priceless art and furniture that surrounded him. It felt as if the life had gone out of it when Meredith had.

Without her the room just seemed stuffy. And stodgy.

He'd liked having her here in his very private space. He'd liked watching the movie with her and how she had not tried to hide the fact she was awed that a president had sat in her chair. He liked how she had acknowledged Bernard who had brought their popcorn and drinks, not treated him as if he was invisible, the way Tiffany always had.

And damn it, he'd liked that movie.

Silly piece of fluff that it was, it was somehow about people finding the courage to be what they were meant to be, to bring themselves to the world, to overcome the strictures of their assigned roles and embrace what was real for them.

And, finally, he had loved how she had come into his space, and how between cream puffs and his genuine interest and concern for her she had become so open. And liked what the afternoon told him about her.

Above all things, Meredith was courageous.

A hardscrabble upbringing, too many losses for one so young, and yet he saw no self-pity in her. She was taking the challenges life had given her and turning them into her greatest assets. She had a quiet bravery to get on with her life.

That's what she was asking of him. To bring his

courage to the dance floor. To dance without barriers, without a mask, and without a safety net.

She was asking him to be who he had been, ever so briefly, when they had chased each other through the mud.

Wholly alive. Completely, unselfconsciously himself.

No guards. No barriers.

And she was asking him to be who he had been just now: deep and compassionate.

Really, what she was asking of him would require more courage than just about anything he had ever done. At the hot springs he had shown that unguarded self to her. And again today there had been something so open and unprotected about their interaction after the movie.

Prince Kiernan felt as if he stood on the very edge of a cliff. Did he take a leap of faith, trusting if he jumped something—or someone—would catch him? Or did he turn away?

"For her sake," he said to himself, "You turn away."

But he didn't know if he was powerful enough to do that. He knew he wanted these last days with her before it was over.

So he could have moments and memories, a secret, something sacredly private in his life, to savor when she was gone.

CHAPTER SEVEN

"FROM THE TOP," Meredith said. Today's dancing session, she knew, was going no better than yesterday's. The movie had changed nothing.

No, that was not true.

It had changed everything.

It had changed her. Maybe not the movie, exactly, but what had happened after.

When Kiernan had held her in her arms, it had felt as if everything she had been fighting for since the death of her mother and baby—independence, strength, self-reliance—it had felt as if those things were melting.

As if some terrible truth had unfolded.

All those qualities that she had striven toward were just distractions from the real truth. And the truth was she was so terribly alone in this world.

And for a moment, for an exquisite, tender moment in the arms of her country's most powerful man, she had not felt that. Sitting beside him on the balcony of his exquisite apartment, surveying all his kingdom, pouring out her heart, telling her secrets, she had not felt that.

For the first time in forever, Meredith had not felt alone.

And it was the most addictive sensation she had ever

felt. She wanted to feel it again. She wanted to never let go of it.

Worse, she had a tormented sense that, though Kiernan walked with kings and presidents, she had seen what was most *real* about him. It was the laughter at the hot springs, it was his confidence in his horse, it was the tenderness in his eyes as he had listened to her yesterday.

And she had to guard against the feeling that he caused in her.

Because just like the wealthy heiress and the dance instructor in the movie, their worlds were so far apart. But unlike the movie, which was pure escapist fantasy after all, they could never be joined. And the sooner she accepted the absoluteness of that the better.

This morning she felt only embarrassed that she had revealed herself so totally to him. Talked, not just about Michael and Carly, which was bad enough, but about her childhood, growing up with a single mom in Wentworth, and then repeating her family's history by becoming one herself.

She'd told him about ballet, and her mother's hope and losing the scholarship when she became pregnant. She'd told him about those desperate days after Carly was born, her mother being there for her, despite her disappointments, Millie loving the baby, but never quite forgiving her daughter.

She told him about the insurance settlement after the tragedy that allowed her to own her own dance studio and form No Princes, and how guilty she felt that her dreams were coming true because the people she had loved the most had died.

Oh, yes, she had said way, way too much. And today, it was affecting *her* dancing.

She was the one with the guard up. She was the one who could not open herself completely. She was the one who could not be vulnerable on the dance floor. She was trying desperately to take back the ground she had lost yesterday.

And she was failing him. Because she could not let him in anymore. She could not be open.

She was as rigid and closed as the prince had been on that first day. It was the worst of ironies that now he seemed as open as she was closed!

"What's wrong?" he asked.

The tender concern in his eyes was what was wrong! The fact she was foolishly, unrealistically falling in love with him was what was wrong!

"You know what?" he said, snapping his fingers. "I know I have the power to fix whatever is wrong!"

Yes, he did. He could get down on one knee and say that though the time had been short he realized he was crazy about her. That he couldn't live without her.

All this work. All this time with No Princes and Meredith's weaknesses were unabated! She despised that about herself.

"One call," he said, and smiled at her and left the room.

When he returned he had a paper bag with him, and with the flourish of a magician about to produce a rabbit, he opened it and handed her a crumpled white piece of fabric.

"Ta-da," he said as she shook out the white smock.

"What is this?"

"I think I've figured it out," he said, pulling another smock from the bag and tugging it over his own shirt.

It had Andy embossed across the breast.

She stared down at the smock in her hand. Sure enough, he had unearthed Molly's smock.

"Remember when you told me this kind of dancing is like acting?"

Meredith nodded.

"Well, I'm going to be Andy for the rest of the rehearsals. And you're going to be Molly."

She stared at him stunned. She wanted to refuse. She wanted to get out of this with her heart in one piece.

But she could not resist the temptation of the absolute brilliance of it. If she could pretend to be someone else, if she could pretend he was someone else, there was a slim chance she could save this thing from catastrophe. And maybe, at the same time, she could save herself from the catastrophe of an unattainable love.

But it seemed the responsibility for saving things had been wrested from her. Kiernan took charge. He went and put on the music, turned and gazed at her, then held out his hands to her.

"Shall we dance, Molly?"

She could only nod. She went and took his hands, felt the way they fit together. Her resolve, which she could have sworn was made of stone, melted at his touch.

"Remember Andy?" he said, smiling down at her as they began the opening waltz.

She gave herself over to this chance to save the dance. "Isn't he that devilish boy who won't do his homework?"

"Except he did watch *Dancing with Heaven*."

"Used class time, though."

"That's true."

Kiernan had those opening steps down *perfect*. A little awkwardness, a faint stiffness, a resolve to keep his distance in his posture.

The transition was coming.

"Andy," she reminded him, getting into the spirit of this, embracing it, "winks at the teacher and makes her blush."

And Kiernan became that young fellow—on the verge of manhood, able to tie his teacher in knots with a blink of sapphire-colored eyes.

"I think he makes her drop things, too," Meredith conceded, and her blush was real. "And forget what she's teaching at all."

Kiernan smiled at her with Andy's wicked devil-may-care-delight. Through dance he became the young man who rode motorcycles, and wore black leather. He was the guy who drove too fast and broke rules.

Something about playing the role of the bad boy unleashed Kiernan. He was playful. He was commanding. He was mischievous. He was *bad*.

His hips moved!

They moved to the next transition, and Kiernan released her hand. He claimed the dance floor as his own.

He claimed it. Then he owned it.

Meredith's mouth dropped open as he tore off the smock that said Andy on it, and tossed it to the floor.

Before her eyes, Kiernan became the man who liked loud music and smoky bars, and girls in too-short skirts and low-cut tops who wiggle their hips when they dance. He became the guy who cooled off in the town fountain, claimed Landers Rock as his own, kept his hat on during the anthem.

He became a man so comfortable with himself that he would delight in swimming in the sea naked under the moonlight.

And then came the final transition.

And he was no longer an immature young man, chasing skirts and adrenaline rushes, breaking rules just for the thrill of having said he had done it.

Now he was a man, claiming the woman he wanted to spend the rest of his life with.

He crossed the floor to her, and they went seamlessly to the finale—dancing together as if nothing else in the world existed except each other, and the heat, the chemistry between them.

Meredith was not Meredith. She was Molly.

And something about being Molly unleashed her just as much as being Andy had unleashed him. She didn't have a history. She was just a girl from the kitchen who wanted something more out of life: not drudgery, but a hint of excitement wherever she could find it.

By playing Molly, Meredith came to understand her younger self.

And forgive her.

Finally, with both of them breathless, the music stopped. But Kiernan did not let her go. He stared at her silently, his eyes saying what his mouth did not.

She pulled away from him. Her smile was tremulous.

"It was perfect," she breathed.

"I know. I could feel it."

She had to get hold of herself; despite this breakthrough she had to find the line between professional and personal. She had to get over the feeling of wanting to take his lips and taste them, of wanting more than she could have, of wanting more than he could offer her.

"You know what would be brilliant?" Meredith said crisply. "We can alter the real performance dream sequence slightly so that it is Andy and Molly, and Andy transforms into a prince."

He was looking at her just as he had on the balcony of his private suite. With eyes that saw right through her professional blither-blather to the longing that was underneath.

She was only human.

And he was only human.

If she was going to keep this thing on the tracks until the performance at *An Evening to Remember* she had to make a drastic decision, and she had to make it right now.

"You know what this means, don't you?"

He shook his head.

"We're finished."

"Finished?"

"We're done, Prince Kiernan." It was self-preservation. She could not dance like that with him every day until the performance and keep her heart on ice, keep him from seeing what was blossoming inside her.

Like a flower that would be cut.

"We've got two practices left," he said, frowning at her.

"No," she said firmly, with false brightness, "there's nothing left to practice. Nothing. I don't think we should do it again. I don't want to lose the freshness of what we just did. We're done, Prince Kiernan. The next time we do that dance, it will be at *An Evening to Remember*."

Instead of looking relieved that dance class was finally over, Kiernan looked stunned.

She felt stunned, too. She was ending it. The suddenness of it made her head spin. And she felt bereft. It was over. They would have one final dance together, but it was already over. She was ending this craziness right here and right now.

"So," she said with forced cheer, holding out her

hand to shake his, "good work, Your Highness. I'll see you opening night of Blossom Week, for *An Evening to Remember*. Gosh. Only a few nights away. How did that happen?"

But instead of shaking her hand, two business people who had done good work together, the prince took her hand, held it, looked with deep and stripping thoughtfulness into her eyes. Then he bowed over her hand, and placed his lips to it.

Meredith could feel that familiar devastating quiver begin in her toes.

"No," he said, straightening and gazing at her.

"No? No *what*?"

"No, it won't be opening night before we meet again."

"It won't?" It felt just like their first meeting, when he had told her she couldn't be Meredith Whitmore. He said things with the certainty of one who had the power to change reality, who *always* had his own way.

"You've shown me your world, Meredith," Kiernan said quietly. "You gave that to me freely, expecting nothing in return. You gave me a gift. But I would like to give you something in return, a gift of my own. Come experience an evening in my world."

Her mouth opened to say *no*. It wasn't possible. She was trying to protect herself. He was storming the walls.

"It's the least I can do for you. I'll send a car to pick you up tonight. We'll have a farewell dinner on the yacht."

Farewell. Did his voice have an odd catch in it when he said that?

Say *no*. Every single thing in her that wanted to survive screamed at her to say no.

But what woman, no matter how strong, no matter how independent, no matter how much or how desperately she wanted to protect her own heart could say no to an evening with a prince, a date out of a dream?

It wasn't as if she could get her hopes up. He'd been very clear. A farewell dinner. One last time to be alone together. The next time they saw each other would be very public, for their performance.

On pure impulse, Meredith decided she would give herself this. She would not or could not walk away from the incredible gift he was offering her.

She would take it, greedily. One night. One last thing to remember him by, to hold to her when these days of dancing with him, laughing with him, baring her soul to him, were but a distant memory.

"Yes," she whispered. "That would be lovely."

It wasn't a *date*, Meredith told herself as she obsessed about what to wear and how to do her hair and her makeup and her nails. It wasn't a date. He had not called it that. A gift, he had said, and even though she knew she should have tried harder to resist the temptation, now that she hadn't, she was giving herself over to the gift wholeheartedly.

She intended to not think about a future that did not include him. She was just going to take it moment by moment, and enjoy it without contemplating what that enjoyment might cost her later.

Hadn't she done that before? Exchanged heated looks and stolen kisses with no thought of the consequences?

No, it was different this time. She was a different person than she had been back then. Wasn't she?

And so, trying to keep her doubts on the back burner, with her makeup subtle and perfect, her nails varnished with clear lacquer, dressed in a simple black cocktail dress with a matching shawl, her hair upswept, the most expensive jewelry she could afford—tiny diamonds set in white gold—twinkling at her ears, she went down her stairs, escorted by a uniformed driver, to where the limousine awaited her. She thanked God that all the years of dancing made her able to handle the incredibly high heels—and the pre-performance jitters—with seeming aplomb.

Passersby and neighbors had stopped to gawk at the black limo, and the chauffeur holding it open for her.

It was not one of the official palace vehicles with the House of Chatam emblem on the door, but still she waved like a celebrity walking the red carpet, and slid inside the door.

The luxury of it was absolutely sumptuous. She was offered a glass of champagne, which she refused. The windows of the backseat were darkly tinted, so all the people staring at her as they passed could not see her staring back at them.

The car glided through the streets of Chatam into the harbor area, and finally arrived at a private dock. The yacht, called *Royal Blue*, bobbed gently on its moorings.

A carpet had been laid out to prevent her high heels from slipping through the wide-spaced wooden planks of the dock. Light spilled out every window of the yacht, danced down the dock and splashed out over inky dark waters.

The lights illuminated interior rooms. It wasn't a boat. It was a floating palace.

And against the midnight darkness of the sky, she could see Prince Kiernan. He was outside on an upper deck, silhouetted by the lights behind him, leaning on a railing, waiting.

For her.

She wanted to run to him, as if he was not a prince at all, but her safe place in this unfamiliar world of incredible wealth.

Instead, she walked up the carpet, and up the slightly swaying gangway with all the pose and grace years of dancing had given her. She knew his eyes were only for her, and she breathed it in, intending to enjoy every second of this gift.

The crew saluted her, and her prince waited at the top of the gangway.

Prince Kieran greeted her by meeting her eyes and holding her gaze for a long time, until her heart was beating crazily in her throat. Then he took her hand, much as he had in the ballroom, bowed low over it, and kissed it.

"Welcome," he said, and his eyes swept her.

Every moment she had taken with her hair and her makeup, her jewelry and her dress was rewarded with the light in his eyes. Except that he seemed to be memorizing her. He had said *welcome*, but really, hadn't he meant goodbye?

"You are so beautiful," he said, the faintest hoarseness in that cultured voice.

"Thank you," she stammered. She could have told him he looked beautiful, too, because he did, dressed in a dark suit with a crisp white shirt under it. At the moment, Kiernan was every girl's fairy-tale prince.

"Come," he said, and he slipped his hand in hers, and led her to a deeply padded white leather bench in the bow of the boat.

As the crew called muted orders to each other the

yacht floated out of its slip and they headed out of the mouth of the harbor.

"I just have to let you know in advance, that as hard as I tried to completely clear my calendar for this evening, I'm expecting an overseas call from the Minister of Business. I'll have to take it. I hope it will be brief, but possibly not. I hope you won't be bored."

Meredith was used to these kinds of interruptions from their dance classes.

"Bored? How could I be bored when I have this to experience?" She gestured over the view of dark sea, the island growing more distant. "It looks like a place out of a dream."

The lights of Chatam, reflected in the dark water, grew further away.

"It will be breezy now that we're underway. Do you want to go in?"

She shook her head, and he opened a storage unit under a leather bench, found a light blanket and settled it on her shoulders. Then Kiernan pressed against her to lend her his warmth.

As the boat cut quietly around the crags of the island, she found she and Kiernan talked easily of small things. The girls' excitement for the upcoming performance, Erin Fisher's remarkable talent and potential, Prince Adrian's recovery from his injury, the overseas call Kiernan was expecting about a business deal that could mean good things for the future of Chatam.

After half an hour of following the rugged coastline of Chatam, the yacht pulled into a small cove, the engines were cut, and the quiet encircled them as she heard the chain for the anchor drop.

"It's called Firefly Cove," he said. "Can you see why?"

"Oh," she breathed as thousands and thousands of small lights pricked the darkness, "it is so beautiful."

The breeze picked up, and he took the blanket and offered her his hand. They went inside.

It was as beautiful as outside.

There was really nothing to indicate they were on a boat, except for the huge windows and the slight bobbing motion.

Other than that the décor was fabulous—modern furniture covered in rich linens, paintings, rugs, an incredible chandelier hung over a dining table set for two with the most exquisite china.

All of it could have made her feel totally out of place and uncomfortable. But Kiernan was with her, teasing, laughing, putting her at ease.

Dinner came out, course after course of the most incredible food, priceless wines that an ordinary girl like her would never have tasted under other circumstances.

But rather than being intimidated Meredith delighted in the new experiences, made easy because of how her prince guided her through them.

They went back out on the deck for after-dinner coffee, he draped the blanket around her shoulders again, and tucked her into him. They sat amongst the fireflies and talked. At first of light things: the exquisiteness of the food they had just eaten, the rareness of the wines, the extraordinary beauty of the fireflies; the stars that filled the night sky.

But Meredith found herself yearning for his trust, the same trust that she had shown him the day they had watched the movie.

With a certain boldness, she took his hand, and said, "Tell me how you came to earn all those horrible nicknames. Playboy Prince. Prince of Heartaches. Prince Heartbreaker. I feel as if I've come to know you, and those names seem untrue and unfair."

But was it? Wasn't he setting her up for heartbreak right now? Without even knowing it? He'd been clear. Tonight was not hello. It was goodbye.

But she wasn't allowing herself to think of that.

No, she was staying in this moment: the gentle sway of the sea beneath her, his hand in hers, his shoulder touching hers.

She was staying in this moment, and moving it toward deeper intimacy even if that was crazy. She wanted him to know, even after they'd said goodbye, that she had known his heart.

"Thank you," he said with such sincerity, as if she had *seen* him that she quivered from it, and could not resist moving a little more closely into his warmth. "Though, of those titles, the Playboy Prince was probably neither untrue nor unfair."

He recounted his eighteenth summer. "I found myself free, in between getting out of private school and going into the military. Until I was eighteen, my mother had been very vigilant in restricting the press's access to me. And women hadn't been part of my all-male world, except as something desired from a distance, movie star posters on dorm room walls. So, I wasn't quite used to the onslaught of interest on both fronts.

"And like many young men of that age, I embraced all the perks of that freedom and none of the responsibility. Unfortunately, my forum was so public. There was a frenzy, like a new rock star had been unveiled to the world. I didn't see a dark side or a downside. I was flattered by the attention of the press and the young women. I dated every beautiful woman who showed the least interest in me."

"And that was many," Meredith said dryly.

Still, she could feel the openness of him, and something sighed within her. She had trusted him, and now he was trusting her.

"That's what I mean about the Playboy Prince title having truth to it," he said ruefully. "But after that summer of my whole life becoming so public, I became more discerning, and certainly more cynical. I started to understand that very few of those young women were really interested in *me*. It was all about the title, the lifestyle, and the fairy tale. I could be with the most beautiful woman in the world and feel so abjectly lonely.

"But for a short while, I searched, almost frantically for *the* one. I'm sure I broke hearts right and left because I could tell after the first or second date that it just wasn't going to work, and I extricated myself quickly. Somehow, though, I was always the one seen as responsible for the fact others pinned their unrealistic hopes and dreams on me."

Was that what she was doing? By sitting here, enjoying his world and his company, was she investing, again, in unrealistic hopes and dreams?

Just one night. She would give herself that. It wasn't really pinning hopes and dreams on him. It was about knowing him as completely as she could before she let him go back to his world, and she went back to hers.

"I'd known Francine Lacourte since I was a child," Kiernan continued. "We'd always been close, always the best of friends."

"The duchess." She felt the faintest pang of jealousy at the way he said that name. With a tender reverence.

"She was the funniest, smartest woman I ever met.

She was also the deepest. She had a quality about her, a glow that was so attractive. She shunned publicity, which I loved."

"You were engaged to her, weren't you?"

"Ever so briefly."

"And you broke it off, bringing us to nickname number two, the Prince of Heartaches. Because she never recovered, did she?"

Which, now that she thought about it, Meredith could see was a very real danger.

But Kiernan smiled absently. "The truth that no one knows? I didn't break it off. She did."

He was telling her a truth that no one else knew? That amount of trust felt exquisite.

"But that's not what the press said! In fact, they still say she is in mourning for you. She has become very reclusive. I don't think I've seen one photograph of her in the paper since you broke with her. And that's years ago. It really is like she has disappeared off the face of the earth."

"Our friends at the press take a fact—like Francine being reclusive—and then they build a story around it that suits their purposes. It has nothing to do with the truth. For a while there was even a rumor started by one of the most bottom feeding of all the publications that I had murdered her. How ridiculous is that?"

"That's terrible!"

"I am going to tell you a truth that very few people on this earth know. I know I don't have to tell you how deeply private this conversation is."

Again, Meredith relished this trust he had in her, even as she acknowledged it moved her dangerously closer to pinning unrealistic hopes and dreams on him!

"That depth and quality and glow in Francine that I

found so attractive? She had a deep spiritual longing. Francine joined a convent. She had wanted to do so for a long, long time. She loved me, I think. But not the way she loved God."

"She's a nun?" Meredith breathed, thinking of pictures of her that had been republished after his broken engagement to Tiffany Wells. Francine Lacourte was gorgeous, the last person one would think of as a nun!

He nodded. "She chose a cloister. Can you imagine the nightmare her new life would have been if the paparazzi got hold of that? Because I have a network around me that can protect me from the worst of their viciousness, I chose to let them create the story that titillated the world."

"You protected her," Meredith whispered.

"I don't really see it like that. She gave me incredible gifts in the times we spent together. I was able to return to her the privacy she so treasured."

"By taking the heat."

"Well, as I say, I have a well-oiled machine around me that protects me from the worst of it. The press can say whatever they want. I'm quite adept at dodging the arrows, not letting them affect me at all. So, if I could do that for Francine, why wouldn't I?"

Hadn't she known this for weeks? In her heart, with her sense of *knowing* him growing? That the prince was actually the opposite of how he was portrayed by the press?

"And then you graduated to being the Prince Heartbreaker," Meredith said.

"Tiffany came along later, and I was well aware it was *time*. Very subtle pressure was being brought on me to find a suitable partner. I had been deeply hurt by Francine's choice, even as I commended her for making it. At some level I think I was looking for a woman who was the antithesis of her, which Tiffany certainly was. Bubbly. Beautiful. Light. Lively. Tiffany Wells was certain of her womanly wiles in this seductive, confident way that initially I was bowled over by."

There were few men who wouldn't be, Meredith thought, with just a touch of envy.

"I was a mature man. She was a mature woman. Eventually, we did what mature adults do," he admitted. "I'm ashamed to say for the longest time I mistook the sexual sizzle between us as love. Still, we were extremely responsible. Double protected.

"But as that sexual sizzle had cooled to an occasional hiss, I realized it was really the only thing we had in common."

"She bored you!" Meredith deduced.

He looked pained. "Her constant chatter about *nothing* made my head hurt. I was feeling increasingly disillusioned and she, unfortunately, seemed increasingly enamored.

"I told her it was over. She told me she was pregnant."

Meredith gasped, but he held her hand tighter, looked at her deeply. "No, Meredith, it is not your story. I did not abandon a pregnant woman."

CHAPTER EIGHT

PRINCE KIERNAN TOLD Meredith the rest of the story haltingly. After overcoming the initial shock of Tiffany's announcement he had weighed his options with the sense of urgency that the situation demanded.

He had done what he felt was the honorable thing, a man prepared to accept full responsibility for his moment of indiscretion.

His engagement had been announced, and they had set a date for the very near future, so that Tiffany's pregnancy would not be showing at the wedding. The press had gone into a feeding frenzy. Tiffany had appeared to adore the attention as much as he was appalled by it. She was "caught" out shopping for her gown and flowers, having bachelorette celebrations with her friends, even looking at bassinettes.

"When we were together, we could not have one moment of privacy. The cameras were always there, we were chased, questions were shouted, the press always seemed to know where we were. Now, uncharitably, I wonder if she didn't tip them off. But regardless, our lives became helicopters flying over the palace, the yacht, the polo fields, men with cameras up trees and in shrubs.

"On this point, Meredith, you were absolutely correct

in what you said to me on the day we began dance practice. Romance is glorious entertainment. It sells newspapers and magazines and it ups ratings. Interest in us, as a couple, was nothing short of insatiable."

"How horrible!" Meredith said.

"You'd think," he said dryly. "Tiffany loved every moment of it. For me, it felt as if I was riding a runaway train that I couldn't stop and couldn't get off of."

"But you did stop it. But what of the baby? In all the publicity that followed, I never once heard she was pregnant."

"Because she wasn't."

"What?"

"Before that incident it had never occurred to me that a person—particularly one who claimed to love you—could be capable of a deception of such monstrous proportions as that. Luckily for me, the truth was revealed before we were married. Unluckily, it was the night before the wedding."

He went on to say a loyal servant, assigned to Tiffany, had come in obvious distress late on the eve of the wedding to tell him something that under normal circumstances he would have found embarrassing. But the fact that *pregnant* Tiffany was having her period had saved him. Despite the lateness of the hour, he had confronted Tiffany immediately, and the wedding had been cancelled.

But now the whole world saw him as the man who had coldheartedly broken a bride's heart on the eve of all her dreams coming true. The press seemed tickled by the new role they had assigned him, Prince Heartbreaker.

Tiffany, on the other hand, seemed to be enjoying the attention as much as ever, photographed often, sunglasses in place, shoulders slumped, enthusiastically playing the part of the party who was suffering the most and who had been grievously wronged.

"Why on earth wouldn't you let the world know what and who she really is?" Meredith demanded, shocked at how protective she felt of him. "Why are you taking the brunt of the whole world's disappointment that the fairy tale has fallen apart?"

"Now you sound like Adrian." He paused before he spoke. "I saw something in Tiffany's desperate attempt to capture me that was not evil. It was very sad and very sick. I glimpsed a frightening fragility behind her mask of supreme confidence.

"How fragile only a very few people know. Tiffany had attempted suicide after I uncovered her deception."

"It sounds like more manipulation to me," Meredith said angrily.

"Regardless, I was not blameless. I gave in to temptation, let go of control when I most needed to keep it. I put Tiffany in a position where she hoped for more than what I was prepared to offer, I put myself in a position of extreme vulnerability.

"I don't think Tiffany could have handled her deception being made public, the scorn that would have been heaped on her."

"She certainly seems to handle it being heaped on you rather well. Her total lack of culpability enrages me, Kiernan."

He shrugged. "I've been putting up with the attacks of the press since I was a young man. I'm basically indifferent to what they have to say."

"You protected her, too. Even though she is not the least deserving of your protection!"

He shrugged it off. "Don't read too much into it, Meredith. I'm no hero."

"Just a prince," she said and was rewarded with his laughter.

"Just a man," he said. "Underneath it all, just a man."

But a good one, she thought. A man with a sense of decency and honor. A man who had not abandoned the woman he thought carried his child.

The man of her dreams. So, so easy to fall in love with him.

A steward came and whispered in his ear.

"I'm so sorry. That's the call I have to take."

The truth? She was glad for a moment alone to sort through the new surge of emotion she felt at his innate decency, at his deeply ingrained sense of honor.

"Don't think anything of it," she assured him. She didn't mind. She wanted to sit here and savor his trust and the world he had opened to her. But she badly needed distance, too.

The steward brought her a refill for her coffee, the day's paper, and a selection of magazines.

After staring pensively at the sea for a long time, she needed any kind of distraction to stop the whirling of her thoughts. She picked up the paper.

In the entertainment section she stopped dead.

There was a picture of society beauty Brianna Morrison under the headline Prince Heartbreaker's New Victim?

But Miss Morrison looked like anything but a victim! She was hugging a gossamer green dress to her, her choice for the Blossom Week Ball, the event that would culminate the week's celebrations.

"I couldn't believe it when I was asked," she gushed to the interviewer. "It is like a dream come true."

It seemed something went very still in Meredith. She was sharing the prince's yacht tonight. But he had been very clear. This was farewell.

The prince giving the peasant girl a final gift of himself before moving back to his real life.

But he had asked another woman to the ball.

Well, of course he had. Meredith had always known she didn't belong in this world. Brianna Morrison's family was old money, the Morrisons owned factories and businesses, real estate, and shipping yards.

And tonight he had said pressure, subtle or not, was being brought on him to find a suitable partner. Brianna was beautiful and accomplished. Her family's interests and the interests of the Chatams had been linked for centuries.

And then there was Meredith Whitmore. A dance instructor, more devoted to her charity than her business, a woman with a hard past.

No, the prince had decided to give his dance instructor a lovely night out.

A small token of appreciation. He had never claimed it was anything more than a way of saying goodbye to her and the world they had shared for a few light-filled days.

She had been crazy to encourage his confidences, some part of her hoping and praying she was in some way suitable for his world and that he would see it.

She set down the paper and called the steward. "Could we go back to Chatam, please? I'm not feeling well."

In seconds, Kiernan was at her side.

"I hope you didn't end your phone call on my behalf," she said coolly, not wanting to see the concern on his face, deliberately looking to the sea that was beginning to chop under a strengthening wind.

"Of course I did! You're not feeling well? It's probably the roughening sea, but I can have my physician waiting at the dock."

"No, it's not that serious," she said, trying not to melt at his tender concern, trying to steel herself against it. "I'm sure it is the sea. I just need to go home."

"I'll give the order to get underway immediately." He rose, scanned her face, and frowned.

Then he saw the open newspaper.

She leaned forward to close it, but he stayed her hand, bent over and scanned the headline.

"You read this?" he asked her.

She said nothing, tilted her chin proudly, refused to look at him.

"Is this why you're suddenly not feeling well? It was arranged months ago," he said quietly.

"It's none of my business. I'm well aware I don't belong in your world, Prince Kiernan. That this has been a nice little treat for a peasant you've taken a liking to."

"It is not that I don't think you belong in my world," he said with a touch of heat. "That's not it at all! And I don't think of you as a peasant."

"Of course not," she said woodenly.

"Meredith, you don't understand the repercussions of being seen publicly with me."

"I might use the wrong fork?"

"Stop it."

"I thought this was such a nice outfit. You probably noticed it was off the rack."

"I noticed no such thing. It's a gorgeous outfit. You are gorgeous."

"Apparently. Gorgeous enough to see you privately."

"Meredith, you need to understand the moment you are seen with me, publicly, your life will never be the same again. Taking you to that ball would be like throwing you into a pail of piranhas. The press would have started to rip you apart. You've told me some shattering secrets about yourself. Do you want those secrets on all the front pages providing titillation for the mob? I won't do that to you."

"Of course," she said, "You're protecting me. That's what you do."

"I am trying to protect you," he said. "A little appreciation might be in order."

"Appreciation? You deluded fool."

He looked stunned by that and that made her happy in an angry sort of way so she kept going.

"You've chosen women in the past that build you up with their weakness, who need their big strong prince to protect them, but I'm not like that."

"I've chosen weak women?" he sputtered.

"It's obvious."

"I'm sorry I ever told you a personal thing about myself."

She was sorry he had, too. Because it had made her hope for things she couldn't have. She couldn't stop herself now if she wanted to.

"I'm a girl from Wentworth. Do you think there's anything in your world that could frighten me? I've walked in places where I've had a knife hidden under my coat. I've been hungry, for God's sake. And so exhausted from working and raising a baby I couldn't even hold my feet under me. I've buried my child. And my mother. Do you think anything in your cozy, pampered little world could frighten me? The press? I could handle the press with both my hands tied behind my back.

"Don't you dare pretend that's about protecting me. Your Royal Highness, you are protecting yourself. You don't want anyone to know about tonight. Or about me. I'm the sullied girl from the wrong side of the tracks. You're right. They would dig up my whole sordid past. What an embarrassment to you! To be romantically linked to the likes of me!"

"I told you everything there is to know about me," he said quietly, "and you would reach that conclusion?"

"That's right!" she snapped, her anger making her feel so much more powerful than her despair. "It's all about you!"

She banished everything in her that was weak. There would be plenty of time for crying when she got home.

After the trust they had shared, the intimacy of their dinner, the growing friendship of the last few days, this was *exactly* what was needed.

Distance.

Anger.

Distrust.

And finally, when she got home, then there would be time for the despair that could only be brought on from believing, even briefly, in unrealistic dreams.

But when she got home, she realized she had done it on purpose, created that terrible scene on purpose, driven a wedge between them on purpose.

Because she had done the dumbest thing of her whole life, even dumber than believing Michael Morgan was a prince.

She had come to love a real prince. And she did not think she could survive another love going wrong.

And the truth? How could it possibly go right?

"What is wrong with you?" Adrian asked Kiernan the next day.

"What do you mean by that?"

"Kiernan! You're not yourself. You're impatient. You're snapping at people. You're canceling engagements."

"What engagement?"

"You were supposed to bring Brianna Morrison to the ball. The worst thing you could have done is cancelled that. One more tearstained face attached to your name. She's been getting ready for months. Prince Heartbreaker rides again."

"Is that a direct quote from the tabs?"

"No. That is so much kinder than the tabs. They're having a heyday at your expense. This morning they showed Brianna Morrison throwing her ball dress off a bridge into Chatam River."

"Make sure she's charged with littering a public waterway."

"Kiernan! That's cold! You are just about the most hated man on the planet right now."

Yes. And by the only one that mattered, too.

Adrian was watching him closely. "And there's that look again."

"What look?"

"I don't know. Moody. *Desperate.*"

"Adrian, just leave it alone," he said wearily.

"If something is wrong, I want to help."

"You can't. Not unless you can learn to dance in—" he glanced at his watch "—about four hours."

Adrian's eyes widened. "I should have known."

"What?" Kiernan said. What had he inadvertently revealed?

"Dragon-heart. She's at the bottom of this."

Kiernan stepped in very close to his young cousin. "Don't you ever call her that again within my hearing. Do you understand me?"

"She did something to make you so mad," Adrian said. "I know it."

"No, she didn't," Kiernan said. "I did. I did something that made me so mad. I gave my trust to the wrong person."

Adrian was watching him, his brow drawn down in puzzlement. "I'll be damned," he said. "You aren't angry. You're in love."

Kiernan thought it would be an excellent time for a vehement denial. But when he opened his mouth, the denial didn't come out.

"With Dra— Meredith?"

"It doesn't matter. It's going nowhere. After I revealed my deepest truths to her do you know what she did? She called me a deluded fool!"

Adrian actually smiled.

"It's not funny."

"No, it's a cause for celebration. Finally, someone who will take you to task when you need it."

"Don't side with her. You don't even like her."

"Actually, I always did like her. Immensely. She wouldn't settle for anything less than my best. She was strong and sure of herself and intimidating as hell, but I liked her a great deal."

"Do you know what she said to me? She said I deliberately chose weak women. What do you think about that?"

"That she's unusually astute. Finally, someone who will tell you exactly what they think instead of filtering it through what they think you want to hear."

"You never told me you thought my women were weak," Kiernan said accusingly.

"Because they were heart-stoppingly beautiful. I thought that probably made up for it. I always knew you never dated anyone who would require you to be more than you were before. I thought it was your choice. That you had decided love would take a minor role in your life. Behind your duties."

"I think I had thought that. Until I fell in love. It doesn't accept minor roles."

"So, you do love her!" Adrian crowed.

"It doesn't matter. I had her to the yacht for dinner last night, and she opened the paper and saw I was escorting Brianna to the ball. She left in a temper."

"Uh, real world to Kiernan: any woman who is having dinner with a man will be upset to find he has plans with another woman for later in the week."

"I told her it had been planned for months."

"Instead of *I'll cancel immediately*?" Adrian shook his head and tut-tutted.

"I told her it was for her own good. She has some things in her past I don't want the press to get their hands on. I was protecting her!"

"I bet she loved that one."

"It's true!"

"She isn't the kind who would take kindly to you micromanaging her world."

"She's not. She doesn't trust me. I showed her everything I was, and she rejected it. She believed the worst of me, just like everyone else is so quick to do."

"Kiernan, you are making excuses."

"Why would I do that?"

"You are terrified of what that woman would require of you."

"I'm not."

"Don't you get it? This is your chance. You might only get one. Take it. Be happy. Do something for yourself for once. Go sweep old Dragon-heart right off her feet."

"Don't call her that."

"I can't believe I missed it!" His cousin became uncharacteristically serious. "She's worthy of you, Kiernan. She's strong. And spunky. She's probably the best thing that ever happened to you. Don't let it slip away."

And suddenly Kiernan thought of how awful she had looked when she had left the yacht. She was afraid. He'd taken that personally, as if it was about him. But of course she was afraid! She had lost everything to love once before. She was terrified to believe in him, to trust.

And Adrian was right. He was *not* doing the right thing. Sulking because she didn't trust him, not seeing what lay beneath that lack of trust. Why should she trust the world? Or him? Had the world brought her good things? No, it had taken them. Had love brought her good things? No, it had shattered her.

Instead of seeing that, he had insisted on making it about him.

He was going to have to be a better man than that to be worthy of her. He was going to have to go get her from that lonely world she had fled to in her fear and distrust.

Kiernan of Chatam was going to have to learn what it really meant to be a woman's prince.

Something sighed within him.

He was ready for the challenge. He was about to go
rescue the maiden from the dragon of fear and loneliness
she had allowed to take up residence in her heart.

"I don't know what to do," he admitted.

Adrian smiled. "Sure, you do. You have to woo the
girl. Just the same as any old Joe out there on the street.
She isn't going to just fall at your feet because you're a
prince, you know. For God's sake, she runs an organization called No Princes. Playing hard to get is going to
be a point of pride with her.

"And don't look so solemn. For once in your life,
Kiernan, have some fun."

The show must go on, Meredith thought as she found
herself, in a white smock in a crowded dressing room,
waiting, her heart nearly pounding out of her chest. She
had never been this nervous about a performance.

"Miss Whit," one of the girls said excitedly. "He's
here. He's come. Ohmygod, he's the most glorious man
I ever laid me eyes on."

"*My* eyes," Meredith corrected woodenly.

"The music's starting," Erin whispered. "Oh, I can't
believe this is happening to me. My production is becoming a reality. I just looked out the curtain. Miss
Whit, it's standing room only out there."

For them. She had to pull this off for them, her girls,
all that she had left in her world.

"I'm on," Erin said. "I'm so scared."

Meredith shook herself out of her own fear, and went
and gave her protégée a hard hug.

"Dazzle them!" she said firmly.

And then she stood in the wings. And despite her
gloom, her heart began to swell with pride as she saw
Erin's vision come to life. The girls in the opening

number carried the buckets of cleaning ladies, or wore waitresses' uniforms. Some of them carried school bags. All had on too much makeup. They were hanging around a street lamp, targets for trouble.

And here came trouble. Boys in carpenter's aprons, and baker's hats, leather jackets with cigarettes dangling from their lips.

The girls and the guys were dancing together, shy, flirtatious, bold, by turns.

And then Erin, who had been given the starring role, was front and center in her white smock that said Molly over the pocket, and she was staring worshipfully at a boy in a white jacket that said Andy on the pocket.

The lights went off them, and the empty spot on the stage filled with mist.

It was time for the dream sequence.

The three-step bridal waltz began to play, and feeling as if she was made of wood, Meredith came on stage.

Kiernan was coming toward her.

How unfair that while she suffered, he looked better than ever! No doubt to make his costume more realistic, he had a few days growth of unshaven beard.

Meredith went to him, felt her hand settle into his, his hand on her waist.

Her eyes closed against the pain of it.

Last time.

Even as she thought it, she could hear a whisper ripple through the crowd. It became a rumble as the spotlight fell on them, and recognition of Kiernan grew.

"You look awful," he said in her ear.

"I've been working very hard with the girls," she whispered back haughtily. She stumbled slightly. He covered for her.

"Liar. Pining for me."

She tried to hide her shock. "Why would a girl like me pine for you?" she snapped at him. "We both know it's impossible."

He was looking at her way too hard.

"You're afraid," he said in an undertone. "It was never really horses you were afraid of. It was this."

The crowd was going crazy. Not only had they recognized their prince, but he was doing something completely unexpected. Kiernan and Meredith picked up the pace, and he found his feet. She tried not to look at the expression on his face.

"Don't be silly," she told him in an undertone. "I told you nothing about your world frightens me."

"You're afraid of loving me. You have been from the moment we met."

"Arrogant ass," she hissed.

"Stubborn lass," he shot back.

She could feel the fire between them coming out in the way they were dancing. It was unrehearsed, but the audience was reacting to the pure sizzling chemistry.

She couldn't look away from him. His look had become so fierce. So tender. So protective. So filled with longing.

He knew the truth, anyway, why try to hide it? Why not let it come out in this dance?

It occurred to her that even if he couldn't have her, even if she would never be suitable for his world, that he wanted her, and that he wished things were not the way they were.

One last time, she would give herself this gift.

She would be Molly and he would be Andy, just two crazy ordinary kids in love. Everything changed the moment she made that decision. She would say to him with this dance what she intended to never admit to him in person.

She found her feet. She found his rhythm.

And they danced. She let go of all her armor. She let go of all her past hurt. She let go of all her fear. She let go of that little worm of self-doubt that she was not good enough.

Meredith danced as she had never danced, every single secret thing she had ever felt right out there in the open for all the world to see.

At some point, she was not Molly. Not at all. She was completely herself, Meredith Whitmore.

For this one priceless moment, she didn't care who saw her truth. Though thousands watched, they were alone, dancing for each other.

And then he let her go, and the crowd became frenzied as he moved into his solo piece.

He tore off the white smock.

And suddenly she saw his truth. It was not dancing as Andy that allowed him to dance like this.

It was dancing as Kiernan.

Everything he truly was came out now: sensual, strong, commanding, tender. Everything.

By the time he came across the floor to her that one last time, the tears were streaming down her face for the gift he had given her.

He had given her his everything.

He had put every single thing he was into that dance. Not for the audience who was going wild with delight.

Not for the girls who cheered and screamed from the wings.

For her. He stared down at her.

It was not in any way a scripted part of the performance. He took her lips with exquisite tenderness.

She tasted him, savored, tried to memorize it.

With the cheering in the building so loud it sounded as if the rafters would collapse on them, she pulled away from the heaven of his lips, touched his cheek. Though the whole world watched it felt, still, as if they were alone.

Goodbye.

"Thank you," she whispered through her tears. "Thank you, Kiernan." And then she turned and fled.

CHAPTER NINE

IT WAS THE DAY AFTER *An Evening to Remember*. Meredith's phone had been ringing off the hook, but she wouldn't answer.

Still, people left messages. They wanted lessons from her dance school. They wanted to donate money to No Princes.

Erin Fisher's excited voice told her she had been offered a full scholarship to Chatam University.

The press wanted to know what it felt like to dance with a prince. They wanted to know if she had been the one to teach the prince with two left feet to dance like that. They especially wanted to know if there was *something* going on, or if it had all been a performance.

After several hours of the phone ringing she went and pulled the connection out of the wall.

She didn't want to talk to anybody.

Maybe not for a long, long time.

Just as she had suspected, the video had been posted online within seconds of the performance finishing.

The website had collapsed this morning, for the first time in its history, from too many hits on that video.

"Most of those hits from me," Meredith admitted ruefully. She had watched their dance together at least a dozen times before the site had crashed.

Seeing something in it, basking in it.

Was love too strong a word?

Probably. She used it anyway.

There was a knock on her door. She hoped the press had not discovered where she lived. She tried to ignore it, but it came again, more insistent than the last time. She pulled a pillow over her head. More rapping.

"Meredith, open the damn door before I kick it down!"

She pulled the pillow away from her face, sat up, stunned, hugging it to her.

"I mean it. I'm counting to three."

She went and peered out her security peephole.

"One."

Prince Kiernan of Chatam was out on her stoop, in an Andy jacket and dark glasses.

"Two."

She threw open the door, and then didn't know what to do. Throw herself at him? Play it cool? Weep? Laugh?

"Lo, Molly," he said casually.

Don't melt.

"Just wondered if you might like to come down to the pub with me. We'll have a pint and throw some darts."

"Once you lose the sunglasses everyone will know who you are." Plus, they'd probably all seen the Andy getup on the video. He'd be swamped.

"Let's live dangerously. I'll leave the glasses on. You can tell people I have a black eye from fighting for your honor."

"Kiernan—"

"Andy," he told her sternly.

"Okay, Andy." She folded her arms protectively over her chest. "Why are you doing this?"

He hesitated a heartbeat, lifted the glasses so she could look into his eyes. "I want us to get to know each other. Like this. As Andy and Molly. Without the pressure of the press following us and speculating. I want us to build a solid foundation before I introduce you to the world. I want you to know I have your back when they start coming at you."

"You're going to introduce me to the world?" she whispered. "You're going to have my back?"

"Meredith, I miss you. Not seeing you was like living in a world without the sun. It was dark and it was cold."

She could feel the utter truth of it to her toenails.

"I miss the freedom I felt with you," he went on quietly. "I miss the sense of being myself in a way I never was before. I miss being spontaneous. I miss having fun. Will you come out and play with me? Please?"

She nodded, not trusting herself to speak.

"Come on, then. Your chariot awaits."

She could not resist him. She had never been able to resist him.

"I'm in my pajamas."

"So you are. Ghastly things, too. I picture you in white lace."

She gulped from the heat in his eyes.

"Go change," he said, and there was no missing the fact she had just been issued a royal order.

"Royal pain in the butt," she muttered, but she stood back from the door, and let him in.

Surely once he saw how ordinary people lived—tiny quarters, hotplate, faded furniture—he would realize he was in the wrong world and turn tail and run.

But he didn't. True to Andy he went and flung himself on her worse-for-wear couch, picked up a book she hadn't looked at for weeks and raised wicked eyebrows at her.

"Did you dream of me when you read this?" he asked.

"No!" She went and slammed her bedroom door, made herself put on the outfit—faded jeans, a prim blouse—that was the least like the one she had worn the other night on the yacht. It was the casual outfit of an ordinary girl.

But when she reemerged from the bedroom, the look in his eyes made her feel like a queen.

Feeling as if she was in a dream, Meredith followed him down the steep stairs that led from her apartment to the alley. Leaning at the bottom of the stairs was the most horrible-looking bike she had ever seen.

Kiernan straddled it, lowered his sunglasses, patted the handlebars. "Get on."

"Are you kidding? You'll kill us both."

"Ah, but what a way to go."

"There is that," she said, with a sigh. She settled herself on the handlebars.

His bike riding was terrible. She suspected he could barely ride a bike solo, let alone riding double. He got off to a shaky start, nearly crashing three times before they got out of her laneway.

Once he got into the main street he was even more hazardous, weaving in and out of traffic, wobbling in front of a double-decker bus.

"Give 'em the bird, love," he called when someone honked angrily when he wobbled out in front of them.

She giggled and did just that.

At the pub, true to his word, he left the glasses on.

She thought people might recognize him, but perhaps because of the plain lucridness of the whole thought that a prince would be in the neighborhood pub, no one did.

They ordered fish and chips, had a pint of tap beer, they threw darts. Then they got back on the bike and he took the long way home, pedaling along the river. She wasn't sure if her heart was beating that fast because of all the times he nearly dumped them both in the inky water of the Chatam Channel, or because she was so exhilarated by this experience.

"Where is this going?" Meredith asked sternly when he dropped her at her doorstep with a light kiss on the nose.

"My whole life," he said solemnly, "I've known where everything was going. I've always had an agenda, a protocol, a map, a plan. The very first time I saw you dance, I knew you had something I needed.

"I didn't know what it was, but whatever it was, it was what made me say yes to learning the number for *An Evening to Remember.*"

"And do you know what it was now?" she asked, curious, intrigued despite herself.

"Passion," he said. "My whole life has been about order and control. And when I saw you dance that day I caught a glimpse of what I had missed. The thing is, I felt bereft that I had missed it.

"Meredith, you take me to places I have never been before. And I don't mean a hot spring or a pub. Places inside myself that I have never been before. Now that I've been there, I can't live with the thought of not going there anymore."

He kissed her on the nose again. "I'll see you tomorrow."

"Look," she said, trying to gain some control back, "I just can't put my whole life on hold because you want me to take you places!"

He laughed, and leaned close to her. "But I've been saving my money so I can get us a Triple Widgie Hot Fudge Sundae from Lawrence's. To share."

"That's incredibly hard to resist," she admitted.

"The sundae or me?"

"The sharing."

"Ah." He looked at her long and hard. "Embrace it, Molly. Just embrace it."

"All right." She surrendered.

And that's what she did. She put her whole life on hold.

But not really.

She just embraced a different life.

Carefree and full of adventure.

Over the next few weeks, as Andy and Molly, they biked every inch of that island. They discovered hidden beaches. They ate ice cream at roadside stands. They laughed until their sides hurt. They went to movies. They roller-skated.

And just when she was getting used to it all, that familiar knock came on the door, but it was not Andy who stood there. Not this time.

This time it was Prince Kiernan of Chatam, in dark suit trousers and a jacket, a crisp white shirt, a dark silk tie.

He bowed low over her hand, kissed it.

"Aren't we going bike riding?" she asked.

"I love your world, Meredith, but now it's time for you to come into mine."

"I—I— I'll have to change," she said, casting a

disparaging look down at her faded T-shirt, her pedal pushers, and old sneakers.

"Only your clothes," he said quietly. "Nothing else. Don't change one other thing about you. Promise me."

"I promise," she said, and scooted back into her bedroom to find something suitable to wear for an outing with a prince. A few minutes later, in a pencil skirt of white linen and a blue silk top, she joined him.

"Are you ready for this?" he asked, holding out his hand to her.

"Ready for what, exactly?" She took his hand, gazed up at him, still unable to quite grasp that a prince was wooing an ordinary girl like her.

"My mother wants to meet you."

"She does?" Meredith gulped. "Why?"

"Because I told her I've met the woman I intend to spend the rest of my life with."

Meredith took a step back from him, not sure she had heard him correctly, her heart beating an ecstatic tattoo within her chest. "But you haven't told me that yet!"

He cocked his head at her, and grinned. "I guess I just did."

She flew into his arms, and it felt like going home. It felt exactly the way she had wanted to feel her whole life.

"You know how I feel right now?" she whispered into his chest. "I feel safe. And protected. I feel cared about. I feel cherished."

"You make me feel those things, too," he whispered back.

"And I feel absolutely terrified. Your mother? That makes everything seem rather official."

"You see, that's the thing. After you've met my

mother, it's going to be official. You're going to be my girl. And then my fiancée. And then my wife."

"Huh. Is that your excuse for a proposal?"

He laughed. "No. Just forewarning you of what's to come." And then he frowned. "If you can handle the pressure. You won't believe the pressure, Meredith. I'm afraid your life will never be the same. Be sure you know what you want before you walk out that door with me."

But she had been sure a long time ago. She knew exactly what she wanted. She placed her hand back in his, and felt her whole world was complete.

Someone with a camera had already discovered the limousine parked at her curb, because this time the royal emblem shone gold on the door. The camera was raised and their picture was taken getting into the car together.

He sighed.

But she squeezed his hand and laughed.

"I may be terrified of your mother," she said, as he settled in the deep leather of the seat beside her, "but I'm not afraid of anything else about being with you. Nothing." She laid her head on his shoulder and soaked in the strength and solidity of him, soaked in how very right it felt to be at his side.

For a moment there was the most comfortable of silences between them.

"Did you hear that?" he asked, as the car pulled away.

"I'm sorry, did I hear what?"

He looked out the window, twisted over his shoulder to look behind them, settled back with a puzzled look on his face.

"Meredith, I could have sworn I heard a baby laugh."

She smiled, and the feeling of everything in the world being absolutely right deepened around her.

"No," she said softly, "I didn't hear it. But I felt it. I felt it all the way to my soul."

Kiernan raised his hand to knock on the door of his mother's quarters. He'd been annoyed that upon delivering Meredith his mother had dismissed him with an instruction to come back in an hour. She had drawn Meredith in and closed the door firmly behind them.

He knew his mother! The inquisition had probably started. Especially after Tiffany, whom his mother had not liked from the beginning, Queen Aleda would feel justified in asking aggressive questions, making quick judgments. Meredith was probably backed into a corner, quivering and in tears.

But as he stood at the door, he was astounded to hear laughter coming through the closed door. He knocked and opened it.

Both women looked up. Meredith was seated, his mother looking over her shoulder. He saw he had underestimated Meredith again. He was going to have to stop doing that.

He noticed his mother had one hand resting companionably on Meredith's shoulder. His mother did not touch people!

Both women were focused on something on the table, and he recognized what it was.

"Photo albums?" he sputtered. "You've just met!"

"Never too soon to look at pictures of you as a baby," Meredith said. "That one of you in the tub? Adorable."

"The tub picture?" He glared at his mother, outraged.

"What could I do?" Queen Aleda said with a smile. "Meredith asked me what my greatest treasure was."

And then the two women exchanged a glance, and he was silent, in awe of the fact their mutual love of him could make such a strong and instant bond between these two amazing women.

In the days and weeks that followed, Kiernan's amazement at Meredith grew and grew and grew.

The day after their first official public outing, when he had taken her to watch a royal horse run in the Chatam Cup, speculation began to run high. Some version of the picture of Meredith leaning over the royal box to kiss the nose of the horse had made every front page of every major paper around the world.

His press corps was instantly swamped with enquiries. When had he begun dating his dance instructor? Who was she? And especially, what was her background?

"This is the beginning," he'd told her. "How do you want to handle it?" Meredith called her own press conference.

Yes, she was dating the prince. Yes, they had met while she taught him the dance number for *An Evening to Remember*. No, she was not worried about his history, because she had a history of her own.

And in a strong, steady voice, without any apology Meredith had laid herself bare. All of it. Wentworth. The too-young pregnancy. Her abandonment by the father of her child. The baby. The lost dance dreams. The grinding poverty. The tragedy that took her mother and her child. The insurance money that had allowed her to start No Princes.

She had left the press without a single thing to dig

for. And instead of devouring her, the press had *adored* her honesty, and the fact she was just one of the people. Unlike so many celebrities that the press waited breathlessly to turn on, their love affair with Meredith was like his own.

And like that of all the people of Chatam.

The more they knew her, the more they loved her.

And she loved them right back. She became the star of every event they attended, the new and quickly beloved celebrity. From film festivals at Cannes to her first ski trip to catch the last spring snow in Colorado, she bewitched everyone who met her.

She was astonishingly at home, no matter where he took her.

But the part he loved the most was that none of it went to her head. She was still the girl he had first met. Maybe even more that girl as she came into herself, as love gave her a confidence and a glow that never turned off.

Meredith could be on the red carpet at a film premiere one day, and the next day she was just as at home on her bicycle, visiting a Chatam farmer's market. She delighted in surprising brides and grooms in Chatam on their wedding days by dropping by the reception to offer her good wishes.

When he begged her to allow him to offer her security, she just laughed at him. "I've already been through the worst life can give out, Kiernan. I'm not afraid."

And she really wasn't. Meredith was born to love. It seemed her capacity to give and receive love was endless.

And since he was the major benefactor of all that love, who was he to stop her?

Besides, he knew something he had not known a few

months ago, and probably would not have believed if someone had tried to tell him.

There were angels. And Meredith had two who protected and guided her. What other explanation for the series of coincidences that had brought them together? How had she landed right on his doorstep? How had Adrian come to be injured so that the right prince could meet her? How was it that Kiernan had gone against his own nature, and agreed to learn to dance? How was it he had seen something in her from the very beginning, that he could not resist?

From that first moment, watching her dance, Kiernan had known she held a secret that could change his life. Known it with his heart and not his head.

And only angels could have made him listen to his heart instead of his head.

But angels aside, there was no ignoring the very human side of what was happening to them.

He *wanted* her. He wanted her in every way that a man could want a woman. Their kisses were becoming more fevered. The times when they were alone were becoming a kind of torture of *wanting*.

The thing was, he would never take her without honor.

Never. What that other man had done to her was unconscionable. He would never be like him, never, ever remind Meredith of him. He would not use her obvious passion for him, or her willingness to have his way with her. He always backed away at the last possible moment.

There were honorable steps a man had to take to be with his woman. He had to earn his way there. It did not matter that it was his intention to marry her, and it was, even though he knew they had only known each other a short while, only months.

But he knew his own heart, too.

And he knew it was time.

CHAPTER TEN

MEREDITH WOKE UP to a sound at her window. Something was hitting against it. She groaned and pulled the pillow over her head.

Kiernan was probably right. She was going to have to move to a building with security. That was probably some fledgling reporter out there hoping to get the shot that would make his career.

Despite her attempts to ignore it, the sound came again, louder. A scattering of pebbles across her pane.

And then louder yet!

She got up, annoyed. They were going to break the window! But when she shoved it up, and leaned out, ready to give someone a piece of her mind, it was Kiernan who stood below her.

"What are you doing?" Her annoyance now was completely faked. Sometimes she could still not believe this man, a prince outside, and a prince inside, too, was looking at her like that. With such open adoration in his eyes.

Of course the feeling was completely mutual!

"I have a surprise for you."

"What time is it?" she asked with completely faked grumpiness.

"Going on midnight."

"Kiernan, go home and go to bed."

"Quit pretending you can resist me. Get dressed and come down here."

She stuck out her tongue at him and slammed the window shut, but she quickly changed out of her pajamas, yanking on an old dance sweatsuit.

"I see you are working hard at impressing me," he said, kissing her on the nose as she reached the bottom of her stairs.

"As you are me," she teased back. "Waking me at midnight. I have work tomorrow. We don't all have lives of leisure."

This was said completely jokingly. She seemed, more than anyone else, to respect how hard he worked, and how many different directions he was pulled in a day. He was still savoring the newness of having someone at his side who was willing to back him up, to do whatever she needed to do to ease his burdens, to make his life simpler.

He held open the door of an unmarked car for her. Tonight as no other he did not want the press trailing them.

She snuggled under his arm. "What are you up to?"

But he wouldn't tell her.

They sailed through the roadblock he'd had put up to close the popular road, just for this one night. Meredith peeked out the car window with curiosity, and then recognition. "Are we going where I think we are going?"

The car stopped at the pull-out for Chatam Hot Springs. He held out his hand to her and drew her out of the car, led her up the path, lit by torches tonight, that led the way to the springs.

When they got there, he savored the look on her face. No detail had been overlooked.

There were torches flaming around the pool, but the bubbling waters of the springs were mostly illuminated by thousands upon thousands of candles that glowed from every rock and every surface.

"I didn't bring a suit," she whispered, looking around with that look he had come to live for.

A kind of *pinch me I must be dreaming* look.

"There's a change tent for you over there," he said. "You'll find a number of bathing suits to choose from."

She emerged from the tent a few minutes later, and he, already changed, was waiting on the edge of a rock with his feet dangling in the water. He smiled at her choice. Though there was staff here, they were invisible at the moment.

"The black one," he said with a shake of his head. "I was hoping for something skimpier. The red one, with the polka dots."

"How did you know about the red one with the polka dots?" she demanded.

"Because I picked each one myself, Meredith."

"That must have been very embarrassing for you," she said. "Careful, the press will dub you the pervert prince."

He leered at her playfully. "And let's hope it's deserved."

This is how it was with them. Endlessly playful. Teasing. Comfortable. Fun. And yet the respect between them also grew.

As did the heat.

As she crossed the slippery rock to him he could easily see that the black tank-style suit was so much more sexy than the polka dot bikini! Instead of sitting demurely beside him, Meredith pretended to touch his shoulders lovingly and then shoved with all her might.

And then turned and ran.

He caught up with her at the mud pool.

And they played in the mud, and swam and played some more until they were both exhausted with joy.

And then he sent her back to the change tent.

Where he knew all the rejected bathing suits had been whisked away, and in their place were designer gowns like the ones she had refused to let him buy for her for all the public outings they had attended.

While she changed, a table was set up for them and waiters appeared, along with a chef fussing about the primitive conditions he'd had to prepare his food in.

When she'd emerged from the change tent this time, Kiernan's mouth fell open. Meredith had stunned him with her beauty even in the off-the-rack dresses she insisted on wearing.

But now she had chosen the most racy of the gowns that he had picked out for her. It was red and low-cut.

She had even put on some of the jewelry he had put out for her, and a diamond necklace blazed at her neck and diamond droplets fell from her ears.

"I am looking at a princess," he said, bowing low over her hand and kissing it.

"I've told you *no* to this extravagance, Kiernan."

And yet, despite her protest, he could not help but notice that she was glowing with a certain feminine delight. She knew she looked incredible.

He led her to the table, laid out with fine linen and the best of china, and the waiters served a sumptuous feast.

She knew most of the palace staff by name, and addressed each of them.

When they had finished eating, she smiled at him. "Okay. I give it to you, you can't ever top this."

"But I will."

"You can't."

He called one of the waiters and a cooler was brought to their table. Inside it was one Triple Widgie Hot Fudge Sundae and two spoons.

In that perfect environment, their worlds combined effortlessly.

"I love it all," she said. "But you shouldn't have bought all the dresses, Kiernan. I can't accept them, and you probably can't return them."

"I'm afraid as my wife you'll be expected to keep a certain standard," he said. "And as your husband I will be proud to provide it for you."

He dropped down on his knee in front of her, slid a box from his pocket and opened it.

Inside was a diamond of elegant simplicity. He knew her. He knew she would never want the flashy ring, the large karat, the showpiece.

And he knew her answer.

He saw it in her eyes, in the tears that streamed down her face, in the smile that would not stop, despite the tears.

"Will you marry me?" he asked. "Will you make my world complete, Meredith?"

"Yes," she whispered. "Of course yes, a thousand times yes."

He rose to his feet, gathered her in his arms and held her. And his world finally was complete.

* * *

Meredith stared at herself in the mirror. She was in her slip at the dressing table, the bridal gown hung behind her. For a moment her eyes caught on it, and she felt a delicious quiver of disbelief.

Could this really be her life? A wedding gown out of a dream, yards and yards of ivory silk and seed pearls. Could this really be her life? Crowds had begun to form early this morning, lining the streets of Chatam from downtown all the way to Chatam Cathedral.

"You look so beautiful," Erin murmured.

Meredith gazed at the girl behind her.

Despite the pressure to have a huge wedding party, Meredith had chosen to have one attendant, Erin Fisher.

"So do you," she said.

"It's your day," Erin said, nonetheless pleased, "just focus on yourself for once, Miss Whit."

"All right."

"Now don't you look beautiful?"

She *did* look beautiful. More beautiful than she could have ever imagined she was going to look.

And it wasn't just the wedding gown, the hair, the makeup.

No, a radiance was pouring out of her, too big to contain within her skin.

"Are you crying?" Erin asked in horror. "Don't! We just did the makeup."

Meredith had been offered a room at the palace to get ready, and ladies in waiting to help her. She had said no to both. She wanted to be in this little apartment over her studio one last time. She wanted *her* girls to be around her.

Erin handed her a tissue and scolded. "I hope those are happy tears."

Meredith thought about it for a moment. "Not really, no."

"You are about to marry the most glorious man who ever walked and those aren't happy tears? Honestly, Miss Whit, I'm going to pinch you!"

"Don't pinch me. I might wake up."

"Tell me why they aren't happy tears."

"I was crying for the girl I used to be, the one who expected so little of life, who had such small dreams for herself. I was thinking of the girl who stood on those city hall steps, in a cheap dress, holding a tiny posy of flowers. I was thinking of the girl who felt so broken, as if it was her fault, some defect in her that caused him not to come, not to want to share the dream with her.

"If she could have seen the future she would have been dancing on those steps instead of crying. The truth? A different life awaited her. One that was beyond the smallness of her dreams."

"My dreams were so small, too," Erin whispered. "What would have become of me, if all that stuff hadn't happened to you? There would have been no Fairytale Ending group for me."

By vote, just last week, the girls, with Meredith's blessing, had changed the name of No Princes.

Because sometimes there just were princes.

And because, even when there weren't, everyone could make their own fairy-tale ending, no matter what.

"I think the universe has dreams for all of us that are bigger than what we would ever dare dream for ourselves," Meredith said quietly. "I even have to trust that losing my baby was part of a bigger plan that I will never totally understand. Maybe it made me stronger, deeper, more able to love. Worthy of that incredible man who loves me."

"Okay, stop!" Erin insisted, dabbing at her eyes. "My makeup is already done, too. Promise me, Miss Whit, that this day will be just about you and him. Not one more unhappy thought."

"All right," Meredith agreed, more to mollify the girl than anything else.

"We can't be walking down the cathedral aisle looking like a pair of raccoons," Erin said.

"Maybe you should have invested in waterproof makeup," a voice behind them said.

Erin whirled. "Prince Kiernan! Get out!" She tried to shield Meredith with her body. "You can't see her right now. It's bad luck."

"Luckily, I'm not superstitious. Could you give us a moment?"

For all the confidence she was developing, Erin wasn't about to make a stand with the prince of her country. She whirled and left the room.

Kiernan came up behind Meredith, rested his hand on her nearly naked shoulder. "This is pretty," he said touching her hair.

See? That was the problem with the promise she had made to Erin. This day could not be exclusively about the two of them.

"I thought it might be a little, er, too much," Meredith said, "but Denise is in hairdressing school. It was her gift to me. How can you refuse something like that?"

"You can't," he agreed. "Besides, it truly is beautiful."

"You really shouldn't be here," she chided him gently,

but the fact that he was here was so much better than a pinch.

This man was her life, her reason, her love, her reality.

"I had to see you," he said softly, "I have a gift for you and suddenly I realized that you needed to have it now, that I wanted you to have it close to your heart today."

All the gifts he had brought her over the course of their courtship could fill a small cottage. After they had become engaged, Meredith had quit asking him to stop. It filled him with such transparent joy to give her, a girl who had spent so much of her life with nothing, lovely things. She had learned to accept each gift graciously, because by doing so, she would receive the *real* gift.

His smile. A moment together in a busy, busy world. His touch on her arm. His eyes looking into her eyes with such wonder.

Now, Kiernan produced a small silver necklace, a cameo.

He pressed it into her hand, and she hesitated. When she touched a concealed button on the bottom of the locket it sprang open, revealing two tiny photos.

One was a picture of Carly, her head thrown back in laughter. And the other was a picture of her mother, looking young and strangely joyous.

"Where did you get this? My mother hated having her picture taken. And she so rarely looked like this, Kiernan. She looks so happy here."

"Ah, princedom has its privileges. I had the whole island scoured until I found just the right photos of both of them. Do you know when that was taken, Meredith? The picture of your mother?"

"No."

He named the date.

The tears spilled. The picture had been taken on the day of Meredith's birth.

"I wanted them to be with us," he said gently, "as close to your heart as I could get them."

"There goes the makeup," she accused him, and there went her idea that the day belonged to him and her, exclusively. What a selfish thought to entertain! This day belonged to Carly and her mother, too.

"You look better without it. The makeup."

"I know, but Rachel is in cosmetology."

"Let me guess. A gift?"

"Yes."

"And by accepting it, you *give* the gift just like the day you agreed to marry me."

The door to the room whispered open again.

"Kiernan! Out!"

There was no question of talking his way out of it this time, because it was his mother who had entered the room.

"Queen Aleda," Meredith said, truly surprised. "What are you doing here?" She had never been embarrassed about her tiny apartment, but she had certainly never expected to entertain a queen here, either.

"There are days when a girl needs her mother," the queen said. "Since your own cannot be here, I was hoping you would do me the grave honor of allowing me to take her place."

"Oh, Aleda," Meredith whispered. Of all the surprises of becoming Kiernan's love, wasn't his mother one of the best of them?

She was seen as reserved and cool, much as her son was. The truth about these two people? They guarded what was theirs, and chose very carefully who to give it to. And when they did give it?

It was with their entire hearts and whole souls.

Kiernan kissed her on her cheek, and bussed his mother, too, before quickly taking his leave. He left whistling *Get Me to the Church on Time*.

Queen Aleda quickly did what she did best—she took charge.

And Meredith realized, warmly, that this day belonged to Queen Aleda, too.

"None of that," Meredith was chastened for the new tears, "It will spoil your makeup."

Queen Aleda gathered the dress, hugged it to her briefly, looked at her soon-to-be daughter-in-law tenderly.

"Come," she said, "I'll help you get into it. The carriage will be here shortly."

Meredith was delivered to the cathedral in a white carriage, drawn by six white horses.

The people of Chatam, who seemed to have embraced her *more* for her past than less, lined the cobblestone streets, and threw rose petals in front of the carriage. The petals floated through the air and were stirred up by the horses' feet. It was as if it was snowing rose petals.

So, this day also belonged to them, to those people who had patiently lined the street for hours, waiting for this moment, a glimpse of the woman they considered to be *their* princess. They called her the people's favorite princess, and every day she tried to live up to what they needed from her. It had been a thought of pure selfishness to think this day was only about her and Kiernan.

The cathedral was packed. A choir sang.

And he waited.

At the end of that long, stone aisle, Kiernan waited

for her, strong, sure, ready. Her prince in a world she had once believed did not have princes, her very own fairy-tale ending.

Meredith moved toward him with the certainty, with the inevitability of a wave moving to shore.

And realized this day, and her whole life to follow, didn't really belong to her. And not to him, either.

It belonged to the force that had served them so well, the force that they would now use the days of their life serving.

It belonged to Love.

EPILOGUE

HE WENT HERE SOMETIMES, by himself, usually when he had a special occasion to celebrate. A birthday. An anniversary. They were part of it, and he could not leave them out.

It was not the nicest of graveyards, just row after row of simple crosses, no shrubs, or green spaces, no elaborate headstones, few flower arrangements.

The world would have been shocked, probably, to see Prince Kiernan of Chatam in this place, a grim, gray yard in the middle of Wentworth.

But he was always extra careful that he was not followed here, that no one hid with their cameras to capture this most private image of him.

It had become a most special place to him. He always brought flowers, two bouquets. He paused now in front of the heartbreakingly small grave, next to a larger one, brushed some dust from the plain stones set in the ground and read out loud.

"Carly, beloved." He set the tiny pink roses on her stone.

"Millicent Whitmore, beloved." He set the white roses there.

He did not know how the world worked. He felt a

tingle as he read that word. *Beloved*. How had a child long dead, whom he had never even met, become so beloved to him?

How could he feel as if he *knew* Millicent Whitmore, Millie as he called her affectionately, when he had never met her either?

Kiernan understood now, as he had not before marrying Meredith, that there was a larger picture, and despite his power and prestige he was just a tiny part of that.

He understood, as he had not before marrying Meredith, that sometimes great things could transpire out of great tragedies.

The death of a child, and her grandmother, had set a whole series of events in motion that not one single person could have ever foreseen or predicted.

Still, this is what love did: if he could give Meredith back her baby, even if it meant he would never meet her, and never have the life he had now, he would do it in a breath, in a heartbeat.

"I want you to know, Carly," he said softly, "that the new baby in no way replaces you. You are a sacred member of our family. Always and forever."

He felt her then, as he sometimes did, a breath on his cheek, a softness on his shoulder, a faint smell in the air that was so good.

"I brought you a picture of her. We've named her Amalee." He laid the picture, framed in silver, of his new baby and her mother between the two graves.

The picture he laid down was a private portrait, one that had never been released to the press. The baby had a wrinkled face, piercing gray eyes, and a tangle of the most shockingly red hair.

And Meredith in that picture looked like what she was: a mother who had already lost a child and would guard this one with a fierceness that was both awe-inspiring and a little frightening.

She looked like what she was: a woman certain in her own power, a woman who knew she was loved above all things.

Meredith was a woman who knew that if her husband ever had the choice to make: Chatam, his kingdom, or her, he would not even hesitate.

She was his kingdom.

He stepped back then, and sighed, asked silently for a blessing on the christening that would happen today, his baby's first public appearance. Already the people of Chatam lined the streets, waiting to welcome this new love to their lives.

He was left feeling humbled by the goodness of it all.

Each day his and Meredith's relationship became closer, deeper, stronger. The new baby, Amalee, felt as if she was part of a tapestry that wove his heart ever more intricately into its pattern.

Kiernan now knew, absolutely, what he had been so drawn to that first day that he had seen Meredith dance when she thought she was alone.

He had witnessed the dance of life.

And known, at a level that went so deep, that by-passed his mind and went straight to his heart, she was the one who could teach him the steps.

He learned a new one every day.

Love was a dance that you never knew completely,

that taught you new steps, that made you reach deeper and try harder.

Love was the dance that brought you right to heaven's door.

"Thank you," he whispered. And then louder. "Thank you."

Cherish

CINDERELLA AND THE PLAYBOY
by *Lois Faye Dyer*

Jenny knows she shouldn't be attending a posh ball with a scandal-plagued playboy. But as the clock strikes twelve she's *still* wrapped in Chance's big strong arms...

THE TEXAN'S HAPPILY–EVER–AFTER
by *Karen Rose Smith*

Rancher Shep's mad about Rania, so when she discovers she's pregnant a convenient marriage is the perfect solution. Until their real feelings begin to bloom...

IN THE AUSTRALIAN BILLIONAIRE'S ARMS
by *Margaret Way*

Stunningly sexy billionaire David vows to stop Sonya taking advantage of his uncle. Until he discovers her real intentions...and his undeniable attraction to her.

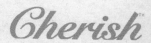

0311/06

The Man She Loves to Hate
by Kelly Hunter
Three reasons to keep away from Cole Rees...
Our families are enemies.
His arrogance drives me mad.
Every time he touches me I go up in flames...and
it's infuriating!

The End of Faking It
by Natalie Anderson
Perfect Penny Fairburn has long learnt that faking it is the
only way—until she meets Carter Dodds... But can Carter get
her to drop the act outside the bedroom as well?

The Road Not Taken
by Jackie Braun
Rescued from a blizzard by ex-cop Jake McCabe, Caro finds
the hero she's been looking for—but to claim him she risks
losing her son to her jerk of an ex...

Shipwrecked With Mr Wrong
by Nikki Logan
Being marooned with a playboy is NOT Honor Brier's idea of
fun! Yet Rob Dalton is hard to resist. Slowly she discovers that
pleasure-seekers have their good points...

On sale from 1st April 2011
Don't miss out!

*Available at WHSmith, Tesco, ASDA, Eason
and all good bookshops*
www.millsandboon.co.uk

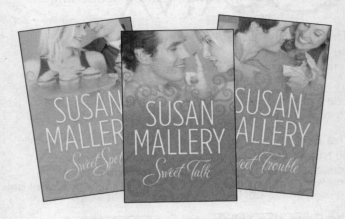

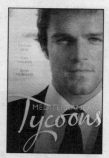

Nora Roberts' *The O'Hurleys*

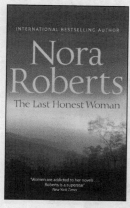

4th March 2011

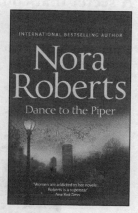

1st April 2011

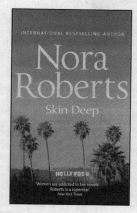

6th May 2011

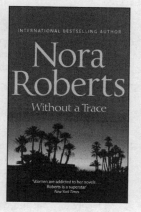

3rd June 2011

One innocent child
A secret that could destroy his life

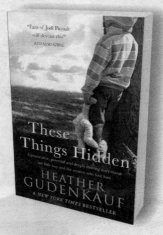

"Fans of Jodi Picoult
will devour this"
RED MAGAZINE

These
Things Hidden

A provocative, powerful and deeply moving story about
one little boy and the women who love him

HEATHER
GUDENKAUF

A NEW YORK TIMES BESTSELLER

Imprisoned for a heinous crime when she was a just a
teenager, Allison Glenn is now free. Desperate for a second
chance, Allison discovers that the world has moved
on without her...

Shunned by those who once loved her, Allison is determined
to make contact with her sister. But Brynn is trapped in
her own world of regret and torment.

Their legacy of secrets is focused on one little boy. And if
the truth is revealed, the consequences will be unimaginable
for the adoptive mother who loves him, the girl who tried
to protect him and the two sisters who hold the key
to all that is hidden...

"Deeply moving and lyrical...it will haunt you..."
—*Company* magazine on *The Weight of Silence*

www.mirabooks.co.uk

How far would you go to protect your sister?

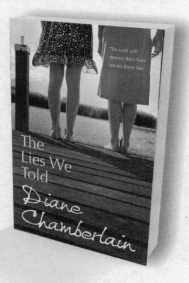

As teenagers, Maya and Rebecca Ward witnessed
their parents' murder. Now doctors, Rebecca has
become the risk taker whilst her sister Maya lives a
quiet life with her husband Adam, unwilling to deal
with her secrets from the night her parents died.

When a hurricane hits North Carolina, Maya is
feared dead. As hope fades, Adam and Rebecca
face unexpected feelings. And Rebecca finds
some buried secrets of her own.

www.mirabooks.co.uk

From the bestselling author of *The Lost Daughter*

Laura's promise to her dying father was to visit an elderly woman she'd never heard of before. But the consequences led to her husband's suicide.

Tragically, their five-year-old daughter Emma witnessed it and now refuses to talk. Laura contacts one person who can help—a man who doesn't know he's Emma's real father. Guided by an old woman's fading memories, the two unravel a tale of love, despair and unspeakable evil that links them all.

www.mirabooks.co.uk

MIRA

2 FREE BOOKS
AND A SURPRISE GIFT

We would like to take this opportunity to thank you for reading this Mills & Boon® book by offering you the chance to take TWO more specially selected books from the Cherish™ series absolutely FREE! We're also making this offer to introduce you to the benefits of the Mills & Boon® Book Club™—

- **FREE home delivery**
- **FREE gifts and competitions**
- **FREE monthly Newsletter**
- **Exclusive Mills & Boon Book Club offers**
- **Books available before they're in the shops**

Accepting these FREE books and gift places you under no obligation to buy, you may cancel at any time, even after receiving your free books. Simply complete your details below and return the entire page to the address below. You don't even need a stamp!

YES Please send me 2 free Cherish books and a surprise gift. I understand that unless you hear from me, I will receive 5 superb new stories every month, including two 2-in-1 books priced at £5.30 each, and a single book priced at £3.30, postage and packing free. I am under no obligation to purchase any books and may cancel my subscription at any time. The free books and gift will be mine to keep in any case.

Ms/Mrs/Miss/Mr _____ Initials _____

Surname _____

Address _____

_____ Postcode _____

E-mail _____

Send this whole page to: Mills & Boon Book Club, Free Book Offer, FREEPOST NAT 10298, Richmond, TW9 1BR